Only the Moon Rages

Only the Moon Rages

Rushton Beech

iUniverse, Inc.
Bloomington

Only the Moon Rages

iUniverse books may be ordered through booksellers or by contacting:

iUniverse
1663 Liberty Drive
Bloomington, IN 47403
www.iuniverse.com
1-800-Authors (1-800-288-4677)

ISBN: 978-1-4759-4828-8 (sc)
ISBN: 978-1-4759-4827-1 (hc)
ISBN: 978-1-4759-4826-4 (ebk)

Library of Congress Control Number: 2012916759

Printed in the United States of America

iUniverse rev. date: 09/25/2012

ACKNOWLEDGEMENTS

I want to acknowledge the important contribution of my first editor Patricia Ann Thomas who had the unenviable task of being first on the scene. Without her assistance and encouragement this book would have languished in the TBD file.

Most successful writers these days have teams of editors, editorial assistants, researchers and project managers. For this book all of these titles and more are bestowed upon Anne Elizabeth Hewat Vaughan. Without Anne this work would never have begun and it most certainly would have never been published. This book is a testimony to Anne's tenacity and conviction both in the work and in me. I dedicate this book to Anne. Thank you Anne.

PROLOGUE

Surely a man in a howling fit believes his supplication to the red planet of greed is *not* a Sisyphus of futility driven to harsh measures by tragic circumstance, even though his NASDAQ losses make his wallet ache. To the contrary, the fool fervently believes it is an action based on the game's luck, a calculated risk, and in trusting, the fool gambles all on *hope*, a tide of reckless emotion swept upon wishful believing somehow the fool is special and has insight no one else possesses, an arcane knowledge perhaps derived from a secret dark energy buried long ago. You laugh and the fool laughs with you.

Yet, within the Van Allen Belt of charged particles that hug our blue earth growing ever hotter, there is a repository of Time, a place—no better, a well or maelstrom of ancient spider webs growing stronger and more complete as the Digital Express hurls unseen 0s and 1s outward to the magnetic *Noosphere* of the universe.

A fool might think that some future race, the fool laughs best at this, one from the past could have understood and read the writing etched invisibly in the sky as surely as the underground stream trickles quietly unseen.

A fool looks for a key to understanding in dreams, omens, and words: one crow sorrow, two crows joy—the fool cries skipping along the sidewalk of semantics, careful not to step on cracks.

The word Time is such a fracture. And the fool who peers down that snapping asynchronous gully is at risk of contracting a perplexing disease. Everything must have its place; order is the bastion against chaos. Mothers against uncertainty—unite!

So, when the wise fool sees two eagles in the leafless oak tree beside the interior expressway that clogs the arterial route to the brain, the wise fool says nothing.

The wise fool knows they are a fool. Welcome to our world.

ONE

In the sweltering heat of the jungle the excavation team worked feverishly. Dr. Greg Fallows, along with senior team leader, Dr. Jana deVries, set out to reach a ridge near the Belize border early in the morning. Jana was on faculty of the Allard Pierson Archeology Institute in the Netherlands, and a first rate hands-on digger. She had a typical Dutch sensibility about her, straightforward and quietly competent. She had shoulder length blonde hair brilliant blue eyes and an easy-going personality that friends would later describe as open, honest and perhaps overly trusting. She loved fieldwork. And now as a newly minted full professor, she was in charge of the evolving Meso-American exhibit at the Museum.

On this morning, one of their guides spotted a shiny object reflected in the brilliant sun near a Temple designated simply as Number 8 on the map of Guatemala.

When they arrived at the site some three hours after leaving the base camp they found a relatively small clump of earth covered with jungle foliage. From the next nearest hill, it looked like all the other mounds. Without the aid of their guide, they surely would have missed it. As luck would have it they trekked to the pyramid just in time to set-up a campsite before sunset.

Over the next few hours they settled in for the night. The Howler monkeys, aptly named, swung from the treetops waking Greg early. When he got up, Jana was already busy at work making her notes. It didn't strike Greg as unusual at all. In fact it made a great deal of sense to dig in the morning before it got too hot.

Greg walked over to where she was sitting on the ground; he startled her when he walked up behind her.

"Morning Jana. What's happening?"

"Greg, you nearly scared the shit out of me!" She took a deep breath. "We should be looking over here." She pointed to several partially dug mounds they surveyed the day before.

After breakfast they began the meticulous work of excavating. Inch by inch they made their way down, and back in time. After long hours of teamwork they reached an entrance to what looked to Jana like a tomb. With a little effort they were able to force their way in. Greg and Jana's eyes met locked in a tractor beam of anticipation.

What followed was one of the most remarkable events in Greg Fallows' life. And what he saw would change him and alter his life—forever. From the dark crevice their flashlights fell upon a sarcophagus. Jana dug furiously with a small trowel, careful as always, to put the precious layers of dirt aside for analysis later. Opening the tomb they found two perfectly preserved and mummified bodies. As a medical archeologist, Greg couldn't have hoped for a more important discovery. He was ecstatic. But what lay beside one of the mummies was to prove even more important. Jana and Greg both sighted the object simultaneously. It was a life size perfectly preserved crystalloid skull. And it glowed like the radiant jewel it was. They stared at each other in disbelief.

"What is it?" Jana cried, barely able to speak.

"It has to be worth millions," Greg sat down beside her to get a better view.

From behind, one of their Guatemalan companions, Tomas muttered something under his breath.

"Tomas says it is the Maya *skull of doom*." Jana simply stared at the eerie glowing object. Greg, transfixed by the beauty of it couldn't take his eyes off the pulsating jewel. Finally he reached out to touch the skull.

"No!" Jana cried, grabbing him by the shoulders.

His hands tingled slightly, not in an unpleasant way but in an almost drug-induced anesthetic way, as he lifted it out of the burial chamber. It was a most magnificent piece of craftsmanship, a perfect tiny replica of a human skull. It was amazingly accurate in every detail, including a full sized jaw, eye sockets and foramina for the trigeminal nerves to exit the skull above the eye, cheekbones and lower jaw. Clearly it was extremely rare, and probably priceless.

"We'll need to take all necessary security precautions," Jana fell back onto the ground smiling at Greg. "This is going to be big, really big."

Tomas stood watching a safe distance from the hole in the ground. His dark skin was pale and his deep brown eyes dilated wildly with fear.

"Holy Father pray for us," he repeated softly under his breath.

"What's Tomas muttering about?" Greg grew increasingly irritated looking over his shoulder at Tomas.

"According to local legend The Pearl was the embodiment of evil in the world, and whoever possessed The Pearl could use its power for good, or evil. The local Indians say the skull or pearl was used when an old man was dying. The old man would lie next to the skull and opposite to him a young man would lay down. As the old man died, his knowledge would be acquired by the young man; in this way the ancient knowledge of the past was handed to future generations."

A strange bubbling cauldron of emotions rose deep inside Greg. He was hot, nauseated, alienated from his surroundings and violently uncomfortable holding this thing that increasingly disgusted him as he held it in his hand. In a flash an overwhelming sense of regret, a fear of repeating past mistakes, a dark existential cloud washed over him. Everything he did up to this point seemed wrong, misguided, stained like a bloody curtain before his eyes. The more he struggled to shake this feeling, the more it seemed to tighten its grip around him, constricting his very soul to a meanness no man, or woman could escape. He was going to explode.

What's happening to me? He tried to wrestle himself back from the dread that was squeezing the life out of him.

What should I have done? He would ask himself a million times.

Like someone had speed dialed the meanest moments of his existence, catalogued and paraded them before his eyes, exposed, a cinematic nightmare only he could see was about to unfold before his eyes as he watched himself.

Jana is going to cheat me—take all the credit and leave me with nothing, nothing but the smoldering regret of fortune lost. This fear consumed every fiber of his being.

At that moment he was certain Jana would cheat him out of this important discovery. It rightly belonged to him too! It was his work that brought them here. He wasn't about to now share it with anyone. It was increasingly clear to him that it was his destiny to possess, to have, to own the thing. This was his treasure. He wanted the artifact for myself. He would not play second fiddle to Jana, whose pride in the discovery was already visible. He could see her reveling in the beauty of the craftsmanship as she held it in her hands. He believed she would attribute the glow of the artifact to a natural phenomenon such as radioactive energy and give no credence to the idea that there was a hidden power undetectable by science.

The sun seemed to energize the iridescent crystalloid skull by the minute like a solar circuit now exposed to the light of day. Greg knew instinctively their find transcended mere academic archeological interest. It wasn't something to be put on a pedestal and left there for swarms of school children to gawk at, as Jana would have done at the Allard Pierson Museum. Here was something of true historical significance. Who knows, it could even have medical applications. He'd heard of the power of ancient charms and he'd always been open to alternative medicine when he was in practice. What if it was a cure for cancer? Should he simply leave it to glow in a museum in Amsterdam? No, it deserved a thorough scientific study. It required someone with a medical background to take charge of it. He needed that skull—for his own purposes. And if Jana wouldn't share it he would have to take it by forces, if necessary. It was just too valuable.

"I need to chill." Greg headed out alone to clear his head.

When he returned to base camp he was in a terrible frenzy. He related a story of how they had been attacked by armed guerrillas. He described how the poor unfortunate Dr. deVries and the guides were killed in their sleep. As he related the horror, he told how he escaped by running through the jungle like a wild animal. Yes, he had been lucky, very lucky. And no, he couldn't identify the killers. It was dark. Yes, perhaps the expedition should return home. Yes, all agreed this was the only thing to do. He packed his bags and headed for the seclusion of the west coast of Mexico. He needed time to think. Confusion pumped agonizing images though his mind. *What have I done?*

TWO

The Philadelphia airport was crowded with travelers waiting to catch flights or make connections. Some were happy and anxious to get where they were going—to close business deals, to interview for new jobs, to see family or old friends; others were modern day refugees fleeing wars in familiar and unfamiliar places. But if you look carefully into their eyes you could see a void. Some are branded with a secret. Dark and painful family secrets in some cases, like rape and abuse at the hands of dirty men who smelled of slivovitz and stumbled in the ruins of a Sarajevo neighborhood. Other secrets were as deep as a broad keloid scar across the face punctuated by eyes that gave reason to pause and think twice about the suffering that was well and truly laid upon the soul therein. There are some things too painful for words. Some secrets are icy cold and send spasmodic shivers down one's spine. And some secrets decay with age into a fine rusty mold, stinking up the psyche, infecting everyone and everything they contact.

Christie Hammond Fallows wore a secret brand but it was not yet ripe. She stood outside the Discovery store tapping her foot nervously. It was early morning. She seemed to be waiting anxiously for relief. She looked at her watch and eyed with envy those lucky enough to have snagged one of the few rocking chairs that lined the vast Philadelphia airport hallway. Alas, there were none available, so she paced in front of the Discovery storefront window.

Christie was a strong, good-looking woman in her thirties. Her face was kind and trusting, framed by straight blond shoulder length hair. Her nose was small with wide nostrils that seem to hover over thick intriguing triangular shaped lips. Her eyes were a brilliant Australian sky blue. She was tall with strong muscular thighs and firm erect breasts.

Yes, she was an attractive and physically fit woman. And she believed in the basic goodness of people. She believed in Christian charity, but she was not what could be called a religious person; she believed in something outside herself. She was intuitive and very intelligent with a nurse's street smarts evident in her eyes.

In her most secret heart she desperately wanted children but had been told by an emotionally repressed reproductive specialist at the university that she couldn't. She filled the grieving void with her music. Her search for deeper meaning was expressed through her hands in her cello's moody voice. She was thinking about music at this moment, as she looked up at the TV monitor permanently tuned to the too familiar American all news cable network.

She didn't see the security camera behind her, or the one down the hall, or even the one at the security checkpoint scrutinizing her.

In airports, in homes, on highways, and on the Internet, the camera's red eye is always looking at us. Beyond Reality TV, The Truman Show, Edtv, Survivor or whatever television series is *au courant*, there are no dress rehearsals. Live is the only game in town. We're all survivors of something—at least we hope, or pray we can survive. But the question is for what? Why?

"Stephen! Thanks for coming so fast." She kissed him on the cheeks three times the way Belgians do.

"No worries," Parmata's Australian drawl a welcome familiarity

"I need your help Stephen. Something is happening to Greg. I don't think he's telling me the truth."

He raised a friendly eyebrow, "no news there, is there Christie?"

"We can't talk here; let's get a coffee."

"Okay, but not here. Let's go to my place, it's private. There are too many cameras here," Parmata led her by the arm toward the exit.

Parmata and Christie disappeared down the escalator heading toward his car. Above on the TV suspended from the ceiling where Christie was standing moments before, the female CNN news anchor announced: "We interrupt the regular newscast to bring you breaking news: Senate hearings into allegations of influence peddling and corruption in the office of the United Nations Information Department continue to raise more questions. Investigations into the mysterious death of White House Chief of Staff Sam Paterson in Amsterdam last week have revealed little, but have raised many questions.

We take you live to Room 419 of the Dirkson Senate Office Building in Washington."

With few notable exceptions Senate hearings are deliberately orchestrated to put everyone to sleep—especially the ill-prepared Committee members. Expert witnesses usually speak in muffled voices guaranteed to bore everyone. But this speaker was different. Dr. Gregory Winston Fallows was arrested at the scene of Paterson's death. He was now testifying for the first time before the Senate Sub-committee in full public hearings.

Greg's face has appeared on every magazine and tabloid television show over the past week. He has been called everything from a techno-terrorist to an unwitting victim. Sitting in the witness box in Room 419 he looked more like a lost child. His clean-shaven innocent face with languid lazy blue eyes stirred the hearts of some in the television audience, and a few of those still awake in the room. One late night talk show caller opined he doubted Greg Fallows would have received half the press attention he has if he were not so good looking. A sign of the times the commentator replied cynically.

Greg had stopped in mid-sentence. He looked more like a teenager in trouble than a terrorist. Turning to the audience he spoke with look of the damned through misty eyes.

"I remember now . . . a cab dropped me just off Dam Square near the Red Light district. One of those small black European taxis. It might have been a Mercedes, I think. It was very late, even for Amsterdam. A blue VW van sped past us, me I mean, almost knocking me down as I stepped out of the cab. There were a few people mulling about as there always are in Amsterdam: addicts, aging hippies, Japanese tourists, burnt out American transvestites. I heard a loud thud and turned just in time to see a blue van knock down a sick elderly man—probably an alcoholic, I really don't know. He was a fat ruddy-faced fellow dressed like a priest. Strange, I remember thinking; he had the look of a defrocked priest—whatever that means. I don't know why that came to mind, or why I remember it now. He looked up and cursed after the car. He shook his fist as he stumbled to his feet. It was getting dark. I think he was very drunk. Anyway, the van didn't stop. It just disappeared over a bridge. Yes, then I remember . . . It's all like a dream now . . . I was trying to read the address on the business card in the dim light of a vestibule. I reached out to knock on the door but something between my hand and my brain stopped me. "I'm sorry," he rubbed his temples. "I have a splitting headache . . ."

"Please, go on, Dr. Fallows," the Committee Chair prompted.

"I don't know why, but everything has so much more meaning for me. Jesus Christ!" Greg stood suddenly. A wave of whispering swept over the room.

"Order! Order! Please sit down Dr. Fallows, or we'll have to take appropriate security measures."

"Yes, sir. Yes, it was Jesus on the cross, the crucifixion . . . a cluster of hanging grapes . . . a heretical motif cast in bronze, mounted on a nameless plaque on the door. I mean . . . I recognized the symbol from my study of groups like the Société de Zion, long since eradicated in the evangelical fervor of past purges of secret societies. My heart raced in anticipation of meeting a Master of the Order of the Poor Knights of the Temple of Solomon."

Stephen Francis Parmata was born in Brisbane, Australia fifty-five years ago. He went to a Christian Brothers boarding school, but escaped the polymorphous perversity that in recent years has branded the Christian Brothers in Australia and Canada as "buggers for the faith." Probably because of his childhood he became a Jesuit priest, but he soon found the work unsuited to his temperament and his colleagues insufferably dull. He left the Jesuits after 3 years. He floundered for some time traveling the world picking up the occasional job reporting the news in trouble spots, and then for a while he worked with Reuter's news service in Frankfurt before settling on his calling as a world-class con man under the respectable guise of art dealer. An Interpol file outlines his connections with foreign currency scams, and amateur art collectors, possibly some stolen from recently opened east block borders via his connection with military intelligence during the Bulgarian communist regime. Parmata believes the world owes him something. His goal is to be very rich, so wealthy that he'd never have to work again, if you can call what he does work. So, when Christie told him on the phone about the thing Greg found in Guatemala he became very interested in Greg, Christie and the discovery.

Christie first met Parmata one summer while she was vacationing on Australia's Sunshine Coast north of Brisbane. Parmata was chilling out from a recent successful sale of a rare religious relic. They met on the beach at Noosa Heads when Christie was backpacking in Queensland one cold Canadian winter. She needed to escape College for a semester. Over beer and delicious Moreton's Bay Snapper Parmata charmed the young Canadian with amazing tales of adventure and intrigue.

He told her how he'd discovered a rare religious relic with a troubled history.

"The scribe, one of the Monks, Thomas probably related by candlelight the sorry tale of an eleven year old boy named Robert Tobin.

"I must tell the tale the way it happened, even if there are certain evil things in it, if for no other reason than to act as a caution to all who may read this, the note read."

Robert is the messenger between the Monastery and the Jewish moneylenders in the town of Brentome. When his body is found near the river outside the Monastery walls near the town on Easter Sunday, the word spread that Jews had crucified the boy.

The new Abby Bruce Tottenham, a staunch anti-Semite, and strict administrator had been plotting to rid the Monastery of its dependence on the Jews. When Robert Tobin was murdered he was handed a convenient excuse to cut those ties.

"In a dream, Abby Bruce sees himself standing before the alter with two other monks holding up a magnificent white sculpture depicting the life of St. Bernard who's fiery rhetoric marshaled thousands to fight to retrieve the Holy Lands from the pagans, igniting the Second Crusade," Parmata took a long sip of his ice cold Fosters lager. "Abby Bruce, you see, commissioned Master William to fashion a sculpture complete with anti-Jewish tirades supposedly from the Bible and peppered liberally with quotations from Endora's *Treatise Against the Jews.*

After the dissolution of the monasteries by Henry VIII in the sixteenth century the monastery fell into ruins and along with it ninety percent of the art treasures of antiquity. The sculpture disappeared."

"How did you find it?" Christie leaned forward, keen to hear more.

"Four centuries later and a continent away, Damien Andrews, a Canadian lawyer came across the sculpture in the home of one of his clients Roseanne Melton, a retired Royal Ontario Museum art historian and collector. Because of her terminal illness, he went to her house to write up her Will. She told him the unique history of the sculpture from an art history perspective, but when she died, the sculpture disappeared. Damien Andrews you see had stolen the sculpture, and he approached me to value it. It was then that I realized the sculpture might actually be carved from a human femur or thighbone. Later, I discovered it was actually fashioned from the femur of St. Bernard, and inside the core of the sculpture I discovered the anti-Jewish inscriptions hidden."

"You can't imagine how excited I was to come across something as valuable as this. I mean, something that rivals *the* famous Bury St. Edmunds ivory sculpture now at the Metropolitan Museum of Art in New York City.

"The sculpture was 18 inches high, not nearly as large as the BSE sculpture, but valuable nonetheless. It had a little door in the back, and inside, there was crushed bone and a scroll."

"How does the story end?" Christie probed, genuinely curious.

"I sold the reliquary, split the money with the crooked lawyer and made enough to travel the world in style." Stephen nonchalantly looked over his shoulder.

But that was a long time ago, on a continent as far away from Philadelphia as say Earth is from Mars.

"It is really good to see you again," Parmata put his arm around her placing a fatherly kiss on her forehead. His loft apartment with a fantastic view overlooking the Delaware River was warm and comfortable, decorated with intriguing works of art from around the world.

"You have a nice comfortable home. I still feel safe with you Stephen, even after all these years" Christie observed. Parmata poured two generous cognacs and handed one to Christie who had already collapsed on his black leather couch. Parmata selected a CD from his vast collection, Pachelbel's Canon in D major, inserted it in the stereo and stood next to the floor to ceiling windows overlooking the river, sipping his cognac, and waiting for her to begin.

She took a gulp of cognac and began: "I'm worried. You see. I don't know what it is . . ."

"An intuition?" He interjected.

"Yes," with a smile, "I think that's what you'd call it."

He turned to look out over the gray city.

"I'm going to need a place to hide. Some place safe. Somewhere Greg can't find me . . ."

Parmata turned around. Their eyes met. He was almost a priest again. *Some things just don't go away*, he thought. A shudder ran down her spine. He looked into her eyes.

"You're in trouble." It was a statement, not a question.

"I think . . . my life could be in danger."

Then she told him about Greg's discovery, the strange change in his personality, and people he'd started working with now. Parmata walked over to the couch and sat down beside her. He put his arm around her. She looked into his eyes. They were soft brown and deep as space. Parmata was strong and fit. His hair was cut short and there was less of it on the top then when they first met on Noosa Heads beach many years ago. His nose was long but not big, and his chin was well defined, but a small neatly trimmed Van Gogh beard hid it. He kissed her again on the forehead; she lunged for him like a hungry child runs home.

"If Greg is mixed up in something, he's probably way over his head," Parmata walked to the kitchen. "Coffee?" He asked, flashing his perfect white teeth.

"Please, with milk," She put on her blue jeans. "You know I have never done this before. Cheat on Greg, I mean."

"You're not really cheating on him are you? Isn't he the one cheating on you?"

"Yeah, but . . ."

"But,"

"Yeah."

They both laughed and the release was good.

"Well, leave it at that. Think of me as your confessor. There are no secrets between us, only pure trust," He disappeared into the kitchen.

When he returned, she stepped closer and spoke.

"Okay, I have a secret to tell you."

"Shoot," he peered over his coffee mug.

"I think I'm in love with you."

"I love you too," and he kissed her softly.

"But I'm married to Greg." He looked away.

"From the sound of it, he's got his hands full, and he may be in greater danger than he or you know. I have contacts with some people in Eastern Europe—SVR, the Russian foreign intelligence service. I've done some work for them, and they owe me. I want you to wear this at all times. Understand?"

He took a small necklace from his pocket and placed it in her hand.

"What is it?" She asked looking him in the eye.

"Our bond." He grinned. She nodded in the affirmative.

"I'll get straight to the point," Professor Hunt glanced sideways out the window at Amsterdam's gingerbread skyline.

Hunt was a toady to the cause; he'd rehearsed this moment over and over in his head. He disliked Samuel Charles Paterson. They'd been rivals for the top position in the Order. Paterson's ruthless cunning had won out once again. But Hunt refused to be defeated by a cultural nematode from America.

"Our people in Switzerland are getting nervous. They're concerned about Mosaic. They want guarantees. Everything we've worked for over the years is at stake. This is too important to let go now."

"Relax will you Hugh," Paterson arrogantly tapped his Blackberry. "Mosaic is on schedule. For once all the pieces are in my hands—I mean, *our* hands—the corporation will have no problem convincing the G10 nations of the importance of a single world currency. It's inevitable. Now is our time. The global credit crisis we created is the perfect rationale. We know it; they know it. Now stop fucking worrying! It's pissing me off."

"It's not that simple. If they get hold of Mosaic they could ruin everything. If there's a leak; if anyone finds out about the existence of G2, a secret intelligence arm of the UN . . ."

"You know Hugh, you worry too much. You always did fucking worry too much. That's why the company chose me, so get the fuck over it. You have to have the nerve for the game. And Hugh, you just ain't got the nerve."

Professor Hunt bristled with anger but Paterson was right. The corporation had chosen Paterson over him with the understanding that once a single world currency was in place, Hunt would rise to the top position within the newly defined Templars.Net Bank Group. The U.S. Presidential Chief of Staff Paterson was in a better position to convince the United States to support the move since the US dollar was the favored currency. And with the tumble in the world currency markets and the beating the US dollar has taken along with the rising US debt, he had been the obvious choice. So, Hunt had reluctantly agreed.

"Look, by the time this thing is finished they'll be begging us to implement Mosaic. It's a perfect plan. Or . . ." Paterson focused on his Blackberry again.

"Or what?" Hunt huffed his irritation. He didn't have a Blackberry or even a "smart phone" as they were now called. People now are increasingly impolite as they suddenly stop mid sentence to answer an email or text message.

"Shit happens," Paterson smirked.

Outside a car screeched to a halt. Hunt could smell sulfur dioxide waft through the window from the congested traffic on the street below.

"Think positive brother. Our work is the culmination of centuries of planning. The religious and economic foundations of the Western world will be finally . . ." he paused choosing his words carefully, . . . corrected."

Out of the ashes a new order will emerge with a powerful new religion and a unified economy. It is an evolution of the human spirit. The lies and real heresies will be exposed. It cannot be stopped. It is our destiny. It is the destiny of our planet."

"You are right my brother." They kissed three times on the cheeks the Belgian way. Then Paterson disappeared, just another reptile, slithering into the dark underbelly of the city.

Outside the clouds took various shapes of great alchemical symbols such as the Uroboros, a snake biting its own tail. The dragon of alchemy as she was once called is a symbol of the endless cycle of destruction and renewal.

It was time to put the final piece of the puzzle in place. The living embodiment of the Templar plan known as Mosaic would be complete. Marvel at the genius of your ancestors. Paterson's time will come. Know that as sure as a surge of warm, glowing energy ignites embers from a long forgotten funeral pyre.

"You have brought your paper or codex as you call it?" the mustached doorman asked, in a thick Arabic accent as he ushered Dr. Greg Fallows into the wonderfully aromatic foyer. The air was filled with spicy cedar incense. It was exhilarating, like breathing flavored oxygen. Police sirens wailed in the background as Greg crossed the threshold. The doorman scanned the darkened street then shut the door with deliberate force.

"Yes." Greg grasped his briefcase with both arms the way a child holds a precious toy. The walls were filled with artists' drawings, sexually explicit and provocative. Together they walked up the stairs, and down a long dark hall to a door marked with three interlocking pentagrams. They entered into a brightly lit circular arbor room filled with exotic trees and bushes from the Amazon and other tropical jungles. Greg squinted to accommodate the sudden change in intensity of the light. Three men stood up when he entered the room. They hurriedly folded their papers as if they had been interrupted. None of them were familiar to Greg. He was a stranger in an even stranger land.

The doorman introduced each of the men in turn seated around a large oak table; then he seemed to evaporate into the darkness that was the aromatic hall. The formality of the introduction was very European as each man introduced himself in turn. The three names were vaguely familiar from obscure journals on subjects ranging from the occult to Jungian phenomenology of dreams. Each in turn shook his hand before he took his place at the end of the table, his back to the door.

One fellow, with a short closely cropped white beard and steel blue eyes, Heinrich Von Hartmann, sat to one side of the table playing nervously with his hands like an expectant father on a maternity ward. An air of anticipation filled the room. Everyone seemed on edge. A tall, thin serious fellow by the name of Hans Brentano nervously fumbled with his papers. The one they called Herr Strumpf flossed his teeth in flagrant violation of all social norms. Such rude behavior seemed out of place with all the Continental formality. Strumpf's eyes were wet and protruded like an iguana's as they darted about to see if anyone was looking at him. He didn't seem to care that Greg stared at him. As soon as Greg sat down they began an intense and heated argument about the meaning of certain obscure archetypes and symbols contained in a painting by Pousson called *The Shepherds of Arcadia.*

Greg did not know the enigmatic painting in question, although he'd heard of Pousson. The way they spun their tale reminded him of a dream. Each seemed to derive an amazingly similar interpretation based on the significance of the angles at which the artist set the scene near Rennes-Les-Bain in southern France. Greg sat silently lost among these later day Pythagoreans.

From the far end of the table Brentano startled Greg as he began to read aloud from one of the papers he'd been shuffling.

"Dream sequence, patient number 906: 'sailing up the Habor river I come to a long wooden trestle; I am looking for a passage through the trestle to reach the other side. I look to my right. I notice a gravel road. It appears parallel to the wooden trestle. I leave the raft I've been sailing on; cautiously I embark on the gravel path. The sky turns dark. The gravel road turns near the end of the long wooden structure, as it curves it also goes back, down into the water. There is a lamplight at the entrance to a tunnel under the water. The lamp is not electric. The light is very blue; too blue. I see it is a gas lamp, archaic yet efficient. The moon is high and full. The light allows me to see my way partially down to the tunnel under the river. I proceed down into the tunnel; it becomes progressively darker; I become increasingly frightened; I start to run; faster and faster. My heart is pounding in my ears. In the darkness I run straight into another faceless figure running from the opposite direction. The force of the other running from the opposite direction knocks me down. We are terrified in the dark. I awake.'"

"Does this sound familiar to you Dr. Fallows?" Brentano peered up from the page he was reading.

"Why should it?" Greg looked perplexed.

"This is your dream is it not?"

Greg gasped. It was. He'd told only one person about that dream. But how could she?

"There is an extraordinary Assyrian manuscript that you would enjoy I believe Dr. Fallows. It describes the building of the Tower of Babel. I think it might interest you," a voice came from the doorway behind Greg.

"Our job consists of adding analogies to what is supplied by the dream," the interloper continued, as he walked toward the large circular table. Greg stood reflexively with the others.

He was a tall man, with a neat white well-trimmed beard. He had round spectacles perched on his long thin nose. He held a Dutch clay pipe in his arthritic right hand. He wore a brown tweed suit, a full size larger than a perfect fit. He had what Greg instantly recognized as the absent-minded professor look. He seemed awkward; not at all what Greg imagined Professor Hugh R. Hunt might look like, and even less like the dust cover photographs on his many books. He seemed frail and elderly like the man he saw knocked down by a van on the street. There was a strange other worldly aura of knowledge about him. *He must be an important person*, Greg thought. He walked to each of the men in turn working his way around the table. He kissed each on the cheek. When he came to Greg he grasped both his hands and shook them gently, yet firmly, the way a diplomat might. His hands were frigid and his eyes, hypnotic more glacial than friendly, a deeper abyss than space itself.

The doorman returned carrying a large, leather bound, ancient text, which he placed on the table, disappearing again into the night without a whisper. Professor Hunt placed the book in front of Greg making sure that he could read the title that was heavily pressed into the thick old cover. The letters, in ancient Greek, spelt *Euphemes.* He looked at Greg, smiled and said in a kind, sympathetic baritone radio voice.

"Some things, like dreams, are best accepted *mente vacua.* That is to say, without preconceived ideas."

The light and noise from the traffic woke Greg from his sleep. He swung his weary legs over the edge of the bed, and sat holding his head. Wow! He supposed he should have gone directly home after the meeting with the Dean instead of staying at the *Hungry Hunter* until 3 A.M. Through his fingers he peered around the apartment. Christie had left for work. He looked at the clock; it was already 8 in the morning. He was going to be late for his second lecture of the term. *Heck of a dream*, he thought. He paused to pour a cup of coffee. Was it a dream? Or did it really happen. He ran his hand through his blond hair with a sigh and stumbled over to the window looking down over the Don River and the morning pile up of cars on the parkway. Orange smog hung over Toronto along the lakeshore for fifty miles to the west. Even on a clear morning the blue sky was filtered through the sulfurous haze. Why did he stay here? He asked himself as he dragged his body into the shower.

At 43, Greg was in his second year of teaching at the University of Toronto. He'd been a physician for 13 years, running a general practice out of a low rent store front office along the Danforth. But there wasn't enough money in it. The overhead was a killer. If only his *ship would come in* as his mother always remarked. Maybe he'd find a treasure and be set for life. Gregory Winston Fallows has always been haunted by a sense of impending doom. Is he really a loser because he hasn't become a millionaire by forty? If money makes the man, what is he? Is success in life measured by how much is in your Swiss bank account? What is the meaning of success? What would his father have thought?

Greg's parents died when he was young. Both died instantly in a tragic car accident on a beautiful sunny Sunday morning. As a teenager he went from having everything to a life of crushing poverty. That fear of poverty drove him to take risks and in so doing he threw things and people away so he wouldn't fear losing them or be attached to them, miss them when they were gone. Was he becoming a fatalist? He wondered. Did he really believe that no matter what you did in life, life would defeat your best efforts? Wasn't death itself proof of that? He couldn't face the mind-numbing routine of hearing people complaining anymore so he applied for a position in medical archeology.

He thought he just might have a chance this time.

Before he went into medicine, he and Christie spent six months working as students on an archeology dig near Lake Atitlan in Guatemala. What if he really did find a treasure of some kind? Something pulled him back to archeology as the likely place to maybe make his mark.

Things had changed at the university since his Master's degree. A cloud of political correctness hung over the institution infecting everyone and everything. He didn't know how long he could stay in academia. He knew he liked the work and teaching, but he could tell from his colleagues' attitudes that he would be lucky to survive the current anti-male purge sweeping the university.

On the subway to the university he couldn't help thinking about the strange dream, especially the dream within a dream, like a Russian doll. He tried to read his lecture notes but found he couldn't concentrate. Each subway stop reminded him of a scene from the dream. He picked up the *Daily Sun at* the newsstand near the exit to the College subway stop. The world was full of violence and chaos as usual. The Dow Jones and NASDAQ were in a tailspin again. The entire globe seemed to be heading for some yet undetermined rendezvous with Armageddon. Disgusted, he threw the paper into the recycle bin and ran up the stairs and through the arched sandstone entrance of the university building.

He rushed into the classroom just as the clock struck 9 o'clock.

"Remember," Greg threw his briefcase onto his desk, "what we were talking about last week? How do you explain evidence of cultural contact between Europe and Central America in the 13th century A.D.?"

"Without appealing to theories about space aliens?" joked Nick, one of his more promising students. "The obvious explanation is that some kind of communication existed between the New World and the Old World before the so-called discovery of the Americas by Christopher Columbus in 1492."

"That's a hypothesis. But where's your proof? It sounds very ethnocentric to me. You are all familiar with speculations that Maya civilization sprang from Phoenician, Egyptian or even the lost continent of Atlantis."

From the back of the room a female student interrupted: "The mathematical probability of building structures . . . exactly the same angles for construction of late Maya temples and the Egyptian pyramids would support the theory. Surely appealing to coincidence reveals an intellectual poverty far more incomprehensible."

Greg was shocked. Ms. Katherine Lockhart, or Kate, as she preferred to be known had never uttered so much as a word in his class before. And now she spoke with real conviction.

Kate Lockhart was a girl who had tasted the fruits of privilege. She was bright and cheery. She had the poise and confidence that comes with a private school education. Her intelligent green eyes and shoulder length brown hair framed her perfect face.

Her father had worked for the British government in the Balkans before the Second World War. He'd retired to Canada. That's all Greg knew about her. He also knew he'd like to know more.

She obviously had a mastery of ideas and men that went beyond the academic learning of the classroom. In other words, this girl also had street smarts.

"You're right," Greg regained his composure. "The end results are there. The final clues are there, but where is the proof?"

"Just because you haven't discovered it doesn't mean it doesn't exist," she baited with a flirtatious smile.

God! This could be an interesting semester, he thought. Greg had many weaknesses, and the so-called "weaker sex" was one of them. In fact, he'd been married three times. When he married Christie he vowed he'd change his ways. But there was a powerful monster raging inside of him—it drove his restless spirit mad.

"The boldness of your statement implies you know more than meets the eye."

"I know that you know more than you're revealing to the class," she mocked him. "I know you've been working on a discovery that could alter history as we know it."

Her statement startled Greg. She seemed to know that he had uncovered evidence to support a link with the New World dating from at least 1309 A.D. But he needed to confirm his findings. Peer review would be a critical first step. The only people who had seen his work so far were Christie, and three independent readers his publisher had arranged. As far as he knew, none of them had commented on it, or even read the codex, as he liked to call the manuscript.

21

"We'll deal with that later. We must return to first principles, and look at the accepted body of information on the issue in this class, before we get carried away with speculation." What bullshit! He hadn't fooled anyone. He couldn't believe he was saying these things. Why shouldn't he talk about his work? His discoveries! Just because his publisher wanted it kept under wraps until the peer reviews were in. He was naked before this class. They wouldn't trust him from now on, and he knew it.

After class Greg went up to Kate in an attempt to apologize. As she was leaving the class he gently touched her arm. She looked up at him with eyes that could have launched a thousand ships.

"Look, I just want to apologize for cutting you down in front of everyone like that."

"Sure, now you apologize, when everyone's gone," she grimaced.

"Look, I am sorry, okay? You caught me off guard when you referred to my unpublished work like that. I just didn't want to get into it with the class, not yet anyway."

After a moment gazing at the floor, she looked him in the eyes and flashed a big smile. "You're forgiven I guess. Now why don't you buy me a beer?"

Greg's brain felt as if it were too small for the tiny skull nature had given him. His pickled gray matter was still swimming from last night's barleycorn romp. He wondered whether he looked that bad.

"*The Hungry Hunter* is just around the corner," taking her arm in his. He fantasized they were skipping like Dorothy and the Lion down the yellow brick road toward Oz, singing yet another chorus of debauchery bop: "If I only had a brain."

At the bustling pub Greg got to know her story. Kate as her friends knew her, grew up pretty much fighting the odds. Her father abused her. Her alcoholic mother committed suicide after several unsuccessful attempts. She worked at the university after high school. Her doting aunt and Presbyterian uncle in the posh suburb of Rosewood had raised her. She had a coarse edge about her that probably kept her alive during those "unspeakable years" as she referred to her early childhood, until the courts gave her aunt and uncle custody over her. She hadn't seen her father since that time.

"I'd walk away if I saw him today. He's just a phantom from some nightmare in my past." She looked into her beer as if the past was visible in the frothing suds.

She worked in the audiovisual department full-time for a year, before enrolling in the Bachelor of Arts program. She had a warm, quietly receptive personality on the outside; on the inside however, something or someone was still tearing her apart. She was seductive and explosively vulnerable at the same time. A combination of emotions Greg found hard to resist.

They talked for hours and after the bar closed he walked her home to her place in the Annex. She rented a loft, the struggling artist kind. They talked some more about archeology and the past. She was a jazz fan. They listened to classics from the Hot Club de Paris and talked, just talked . . . for hours. Greg talked about his work, how digging up the past was like traveling back in time—how medicine had sucked the life out of him. How he discovered one day in Guatemala after a terrible earthquake that to sleep where ancients slept thousands of years ago, or to walk into crypts, to breath the air from a thousand years ago was what really made him feel alive. They kissed like Europeans on both cheeks and nodded good night.

Greg took a cab home just after 3 A.M. and climbed the stairs to his apartment with his tail between his legs like a dog on the lam. Christie was up reading. She'd been home twelve hours earlier from her shift as an intensive care nurse at Queen City General. She made a wonderful dinner. But he didn't have the courtesy to call to say he wasn't coming home. She was angry. He couldn't blame her; she had a right to be. He'd seen this before.

Greg apologized. But that wasn't enough. He'd been so self-centered since his return from the dig in Guatemala. She supposed he'd better smarten up.

"I'm sorry, I didn't mean . . ."

"Never mind. I've done a great deal of thinking over the last little while. It might be best if we live apart for a little while . . . say, a few months."

A wave of confusion swept over Greg. Overcome with a sudden fear for the future, he blurted out in an arrogant tone: "Perhaps you're right." He down at his dirty running shoes; he was unable to look her in the eye.

"I've made arrangements to stay with Jenny for a while. I've been thinking of going back to school. I need to get on with my life. I mean, if I can't have children. I can't just keep waiting around for you to wake-up."

"We both need time to evaluate our priorities," she abruptly headed for the door. *What a cliché,* Greg thought. *This can't be real. Why couldn't she run off with a lover or something? Her brother is a dumb cop over in Hamilton; she could go there, but Jenny, that's too much.* Then he realized he was the cliché.

She quietly closed the door. And then silence. Sweet sleep came as a release. The sound of the pulsing brain waves in his head distorted the cacophony of early morning street sounds. A siren in the distance wailed to a crescendo and then evaporated down the telephone lines, electrons chasing electrons, into the tunnel and over to some other tragedy unfolding on another street, in another world miles away.

In the fog of sleep, scrolling angelic demons, crash through the surface of waters deep and wide; suffocating faces like marionettes dance to the hip beat songs of the sewer heated sweat shops, swirling like mad Dervish dudes in baggy pantaloons, laughing and cajoling each other, reaching out to take his hand. In blind obedience he cried out what every man would: *Why?* But he couldn't speak the words. The question itself was somehow invalid. Why thunder? Why earthquakes? Why matter? Why do tiny butterflies in Ohio affect the weather in New York? The cosmic marshmallow of Time sticks to us like primordial gluons, vibrating and spinning in our neural nebulae, galaxies of perfect copies of the past, hidden yet present just under the rough wart-like surface of a tiny spectrum of this electromagnetic field. Ah . . . sweet dreams brook no reason to anoint the soul of man.

THREE

In his dreams Greg saw Mahacutah's hand tremble under the weight of the sword. The sky darkened even though the mid-day sun still made the humidity rising from the floor of the jungle pour beads of sweat from Mahacutah's forehead. The people assembled at the main temple in the Great Plaza of Dos Pilas know this is the most important ritual of all. The end of another millennium had special significance. Now it was the end of time. Mahacutah's eyes search the crowd below.

"The molten sea of serpents that keep themselves invisible beneath our earth's crust break open every thirty-four thousand years; tearing the sun from the sky and moon from the night," he held his arms up toward the eclipsing sun. The drums beat staccato rhythms across the jungle. In the searing heat of midday the green and red paint on his face ran down over his lips.

"The black dogs of night will soon devour our sacred people." He raised a short jewel handled sword high above his head.

"We must fulfill the destiny of our gods," he cried as he plunged the blade into his chest with both hands. The direct blow to the left ventricle of his heart spurted blood six feet from his body, instantly soaking the Altar. He fell to his knees. His eyes slowly drained of life. The eclipsed moon raced across the face of the disappearing sun.

"He is gone," shouted Balam, one of four deacons, who up to this point had been silent, nervously waiting just a couple of feet away. Balam's moist olive skin was almost white with fear.

The solar eclipse ended and the searing heat of mid-day clotted the blood of Mahacutah as it dripped down the stone steps of the temple. The rushing wind whispered victory to the trees of the jungle.

The deacons dragged the body of Mahacutah from the altar. It is a harsh necessity that requires a people to give up their priest for a greater cause.

The community was beheaded. No one would take Mahacutah's place. It was forbidden. And it would be suicidal.

Balam took Mahacutah's body from the temple and prepared it for burial according to the tradition. He went back to the temple to retrieve the jeweled sword that Mahacutah used to take his own life. It was the same instrument that condemned his people to oblivion.

Greg tossed in his bed. In another dream he heard the Gregorian chant *Tod und Auferstehung* (Death and Resurrection) radiate within the cold walls of a cathedral. The darkness made it impossible for anyone to see the faces of the approaching horsemen. The white robed monks inside the stone and flying-buttressed fortress could not have known the extent of the forces turned against them. Forever, this day would be synonymous with evil perpetrated on holy men for political gain.

"Abbé! Abbé Antoine!" shouted a monk dressed in a cagoule, a sort of white hooded robe, a long sleeveless tunic with a heavy vestment underneath for the cold October night. Gripped by terror, Knight Templar Henri Bieil ran up the aisle of the church toward the altar. He was almost cut in half by the whirling arrows of the King's men waiting in the foyer of the church. He fell before he reached the altar, lying on the cold marble floor; red blood quickly soaked his white mantle like the white fur of a slain rabbit. His black eyes blinked a stare of animal recognition of the end, or was it the beginning? His body shuddered a death rattle in a pool of blood.

The soldiers entered the church from all sides now; their clanging steel, and smell of hot horse breath filled the peaceful church with the pungent odor of a barn.

The Captain of the guard, Jean de Joyneville, a young impulsive man with political ambition, had been in the Seminary of Saint Sulpice in Paris. He was recruited as a spy for the King to infiltrate the Order—a medieval mole—to rise up against the Order of the Hospitallers of Saint John, and to betray his brothers in Christ. He would accuse his brothers of heinous crimes against God, and the Holy Mother Church. He would relate such vivid tales that the hounds of Christ would hunt for heretics within the bosom of the Church for centuries to come. The soldier knights of the Order of the Temple of Solomon, also known as the Knights Templar were the most powerful threat to the established order because of their wealth, power, and influence.

But how could the young ambitious Captain Jean de Joyneville know that he had unleashed the forces of darkness during one of the most diabolical periods—the Inquisition? Centuries later the very word still conjured images of torture and suffering. They believed they were cleansing the Church of foul pagan influences brought back from the Holy land by the 'Poor Knights.' Besides, the path to eternal peace was paved with suffering. Was that not the message the Son of God brought to mankind? Jean believed.

Jean knew of the plot against the Templars. He was the seneschal of Champagne and received his secret orders directly from the King of France, Philippe le Bel. He warned the Abbé of an impending raid so that neither the money, nor the treasure of the Order would be in the Paris Temple that night; nor were there any documents corroborating the accusations Jean himself had related to the King. The Order had a mysterious oath requiring initiates to spit on the cross. It was on the basis of this hearsay evidence that the Pope agreed to support Philippe in his campaign against the very popular Knights Templar.

When King Philippe himself entered the Paris Temple the following day, he was outraged to find the legendary treasure of the Templars gone, and no evidence of any alleged heresy was found. He ordered the soldier monks held captive, and subjected to the most rigorous questioning under torture, until the truth was told.

Meanwhile the entire Templar fleet headed by Etienne Lafoix escaped the round up. Because of De Joyneville's warning they were able to make their way to Amsterdam, and across the ocean to the land of the pyramids and the former Maya kingdom of the jungle. Many years later Christopher Columbus would also cross that same ocean, once again under the sail displaying the Templar cross.

Two Ospreys rode the thermal current overhead and looked down on the waves that crashed against the rugged coastline of southern France. The moaning wind howled. Rain pounded the coastal mountains to the west sweeping in a curtain toward the coast as the Poor Knights loaded crates on three ships moored beside the imposing Chateau Royale. Behind the veil of the black night sky, a force of equal and sullen magnitude stirred under a Moorish crescent Moon. Somewhere high in the mountains, rivers were beginning to burst their banks, soon to release a flood upon the lowlands.

Brother Marc shivered as the sky darkened. He silently folded his belongings and tied the parcel with thick cord. He made his way to the ships docked beside the castle.

There was a beehive of activity around the port. Three ships were being outfitted with supplies for a long journey, one that would take them half way around the world.

The Templar vessel *Sainte Claire* was one of the sturdiest in the fleet. Marc was a young novice. "Are you finished stowing your gear?" the burly First Mate grumped. "You can't take everything you own, you know!"

"I must have my books!" Marc cried.

The Mate laughed. "We can't be too careful you know. There are forces about the country fired up by the King who would dearly love to get their hands on our property and arrest us on some trumped up charge."

"Yes, Mate," Marc hurried past the crusty sailor as the wind and rain began to lash the ship's rigging.

When Marc returned to the top deck the Mate put his hand on his shoulder.

"Marc, come with me to the castle. There is something I need your help with."

"Yes, of course, Mate," the young monk covered his head with his hood. They quickly traveled the distance from the ship to the castle in the driving rain.

"Brother," he shouted running to keep up several strides behind the mate. "What is our destination? I mean, where our we headed tomorrow?"

The mate stopped, stood gravely silent in the rain, and turned to look at the novice trailing behind. In a flash of lightning the mate's face appeared, a weather worn patch of leather with small holes for eyes and a slit where a mouth should go, framed by a graying beard beneath his hood.

"Come inside. You are about to help change the course of history."

After many months at sea the descendants of the great Maya civilization greeted the white-coated knights as gods. The great treasure they brought with them, the sacred crystal skull of Christ, and the secret of Christ's life became one with the people of the forest, incorporated and blended with their own myths.

Years later the missionaries were shocked at the similarities between Christianity and the Maya religious myth of the crucifixion. Their version told that someday his heirs would inherit their rightful kingdom on earth again.

Balam was running out of time. He tucked the ceremonial knife into his belt and fled along with the hordes running past the flickering blue waters and green jungle flora, scaring the birds and fauna as they ran. The Quetzal bird was no longer a visitor to these parts having long since retreated deeper into the rain forest where it was safe from the greedy hands of men who plunder it for its beauty and for its entails to tell the future.

The deeper Balam ran into the jungle the more a permeating fear enveloped him. A monkey squealed from high atop a tree as Balam ran. He tripped over a root and impaled himself on the sharp, business end of the jeweled sword. He collapsed onto the jungle's carpet. He rolled over onto his back and wept until the river of tears flowed no more.

Balaam's blood, like hot molten ooze, spread across the floor of the rain forest. The radiant jeweled handle of the knife attracted the monkey still sitting in the tree. The monkey swung down onto the jungle floor. He looked Balam in the eyes, and touched him gently, recoiling at the sight of the dead man. Then he ever so carefully removed the blade from Balam's abdomen. The sparkle of the jewels reflected in the monkey's dark eyes. If a primate can smile this monkey did as he held the sacred sword in his almost human hands.

The jungle reclaimed all in the silence of Time; eternal defiance whispered on the wind. Twenty-five hundred year old trees stood as living testimony to the relativity of Time. Red, blue, yellow and green flowers rose from the jungle's time-lapse, and crept with their tiny fingers around the remains of Balam and Mahacutah and the others.

As the dust settled on the verdant carpet of the jungle floor, Time reclaimed all to itself. The sword that once cut out the beating heart of the living jaguar and held the power to see and change the future was lost forever in Time's organic web.

The telephone, that intruder of the modern age, woke Greg abruptly from his dreams. His aching body jerked reflexively to the sound of the telephone's summons. He reached into the darkness for the pieces of plastic, magnet, and wire that refused to stop ringing.

"Uh . . . Hello."

"Greg?" It was a woman's voice. It trembled like a wounded animal, a little desperate perhaps but definitely not Christie's. Her voice would be warm, and intuitive like she knew he had strange dreams of knights and Mayans. This voice was whispery smooth, perhaps a little weak and vulnerable too.

"Yes." He resisted to letting the voice in on his temporal confusion.

"You sound like you have a cold." The voice was beginning to sound familiar. For a split second his mind took him to back to the frigid waters of Bayswater beach where his spent his summers as a child. He was surfacing after a deep dive in the cold Atlantic.

"No . . . no, I just woke up. I always sound like this on the phone. People are always asking me if I have a cold. I think its allergies or something," Greg cleared his throat, and reached for the glass of water on the night table beside the bed. A neuron fired and he knew who it was.

"Kate, what's wrong?"

"Look, I can't talk now. Meet me at the ferry terminal." She hung up.

The ferry terminal? It has to be one of the sleaziest places in town—the kind of place where drug dealers, desperados and undercover cops hung out. Why would she be there? He queried, as he stepped into the shower.

The entire city seemed to be on strike, and the cabbies were working to rule, so he walked the eight blocks to the ferry terminal. Everyone was in a foul mood. Winos and derelicts hovered under the rotting supports of the expressway. As he walked by, one of the winos, a particularly aggressive fellow demanded payment. H kept walking, his pace picking up. He ignored the stares and taunts of the residents of this home for the desperately lost.

"Fuck you," came the insolent reply from behind. He glanced over his shoulder in time to see they had already lost interest in him and were huddling around a burning drum for warmth.

Greg stepped over broken whiskey bottles, around wrecked cars abandoned like pieces of lost luggage.

Kate was standing by the phone booth outside the ferry terminal. She looked worried. From the distance he could see something was bothering her. This wasn't the same self-confident girl from his class. This wasn't the young woman who was ready to take him on in front of everyone. She looked lost, not in a geographical sense, but in a spiritual way. Her make-up was thick and she wore a tight little mini-skirt. He almost laughed. But she had a sharp look about her that he had not noticed before, as she paced in front of the phone booth.

31

"Greg!" She gave a big smile, tossing her hair to one side. She reminded him of a horse trying to break free from its harness. For the first time he could see her father still had a hold on her. She looked deeply wounded. Every man was her father; this was her way of giving him what he always wanted, just like when she was a little girl.

"Kate, what are you doing down here alone?"

"Look, don't moralize, okay? I need your help."

She must be in trouble, he thought. *No, not Kate, she was too independent to be caught in a dime store novel.*

"Fine, fine, but can we go someplace else, a café or something?" He grabbed her by the hand and dragged her across the tram tracks under the expressway, her high heels clicked on the pavement all the way. He took a crazy risk. If her father was rich, maybe, just maybe she had money. And with money he could be free of always looking for money. He knew is it was insane, but something called him to follow his instincts, to follow this girl and her troubles.

In the second story seafood restaurant overlooking the harbor, the suit-set drank their morning coffee and some still chain-smoked cigarettes. He ordered 2 regular coffees from the sultry waiter and sat down next to a window with a view of the port. He looked her in the eyes without saying a word.

"Did you ever want to be part of a world you can never have?" she asked, staring blankly out onto the street where crowds of businessmen and women swarmed.

"Sure." His ambition was to be a millionaire by age 40. Just being a doctor would never get him what he wanted. He'd never achieve the kind of wealth he really craved. The freedom to do what he wanted, when he wanted. He knew he didn't have what it took to numb his senses to the reality of the horror, and suffering of his fellow humans for money. There had to be a better way. He looked horror in the face and turned away. He couldn't bear to look at it anymore. It was his failure. It made him sick. It was a part of himself he hated thinking about. It was a personal failure. He would always see himself as a failure. He hadn't reached his goal and he had learned he couldn't just pass time in a career. He remembered an experience from his army days in the Balkans. They had just come across a row of children nailed to the side of a house. He couldn't take it any more. He broke down. He left the army and came back to Canada. He was as confused now as any point in his life. He was throwing away his marriage—again. One career was out the window and another life that seemed so alien to him was emerging through the fog. He silently sipped his coffee and retreated to the safety of the past, where he could see what he wanted to see. A long time ago, in the jungle, he learned there was no such thing as good or evil. Nature doesn't moralize. But something inside of him did. He was torn. The aching heart of man longs for convenient ways to cope with the struggle called existence. No, he wasn't going to moralize. He just smiled warmly.

"My father," she sighed. "He phoned me last night. He's in some sort of trouble . . . and he needs my help." Tears swelled up in her eyes until she could no longer contain them.

"Go on," he reached out to touch her hand, to comfort this wounded creature. He had to remind himself she was his student and there could be ramifications.

"He's involved," she paused again, biting her lower lip. "He's mixed up with some group."

"Organized crime? Drugs?"

"No, something worse." She regained her composure and looked Greg directly in the eyes. "When I was a child, before my parents marriage hit the skids, and he started doing me . . . you know abusing me . . . my father was a big guy in the community. He worked in the British Foreign Office before the Second World War as an attaché, or something—he never liked to talk about the war—in the Balkans. After the war broke out he was sent back to London where he worked for MI6 the famous British Intelligence section. At the end of the war, he and my mom came to Canada where I was born. He was successful in a few real estate transactions, so he never had to work. He was an active volunteer. He joined the Legion, the Lions Club, etc. He attended St. Martin's church every Sunday, and then in 1993 he was invited to join the Masons. He began working for an American firm that did consulting work around the world.

He began traveling again, mainly to Eastern Europe where he had business contacts. He worked out of a temporary office in Sarajevo before Tito's death and then the civil war broke out in Yugoslavia.

"After my mom died—I was sixteen at the time—he began taking me along on his business trips. In the beginning it was fun. There was the excitement of hotels and peculiar food in strange countries. Later I began to realize I was there just to satisfy his urges. It was so awful. He made me feel dirty. After he disappeared, gradually but surely I evolved into what I am today. I always thought I might see him again, you know, by accident. He would have really gotten off on that." She blew a plume of cigarette smoke in the direction of the harbor.

"On one of these trips we were in Amsterdam, he met a man, another 'brother', I think. This fellow was fairly high up in 'the church,' as they called it. Anyway, he met the man, a Frenchman I think he was. I remember thinking it odd because he swore at my father, in French, then spit in his face before walking away. My father mentioned something about him being a heretic, and that people like that had to be taught a lesson, so others wouldn't do the same things. The way he said it made me feel like he was referring to me. I thought he meant that if I told anything about our relationship he would punish me. At the time, I believed he might even kill me if I said anything.

"That night he left without saying a word. The American Hotel I think it was, a stone's throw from the big museum in Amsterdam. I remember the lovely park, the fresh, clean smell of the air, with the artists selling their art.

"I loved the canals most of all, because the next morning the papers ran a piece about a tourist boat that found a man's body in the water crashing against one of those white pillars in the water by the docks. The head had been severed from its body with surgical precision. The picture in the paper showed the body lying supine on the ground beside the canal. The picture didn't show the victim above the shoulders, but I recognized that he didn't have any shoes on. That struck me as odd, because I recalled he wasn't wearing shoes when he was with my father. I know it's not conclusive, but it stuck with me. He had been a priest from the small town of Rennes-les-Bain in southern France.

"I knew then that my father was a dangerous man. But I never thought him capable of killing a man, especially a priest. It sent shivers down my spine. So when he called last night, I remembered Amsterdam."

"Why didn't you hang up? I mean you don't owe him anything after what he did to you."

"He knew he'd ruined my life, and he wanted to make it up to me. He was in some kind of trouble. He couldn't talk on the phone. He wanted to give me something that would set me up for life. He wanted to do this for me because he owed it to me."

"And you believed him?"

"I believed him. I believed him because he sounded like the father I knew as a young girl before my mother died and the pain. Besides, I could sure use the money."

"Did he mention anything about money?"

"No, but he said, I would be 'set for life'."

"Whatever that means!"

"Really, Greg! You're such a cynic."

"Perhaps, or maybe just a realist. But what makes you think he's got money?"

She smiled, obviously amused. It was the first time she smiled since they sat down. Outside the sky grew dark and it began to rain hard. The streets were full of people running for shelter from a sudden rainstorm.

"He's in Europe. He wants me to meet him in Amsterdam. Will you come with me?"

Greg didn't know what to say. He wanted to go, but there was the mess with Christie, and he had responsibilities at the university. It just wasn't possible. He knew he was irresponsible, but was he really that irresponsible? He'd have to get somebody to cover his classes. He might lose his job. Robin Fisher might help out. It could be done. He'd have to lie, but that was something he was getting good at. He'd phone Christie and tell her he'd been asked to give a paper, on short notice, at a conference in the Netherlands. She'd understand. The spontaneity appealed to him. Was he crazy? Was he being catapulted into freedom?

"Okay . . . you think he's got lots of money," Greg threw his hands up. "Call me irresponsible. I've always been a sucker for a treasure quest. But I've got to be back in Toronto by the end of next week. I don't want to lose my job."

She leaned over and kissed him on the cheek.

"Thanks. You won't regret it."

What a strange choice of words, he thought as he watched the traffic police tow away an illegally parked car.

FOUR

Greg picked up the morning paper in the lobby of the Hotel de l' Europe and walked to the hotel next door. He liked to bask in the morning sun from the De Jaren Restaurant terrace beside the Amstel River and watch the canal boats. Throngs of Japanese tourists snapped endless photos of the hotel. It was the only time of the day the sun actually shone in Amsterdam in October.

Greg puzzled over an enigmatic crossword, fifty-five down: *Rant's companion.* He hated crossword puzzles. He couldn't understand why some people wasted their time on the things. A patient he once had, an elderly fellow—nice chap—invented crossword puzzles for syndication. *Should I have stayed in clinical medicine? It wasn't too late,* he thought. *I could always go back. But not right now, something more important to do.* Kate had told him to look for a personal ad in The International Herald Tribune.

He glanced over to a very peculiar ad in bold type with a black box border: "DESPERATELY SEEKING GREG F. Meet at *De Melkweg Café,* 234a Lijnbaansgracht 20.00h. Wear a red tie. Kate." *A rather strange way to contact him,* he thought, *but Kate was rather unconventional, to say the least.* It was a wonder he hadn't noticed the ad earlier. He pictured the place full of Greg Fallows wearing red ties. He smiled, the warm sun on his face. He was on a quest for treasure. Maybe this time he'd win the jackpot.

Nigel Lockhart drew the blinds of his third story window in the Eden Hotel overlooking the Amstel River as he hung the telephone receiver back on its cradle. It wasn't easy for him to phone Kate. Things had been rough for her since Sarajevo. Now again, the world was being turned upside down. History as we know it was about to be blown wide open. And Nigel Lockhart was the one who was going to do it.

He walked to the tiny bathroom to wash his face. Looking in the mirror he saw his once bright eyes were now a cloudy fog. His hand trembled as he put a finger to his eye to expose his yellowing sclera. He looked older than his seventy-five years. He was an old man now. This would be his last secret mission. The cancer eating his liver would soon devour his body. He needed to see Kate, to reconcile with her before he died. He had to warn her.

After he'd relocated back to London from the Balkan trade office, he worked with a branch of MI6 to set up a network of counter-espionage agents in the Balkans during the civil war. These weren't good times; many of his former friends in Sarajevo were captured and later killed.

When the war ended, he jumped at the chance to be a part of the emerging UN information office known simply as G2. The joke around New York at that time was that the bureau was called the "information office" because everyone knew that anyone with any intelligence wouldn't work for the UN. Besides, official policy was the UN had no need for an intelligence department. It smacked of espionage and that was politically incorrect—even back then. Reality, however, was much more insidious. With the fall of the Berlin Wall, the end of the cold war and the never-ending wars in the Balkans, G2 had emerged as the most powerful organization inside the UN. Although officially an information gathering arm of the Secretary General's office, G2's secret membership list included some of the wealthiest men in the world, and some of the most powerful on the planet. Their ambition of global government would soon be within their grasp.

It was time the public knew about the designs this shadowy group had for the world as a result of the power vacuum created by the end of the cold war.

He'd made arrangements to meet with an Israeli journalist Jerry Simon. Simon had been working on a series of articles for the Herald

Tribune-Washington Post on the existence of a powerful and secret lobby group at the UN. Nigel intended to pass to Simon a valuable G2 membership list. As he tucked his comb back into his overnight bag, he remembered Kate. He'd done some terrible things. Could she ever forgive him? Perhaps not, but he'd at least make a difference in her life. Simon was prepared to pay $25,000 for hard evidence. The money would go to Kate. She'd be able to get an education at least.

He locked the door behind him and carefully walked down the narrow stairs of the apartment, breathing deeply, peacefully. He opened the front door and stepped out into the dull drizzle of Amsterdam. He buttoned up his coat and opened his umbrella. In his pants pocket a 9 mm Springfield XD service model pistol bounced against his leg. Two punks rolled out of the Big Fun coffeehouse bumping him onto the narrow road along the canal. A blue VW bus screeched to a halt as two men dressed as policemen jumped out. They quickly thrust the old man into the van and disappeared.

Kate took an earlier flight. She wanted time alone with her father. Greg arranged to meet her a couple of days later. As luck would have it, Greg's colleague Robin Fisher had to rearrange plans for outpatient surgery—a prostate problem—at any rate he was only too glad to postpone it.

Before she left for Amsterdam Kate mentioned her father was now in the diamond business, import-export stuff, nothing big . . . or illegal. She had made a point of saying that.

There was still something very strange about Kate. He folded the paper and drank his thick Dutch coffee. He glanced over the Amstel; the river sparkled as the clouds and short rainstorm turned into brilliant sunlight again.

Greg needed a tie, a red tie (something he didn't own). He walked across Rokin to Vroom and Dressman's department store where he bought a red floral patterned tie for Euro 39.95. *A real extravagance*, he thought as he held it up to his neck. The matronly clerk gave a nod of satisfaction.

He checked his watch. He put on a raincoat, tucked an umbrella under his arm, and headed south along Koningsplein to Leiderstraat.

He wanted to have plenty of time to find a place called *De Melkweg*. He passed the time window-shopping along Leidsestraat. He passed a shop called the Torture Museum. He considered checking it out but decided to pass. As he walked he thought about Christie. No matter what he did life seemed to reach up and smack him. If he could only win big, just this once, he could make things up to her. They could start over. They could even adopt a child if she wanted. He knew she ached over the inability to have children. He was resigned to it being to just another kick in the head. He had to win big this time. He just had to make it work.

De Melkweg was across the street from the police station on Lijnbaansgracht. It was an anachronism by modern standards. Opened in 1970 at the height of the hippie era, it gained a reputation during the seventies and eighties as a sort of counter-culture United Nations. Today it just seemed seedy; with its tacky sixties art deco stars hanging above the door; its avant-garde veneer wearing all too thin.

It was a strange place to meet, an even stranger place to wear a red tie. Nobody wears a tie here. They might not even let him enter wearing a tie, especially a *red tie*.

An androgynous Gothoid with black leather jacket at the ticket counter looked Greg up and down. *I think s/he dislikes red ties as much as I do*, he thought. He fumbled for the right change and decided to wait for Kate at the bar on the main floor. He found his way to the bar and ordered a Heineken. He sipped his beer and looked around the room. The sound level was off the Richter scale as the music blasted from the huge speakers at the end of the long room. The patrons were straight out of the Star Wars movie bar scene. *Such a practical joker, she's going to hear about this.* He looked out the window across the canal to the police station across the street. He decided to check out the club. Maybe Kate was in another part of the building.

Admission to the club cost him Euro 30.00, including Euro 15.00 for a membership Greg would never use again. The place was a maze of activity; two bars, a cinema, a stage with the Fellini twins playing dueling violins. He didn't know for sure but it sounded like a sort of Hungarian rhapsody in F minor. Upstairs there was video, another café, and a black and white video art show where naked women thumped to primitive drums on a large silhouette projected on a wall sized screen.

Off to the sides were several smaller rooms where the smell of burning hemp permeated the air. Throughout the dark clandestine atmosphere a constant beat pounded, mixed with dense cigarette smoke. He found it hard to breath.

From behind came a tap on the shoulder.

"Greg!"

"Kate?" He spun around and stared at her, feeling lost, out of place, and extremely uncomfortable.

"You look great," She planted a big red kiss on his cheek. *More like branded,* he thought.

"You look . . . well, how should I say, pretty . . . stylish, yes, that's the word." In fact, she had an uncanny talent for blending in with her environment beautifully. Her brown hair was pulled tightly into a greasy ponytail. Her pale complexion made her look like a fallen Metal angel.

She wore a form-fitting spandex suit, and a black leather bomber jacket. Her red lips were outlined with a charcoal black liner and she smoked French Gallois cigarettes for full heavy Metal effect.

When she kissed him, she stepped on his toe with her heavy black leather cowboy boots, the kind of boots with elastics and silver ringlets at the back. She looked foreign, something out of this world.

"Why all the mystery?" Greg shouted above the din of the euro-beat. "Why didn't you just call my hotel? You knew where I'd be staying."

"You can't be too careful in A'dam," she replied flippantly, taking a long drag on her cigarette, scanning the room disinterestedly. She took Greg by the hand over to one of the smoking tables in the corner by a wall-sized fish tank.

"Look." She was suddenly serious. "We have to get one thing straight. My father needs my help. If you're going to help, don't ask a lot of questions, okay?"

"Have you spoken with him?" Greg demanded, as the pull of the vortex sucked him into the wind tunnel of Fate.

"Yes, he'll meet us tomorrow at the Rijksmuseum. Two o'clock. Now, let's just try and have some fun tonight. Okay?"

"Okay! Now let's get out of here," Greg stood up. He seized her wrist and began heading for the exit.

"Wait! I'm not finished," she grabbed hold of the table.

"Well I am!" Greg dragged her reluctantly toward the door.

"Look, if you want my help, we play by my rules. Got it?"

"Sure," she flashed a smirk of contempt. "But I have to go."

She walked briskly away from him, disappearing along Marnix Straat. Greg chased after her.

"Wait! What time tomorrow?" He grasped her arm.

"Two o'clock, main foyer, Rijksmuseum, and let go of me." Her look cut him off. He let go.

"See you tomorrow then?" He called after her suddenly noticing the pile of dog shit he'd stepped into and thought *what is it with this city? What is it with me? Why did I follow her to this weird place?*

Everywhere he looked he was reminded of a B movie. The odd and the innocent, glued together in this spot on the planet by God knows what. It sure wasn't the weather. It rained again that night. He stopped at the American Café across the street, where the alleged spy-vamp Mata Hari held her wedding reception. The literati supposedly liked to hang out there, but who could tell the art from the non-art crowd in this city.

He awoke to a sound. Was it a dream? He wasn't sure what it was. European phones have a very different ring.

"Hello,"

"215?"

"Yes."

"A call for you sir . . ." Then silence.

"Greg?"

"Yes . . . Kate is that you? What time is it?"

"Never mind that now; something terrible has happened. It's my father, he's . . . dead." He voice began to break.

"What? I mean, what happened?"

"I don't know. The police found him hanging under one of the bridges near Oude Hoogstraat in the red light district; his hands tied behind his back; his feet dangling in the water."

"Suicide?" The word seemed to get stuck in Greg's throat.

"No. You can't tie your own hands behind your back."

Good point, he thought. *What have I gotten into?*

"Where are you now?" He was genuinely concerned for her safety.

"Just a block from your hotel at De Engelwaarde pub. The police at Kloveniers Burgwal just finished questioning me."

"How . . . ?"

"Not now Greg. I have to see you. Meet me here."

"I'll be there in twenty minutes," He was sitting on the edge of the bed.

"No, right now!" He could hear the excitement in her voice.

"Okay, Okay, I'll be there in a couple of minutes."

Ten minutes later he walked up the steps of De Engelwaarde pub. In its hey-day it was a trendy spot to drink Bokma gin and smoke hand-rolled cigarettes. This time of the day it's empty except for a handful of committed drinkers sipping cognac with their coffee.

Kate sat in the corner by the window nursing a frothy Amstel. She gave no visible sign of emotion as Greg walked in the front door.

"A little early isn't it?" he looked at the beer as he sat down.

"Or a little too late."

The air was tense. It was hard for him not to stare out the window at the brackish water of the canal beside the pub. He wanted to avoid eye contact. He knew he wouldn't know what to say. A house boater was just getting up. He emerged from his floating home. He gave a cough and his breath evaporated in a cloud of damp cold air.

"It was either beer or brandy." She nervously held the glass up to the light beginning to radiate through the window. Her hand shook. This child-woman who dragged him off to Amsterdam was clearly shaken by the news. But there was an inconsistency. Greg couldn't understand really why she was so upset. She behaved like she hated his guts. Something didn't make sense. Then it came to him in a flash. She's not mourning, she's scared.

"My God, he's dead," she burst into tears.

A flood of tears followed. It was the release of a river damned. The force of her tears gushed forth with such pent-up fury that Greg put his arm around her just to calm her.

"What did the police say?" he asked moving closer.

"They believe he was involved in some sort of diamond smuggling scam." She wiped the tears from her face with a curious white handkerchief made of Belgium lace.

"It sounds like you don't believe them." He watched the mascara run down her cheek. *It makes her seem older than she is*, he thought as he flagged the waiter to bring her another beer, and a coffee for himself.

"Of course not," she declared, her wet red eyes flashed a hostile message. Her mascara was now a river of purple tears.

"Look, why don't you tell me what's bothering you. The truth?"

She looked at Greg with that same distracted look he'd seen outside *De Milkweg Café*.

"He was a Knight."

"I know, you told me he was a Mason. But that's not a reason to get murdered. Lots of people are Masons, and Lions and Kiwanians. What about what the police suggested. Maybe he was into something illegal. God knows there's enough trouble to get into in this town."

"No, it's more than you think; some of them are more serious about this stuff than others. You've read Dan Brown.

Sure, in many places that's all it is, secret handshakes and stuff . . . a kind of charity, but it can also be more, a . . ."

"A kind of club?" he interjected sarcastically.

"A real conspiracy." She ignored him. "It's no use. You'll never understand will you?" She stared coldly out the window at the trees tossed about by the wind along the canal. University students came and went through a gate on the other side of the canal. The cruel reality is life goes on. It should stop when a loved one dies, but it doesn't. The world is absorbed in its own arrogant dream.

As they walked along the canal Greg couldn't help but wonder whom this woman really was. He knew her vaguely from one of his classes. She was certainly full of surprises, and now here he was in Amsterdam, and her father was dead—murdered? Maybe. He didn't really know this woman. What had possessed him to come with her? Was he so naive that he fell for the old, family trouble routine? Or was it his magical thinking? Perhaps he was delusional and running away from life. He'd made another mistake. He had his own emotional mess to contend with, his own family trouble.

Greg grew up an only child in Vancouver, Canada. His father was a frustrated but successful stockbroker. His father scorned religion. His mother was a Presbyterian. She had been brought up in an era of declining Edwardian morality. In her home feelings were rarely discussed. There was a benign silence at meal times. Conversation over dinner was discouraged. He didn't bring friends home from school. He learned to nurture a kind of secret world for himself. He read a great deal and spent many quiet hours making model airplanes and drawing pictures of distant, mythical lands. His world changed dramatically when his parents died when he was sixteen. They were killed in a car accident during a rare B.C. blizzard. He went from having everything he needed to abject poverty. He hated poverty. The fear of it drove him to take enormous risks and in so doing to fall into the very thing he feared most. He threw away people and things that came too close because he didn't want to become attached or miss them when they were gone. Life is going to get you in the end. So what's the point? He couldn't win. Death and humiliating defeat were always waiting to cut you down to size. Lack of money was the worst feeling in the world for him.

It wasn't until he left for Dalhousie University in Nova Scotia that he came out of his inner world. It was at Dal that he discovered women. In sex he found the emotional nourishment he'd never received at home. But it seemed he was never satisfied. It was a bottomless pit that had to be constantly refilled—a monster howling to be fed. At the time he married Christie he assumed that feeling had ended, but he couldn't lie to himself any longer. Empty and alone failure gnawed at his heels. Success for Greg meant, pure and simple: money. Once again looking for the answer in a strange woman's eyes. He was running from himself, headfirst into himself.

He remembered the dream, the day Christie left, in which he ran into himself and he awoke terrified. He was chasing his own tail like the dragon described in Professor Hunt's book The Phenomenology of Alchemy.

They walked, just walked for quite some time without saying anything. The city came alive as bicycles zipped around them everywhere. They walked down Leidsestraat again past the Torture Museum. This time it had an existential meaning to him. They stopped and stared at the poster depicting a macabre version of a Madame Tussaud-like medieval nightmare.

"Let's check it out." Kate seemed overly attracted to the ghastly posters. Greg paid for their tickets. They entered by walking down a long dark hall that smelled of urine and cigarettes. They descended a spiral staircase that opened into a well-lit office with wide windows that led to a courtyard behind the building. Through dirty lace curtains Greg could see white wrought iron garden chairs set around a well manicured Dutch garden.

Two men wearing suits, possibly in their late fifties or early sixties, sat at a small table facing the garden. Greg couldn't hear what they were saying, but they were having an animated discussion. One of the men stopped and looked over at Greg and Kate peering through the curtains.

The taller man with short white hair in military style had sharp, high cheekbones, and tanned weathered skin. He approached Greg and introduced himself simply as Brentano. The other man stood up from the table and walked with his hands behind his back over to a wet bar and poured himself a Sourcy. He turned and looked sharply at Kate and Greg. Autumn was in the air; the smell of burning wood from fires across the rooftops permeated the central courtyard.

"You know," Brentano said in English, cut with a heavy German accent, "we have been meeting here in Amsterdam for quite a few years. And this is the first time we've had to bring in an . . . how shall we say . . . an outsider." He motioned for them to sit down at the table. Greg was puzzled, but he was hardly in a position to refuse such truculent hospitality. Brentano's manner and command of English conveyed sophistication bred on superiority.

The other man, a short stocky fellow in a three piece suit that looked too small for his large frame drummed his stubby little fingers on the table impatiently. Brentano continued.

"We have talked around the issue for some time now, but I still have the feeling that there are those who we call loyal, who for personal gain have forgotten the need to be loyal to the church above all else." He looked sharply at Kate, and after a pause he lit a cigarette. He continued shaking his head.

"What do you mean by 'the church?'" Greg interrupted.

"Forgive me. I must have forgotten my manners. Let me introduce my associate, Mr. Hunt."

The balding man in the three-piece suit waved a stubby finger as if bored by the interview. His long nose and fat red face had small slits for eyes, which made him look like an unfriendly caricature of photographs on numerous book covers.

"You have always had too much faith in people." Hunt spoke without any trace of emotion in a perfect Oxford accent. He motioned for Greg to sit next to him at the table. Greg was puzzled by the sudden familiarity.

"Come, sit down. We are anxious to see what news our young colleague Dr. Greg Fallows has brought for us."

"I don't know what you're talking about." Greg sat down, more than a little surprised these strangers knew his name. Kate took a seat in a folding chair in the shadows of a far corner. He couldn't catch her eye.

"Look, all I know is that I was asked to come to Amsterdam by Kate," Greg thrust his chin toward Kate sitting silently. "To help her father," he added nodding his head for emphasis. He was sinking deeper into something he knew nothing about. And he didn't want to know more.

"Look, I'm just a physician with an interest in archeology . . ."

"We know all about your research," Hunt abruptly rose and walked to a window overlooking the courtyard. He turned as if he had blocked this scene many times before and knows his part well.

Greg gasped.

"I don't know what you mean."

"You haven't been asked for anything," Hunt smiled. He took a long leisurely drag on his cigarette.

"Yes, of course," Greg again looked toward Kate.

"We are interested in your work in Guatemala," Hunt's tone changed abruptly, and blowing smoke rings into the air, at the same time he gave his cigarette an arrogant flick.

"How does that concern you?" Greg asked surprised they knew about it.

"The fall of civilizations are a major hobby of ours, doctor," With the word "doctor" he curled his thin lips into a pucker exposing his irregular teeth.

"Yes, of course," Greg felt the intended slight. His eyes searched for a response from Kate. There was none.

Hunt's glare made him nervous. He looked down at the patio stones and fidgeted. He thought, *this couldn't be the same Professor Hugh Hunt*, and looked back at Brentano.

"We are interested in a codex you discovered near the Guatemalan-Mexican border."

Greg was confused. What was happening? Why were they here? Were they waiting for him? Was Kate in on this? Was this a trap? Why were these people interested in his work on the Maya? Did Kate bring him here on purpose? He became dizzy with questions swirling around in his head. Was the some kind of trial?

"Did you bring the manuscript, as instructed?" Hunt barked, looking at Kate.

"Yes." Reaching into her purse she took out a brown manila envelope, the kind that are used for sending everything from form letters to stolen copies of other people's work. Greg already knew she was acquainted with his work, but how could she have gotten a copy? And brought it to Amsterdam? She must have stolen it from the Department. That wouldn't be hard to do, not for a cunningly clever woman like Kate.

"You needn't worry about my colleagues."

"I don't understand," Greg protested.

"Shall we proceed," Brentano ignored him.

"Yes," Greg was feverish with excitement. "I call the codex—which really is a copy of a petroglyph and interpretive manuscript—The Myth of the Skull of Doom."

Hunt chuckled. Brentano looked at Hunt severely as if to say, 'That's not funny.' Then they looked back at him.

"Let's see the manuscript please," Hunt politely held out his hand. Kate handed him a digital photograph of a petroglyph taken in a remote area north of Tikal, near the border between Guatemala and Mexico.

"This is the missing piece," Hunt stroked his fat face. "But we have missed an important element in the sequence of events." He looked troubled for a moment as if the whole meeting was a waste of time. Then he smiled, a knowing, devilish grin.

"All along we have been mislead," he began. "Our journey into the science of history has us led down many blind alleys. We have peeled back a secret membrane of time to reveal your destiny," as Hunt stopped miming the peeling of a banana, Brentano picked up the cue.

"There are many meanings to experience and behavior that are not immediately accessible to us," agreeing with Hunt.

"But what does this have to do with the Myth of the Skull of Doom codex?" Greg asked, puzzled by the vague inferences. "I've been trying to decipher it for almost a year now. How did you know I had it anyway?"

"It means we are very close to putting the pieces of our enigma together," ignoring Greg's question.

"There is one last piece. We must have it!" Brentano hammered his fist on the table.

"I've studied Maya civilization for a few years now, and I confess I don't have any idea what you're talking about," Greg shook his head, truly perplexed. "I spent four months living with the people. I've heard many of their legends and myths."

"Then you are also familiar with legend of the 'Skull of Doom.' That is all for now. You will return to you hotel," Hunt announced abruptly. "You will discuss our visit with no one. Understand? We may contact you again."

"What about Kate?" Greg asked looking at her in the corner. She hadn't acknowledged his existence since their arrival. She had been as cold and aloof as a statue. "Her work is done," and he quickly disappeared down a hallway.

It was all just a bad dream. Brentano dropped Greg off at his hotel. When he opened the door to his room, he was suddenly extremely tired. *Perhaps I've been drugged*, he thought as he flopped down on the bed kicking off his shoes. *But when? And how?* So many questions remained unanswered. As the fog of sleep crept over him an absurd thought flashed across his mind . . . he had found something more important than he'd ever dreamed of. He'd found something profoundly important. He sat bolt upright in bed. So important in fact that someone could get killed over it.

"Christie!"

FIVE

It was getting dark rapidly, as it always does in the tropics. The twilight sky cast a spell over the heavy jungle foliage. The birds began to sing their love songs and warning.

Greg held her. She trembled with fear.

"It's okay Ana. You can tell me. It's okay. Tell me what happened."

Ana, a 15-year-old Guatemalan girl had become lost in the jungle. She came upon a tall grass hut she had never seen before. It grew very dark, so she crawled on her hands and knees into the shelter that led down into a cave. The walls of the cave were brightly painted with pictures depicting the hunt and slaughter of various animals. The air was thick and heavy. Ana found it difficult to breath in the stagnant air.

Within minutes, people appeared wearing long white robes, over their heads they wore jaguar masks with brilliant emerald eyes. They bowed down in front of Ana to offer her food and drink from a special silver chalice. She was very thirsty. But instead of water they gave her warm human blood to drink. She managed to sip some of the blood but its salty taste repulsed her.

Her hosts brought her to a pile of garbage covered with leaves for a bed. She unwillingly laid down on it and tried to sleep. In the darkness millions of eyes stared at her. She was frozen with fear. She didn't know what to do.

In the morning she was given a woven basket. It was fastened shut with the seal of the jaguar people. She was warned not to open it until she was safely at home with her family.

When Ana arrived home she opened the basket. She found a beautiful skull with emerald eyes that seemed to glow in the dark. It was "the skull of Jesus Christ" her mother said making the sign of the cross, eyes wide.

She told Greg, her brother Arturo saw the strange gift and was struck with jealousy. He stole the skull one night and fled the village. The next morning Arturo was pyretic and covered with pustules. He opened the lid and saw a jaguar's heart beating as if alive. Out of the aorta rushed a giant snake that attacked his eyes and covered his body with a million bites until he lay on the ground immobile, stung to death.

Greg awoke with his heart pounding and an impending sense of doom. He was terrified. He sat on the edge of the bed with his head in his hands. He couldn't shake it away. *Was this some kind of omen?* "Another strange dream," he exclaimed aloud. *What's happening to me?* Then it came to him. Christie was in danger. He had to warn her quickly. He picked up the telephone and dialed the front desk.

"Hello, get me the overseas operator please."

Rijkspolitie Inspector Hans Kroode with the water squad of the Amsterdam police, based on De Ruijterkade, was accustomed to chasing speeders in boats, and hauling bodies out of the canals, but in the past year he and his team have pulled 52 bodies from the brown waters of Amsterdam's canals. The bloated bodies spent an average of a month in the water before the decomposing gases in the intestinal tract fermented causing them to float skyward rolling against the canal walls, their disfigured carcasses resembling caricatures of their former human selves.

Most were victims of their own excess, falling into the canal after attempting to urinate while intoxicated. Others had been robbed, murdered and dumped; still others were junkies playing a game that inevitably resulted in death.

But this case was different. The body was found under the bridge over Kloveniersburgwal at Staalstaat, in the heart of the city.

It could be seen by everyone coming to work. Undoubtedly it was meant for someone specifically in this area to see and to be warned, or scared off.

The body was first spotted by a student on her way to the University of Amsterdam around the corner. Lisa, a foreign language student in the translation program, spotted the body swinging, feet below the water line, under the bridge as she stopped to catch the morning rays of the sun as it poured over this 700 year old city that bright fall Monday morning.

Inspector Hans Kroode's police boat came speeding around the Amstel River from its base on De Ruijterkade. At this time of the day it was faster to go by water than to suffer the morning traffic congestion on the streets. As they rounded the corner to Kloveniersburgwal canal the body of an older man wearing a suit, probably late fifties, could be seen. The police doctor, Dr. Pieter Teunon, would be along shortly, to examine the body before removal from the scene.

At thirty-nine, Inspector Kroode was a fifteen-year veteran of the Rijkspolitie's elite water brigade. At five feet eleven inches with thinning blond hair at the crown he looked more like a well-fed monk than a policeman. His serious blue eyes betrayed an intensity that it was wise not to brook. His mouth, like the rest of his features was sharp and boyish. His team traveled by truck and trailer; hauling a high speed eleven foot Zodiac for rapid response

The canal reeked of urine as they pulled alongside under the old drawbridge over Staalstraat. The corpse wore no shoes and the toes below the water had bled, possibly from ritual torture. The vacant eyes of the dead man reflected the mushroom soup water of the canal.

The corpse had been secured with yellow nylon rope. The hands tied behind the back extending to the legs. This caused the body to hang forward on the rope, bobbing to and fro as if acknowledging the icy water below with a respectful nod. There was a single bullet, perhaps 9 mm, in the center of the forehead. The exit site had blown of the back of the head clear off. The eyes were fixed wide open. Their cold stare and deep black pupils were nothing compared to the wide-open mouth gaping for mercy not found. This was an execution style murder. In this city, the chance of finding the murderer was remote, even less than that, probably next to nil. The body tossed about in the gusty October breeze as they waited for Dr. Pieter Teunon. The clouds would soon cover the horizon again and it would rain soon.

Dr. Pieter Teunon was the perfect police doctor. At forty-two he was a medical graduate of the University of Amsterdam with not one but two graduate degrees. A pathology residency research stint at the Allard Pierson Museum had him investigate the cause of death of some of the Egyptian mummies in the Museum. Later he completed a forensic pathology residency program at Johns Hopkins in Baltimore. For the past ten years he'd worked with the Rijkspolitie. Over the years he'd gotten hardened to the smell of his job. It is the smell that gets the first timers. It's always the smell and nobody ever writes about that.

Pieter arrived ten minutes after the Inspector and his team.

"Sorry for the delay," he nodded to Hans as he got out of his black police Mercedes 190E. His was about the same height as the Inspector, but his hair was dark brown and still abundant. He wore round plastic glasses. But his sunken eyes, pale skin and thin lips made him look rather ghoulish. Hans shook the doctor's soft clinical hand.

"Better late than never," and Hans pointed in the direction of the canal.

"He's not going anywhere by the looks of him," Pieter replied sarcastically.

"Have you photographed the scene yet?" Pieter asked the Inspector.

"What do you think we've been doing?" Hans replied, and then added with a smirk, "Just waiting for you, darling."

Pieter waved as if to say: "go on, get out of here." He was a professional, a detail man. He was the right man for the job at hand.

When Pieter gave the okay, three policemen from the homicide team cut the body down and placed it on a sheet of plastic by the edge of the canal. Another team of policeman kept curious onlookers from getting too close.

"I remember a case in London, in '89, I think it was," and held his gloved right finger over the 9 mm hole in the victim's forehead—point blank range for sure. There would be powder burns around the wound.

"Somebody wants to get a message out to someone," Hans droned looking the Inspector in the eyes.

"A guy with the Vatican Bank was found hanged in a similar fashion under a bridge in London in '89. He was involved with a secret sect possibly connected with an ultra-secret group of Masons. There was some sort of conspiracy, as I recall, involving highly placed members of the Italian government and business community . . . and possibly even the Catholic Church. Although it's never been confirmed—or solved," he added.

Hans didn't say anything; he continued to smoke a cigarette he'd bummed from one of the junior policeman on the homicide team.

"See this Hans?" Pieter asked looking up from his position over the body lying on the plastic sheet.

Hans put another cigarette out, stubbing out the butt with his boot on the cobblestone road next to the body. Over the victim's heart was a tattoo: two overlapping stars of David, each about the size of a Dutch coin. The Euro that replaced it was itself about to crash and burn. It was clearly a death with a message: a cold-blooded murder with a warning.

"I hope this isn't some kind of Nazi thing," and bent over to take closer look at the intricate detail of the design. Clearly it wasn't new. It had been a part of this man's body for a long time.

"Looks like its been there for years," Pieter leaned forward. "Whoever killed him thought about removing it after death." He pointed to a cigarette burn in the upper right corner of the double pentagram.

"There can be no doubt now. Does the double pentagram have nothing to do with Judaism? We need to get Intelligence on this one straightaway. Ask them to check out cults, secret societies and shit like that."

"Hell of a way to start the week," said Hans tossed his cigarette into the canal.

SIX

The next morning Christie opened the door to her apartment. She was determined to survive this storm. She was not going to allow Gregory Winston Fallows to throw his life—and hers—away. Whatever demons were torturing him, she vowed that she would lash herself to the mast and hold on. She had an intuition and a confidence that things would be all right. But she had to go after him. She turned the radio on. The sound of Margo Timmins and the Cowboy Junkies played a memory . . . "Misguided angel love you to death . . ." It brought tears to her eyes. She picked up her cello and played along with such passion it shook her to her very core. She had neglected to nurture her soul, and the music fed her hungry spirit.

Christie was an exceptional woman. She had long blonde hair and a well-proportioned athletic figure. She looked great for her late thirties. Her cheeks and lips were naturally rosy. She shunned make-up, and wore baggy comfortable pants and a loose denim shirt. She was a professional and she would take control of her life. She refused to play the victim. But she was hungry for meaning. And if she couldn't have children, she would create her own meaning. The apartment was lonely and cold. She had an apprehensive feeling and it had something to do with Greg. She had an intuitive sense, an instinct. She had an uncanny way of reading her emotions as harbingers of the future. She knew from experience she had to listen to the music of her moods, and the difference it could make. She sensed danger. It came to her in an insight. She had to find Greg. He needed her strength. He needed to understand the future would be all right if she was there. She had to stop him from making a mistake. She didn't know what it was, but she knew he needed her now.

She remembered those endless days of youth they shared, like their first trip to Guatemala when Greg had almost gotten arrested by the army for not carrying his passport. Or the time he got arrested outside the bus station in Vera Cruz in Mexico. Every time he got into trouble she had to bail him out.

But there was a howling wolf out there hunting him. It was a rage suckled by madness. Could it be her imagination? No, she knew she was right and she had to act on her instinct.

Christie moved about the apartment with a renewed sense of purpose. A deep determination told her to get packed. She didn't know where yet, that too would come.

She decided to start with Stephen Parmata, her old Australian friend, himself a "reformed priest" as he referred to himself, now working as a writer and art dealer. He'd made quite a reputation for himself exposing an art scam recently. She looked up his number in her address book and dialed. He wasn't in, so she left a message.

The doorbell rang. In the seconds it took her to cross the room her life would change. That's the way it is with only five senses. We only perceive a defined and narrow part of the spectrum of being. Even beyond the surface of the lives of Christie and Greg, and all life, there is a tension. Not the tension of conflict and plots, but entropy of atoms, an energy wearing down unseen by the senses.

She opened the door without so much as hesitating. She should have left the safety chain on and looked first, not that it would have mattered, but she could have been more cautious. Greg used to warn her about safety and vague notions like street smarts, living downtown and all.

Christie grew up in the gated community of Rexmont Hill, a suburban girl. She was used to leaving the doors unlocked. Nobody ever violated another's privacy in Rexmont Hill when she was growing up, well at least they never used to. Of course, things are different now. Russian and Asian gangs drive Lexus around Rexmont Hill, and people get shot. Things had changed.

She turned the deadbolt. The door flew open. Two men dressed in blue workmen's coveralls burst into the room and slammed the door behind them. They wore nylon masks and surgical gloves. They were armed with the tools of their trade. She wanted to scream but nothing came out. In a flash, before she could say a word they grabbed her and spun her around. One of them held her while the other silver taped her mouth shut. She struggled but they subdued her easily. They bound her legs at the ankles with tape and taped her hands tightly behind her back; all in a matter of seconds, not minutes.

She was determined to remember something about their behavior. She tried to etch every movement into her memory without success. Their nylon masks twisted their faces into hideous shapes. The more she struggled the faster their faces faded into nothing as the burning in her right arm from the injection spread through her entire body. Finally she embraced the balm of sleep.

When ready, they loaded her into a laundry hamper outside the door. They carried her down the stairs to avoid running into neighbors, although that was unlikely—they had been watching her place for 24 hours.

The van with the *Snappy Laundry* service logo disappeared into the morning traffic on Lakeshore Drive.

On the back of a hotel postcard Greg wrote:

> Dear Christie:
> I am left alone and uncertain what I've done. I can't seem clearly to separate dreams from reality. But something deep inside compels me to see this thing through to the end. There are just too many loose ends.
> Love, G.

Greg dropped the postcard in the mailbox and walked down Singel Straat. The hustle and bustle of nightlife made him realize how precious little time there really is in life. Could Kate really work for those strange men? Well, obviously! They weren't the Hollywood version of criminals. But what did he know? They seemed well educated, refined. Okay, there was a darker side. Wait a minute; it occurred to him they might have something to do with Kate's father's death. But why? He walked across Muntplein and crossed over to Nieuwe Dielenstraat dodging the heavy traffic. He couldn't understand how such well-heeled and intelligent men could be so gullible. He didn't understand it.

As he turned the key to his hotel room the phone rang.

"215?"

"Yes . . ."

"We have a package for you. May we send it up?"

"Er . . . sure . . . send it up." Greg hung up the phone. Moments later there was a knock on the door.

"Package for you, sir," the blonde male bellhop looked very happy to be alive, his teeth gleamed a perfect commercial smile.

"What is it?" Greg asked.

"I don't know, sir," the bellhop beamed. He held the parcel out for Greg then disappeared down the lift.

Greg closed the door, and then carefully locked the deadbolt lock behind him. Once inside the sanctuary of his room he placed the envelope on the coffee table for closer scrutiny. It was a standard 81/2 x11 brown manila envelope addressed:

Dr. Gregory Fallows
The Hotel de l' Europe
Amsterdam, NL
Room 215

There was no return address. In fact, there was no postage. It must have been brought by hand. He phoned the front desk.

"Front desk," the pleasant voice answered abruptly after several rings.

"Yes, this is Dr. Fallows in room 215. Someone just dropped a letter off for me. I wanted to thank them, do you know who delivered it?"

"There has been no letter for you, sir," the voice replied without hesitation.

"No . . . I mean the one the bell hop just delivered to my room . . . just now."

"I am the only one taking messages at this time of night, sir . . . and I didn't deliver any letters, sir."

"That's very strange," Greg reflected. "Someone, a blonde bell hop, a very nice fellow, with a very pleasant attitude . . . he just dropped off an envelope for me, and it has no return address, and I was just wondering if you could tell me where it came from?"

"Sorry, sir, I'm the only messenger on right now, and I have brown hair—what little of it there is."

"You're sure?" Greg probed.

"Quite," the voice grew irritated and he hung up the phone.

Greg sat on his divan and opened the envelope. Inside was an onionskin parchment with a list of Grand Masters of the Knights Templar and a digitized photograph of the Tiger of the Moon codex. Greg understood the symbols and knew exactly what they meant. It welcomed the arrival of Dagobert the King to the New World. Dagobert was holding "the Skull of Doom." Greg knew little about the mysterious brotherhood except what he could remember from his medieval French history. He knew, however, they had amassed a great deal of money and power after the Crusades.

What the hell? The names on the list were all foreign, except the last one: Mr. Hugh Hunt.

Could this be the same Professor Hunt? A news clipping fell out of the envelope. He picked it up off the floor.

SECRET MASONIC SECT THOUGHT
RESPONSIBLE FOR DEATH IN PARIS.

It went on to describe a ritualistic execution and hanging according to some "ancient and secret law." According to the article the perpetrator of the crime had to be punished by death and public display, usually by hanging the body under a prominent bridge, with feet below the water line. The victim, a prominent French businessman, was an influential member of the French government's central finance committee.

It all sounded a little too bizarre. He stood up dropping the article on the floor again. He poured himself a Chivas from the mini-bar and turned on the TV.

The lead story on CNN International was about a possible politically motivated killing in Amsterdam. The camera caught pictures of the police cutting down a man in a business suit, bound with rope by the hands and feet, suspended under a canal bridge in the Centrum.

As he sipped his warm Scotch a shiver ran down his spine, as if someone just walked over his grave. *Wait a minute, that's right behind my hotel.*

He turned the TV off. He was being drawn into the television, the way a sudden breeze sweeps a toy boat out to sea. Something big was happening here. He could taste it; his luck was about to change. His energy soared—perhaps it was the Scotch.

Another soul, perhaps restrained by reason, might have called it an error in judgment. Not Greg. He smelled opportunity. He didn't understand it himself. Whatever it was, call it unbridled ambition; he defined his life by it. But he needed to get some sleep.

So it was that silent atoms moved dark energy Greg Fallows' way.

Greg took a sip of water. The television lights were hot and he was perspiring profusely. Millions of eyeballs were tearing at his hot skin. He cleared his throat and continued his testimony.

"No one spoke. Everyone seemed preoccupied. The next morning I packed for my return to Canada. At breakfast Hunt and I briefly agreed that I should return to Guatemala to continue my work. He stipulated no university connections, however, I was to work independently.

"On the long flight to Toronto I had interrupted sleep. I seemed to be dreaming an inordinate amount lately. I dreamt I was lost in a deep forest. My wife Christie was calling out to me, but I couldn't find my way out. An old man appeared and took my hand, silently he lead me out of the woods."

"I don't think this committee is interested in Dr. Fallows' dreams." Senator Wilson leaned forward to catch the eye of the Chairman.

"Please go on Dr. Fallows," directed Chairman Clattmore.

"I opened a note . . . a note from the guy, the one they called the Master. He'd given it to me to read with instructions not to open it until I was aboard the plane. It read: 'Instruments that do harm may also heal. The final result depends on the proficiency of the user, and not just the instrument.' It was signed, 'Et Arcadia Ego'—I am from Arcadia.

"The message absorbed my thoughts for the rest of the flight. Who or what was the instrument? Who or what was Arcadia? A place in ancient Greece?"

"We know this is difficult, but please try not to leave out any details. They may prove very important to us in the end."

"When I finally landed in Toronto after stops in London and New York, I was fatigued and troubled. What would I tell my wife? What was happening? Would she forgive me?

"I took a cab from the airport to my apartment. It was after midnight when I finally got home. The door was unlocked. I was seized by a sense of apprehension. The apartment was dark. Not wanting to wake my wife, I crept into the bedroom and fumbled for the little flashlight I kept by the bed. I found it and turned the bedside light on. I noticed the bed had not been slept in. I turned the overhead light on. I was griped with fear. Where could she be? I shouted, 'Christie!' No answer. Our old gray cat, Hermes, appeared looking for food and affection. She must be out with a friend, or her sister, I tried to rationalize my feelings. I walked to our study. I saw the computer was on. 'That's odd,' I thought. Christie would never leave the computer on. It's not like her. I had that visceral panic again. I went to the computer screen. There was a file with my name on it. 'Dear Dr. Greg Fallows, if you wish to see your wife alive again, come to Chetumal with your Templar files this Friday. Meet at Anita's Café at midnight. Be there, or say good-bye to your wife . . . forever. And remember, no cops or she's dead.' That last word sent a chill up my spine. Chetumal by Friday; what day was today? The clock in the living room struck midnight. Today was now Wednesday. I had three days to get to Chetumal. It was the 'wild west' of Mexico, on the Belize border."

"Mr. Chairman, I don't see how this man's testimony is in any way relevant to our committee," Senator Matt Coyle smiled toward the camera recording the proceedings.

"I believe, Senator, that this committee wants to get the facts of this case and Dr. Gregory Fallows is one of the few people alive who knows what went on. Please continue."

"Yes, sir." Greg cleared his voice and continued. "The university was expecting me back at work in the morning. I quickly phoned my brother Ron, a professor of History at the university. I apologized for waking him at such an ungodly hour, but asked if he would be so kind as to call my department in the morning and tell them I was ill. Ron expressed concern. I said I was okay really, but Christie wasn't feeling well. You know, bad time emotionally; things have been rough for us lately. He said he understood and would take care of everything for me. I thanked him and hung up."

Inside the offices of the National Security Agency are, just like any other large office, rows upon rows of desks with computer terminals on every desk. Except one thing is different. It is noticeably quiet.

Historically, the NSA dates back to the days of the old SIGINT—signals intelligence—Corps of the United States Army during the Second World War. Today the agency's supercomputers are among the biggest and busiest in the world, analyzing every bit of digital and analogue traffic on the electromagnetic spectrum. Echelon is the program that listens in on all communications among "friendly" countries.

Jim Eadey was a junior communications research analyst working on Echelon. He watched the digital traffic spin on his screen. His job was to monitor cellular phone traffic in a defined sector. In this case he was responsible for monitoring traffic north of the 49th parallel. Both Canada and the US had agreements not to spy on each other's citizens—except where matters of national security where at stake. And these days at least, with Canada on the verge of Balkanization, it was very much in America's national interest to monitor communications to and from Canada. Eadey's analysis, therefore, was coded 'top secret cosmic.'

Eadey didn't know all the technical stuff, even though he'd taken the course. He'd slept through most of it. He completed a BA in American government at Boston College and now at 27 he was coping with his first real job, and all the bullshit he could handle.

The office was crackling with the latest flap over CIA's "flabby and complacent" analysis. Talk of impending intelligence community reorganization was rampant—again. Rumor suggested that the next agency to fall into the spotlight of public scrutiny would be the NSA. So far that hadn't happened, although the pressure was mounting, even a junior G-man like Eadey could see it coming.

"Wait . . . message downloading . . . traffic . . . a confirmation. Possibly a terrorist kidnapping . . . the message was scrambled. Not American . . . looks like . . . better get this to the Section Director stat, Eadey" said aloud, as he selected 'print' from the screen's menu.

Greg had 71 hours to get to Chetumal on the Belize-Mexican border. He immediately took a cab back to the airport and caught the red eye to New York with connections to Miami. He had an eight-hour wait at MIA for an Aero México flight to Mérida.

It was late when he checked into the Camino Réal in Mérida, exactly 24 hours after he arrived back from Amsterdam. His life had become a bad dream . . . a nightmare in fact.

He couldn't sleep, so he went for a walk. The people in tropical climates seem to magically come alive at night. There was a carnival atmosphere in the air on that warm October night. He walked to the market decorated in bright colored lights around a beautiful Spanish colonial square. He stopped into Bar Montezuma for a beer. He couldn't get Christie out of his mind. He needed a plan, and he didn't have one.

As he sat sipping his beer watching the activity in the street, another gringo sat down beside him.

"Do you mind if I join you?" the man asked with a southern drawl.

"No, not at all." Greg motioned to the empty seat beside him.

"You look preoccupied," the gringo observed as he sat down, ordering a double tequila and lime. "Some things never change." He looked out over the market while taking a sip of the liquor. "Do they?"

"What do you mean?" Greg asked, already becoming bored with the conversation.

"I've been here for five years now and it still don't feel like home."

Greg nodded and took a sip of beer.

"Carlos." The stranger held out a large callused hand.

"Greg. You don't look like a Carlos," Greg glanced out of the corner of his eye.

"Yeah, everybody says that. They call me Carlos, el gringo," he chuckled heartily.

"What brings you to the Yucatan?" Greg asked, wary of anyone approaching him.

"I was going to ask you the same question," Carlos knocked back a slug of tequila and sucked on a lime.

"No reason, just passing through."

"Not exactly Hawaii," Carlos appraised coolly. "I could think of better places to pass through."

"What about you? What brings you to the expatriates bar and grill?"

"I work here," Carlos became serious.

"Sounds mysterious," Greg noted his reticence.

"Not really. I'm with the DEA. You know, the Drug Enforcement Agency. You're an American?"

Greg remembered how DEA agent Camarrone was murdered brutally by Mexican drug lords.

"I'm a Canadian actually. I'm a medical anthropologist. I examine medical evidence on archeological digs. Sort of like forensic medicine, only without the criminal aspects."

"What are you doing here?" Carlos asked. He made it sound official this time.

Greg hesitated. "Uh, I'm going to Chetumal in the morning. I'm looking into allegations that a bunch of nineteenth century French eccentrics who called themselves 'the Council of 33' might have established a kind of utopian community there," he checked his watch. He could never look anyone in the eye when he lied.

"Weird shit. What was their thing?"

"They were a secret society—popular at the time—who believed in a world government. They traced their origins back to the medieval Knights Templar. They were a spin off sect of the secret society of Freemasons." Greg wondered whether he'd said too much.

Carlos smiled. "I'm headed in country myself."

"Ever been to the Wild West of Mexico before?" Carlos asked changing the subject.

"I've been in the jungle quite a few times on projects," Greg brightened in relief.

"Ever been to Chetumal? The asshole of Mexico, man. A real dangerous outlaw kind of place. I once saw the police in Chetumal driving a stolen Texas police car. No shit man. The car still had Texas plates!"

Greg looked either shocked or guilty because Carlos smiled and asked if he wanted a ride. "It might be safer for you," Carlos added.

"Maybe, maybe not," Greg said sarcastically and took a sip of his beer.

"Maybe not," the DEA man agreed downing the remaining tequila and standing up.

"I'll meet you in one hour. It's safer and cooler to travel at night in the Yucatan. And beside it's a good eight-hour car ride to Chetumal from here. Be here in one hour," Carlos disappeared with a grin into the crowd on Calle de San Cristobal.

Greg finished his beer and went back to his hotel to pack. All he could think about was the message on his computer screen: "No cops or she's dead."

The fact sheet in his hand troubled inspector Kroode. He wasn't having what might be called a good day. The "canal murder" as the papers called it was a player in the Amsterdam diamond scene. He was an expatriate Brit by the name of Nigel Lockhart who had connections with the Bank of Commerce and Industry on Herengracht Straat. To top it off he was a grand potentate of the Masonic Lodge with many influential friends.

The first thing he had to do was to find out more about the Masonic Lodge connection to all this. He picked up the phone on the corner of his desk and dialed Dr. Pieter Teunon's office.

"Pieter?"

"Yes."

"It's Hans. Can I meet you after the office sometime to talk about this Masonic case?"

"You really think it's got something to do with the Masons?"

"I'm not sure what to think, all I know is a guy is dead and the ritual hanging was meant to scare somebody off. You've studied secret societies haven't you?" Hans knew that Pieter spent a number of years exploring the connection between the Knights Templar and secret societies like the Masons after the Dan Brown books came out. In fact, he'd published a book a few years back called *Secret Myths of the Knights Templar.*

"You know I have, Hans." It hadn't sold well, but it was a conversation piece at parties. And at least twice a year he was asked to speak to church groups about the book. Once a theater company called to ask if they could use some of the material for a play they were producing about the Templars.

"Meet me at *D'Admiraal,* on Herengracht, near Oude Spiegelstraat. I'll be waiting for you around 5 o'clock at the café."

"Okay . . . see you at 5."

Hans put the phone back on its cradle and picked up the photo of the tattoo.

SEVEN

"Order . . . order please . . . order," Senator Clattmore called hammering the gavel on the oak table. "I must remind all those in attendance, this committee will not tolerate outbursts."

"Go on Dr. Fallows."

"Yes, sir," Greg steeled himself.

"Carlos drove. I slept most of the way. I should say I tried to sleep. I was awakened by a sudden slowing and sounds of music and saw locals dancing in the dark on the highway. As dawn broke I could see we were driving through tall grass ten feet high. I saw people living in tall grass huts that looked like they were tied at the top.

"We arrived in Chetumal just as the city was awakening. It was an odd city; full of shops selling imported goods from all over the world. Not at all like most Mexican cities. It was hot and humid.

"Carlos dropped me at the bus depot. I thanked him for the ride and I checked into the nearest hotel. I had some time before my rendezvous, so I decided to try and get some sleep. The hotel had no air conditioning, only a large circular fan over the bed. I lay there on the bed for hours as the humidity increased with every passing minute of that very long day . . ."

Night came, a long awaited friend to smugglers and criminals in this town. Greg got up, showered and changed clothes. He ventured out of the hotel and into the night air. There was no tourist business here. It was a city "on the edge." There was a palpable tension in the air. There was a good business buying stolen cars from the US and Canada in the State of Quintana Roo. There were new cars everywhere. They even had mufflers. The lack of noise and pollution was eerie for a Mexican town.

Greg checked out Anita's Café, a fleabag on a corner near the bridge to Belize. He walked around town killing time spotted Carlos' beat up 1969 blue Ford Econoline van following him. It was distinctive because it had no windows in the back and had a large dent in the left side. He started to get paranoid. He ran down several alleys and out along the tree lined boulevard by the harbor. Every time he'd ditch Carlos, Carlos would find him again. Even by amateur standards, he knew he was being followed.

Greg made his way back to his hotel undetected and stayed there until close to midnight. At 11:45 P.M. he left the sanctuary of his hotel and headed out onto the streets now alive with people, making his way the four blocks to Anita's Café. He ordered eggs, beans, tortillas, and a cold beer. He waited, passing the time watching the rats dart out of the kitchen as the cook threatened them with his broom.

At 12:10 A.M. Greg was getting increasingly nervous, still no sign of them, whoever they were. The manuscript, or codex, was getting wet in the humidity and sweat of his hands. He ordered another beer. He wanted a cigarette even though he didn't smoke.

"Dr. Greg Fallows, of course?" asked a short wide man with a white Panama hat and red Hawaiian shirt. He had a heavy Brooklyn accent. The man was unshaven and had large dirty feet and wore plastic flip-flop dime store sandals. Greg feared for Christie more than ever as he looked into these cold sallow eyes. Greg knew immediately this wasn't the kind of person he wanted to get to know better.

"Yes, I've been watching the stage show." Glancing over to the kitchen as the cook swept another squealing rat out.

"Lotta rats down here," the man smiled, showing his yellow teeth.

"I see what you mean," Greg grimaced, looking him in the eye.

"Y'all, bring the package?" the man asked sitting down at Greg's table. Greg could smell the heavy garlic body odor as the man leaned over to get closer.

"Did you bring my wife?" Greg whispered quietly, getting impatient with the man in the red Hawaiian shirt.

"Your wife's a nice lady." The man grinned.

Greg didn't like the way he said that.

"She'd better be okay, or . . ." Greg stood up.

"Or what?" His stare conveyed a million threats. "You'd better sit down." Greg obeyed the command.

"What is it you want from me?" Greg asked bluntly.

"Now that's better," the man picked his teeth with a piece of paper he found in his shirt pocket.

"You have something many people want. Or should I say, some people are willing to pay a great deal of money for." He looked over his left shoulder and glanced back at Greg and whispered: "Your discoveries."

Suddenly Greg understood the danger to Christie. The people in Amsterdam wanted information. Now, somebody else wanted the same information about a Templar connection with Guatemala and Mexico in the 14th century. Who were they and why? *What a bizarre situation*, he thought. *Am I the only one who doesn't know what everybody else seemed to know and want, and were willing to kill to get it?*

"How does my wife fit into all of this?"

"She's our . . . insurance," the man flicked his Panama hat.

"What do you want me to do?" Greg surrendered his former hostility."

Now that's the way to get things done." He spit through his teeth at a rat escaping out the front door.

"What do you want me to do?" Greg demanded again, growing impatient.

"Come with us."

"Where?" Greg threw up his hands in exasperation.

"Belmopan."

"Belmopan?" Greg shouted incredulously. "What about my wife?"

"She's in good hands." As he spoke those words, he pointed outside to a car that slowed down in front of the café. The back door opened and Greg could see what looked like Christie, as someone shined a flashlight briefly on her face.

She looked frightened but unhurt. Greg tried to get up. The fat man grabbed him by the wrist pulling him back into his seat with impressive force. The car door closed. The car sped away to the bridge at the border within sight of the café. It darted away. Greg could see the taillights move across the border into Belize. He understood the border protocol. The only papers needed here were green . . . American dollars.

"When do we leave?"

"Now."

"Let's go"

As they crossed the bridge into Belize, Greg had to remind myself of a line from the Igi-Balam: "there are some places force cannot penetrate, where human destiny may brook no contradiction."

The Petén jungle is dense and unforgiving by day or night. It swallows its quarry with quiet lethal stealth. Like a panther stalking its prey, the night moves invisible against the Moon. Its olive face is a dark mirror drawing light into itself; a secret black hole at the center of lost worlds, mysterious and dangerous, jealous and unforgiving.

Of all the commercial attempts to harvest the mysterious exotic fruits of the rain forest, none has seen more blood shed than the coca plant. It has the power to numb pain and the power to inflict pain—depending on its use. It has the power to make some men rich and other men poor. Coca is money. Cocaine is power. Men who seek more power need money. They are never satisfied. They seek more and more. It is an addiction.

They drove throughout the night in a blue 1970 Toyota Land Cruiser with cracked plastic seats and leaf springs destroyed from many miles on the rough roads of western Belize. They stopped for gas at a tiny village in the middle of nowhere. The fat man went to relieve himself around the corner next to a corrugated fence beside several grunting pigs

The lights of a small cantina across from the gas bar attracted Greg who was ready for something to eat. The Dunlop tire clock on the wall read 3 A.M. After waiting for several minutes a tall Englishman asked Greg if he wanted something to eat. Greg gave an affirmative nod and the Englishman motioned for him to follow.

He led Greg to a courtyard with a large open kitchen and he began to prepare a meal of eggs, grouper and mango. Greg sat at the outdoor table gratefully eating the meal. The Englishman had a television set next to his table outside. He told stories about things he had seen on television. He talked about space ships and beings from other planets that he had seen on television. He also believed he'd seen similar things in Belize, around this area. He pointed to the corn behind his house and lowered his voice as if someone might hear him reveal a great secret.

"Sometimes I put special herbs in my bath, and I can talk with these beings from other worlds."

Greg stopped eating for a moment. He looked at the stranger with a mixture of amazement and confusion. Then he continued eating the very tasty eggs.

The bird and animal sounds of the jungle made excellent background for the stranger's odd story. But Greg Fallows was starting to think he was a dangerous madman, a pleasant, amicable host, but crazy nonetheless. Greg began wondering where his fat little escort had gone. Surely he wouldn't leave without him. He hadn't heard the engine start. How long does it take to go for a piss? He needed that disagreeable man to find Christie.

Greg abruptly got up from the table. He thanked his host and walked back across the street to the gas bar. There was an eerie silence about the place, broken only by the sound of an occasional croaking frog.

From nowhere a flood of lights blinded him. He raised his arm to shield his eyes from the intense bright light.

"Put your hands up!" came the command from behind him. He turned around but could not see, temporarily blinded by the white light.

"Where's Christie?" he shouted nervously, standing with his arms above his head, his knees beginning to shake with fear.

"Arrest him!" came the reply from behind the lights.

Two soldiers grabbed him by each arm and put him into the back of a military Jeep. The lights went out and the convoy of Jeeps sped away.

"What's going on?" Greg asked leaning forward from the back seat.

"Shut up, or you'll end up like him," the uniformed man said from the front of the jeep. He pointed a flashlight at the dead body of the fat man lying just behind Greg in the back of the jeep. His throat had been cut—expertly.

Greg wished he were back at the university sitting through one of Professor Gowan's endless diatribes at the faculty club on the historical and archeological importance of Dr. Schliemann's excavations at Hissarlik. At that moment, however, he wished he'd never heard of anthropology, archeology, or medicine. *Black operations military experience might be more helpful right now*, he thought. *What have they done to Christie?*

They pulled into a military camp in the middle of the jungle. He was taken to an office and seated across from a large empty desk. On the wall were maps of Belize and Guatemala. His two escorts left the room and closed the door behind them. He was alone. He stood up and walked over to one of the maps on the wall behind the desk. There were red and green dots throughout the area on either side of the Belize-Guatemalan border.

The door opened. Greg turned around expecting to see an interrogation team. But it was Carlos "el gringo" smiling and holding two cold cans of Heineken beer. He walked over and handed one to Greg.

"Have a nice trip?" he asked as he lit up a Pall Mall, and sat back on a wooden swivel chair swinging his feet up on the desk. He looked very comfortable. He looked like a man who was meant to be doing what he was doing.

"You don't mind if I ask: what the hell's going on?" Greg asked stunned.

"What do you know?" Carlos retorted pointedly.

Greg told him the story of Christie's kidnapping.

"You left one thing out."

"What's that?"

"Your role in all this."

"I'm just an innocent victim," Greg's voice rose. Carlos laughed. Greg nervously did too. The sound of laughter seemed to diminish the tension in the air.

Carlos explained the DEA was investigating an especially notorious group of cocaine barons who had fled Columbia after the Cali crackdown. They had set up shop in a politically disputed area around the Guatemalan-Belize border. Apparently British Intelligence in Belize intercepted some communications from the border area relating to a kidnapping plan in Toronto. The information was passed to the DEA in Washington and CSIS authorities in Ottawa.

"We didn't know who was going to be nabbed, so we couldn't set-up a sting type operation. Besides, we wanted to catch the big fish, and shut down the whole enchilada. The US government wants these criminals extradited to stand trial."

"There's more to it than that."

Carlos took a long puff on his Pall Mall and waited for Greg to continue.

"I discovered some incredible evidence in an excavation down here that I had hoped to publish in the *British Journal of Archaeology and Anthropology*. I sent the manuscript three months ago. Ever since then my life has changed. It's become a kind of surrealist dream, filled with people like you. Don't take that the wrong way . . . I mean . . . well, you know what I mean . . ."

Carols ignored the comment and opened another pack of Pall Mall. He lit a cigarette, blowing smoke in the air as if checking the direction of the wind.

"In the article I intend to expound a theory based on evidence I uncovered near the Temple of the Iqi-Balam, or what I translated as Tiger of the Moon. Based on new evidence, I postulated the mysterious missing fleet of the Knights Templar fled to the New World with their secret treasure in the 14th century—one hundred years before Columbus. In my opinion, the transcription or codex clearly suggests Jacques De Molnay (the last Grand Master of the

Knights Templar) saved the treasure of the Templars by sending the Templar fleet away. I believe he was tipped off and knew the King's men were going to round up him and his warrior-monks. He didn't escape, and his followers were later tortured and burned at the stake as heretics.

"But, this is the interesting part, I believe their treasure was taken to the New World where it ended up in the Mexico-Guatemala border area, in the hands of Maya priest-kings. On a recent trip to Amsterdam I was shown a copy of my codex by some people who were very interested in my work."

"Who?" He asked with growing interest.

"A group of academics, I think."

"And you believed them? Are you sure they were academics?"

"Why no," Greg asserted defensively. "But they did seem extremely knowledgeable."

"I believe that." Carlos paused while playing with the cigarette butt in the ashtray.

"Are you implying I shouldn't have trusted them?" Greg asked. "They were into something they called 'hermeneutic phenomenology,' which sounded academic to me."

"Right! They wanted information from you." Carlos rebuked. "They were bound to be nice to you." He paused for a moment, as if carefully choosing his words before he continued. "They could always kill you later, you know. They presented themselves to you in a way they knew would be acceptable to you—academics, interested in the pure pursuit of knowledge."

Greg had missed it, but Carlos was right. He cursed his own naiveté.

"Did they kidnap Christie?" Greg asked unsure of what to think next, or what to believe. "They knew when I'd be away and when I'd return."

"So did everyone at the university. Didn't they?" he observed astutely. "What were their names? The people in Amsterdam, I mean."

Greg told him about Strumpf, Brentano, Von Hartmann and Hunt. He told him everything he could remember. He was doing it again, trusting someone he didn't' know. He sensed he had to trust someone. Who else could he trust?

"I don't think they kidnapped your Christie, if that's any consolation to you." He got up and walked over to the map on the wall.

Greg supposed Carlos must be about 37 going on 50. He had been around as they say. Greg guessed he was probably a Vietnam War vet.

"Listen carefully. I have a plan," Carlos said looking at the map.

"Good, that's what I need . . . a plan!"

"You might not like it so much after you hear It." he gave Greg that same crooked smile he flashed in the bar the night they met in Merida.

"I'll do whatever you say right now. Besides, what choice do I have?" Greg joined him at the map.

"Good. Get some sleep, and we'll go over it in a couple of hours. They'll be expecting you and your buddy soon. My people will have to create a diversion. We'll have to get them to think that a rival killed the fat boy before he picked you up and I'll have to pose as your escort. It's risky, but it's all we've got."

"Oh, yeah, one last thing," he paused, "You're going to have to be our decoy."

"I'll do anything to get Christie back." Greg knew what was meant by decoy.

"Get some rest," Carlos clipped as he left the room. "There's a fold-out cot in that closet."

"Sure."

EIGHT

The sound of cicadas broke the silence of the tropical night. As Greg stood outside listening to the cacophony, the beauty of the place overwhelmed him. A thick mist filled his nostrils with the air of an enduring place, more comfortable with mango and millennia than rifles, flacks and governments. Years meant nothing, measured against its bleak balance sheet of gains and losses. Here, standing in this place of amoral judgment, Greg could feel the Maya seduction with capturing and disarming time by ending it. Like a lover's heart beat, a steady droning hammer forged harsh alliances between the contradiction of time sleeping and time raging camouflaged in the harmless green and brown foliage of thousands of thousands of years. His mind turned to Christie, and he was swallowed by a powerful terror. A monsoon of tears flowed in torrents from his tired eyes. Gregory Winston Fallows was changing. He was beginning to see and to feel, to break through the technological numbness that is modern life.

They met as undergraduates. They sat next to each other on the first day of Professor Melcher's anatomy class. When she looked at him there was a power surge of energy. A curious new vitality rushed through him as if awakened from a deep sleep.

She convinced Greg to skip their next class to attend an ecology lecture by an activist/professor from New York City who probably had never been outside of Manhattan in his life, but he liked the sound of his own voice.

They became good friends. When she touched him or kissed him on the cheek something stirred in him that he'd never felt before—something honest.

They first made love several weeks after they started seeing each other. He borrowed his brother's van and they drove out of the city on a sunny spring day. The air smelled fresh and clean. They drove to the country to a little park southwest of the city. They devoured a picnic lunch in a place of solitude high on a tree covered limestone cliff overlooking the world and the gentle waters of a river far below.

She rolled over on her back her breasts high and firm bulging beneath her top, bursting for freedom. He leaned over and kissed her on the lips for the first time. They made love el fresco.

They were married in October and settled into married student life. Christie continued her music studies and Greg returned to his pre-med classes. She was a gifted musician and played many instruments, but her first love was the cello. She studied classical cello and practiced at home in their basement apartment. These were their poor student days. The icy winter of his discontent had not yet descended upon him.

When Christie finished school there was very little she could do with her music professionally without further studies. They talked about children, but Greg was just starting graduate school and they didn't have the money to support a family. Later they discovered she couldn't have children. She went back to school and graduated in nursing. Greg knew she hated it, and felt she resented him. He increasingly fell under the spell of anthropology and archeology. He spent hours studying ancient dead languages. It was natural therefore that he should be drawn into medical anthropology.

"It's time to go." Carlos lit a cigarette, throwing the match on the ground. He ground it into the dirt with his foot in an effort to deliberately waste time the way smokers do.

Greg walked over to the Toyota and threw his bag in the back. Carlos watched Greg return from the vehicle.

"Your wife's waiting, pal."

"I know. She's been waiting for years."

NINE

The whining of the Landcruiser's engine misfired like random gunshots taxing Greg's already frayed nerves as they drove. Dawn's bright light crept over the trees behind them as they drove west toward Guatemala. The cries of howler and spider monkeys high in the trees echoed across the jungle.

About a mile from the Guatemalan border a group of five men walked out of the jungle fifty meters in front of them, armed to the teeth with M16s. Dressed in jungle camouflage they stopped the Toyota in the middle of the road. The brilliant morning sun blinded Greg as he stood outside the truck. This was a tactic crafted in the unwritten policy of guerrilla necessity. Fear was a powerful motivator and it made everybody suspicious of everyone. In war, trust was the first luxury no one could afford. War was greed. It doesn't matter where you are. From bombed out streets in Sarajevo to fortress Nebaj in the Guatemalan highlands, it was always the same: anything for a buck.

The soldiers approached the Landcruiser with the caution of a panther who has trapped its prey. A panther relishes the taste of victory—the triumph of power over weakness. As they approached Greg could see the insignia badges on their jackets.

"They're Belizean regulars!" looking at Carlos in disbelief.

"In this war the enemy is invisible." Carlos put on his sunglasses as they watched twenty meters shrink between them.

"Now what?"

A world-weary sergeant approached Carlos. He had a small round face with broad protruding lips, and dark circles under his eyes. He made grunting sounds through his nose when he spoke.

"We were . . . expecting . . . Hardin'." He leaned through the jeep window looking at Carlos. He had the carrion odor of decay about him.

"Where's Hardin'?" he asked looking suspiciously in the back of the jeep. "He got drunk in Chetumal and fucked up," replied Carlos.

"Yeah, that's Hardin'" the sergeant laughed.

"They brought me in from Mérida, I'm supposed to take this asshole to 'the shooting gallery'" gesturing toward me with the back of his hand in a flippant tone.

"Yeah . . . follow . . . me," the sergeant motioned for his comrades to come closer.

"The dick head here will have to be blind folded," Carlos said in the same contemptuous tone.

"Yeah, sure," the sergeant grunted, properly admonished for his forgetfulness. Greg was blindfolded and led by two of the soldiers a few hundred meters down the road where he was strapped into some kind of seat. He could hear the roar of turbines and feel the thrust as they took off.

Shit! I'm in a helicopter, he thought. He shook his head in disbelief. He could only wonder at his predicament. Why did all these people care so much about the past? He was more concerned with the present, and more ominously, the future.

After what seemed an eternity they suddenly banked forty-five degrees to the right and quickly landed. Greg nearly retched as the G-force thrust him back in his seat.

"We weave to the right then to the left rapidly, with about twenty degrees bank each turn. After what seems like forever we make a break to the right then land with a sudden thud. The engines wind down, and then shut off. The air is more humid here. I can hear the jungle sounds of birds and monkeys when the engines finally cut out. My blindfold is taken off by one of the soldiers seated on my right.

Only then I see we've been flying in a military Jet Ranger helicopter. As I step out of the helicopter I can see for the first time that we are in the heart of the Petén, and probably, I think, in Guatemala."

The CNN TV camera pans from a close-up of Greg to a wide-angle of the entire Senate hearing room. From a door off to the right of the room, a blue suited man with a military haircut, moves behind the committee members and whispers in the Chairman's ear.

Greg continued, "The base is active. More helicopters are taking off, and ground troops drill in a clearing not far from the banks of a beautiful river. I glance behind me at the Jet Ranger and notice . . . they're American! I can't control my sense of shock. I turned to Carlos who was standing near the front of the Jet Ranger talking to the pilot, another American! 'What the fuck's going on?' I yelled. Carlos continues to ignore me, deep in conversation with the pilot. My two armed escorts each grab me by an arm and insist 'come along.' I felt sick and betrayed."

"If no one objects, I think this is an excellent time for a short recess?" the Chairman rose to escort the blue suited man to his office.

"What the fuck is going on?" Greg erupted, very much alone face to face with a US Army Colonel. Colonel Ray Ban's gold-rimmed mirror sunglasses reflected a cabin by the edge of the river. Colonel Bruce studied aerial photos of the jungle terrain.

"Excuse me, Sir. I'm looking for my wife, Christie Fallows."

Colonel Bruce looked up and motioned to the two Belizean soldiers. Bruce is a middle-aged soldier of fortune whose time had come, and gone. His face was a quilt of brown speckles with deep furrows.

A slight tremor shook the Colonel's left hand. *Perhaps early Parkinson's disease*, Greg thought, emanating hostility, "I was told somebody kidnapped my wife and was holding her hostage."

"Hang on, man," the Colonel Bruce snapped. "To them it's more like insurance. And we are going to get your wife, but we need some information from you that can help us. We can't just waltz in there and ask politely for your wife. We'd all get killed. And that includes your wife too."

"Yes, of course," somewhat reassured by the inescapable logic.

81

"What is it you want to know?"

"Well, that's the problem. You see, everyone seems to think I know more than I do."

"I find that hard to believe. Here, look a these . . ."

Greg and Colonel Bruce reviewed the aerial photos together. Colonel Bruce was concerned that an over zealous assault might damage important archeological artifacts in the region. This impressed Greg. Colonel Bruce was also worried about unnecessary risk. In a raid, they mustn't do anything that posed a personal danger. Greg told him he was not familiar with the area they were in. He told the Colonel about the codex he found in Guatemala, southwest of the border with Mexico. It came as no shock that the Colonel was familiar with Greg's discovery too.

"How can a very old manuscript, or codex, as you call it, change the course of history?" Colonel Bruce asked placing his glasses on the map.

"Well, according to the codex/manuscript, certain things—events—are supposed to come together at the beginning of the new millennium. I don't know exactly when. This will lead to a New World Epoch. It doesn't say how this will happen or who will make it happen. However, it gives several very cryptic messages. It says whoever uncovers the ancient secrets locked in the jungle controls the power to change the future—and the past. It's an enigma. I mean, how can you alter the past? But in order to change the future, you have to change the past. Get it? It goes on to say reason is the obsession of our time. The source of our success as a civilization perhaps, but according to the codex at least, it is the hubris, or faith in reason that leads us to destroy the planet in an environmental disaster. Our dreams, I mean our normal nocturnal dreams, are the key to unlocking the mysteries of ancient wonders, deep in the Petén jungle. I know, it's weird, and Jungian and all that, and that's why the level of interest in this whacko discovery surprises me. I didn't think anyone would believe my translation, let alone kidnap and kill for it."

"Sounds like some sort of faith healing bullshit to me." Colonel Bruce rubbed his eyes. They were cold, gray and tired eyes. From the expression on his face, Greg sensed that the Colonel didn't believe what he had just said. It was like somebody had already briefed him and the explanation Greg just gave didn't fit

"Look, this kind of shit gets some people worked up. Not me. For some reason the people in D.C. want this secret shit of yours before anyone else gets it. That's all I know."

"Sure, that makes at least three different groups who want something I don't have. Nobody believes me. Every one of you thinks I'm trying to hide something. You simply can't get it through your skulls. I don't have any secrets."

"You don't get it do you? You're their ticket to ride." Colonel Bruce grinned. Greg detected a hint of irony. "I have strict orders to take you back to Washington as soon as you take us to where you found the codex." He looked Greg Fallows straight in the eye as if he were a sniper looking through the sights of a .50-caliber Barrett machine gun on a clear desert morning.

"I'm not going to show anyone anything anywhere until I get some real explanations," Greg pleaded with passion. *If I'm their ticket to ride*, he thought, *I'm going to call the shots.*

"Have it your way, doc," and Colonel Bruce folded the map.

Two veteran US Army twin Huey helicopters loaded with Carlos, the Colonel and a platoon of Belizean regulars lift off from "the Gallery" and worked their way down river, careful to stay below the tree tops to avoid giving advance notice of their arrival, or their identity. About 20 minutes out they land in a clearing and proceeded to load inflatable Zodiac boats for another half hour trip down the river.

Carlos "el gringo" and Greg hadn't spoken a word to each other since the roadblock. Now in the same boat together their eyes meet. *Perhaps I have misjudged him . . . again*, Greg thought. Carlos looked away, far away into the jungle. The Colonel gave the command to pull in near an area of dense foliage a little further up stream. It was starting to get dark. It gets dark quickly in the tropics. Greg was beginning to understand, they were waiting for the cover of darkness. And so they waited. The soldiers smeared their faces with black. Carlos gave Greg some blacken to apply to his face. Greg could sense a quiet apprehension in Carlos. Everyone was distant, very alone with his or her private thoughts and fears. Such was the calm before the storm.

After dark they made their way along the shore, until they could see a campfire up ahead. The closer they got the clearer they could hear the thumping of a primal rhythm. The sound of ZZ Top blasted through the night. Greg could make out at least 30 people milling around rustic thatch huts, and the hum of a Honda generator behind the wall of sound. Some were hauling 45-gallon drums of what could be chemicals to a building on stilts at the edge of the river.

Colonel Bruce gave a hand signal for the group to rest for a while. He took out his night scope to observe the encampment. There was no moon that night which was good for an attack. The soldiers seemed confident and unafraid. They were seasoned troops

"Surprise is the key," the Colonel had advised during his pre-engagement briefing. He divided the platoon into three. One for each flank and the main strike force including him would head up the middle. Carlos and Greg were to be part of a frontal assault once the flank forces had silently neutralized the few guards posted around what appeared to be the main building on stilts by the river. The Colonel quietly handed Greg a 9 mm pistol.

"You might need this for self-defense." The whites of his eyes were barely visible behind his blackened face.

"These guys make more coke than anyone in Cali today. And remember, keep your eyes peeled for the hostage." "Let's go," Colonel Bruce ordered.

The left flank headed around the back of the camp, while the right flank crawled on their stomachs up the beach under the main building by the river. The first man killed was a half drunk sentry sitting by the water. A muscular black soldier cut the man's throat with the skill of a surgeon. They dragged him still kicking under the stilted building. The rest moved deliberately toward the main area of huts. They fanned out as they reached the perimeter of the camp. Without warning, gunfire and explosions came from all directions. Huts were on fire, there was screaming and mayhem everywhere. Greg dashed across a central open square to the building on stilts.

Men firing M16s randomly into the night came running out the front door and ran left and right. Miraculously, Greg bolted straight into the building without taking any hits. In his sweating right hand he held the 9 mm and behind him was Carlos. His eyes were wide open and glazed. He shot three men in the chest in rapid succession. Suddenly the building exploded into flames. In the chaos stray bullets had hit chemicals stored there. Once inside the smoke and flames obscured Greg vision.

"Christie!" he called out, searching the burning building, as it started to collapse upon itself. Greg heard a muffled banging sound coming from one of the drums. Covering his face he made his way to the barrel. He frantically pulled the lids off several barrels at random. In the third drum he found Christie, bound and gagged with adhesive tape. He lifted her out and pulled the tape off her mouth. He released her bound hands with the skill of Houdini. From behind two men who had come back to the hut to get Christie crashed through the front door firing. Carlos returned their fire but took several hits in the chest. However he killed one of them, before they shot him. Greg turned and fired three shots. He hit the second intruder in the leg and face, splattering blood and brains throughout the room. Greg grabbed Christie's hand as they fell through the burning floor into the river below. They swam across the river and sat on the bank cold and wet. They held each other as the battle continued to rage in the distance for another few minutes. Long into the night the chemicals that fed the flames lit up the sky.

"Carlos is dead. And you are here with me. It's like a dream, a nightmare," Greg shivered as they huddled together.

"Who's Carlos? Why is this happening?" Christie shivered.

"I'm not sure. I'll tell you what I know later. We need to keep quiet"

They held each other out of fear and love. "I love you." Greg stroked Christie's radiant blonde hair.

"I love you too. I thought I'd never see you again."

For a timeless moment they held each other while the fire burned through the night. It was far from over. But all that didn't seem to matter now. What did matter was that he and Christie were together again, and from now on nothing else mattered. They were together. All of their past troubles were gone like storm clouds blown out to sea by the winds of a changing sky. Greg was scared, but in a strange way, for the first time in his life he had a purpose.

TEN

The jungle at night had a million eyes; invisible sensors scanned every corner of the dark. A smoldering fire flickered silently across the river. Greg saw no sign of life. How quickly the jungle reclaimed its superiority over all things under natural law. The jaguar heard under cover of darkness, the primal screams of its victim echo through the long night. In that terror of mind, Greg held his direction. As if by some cosmic design, Greg had a task to fulfill. Confidence overcame his instinctive fear. An odd alchemy of emotion, brewed in Merlin's cauldron; hot and vapid sauces of secret recipes, a mixture of virtue and sin; incantations whispered over cold damp stones at the bewitching hour by Templars wearing crimson robes; bending in ritual adoration to kiss the sword placed at the throat, a sacrifice before the alter of reason.

Christie fell asleep in Greg's arms. Their wet clothes stuck together. Her chest moved rhythmically with every respiration. Primitive desires stirred within him. A kundalini of emotion rose up from the base of his spine milking his tear ducts of their salty concern. It was a catharsis more cleansing than he had ever known. There is no renewal more energizing, no sorrow more sweet, and no joy more deflating. He wept as the jungle watched without emotion. Human emotion imbued meaning into an otherwise heartless night.

In sleep dreams came again . . . Greg entered his apartment, overlooking the beach. The unfamiliar furniture startled him . . . someone else's house where he once lived. He walked down a long dark hallway held up by beams, perhaps six feet apart. The beams overhead had inscriptions like those at the Museum of Natural History—stolen from tombs of the Pharaohs. He saw a light in a room off to the left of the hall. He heard a German accent beckon him: 'come in, Dr. Fallows, don't fear your own shadow,' the voice beckoned. He walked toward the light with a mixture of trepidation and curiosity. His heart thumped a deafening beat. It reminded him of the sound of a submarine diesel engine.

In the light stood a roll top desk, an old man with white hair and pipe in his right hand. He seemed busy with a manuscript. He swung around in his chair and looked at Greg over his glasses. Behind him, three large stained glass windows with various scenes of the crucifixion of Christ, and one of St. George slaying a dragon covered one wall. Hunt was dressed in a tweed jacket, college tie, heavy wool pants, green argyle socks, and no shoes. He extended a friendly hand inviting Greg to sit down. The socks and no shoes stood out as important in a dream-logic way. His disarming smile put Greg at ease. It was like home, even if it wasn't *his* home.

In the dream, Hunt motioned to Greg to sit down beside him at the desk. A strange odor of musk and mothballs filled the air. Professor Hunt took a puff from his clay pipe. Greg followed Hunt's eyes down to a book on the desk. An ancient manuscript of some archeological and monetary importance took up the entire desktop. Hunt put a white glove on his right hand so the oil from his fingers would not stain the pages as he turned them.

'Please, let me read it,' Greg was, anxious to see the document.

Professor Hunt grew very serious, as if Greg had made a terrible faux pas.

'The laws of physics reveal a symbolic, mathematical understanding of the world . . . '

The musk and mothballs nauseated Greg. Hunt gestured toward the stained glass window behind him. St. George the dragon slayer, self-satisfied and omnipotent, ripped open the throat of the dragon with his broad sword.

'Since the very first Homo Sapiens gazed up at the sky, awe struck by the regular, measured laws of the sun and the moon; the science of astronomy has guided our understanding of time's light, flickering still as it dies some millions of light years away; clinging like dust to silk on the tail of light's bright spectrum. Numerology's autochthonic symbols arise from the secrets of Nature herself. An elegant math communicates meaning and purpose about this esoteric world, expressed linearly and conceptually as Time. The jungle has kept our secret for the right moment, when our destiny will be fulfilled.

'Remember,' Hunt's eyes closed as if in deep meditation, 'mathematics is the key to unlocking the mysteries of the past and the future.'

He looked back at the text.

'What modern physics seeks to discover is a primary and palpable connection between matter and soul . . . ' He pointed to the manuscript. 'We found the Maya knew what the Pythagoreans deduced: the power of God is attainable through understanding numbers and their relationship to Time . . . the mastery of Time's secret formula.' He looked up again. 'The poet T.S. Eliot put it most elegantly: 'Time present and time past are both perhaps present in time future, and time future contained in time past.'

'Your manuscript, or codex as you call it, is very modern and . . . potent.'

In this dream world between worlds, an intense heat burned deep within his being, as if he were struck by lightning from the inside. Although their approaches may have differed, the alchemists' search for the philosopher's stone, and the Templars' obsession with the Holy Grail . . . The prize was one and the same. Dreams can pose questions. They rarely, if ever, give complete answers. But this one was giving answers.

'Take this book and guard it with your life.' The dream Mr. Hunt hesitated before passing it over to Greg. 'Some people would use this knowledge for their own material gain. It cannot be sold.' As he said this he handed Greg the heavy tome.

Greg looked at the dusty book; by its weight it seemed to contain all the lost knowledge of the ancients. On the thick leather cover embossed in ancient Greek letters. A woman's voice whispered the word . . . *Euphemes*. In the dream, Greg understood it to be an omen.

As he picked up the text, the weight of the immense book brought him to his knees. He crashed through the floor, tumbling into darkness as pages were torn from his hands by the force of his rapid descent. He fell screaming and he awoke sitting bolt upright as dawn's first light cast its brilliant red calligraphy across the morning sky.

He focused his eyes as the first rays of light cast. A shadow of a figure stood in a clearing a few feet from the water's edge. The morning light had the effect of a curtain opening as the sunlight cast center stage upon the figure of a man. It was an unmistakably Mayan face with dark friendly eyes. His age was difficult to discern. He could be 40 or 60. His bearing betrayed the taunt body of a small but mighty warrior. He looked fierce as a tiger, yet his eyes had the gentleness of a deer. He wore a cloth-like codpiece strapped around his scrotum, held in place by a single piece of twine around his waist. Brightly painted jaguars and Quetzal birds adorned his chest. He carried a long spear. For some peculiar reason, he reminded Greg of the St. George in his bizarre dream.

The sound of the rushing river distracted him as the birds and Howler monkeys greeted the new day. The stranger studied Greg. There was no fear in his eyes. The fire across the river probably attracted him—an omen from the gods.

Christie, already up, bathed by the river the way people have since the beginning of time. She was oblivious to the visitor watching them. The stranger muttered several words in a language Greg did not understand. The stranger's tone, however, was not angry or hostile. He clearly did not intend to harm them or he would have done so by now. Without warning the stranger walked over to him. Greg stood up reflexively. His six-foot height towered over the stranger. The stranger extended his hand. But he didn't let go of Greg's hand. He pulled Greg. He wanted Greg to follow him.

"Christie!" Greg called out, "Quick! Come quickly."

ELEVEN

A runic air hung over the jungle like the aroma of burnt coffee. The forest was thick with the sweet smell of hibiscus flowers. The women doted on Christie with a special kinship. Christie laughed and hugged the children as they surged excitedly around her. She picked up one child, tossing her in the air. The little girl squealed with delight, the way children do at fairs, or circuses when the clowns fall in front of wild animals. In the heart of the Petén jungle the same simple pleasures of human affection live untouched by the godless modern world. Here, the ancient and modern oscillate in tandem, accelerated quarks, worlds set on a collision course.

The trek from the river took most of the day. Greg's Seiko waterproof watch hadn't worked since their swim across the river. These ancestors of the ancient Maya who fled the temple at 'Iqi-Balam' have lived the same way for a thousand years. They had no need for watches.

Their guide was a man who knew the impenetrable rain forest the way Greg knew his way around Toronto. However, the stranger didn't need fossil fuels to get where he was going. Simplicity was his key to freedom. But Greg and Christie were not so free.

Around phallic stelae, a group of elder tribesmen held court earnestly discussing a matter at hand. Their escort described at length the events leading up to a fiery battle of the gods near the river by the flying spirits from the north. His language was unfamiliar. Greg had no idea what the stranger actually said, but he imagined it was a situation report. There was a drama inherent in the rapid clicking of the Maya tongue. It made Greg think about the difficult times ahead for all the indigenous peoples on this planet. Every now and then one of the elders smiled and pointed at Greg, nodding his head in acknowledgment. After about an hour their escort finished his story. The cross-examination would now begin. Several of the older men fired questions at the escort in quick succession. *Was he angry or was he just over acting?* Greg couldn't tell. On and on it went. A gong sounded and the men brought their disagreement to an abrupt end. Their heated disagreement came to a sudden agreement, as if prompted by the sound of the gong. All parties seemed satisfied with the report. The supreme and final court of jungle tort had moved to adjourn.

All the while the women and children gathered around Christie. They seemed to accept her into their circle without the inquisition required of men. Greg understood that they accepted women because they did not see women as a threat to the safety and security of their society. Men, on the other hand, had to pass the scrutiny of elders. While Greg understood instinctively that rejection by the clan elders could mean a sudden and harsh return to the mercy of the jungle, and certain death.

The women, Christie included, began preparing a meal. Their escort led Greg to a hut where Greg presumed he and Christie would stay. Greg hadn't talked to Christie since their arrival at the village. She took to the people and the place with uncanny naturalness. She looked more at peace here than at any time he could remember. A magic web of radiant beauty surrounded her. She was bathed in pure poetic light. She laughed and smiled freely. It reminded him of the first real day of spring. The ambiance conveyed an aura of hope and purity. Seeing Christie this way made him happy too. He stood watching her outside their new home. She was strong and beautiful. She was more alive than he had ever seen her before. An inappropriate sense of euphoria enwrapped him.

Several days of bucolic bliss passed into a rhythm of endless weeks. He couldn't really say how long it had been. Their final acceptance into the tribal family would be marked by a ceremony called 'Uxu.' To Greg it meant the holy right of transformation and escape from both the present and the past.

In the months that followed Greg rediscovered his medical talents and rekindled his field analysis skills. He trained his memory with daily exercises he designed. Yet he retained an anthropologist's keen eye for detail. The retrieval of bone artifacts occupied his time. He would send these back to Oxford University's Cherwell Laboratory for DNA analysis. He began to remember why he went into medical anthropology and archeology in the first place. The long voyage to this paradise of discovery had been years of hard work.

It was here, on their first trip to Guatemala as students, that he and Christie finally had their honeymoon. He tried to remember every sensation from that trip as he glided his dugout canoe across the Crystal Lake. The forest all around threatened Greg's peace of mind and he was filled with a sense of apprehension.

To some it might seem peculiar, but to the jaguar people relics of their dead ancestors were an essential part of their coming to terms with the human comedy—life and death. Many of them wore amulets or pendants made from the bones of dead animals. Greg was reminded of tales of pilgrimages to Santiago de Compostella in Spain during the middle ages. According to legend the bones of James the Apostle were buried there after he died in 42 A.D. Is it really so very different from the thousands who line up every year outside of Elvis Presley's house in Memphis, or those who flocked to see Achilles' spear at the temple of Athena in Phaselis? Mankind, Greg was beginning to understand, needed a way of connecting to the past and to bring the past alive in the present. Would that be real magic—or real science? It all depended on how you saw the world.

Greg's plan was to apply himself completely to the task of solving the mystery of the treasure of the Templars. If he could find the treasure it would surely bring him great wealth and academic credibility. But he would need to find a way out of the jungle.

In preparation for the ritual they were made to fast for twenty-four hours. Nothing but water could touch their lips. Even water was allowed only to moisten their lips during the humid heat of the day. Each had a guide who assisted them with their preparation for their rite of passage. Greg was beginning to get very tired waiting for this 'Uxu.' He wanted to get on with his mission.

Greg had a great deal of time to think over the past several weeks and he believed he should sell his manuscript to the highest bidder. If they wanted it bad enough to kill someone, surely they would be interested in selling the information for a few million. Greg rationalized this by thinking of it as a 'consulting fee.' Would international law back him up? He wasn't sure about that one. He'd convinced himself he was owed the money. He was getting anxious to get back to civilization to collect the money. He worked it out in his head that if he could get, say $2 million dollars, he and Christie could retire to one of the villages near Lake Atitlan. It was either that or to win the lottery but Greg couldn't see himself going back to a medical job in the city. He knew he was finished at the university. But he could always practice medicine if he had too, especially in the Third World.

Greg worried about the decline of Western medicine. There was a great deal of instability in medicine and science. The absolute fear of what governments and insurance companies might do to doctors under the banner of fiscal responsibility had demoralized a once proud profession around the world. For many years now there has been a brain drain of the best and the brightest. From one country to another the exodus continued. Confrontation and a succession of poorly conceived reforms had grown tiresome to him. He vowed to himself he would never work under such grim conditions again. He had a plan. He just wasn't sure how he was going to accomplish it. But he was more interested now in discovering whom these mysterious people were, as his canoe glided smoothly onto the sandy beach.

Christie gathered flowers and small red berries. In turn, Greg followed his guide into the forest beyond the village. She was a girl in her mid teens with dark olive skin, hazel eyes and pitch-black hair. She spotted an open area where a patch of wild mushrooms grew in abundance. She gathered several in a small pouch. Once she was satisfied and she had enough they returned to the dugout canoe and paddled back across the lake to their village.

The preparations for 'Uxu' complete, Greg sat by myself near a small stream that worked its way through the jungle and fed the

Oro River. From high in the trees, the sound of Macao and Howler monkeys reached the sky like long fingers from the earth, a broad chorus of sound disturbing leaves, releasing precious molecules of oxygen to the world as it had for millions of millions of years. The thick smell of humus and a gentle breeze that blew up river caressed Greg's face. A joy and power swept over him, serendipity revealed in the magic glow of an oasis away from the violence and dirt of modernity—nestled, hidden from the churning combines of industrial strength smoke and grit. For a thousand years they have maintained their spiritual whole in the face of overwhelming odds. But their peace must come to an end. It would crash down around them in a blinding storm. The heat and smell of engine oil from the bulldozers filled the air at the edge of the forest where they waited to pounce with sweaty machine hearts of steel. They would be torn from their forest, and the forest would be lost . . . Forever.

Awakening from his vision of flames, his little 'helper,' the one they called Itza touched his shoulder from behind. Her broad, innocent smile made him forget his apocalyptic vision. He took her hand and followed her back along the dark path to the village. He had a sense of apprehension. He thought of the cats that disappeared before Pompeii's fatal volcanic eruption. There was an inexplicable sense of imminent doom within him. He feared for Itza. Her dark skin, mysterious dark eyes, and long black hair already seemed like a mirage to him. Was it a dream, a phantom, or maybe he did die back at the river and this was Paradise? Who were these people?

When they reached the village, it was somehow different. The brown and green of the village replaced by bright red, yellow and blue feathers. The whole tribe gathered painted with many colors. The chief wore a mask. He sat surrounded by his warriors dressed in ancient battle dress. Greg sat next to Itza across from a large open fire. The chief sat cross-legged directly across from Greg on the other side of the fire. The men sat in a circle around Greg. Itza fetched Christie and sat her down next to Greg. Christie was dressed in bright colors. She kissed his cheek. Greg smiled back at her. He took her hand, drawing her to his side. They sat by the fire. The whole village surrounded them, perhaps a hundred people in all.

The crackling of the fire and smell of the burning wood took Greg back a thousand years. The hollow log drummers beat a syncopated rhythm. Twilight turned to dusk as the jungle slipped into night.

Greg's heart thumped in anticipation as one of the men painted his face. The tepid thick paint that smelled like pumpkin was smeared over his face. A moist night air arose from the jungle floor. A mystical fog invaded every orifice of his body with its shuddering cold. A shaman wore quetzal feathers and chanted. He presented Greg with a small wooden bowl of ground mushroom mixed in a paste. Greg knew the mushrooms Itza gathered had to be members of the hallucinogenic Amanita species. The drug flowed down his esophagus on its speed of light journey to his central nervous system creating shocking sensual intensity.

A welter of flashing images surrounded the drummers as they reached a crescendo. Each beat of the drum mirrored Greg's own pounding heart. The blood that flowed to his brain was forced under extreme pressure by the rhythmic contraction of that perfect muscle. His strong legs and padded feet seemed to know the trails of the forest as if patterned and ingrained by millions of years of ancestral experience. His eyes flashed alert. He panted pheromones of adrenaline searching for traces of prey on every branch and blade of grass. His voice took on a deep rich guttural sound. His regal steps with padded purpose, clawed supremacy, and emerald eye to capture under taunt reign of muscle. Neck bent, searching, with nostrils of opportunity. Fortune gave him the name—jaguar. He knew of no synapsed power greater, no black confidence superior to the palpable fear of his natural thrusting forward into the kill of the night. This power was nemesis in his greatness, and his greatest weakness. His secret was what wise men seek. They stalked him like he stalked them. They covet his heart chained in its feline cage. They steal his life in the primordial race against time's dark corruption—death.

The jaguar Greg was caught; captured by the greed of men. Natural justice was no match for his or her cunning. Trapped in time as real as when he was a man. Just like the men who trapped him, a crazy unity of life. The natural order of things: Man and animal as one spiritual species not separate but one. No need to look to the sky for a god. The kingdom of God was within the river of Time, hidden in the tribal images of myth, in religion and especially in the elegance of mathematics. A swell of entropy unlocked the mystery, not in the earth or the sky, but in dreams. Action became an imperative, a thread that binds us to the law of nature. This natural justice was hidden from humanity's eyes; yet it was present in the physics of the Van Allen belt that surround the earth and is stored there for Time eternal.

The assembly went to the temple of 'Iqi-Balam' high atop the forest. A dark cloud churned above Greg's head. Thunder cracked as the emerald sword was presented to Greg's throat. To kiss the blade, the Mason's believed, was a sign of supreme homage.

Awakening as from a heavy sleep, Greg stood on the top of the temple of 'Iqi-Balam.' The rain smeared paint on his face. The torchlights flickered in the wind. He could see Christie at the bottom of the temple stairs. A hundred dark eyes stared up at him. The 'Uxu' has ended. Greg kissed the ancient sword of trust. He had become one with the jaguar people. His heart was one with the jaguar's heart. Time future and time past, a contradiction contained in time present.

The dawn of Greg's awakening coincided with sunrise over the forest. From the temple top he could see for miles over the sprawling jungle. It stretched endlessly, and yet it was threatened. As the sun broke across the horizon Greg saw what at first looked like dragonflies in his direct line of sight. The longer he stared the clearer they became. They were not dragonflies. These were Cobra attack helicopters. Greg instantly recalled that he was in Guatemala where a bloody civil war had been raging for almost 40 years.

The sound of the approaching helicopters brought fear to the faces of the jaguar people. They scattered, screaming as 50 caliber canons opened fire on the temple. The incendiary bullets burst its victims into a fiery eternity on impact. The chief beside Greg burst into a Roman candle as he fell forward down the steps of the temple. Greg raced down the steps as fast as his feet could maneuver the steep incline. Christie, just as anxious, raced up to meet Greg.

All around them people were being vaporized. Their hot blood was splattered over the temple, a sad parody of Greg's amanita inspired hallucination. He motioned for Christie to follow him and together they dashed into the jungle. Greg ran ahead as fast as his legs would carry him. They would have to make it to Palenque. That meant trekking through thick triple canopy jungle and mountains for several hundred miles—a daunting task at the best of times. Greg's heart sank. As he ran he inhaled the freshness of the morning air mixed with the smell of blood and gunpowder—truly macabre combination. The gunfire stopped behind them and the Cobra's went silent. He turned around to absorb the stillness of the jungle. Christie was gone.

Panicking, he shouted foolishly, "Christie! Christie!" A noise from behind, like a rifle cocking, startled him into reality. He turned to face the direction of the temple and saw a squad of soldiers restraining Christie. She struggled in vain to free herself from their grasp. With the squad of soldiers, Greg recognized one of the men. He was tall with curly black hair and a thick black mustache. He seemed familiar, but Greg couldn't quite place him.

From behind him came a voice Greg knew.

"We've been looking for you Dr. Fallows."

TWELVE

Vapor trails of cloud sketched chiaroscuro across the early morning sky. The silver wings of the Lear jet disappeared into the rising sun. Somewhere a leaf drifted down the Oro River. The poetry of movement beat its bruised head against invisible atoms. The great condor soared high, free from extinction in an age when only birds and gods knew the perfect freedom of flight. Cast not in bronze busts of vanity, nor the eclipsed desire of pleasure; this rare bird hovers in perfect form, an archetype of perfect flight.

An explosion rocked the silence of the dawn, and in a flash of light it was no more. A small plane fell into pieces from the sky like tears raining down on the blue Caribbean Sea. A sweet, sweet love was gone forever. Was it an accident or geopolitical incident? Causality's secret mystery is hidden from today's irrelevant questions. Where was she? Was she even alive? Greg could remember nothing of what happened after Guatemala. His brain, a sore and aching gland had been squeezed of its intelligence juice.

The great pyramid at Uxmal rose thirty meters above the overgrown flora of the jungle floor. Twisted vines and iguana roam in the silent moonlight. Chirping harpies of decay chart a course between order and chaos. Greg's pale face reflected in the cold green water of the sacred well at Chichén Itza. A stone serpent's stare is timeless and without emotion, visible remnant of a civilization whose cultural symbols do not speak the voodoo mantra of our mass media dragons. Quetzalcoatl coated gurus at the end of the second millennium, another civilization abandoned by its high priests, left to fend for itself in a universe void of meaning, a new spiritual dark age of silicon hearted temples, the last sacrifice to the mushroom god of modern destruction.

A naked female body stood next to the pool; a gentle breeze blew a cool wind across Greg's face. The smell of warm cinnamon filled the air. The hot slabs of stone beneath his feet retained the heat of the day as the sky's orange glow slowly etched itself into darkness. Her dark hair and olive eyes, deep tanned brown skin, painted with radiant color, stood before the shimmering waters of the pool, as drums beat a ventricular rhythm. The dance rode a crescendo to the moment when she swam in whirlpools of blood. She gave herself as a sacrifice to the secret voices of the winged-serpent that lived in the well, under the surface, as she crashed through that thin membrane of time, all becomes clear.

Greg opened his eyes on the world. Were these nightmares suppressed memories or creative fiction? He couldn't decide. They were expressions of post-traumatic anxiety, his doctors instructed. He couldn't remember. All he knew was what he was told. He learned that he had fallen in the jungle and hit his head. He was found and rescued by a group of missionaries who contacted the embassy and arranged for his repatriation.

The dreams were as real to him as the manicured environment of the Holmewood Sanitarium that had been his home for the past month. He couldn't confront the bitter memory of Christie's disappearance. He couldn't believe she was dead. It just wasn't possible. She was alive. She had to be. Even though they told him she died in a plane crash. He just didn't know what to believe. In the bleakness of winter he stared out at the cold Canadian landscape. He filled his days in a drug-induced silence. He stared aimlessly out the window from his blue chair. It is his strength, an allegory for his blue soul. In his mind he sometimes walks with Christie as they browse Brentano's bookstore on Fifth Avenue in New York City. He climbs the spiral staircase to the mythology section near the front of the store. They thumb through the large bound picture books of ancient drawings. He imagines what it must be like to live again, to wear those clothes, to eat really good food. They stroll out onto the streets of Manhattan, holding each other tight, lovers on their honeymoon. They are carefree, not aware of the pain in life's hidden dossier on each of us. They make love on clean white sheets in hotels with cosmopolitan names like St. Moritz on Central Park. They laugh and toast the Gatsby's' with champagne. His heart ached for the time they climbed the Empire State building as they watched the people of the world race around like ants. How they laughed. Now reservoirs of tears held captive by chemical restraints held him in his blue period.

"Good morning Greg," Rhonda Hardwell bubbled over with stilted institutional enthusiasm. She flung the heavy curtains open with gusto allowing the morning light to flood Greg's hotel-like hospital room.

Rhonda Hardwell is a precocious twenty something nurse with a flirtatious attitude. But she was more akin to General Patten than a nurse. Still, she was a woman, and a pretty good looking one at that.

"You really should be thinking about getting on with your life," she reproached. She hauled back the covers and dragged Greg out of bed with a single yank of her well-developed arm.

"You really are a scoundrel staying in bed so long. You can get yourself dressed ASAP." The way she murmured "A.S.A.P." was almost sexual. He dropped his half aching body back onto the bed. *Maybe these drugs have weird side effects.*

Mornings were the most difficult times, the endless monotony of the day, the dull routine of cloistered life. He was stuck in time between no future and no past. The doctors advised he was making progress and that his dreams were the key to releasing his suppressed memories.

"You have a visitor today," Rhonda Hardwell poked her head into his room. She rolled her eyes at Greg, and then flashed a big knowing smile before she disappeared down the corridor.

Dr. Gustav Rolf, his *numero uno* shrink, was a tall thin balding man in his late forties. He wore round spectacles like the kind that were in style in the Sixties. He reminded Greg of a balding and slightly overweight John Lennon. He rarely smiled, but he always

101

nodded in a supportive way shrinks always do. There was a certain innate goodness about him. Rolf's expertise was dream analysis and his reputation was legendary. They spent at least one-hour everyday going over his nightmares. Rolf said that when Greg recovered—a thought that energized Greg—he wanted to write a book about Greg's dreams. He suggested he might call it *Rolfing for Trout*, but Greg didn't get the joke.

Rolf had a stranger with him. He ushered the stranger to a wicker chair next to Greg's blue rocker by the window. Rolf settled into a chair by the door.

"Do you mind if I smoke?" the stranger asked with a slight accent. The voice and mannerisms were vaguely familiar. Sparks of electricity fired synapses between neurons in Greg's brain. *Deja vu's* micro-seizures pulsed. The stranger pulled out a pack of Pall Mall's and lit a cigarette. Greg's whole nervous system was on fire. He wanted to explode, to call out for nurse Rhonda Hardwell, but he couldn't. He just stared at the cigarette pack. Pall Mall, Pall Mall. It had meaning. He remembered, Rolf told him it would be like this. Remembering would be painful and exhilarating at the same time.

It began with an odor—the faint smell of burning rubber. It took Greg back to a small hotel with a colonial style courtyard near a Plaza, the Plaza de la Independencia! He could remember the name! Memories flooded his mind like amoebic dysentery. The hotel had a pool, and white wicker lounge chairs, set against a backdrop of ivy covered yellow brick walls. He could see brightly painted tiled floors, antique furniture, wrought iron rails and *huevos revueltos* piping hot in the morning sun where the coffee mixed with the sweet moist air. It filled his lungs, as his brain pumped out memories of Mérida.

"You look preoccupied," the man observed sitting down. "Is this a bad time?" No answer. "Some things never change," he added as their eyes met.

"What do you mean?" Greg looked out the window over the grounds of this famous institution for the 'minds of the rich and famous.'

"Not exactly Hawaii," the man took a drag on his cigarette.

"And this isn't Mérida either," Greg smiled looking back at him. He swelled with a confusing combination of rage and joy; a visceral collision of raw emotion twitched his cheek.

"Car . . . Car . . . Carlos . . . I thought you were dead! I saw you die with my own eyes!"

"Look Greg, I think you have a right to know some things, and your doctors think you're ready. It might even help you get well again. Obviously, I didn't die. I was wearing a vest—you know the kind. However, I did want you and some other people to think I was dead. Believe me, I'm sorry. It had to be this way."

"What about Christie?" Greg asked growing confused. In his heart he hoped like Lazarus others might also arise from the dead.

"I'm sorry," Carlos apologized sincerely. "We don't know." He looked down at his cowboy boots. Greg could see it wasn't easy for him either.

"Look," Greg took hold of a hand of friendship, "I want to know the truth. It's important to me. Up to this point, it has all a bad dream. My life is over, there is nothing left for me."

Carlos lit another cigarette, and took a long drag. Greg watched his every movement. He wanted so much to trust, to believe in something, or someone. But he knew better. One time he thought he new this man. He knew strangers on the street better than he knew this man. Carlos was an enigma, but he was the only connection Greg had to the past.

"I have to come clean on this. My real name isn't Carlos," he hesitated unsure of where to start. "It's Steve . . . Steven Knight. I'm from Anaheim California, and I worked for the National Security Agency, not the DEA. I lived in a world of deception. I left all that almost a year ago, partly because of you and what you discovered. People like you are just innocent victims of institutional greed." He paused, staring out the window. The wind blew snow around the trees. His chest tightened. He wanted to lash out at this world of deception. He stood up and walked over to the window. He pressed his hot forehead against the cold windowpane for relief. The grounds of this beautiful home for "nervous diseases and inebriates" as it was once known seemed a prison to him now. The world outside was an icy cold place. Could he ever return? But somewhere from deep within his spirit, a hot lava of emotion waited for release. As if under pressure, suddenly like a reflex, Greg swung around and faced Carlos—Steven—or whomever he was this time. His pain was transformed to anger.

"For Christ's sake Carlos . . . Steven! Did you kill Christie?"

"Settle down," Dr. Rolf appeared from the hallway, "He's here to help."

"Like fuck, he is," Greg lunged for Steven Knight aka Carlos el gringo. Rhonda Hardwell appeared out of nowhere in time for her to help Dr. Rolf to restrain Greg. She quickly gave Greg an intramuscular injection of the major tranquilizer Largactil. Greg could see Dr. Rolf and Steven Knight talking just outside his door, they shook hands and disappeared in opposite directions down the corridor. In an instant Greg was released from this world of cunning men with strategic interests, to the mythic dream world of the gods.

Who knows the devil's business plan? The prince of darkness does his wet work well. The painful groaning before the last gasp of air, the tragedy of small lives drowned in ageless chaotic wars of interests. The illusion of reason is a potent anesthetic for modernity. It is the sugar pills that coat our hollow lives, lives devoid of mystery.

This inner war is fought in silence. It is locked in individual DNA, invisible as RNA enveloping our thin fabric of mortal skin. We suffer because we cannot see the chaos around us; our chemistry is set to want order, and our chemistry is, shall we say, limited by its design. We become martyrs, saints and mentally ill, locked in a societal scheme that cannot cope with Nature's disorder. Facing chaos can be deadly; suicide seems a natural defense, but it is not, it is succor for it. Greg knew the devil's business all right. He met the devil, and he was charming.

THIRTEEN

"Determined to regain my memory and my former life I threw myself into analysis . . . Jungian analysis. At first this reflection seemed self-indulgent, a waste of time. But as the days passed to months and the eclipse of my discontent turned again to light of optimism, I began to see the value in Dr. Rolf's methods.

"I had an increasing desire to meet with the man who called himself Steven Knight aka Carlos. He was my connection to the past. I had to discover the *truth* of why Christie disappeared—and for what? This became my life's motivating force. It was something I had to do, you see. It was—no—it still is, my purpose in being here, in testifying before your committee, I mean."

"I'm not entirely clear on why you are here," Senator Clattmore barked, jowls flapping angrily. "It would appear that you are involved in many unethical, if not down right illegal activities, Dr. Fallows."

A murmur arose among the small cadre of journalists at the back of the hall as Stephen Francis Parmata entered the room. Cub reporters and twenty something wasters, Bart Molanson and Basil Johnson looked at each other and grinned from ear to ear like schoolgirls on a double date. There could actually be a story here that could catapult their nothing careers out of the doldrums and into the bright sun light of an online wire service, where reporters could play games, even snooker, on company time. Now that's a job that a job!

Parmata was one of those rare people who had done it, and seen it all, as Bart Molanson would say. He was an ex-everything:

ex-physician, ex-priest, ex-international banker and now he claimed to be a writer, although he was believed to be independently wealthy and didn't have to work. This made him suspect to the other flacks in the room. Everyone knew he was the one who broke the story of the strange death of White House Chief of Staff Sam Paterson that led to these hearings. He had connections in high places and worked the network to his advantage. If he was here, there had to be a big story to follow, even Bart Molanson and Basil Johnson could figure that out.

Parmata wore a white shirt and gold silk tie under a long black trench coat with black Hugo Boss pants and black shoes. A wool gray scarf hung around his neck. His long beak-like nose, slick black hair and intense gaze gave him a sharp edge.

An expatriate Aussie: while he gave the impression of having wealth, he had no money. He wanted money. He carried himself with an air of refined wealth and nobility, an attitude he affected for his audience. He was an actor of sorts, and not a very good one; actually he was broke. He was one of those who had to keep up the appearance of having money. Without money, friends and opportunities were scant.

Parmata believed the world owed him something and he intended to collect. His MO was not what it appeared. He'd gone from a petty North Sydney thief to world-class con. There were rumors an Interpol dossier outlined his connections with foreign currency scams, and stolen art. His friends in Israeli and Bulgarian intelligence kept him well supplied with just the right information when he needed it.

He took a seat next to Bart and Basil.

"You think you're ready to leave, do you?" Dr. Rolf stroked his bald forehead as if looking for something.

Greg felt judged and he didn't like it. He'd never liked being judged. "Yes . . . I do. That's not to say I have no fear. Do you ever know with certainty that what you are about to do in life is the right choice?" Yet Greg knew he had to leave now, or forever be locked-in by the past.

The next morning the limousine picked him at the front door. He was leaving the comfort and security of Holmewood. Dr. Rolf told him to expect a certain amount of apprehension when he first left. Rolf also said he must get on with his life; that, at least, Greg intended to do.

"Seize the moment," Rolf directed Greg as he stepped into the car, closing the door behind him.

The driver, a very fat man in his mid-fifties, glanced in the rear-view mirror as they drove along the tree lined driveway of the sanitarium to the main street of the rural southern Ontario community. The traffic was heavy as usual as they drove east to Toronto International Airport. Greg looked out over the rapidly industrializing fields, and thought how Christie used to tirade about environmental causes every time they drove along that stretch of the 401 highway.

As he looked over the sprawl he could see her face, a chimera floating above the dying countryside says: "It's a crime that the best farmland in the country is being gobbled up by rampant urban expansion."

Greg stepped up to the American Airlines ticket counter at Terminal 3. He was daydreaming about New York when the attendant handed him his boarding pass. She was a pretty woman. He hadn't thought about women since before Christie's disappearance. It stirred a mixture of confusing memories. Her perfume reminded him of the hibiscus flowers in the jungle.

Steve Knight had sent a message via Dr. Rolf. He was to meet him at Brentano's bookstore in New York. Knight made all the limo, airline and hotel arrangements—first class all the way. As Greg stepped through the security booth he stepped into the past, to a time when he was racing to find Christie. Now he was driven to discover the lost truth.

As he handed his Canadian passport to the Immigration officer, and she punched his name into the computer alarms bells went off in his head. He wanted to run, but his feet wouldn't move.

"Would you come this way please, Dr. Fallows," she invited in a pleasant efficient voice. "Is there a problem?" Greg asked.

"No, sir. Just a routine matter," and she led him to the glassed office with the US flag and framed picture of the President on the oak paneled wall.

When the door closed Greg began to see his nightmare hadn't ended. The faces before him shattered his thin layer of sanity. He wheeled around in an effort to escape, away from the shadows of the past. He froze, he couldn't move.

"Greg," he heard a kind, clear voice and turned to see the same faces he'd seen in Amsterdam. Or was it a dream?

"You people!" Greg cried as the light receded from their faces. He could clearly recognize the UN pin on Strumpf's lapel. Perhaps it was only the badge of a Masonic lodge, or the descendants the Knights Templar—the warrior-monks of medieval France.

Greg's mind raced. He tried to remember everything he'd read about the Templars during his convalescence. *It just might save my life,* he thought.

"Be seated." Hunt spoke with authority and reassurance. "You needn't fear any longer Greg." He paused for a moment as if troubled by something, searching for the right words.

"You have a right to know of your contribution in this great restructuring of the United Nations.

"Because of Christie and what you've done?"

"No," he continued. "We had nothing to do with what . . ."

"Who did then?" Greg shouted. His recharged anger surprised even himself. "The Cali cartel likes to explode airplanes," as he pointed to a map of Columbia on the wall.

"Exploding planes is what it's all about," Brentano added excitedly. His smile revealed new gold-capped teeth.

"Sit down," Hunt placed a hand on his shoulder, at the same time he motioned to the others to have a seat. "We are here to tell you the truth."

"And what's that?" Greg glowered back.

"Your amnesia is a result of the horror you witnessed during the destruction of a Maya village in Guatemala. You saw the slaughter of innocent people; destruction of the rainforest by bulldozers to build airports that bring more development to harvest the rich mineral deposits hidden in the jungle.

"Your discoveries had nothing to do with the Maya destruction except in the sense that greed destroys all, like your myth of the Jaguar's heart. The codex revealed the rough location of ore deposits, rare minerals needed for construction of stealth-fighter technology. The only place on earth it is found. Right where you were working in the jungles of Central America.

"Governments around the world are trying to get their hands on it. They obviously want to monopolize the source.

"For instance, Israel wants it badly to achieve a major technological advantage before the next war in the Middle East breaks out. It would give them air superiority. It's the kind of edge that up to now only the United States has had. And the US has coveted that advantage.

"Human sacrifices are inevitable in this game." He drummed his hand nervously on the table. "Lives are expendable and minds are lost in the need to maintain secrecy, and shroud it in mystery."

Greg understood what Hunt was getting at. He also knew there must be a reason Hunt was telling him all of this. By now Greg knew only one reason why spooks ever told the truth and that was to recruit or to neutralize. *A quaint euphemism*, he thought. *But which ticket had his name on it?*

"In the beginning the European Union hoped to mine the secret technology for themselves. Israel however, always an outsider, wanted the military advantage and was willing to do anything in the name of national security. Preferring to work alone, Israel set on a parallel course along side the EU to find the mineral laden deposits."

But what they found instead was what Greg knew. He knew what he'd really discovered was a codex that outlined a series of interconnecting world political events that would signal the beginning of a New World Order. A special branch within the labyrinth of the UN Information office would oversee this New World Order. As world events fell into place a group of businessmen, government men and woman in different corners of the world would simultaneously open ancient envelopes on the order of the last Grand Master of the Knights Templar, Jacques De Molnay. It was his foresight and genius that saved the Templars treasure by bringing it to Central America in 1313.

"Steven Knight (aka Carlos) worked for a top secret branch of the National Security Agency. He attempted to thwart all efforts to obtain the minerals.

"You were our ticket Greg. You were our smoke screen, our plausibly deniable pretext for being there in the first place. As an academic engaged in bona fide field research you were above suspicion in most places.

"Knight tried to block others from getting the technology. His death was set up to make Mossad believe, and the contact group of governments to believe you and the secrets were lost again. In reality you and Christie were set free from the hands of Mossad agents, back to the safety of the jungle, until Mossad recaptured you and Christie again."

"The die is cast?" Greg asked.

"Yes."

"And Steven Knight?"

"He's waiting in New York with instructions to kill you." Greg knew it was coming, but it still hit him like a sledgehammer.

"Is there any way out?" Greg asked.

"If you kill him first." Hunt looked away.

"Kill him for you—you mean," Greg snapped back.

"As you like it," Hunt grinned. "He's working for both Mossad and NSA. He might still have Christie. I don't know. He's a problem for both of us."

"Checkmate." Finally, it all made sense. But as anxious as he was to find Christie there was part of him that kept telling him he was getting more involved with things that shouldn't concern him. Yet, he was being drawn into a web of international conspiracy. He wanted to find out more about the United Nations and the development of a world government. And this he couldn't miss. The story Hunt told was only a half-truth. Surely there was more to it than procuring the mineral rights to stealth fighter radar avoidant technology. But what was it? It had to have something to do with him or they would have gotten rid of him a long time ago. It had to do with the Templar codex found at Igi Balam.

The flight to LaGuardia was a short one. A limo met him at the airport and drove through Queens, over the mid-town bridge to Manhattan. At Brentano's bookstore he stopped outside to appreciate the irony for a moment. *Nice sense of humor*, he thought to myself. He climbed the spiral staircase to the second floor and walked along the railing to the front of the store, browsing in the mythology section as he went.

"You made it alright?" Steven smiled. "Come on, let's get a bite to eat."

"No, I feel like a walk."

"But it's almost dark," Steven hesitated. "This is New York. No one in their right mind goes out walking after dark." He had things planned as always. This would disrupt his plans. Greg knew it.

"Nothing frightens me anymore . . . Carlos. Why don't we walk up through the Park?"

"You are adventurous," he flexed his arms, mildly irritated. "Come on then let's get going." He headed down the stairs, out onto a hectic Fifth Avenue.

When they arrived at the park, Greg crossed the lawn toward the old dairy. He walked inside the darkened old dairy building. It was empty as he expected it to be this time of night. Steven followed a couple of steps behind.

"What's going on?" Knight asked. "Are you fuckin' crazy, or what?"

"You tell me." Greg took a hypodermic needle from his pocket—given to him by Hunt. It was filled with succinylcholine and potassium chloride. The combination of a fast-acting muscle relaxant produces rapid onset of flaccid paralysis—within one minute and lasts 4-6 minutes. The potassium chloride causes sudden hyperkalemia and cardiac arrest—instant death.

Greg stabbed him in the upper right shoulder. Knight struggled for a second or two, and then fell to the floor gasping for breath. In a moment he stopped breathing. His heart stopped. He was dead. It would look like another overdose in Central Park. Greg removed the syringe and dropped it beside the lifeless body. He put his gloves in his coat pocket. He knew the postmortem would indicate the probable cause of death to be a malignant cardiac arrhythmia. Greg slipped out the door onto the roadway leading to South Central Park. He stretched, energized. He had killed Carlos. He should feel free, but his stomach balked. He had the uncomfortable feeling that he'd just killed the wrong man. But he knew he couldn't go back. There was no turning back now. *God, forgive me,* he thought.

As he walked past the Park Plaza Hotel heated with anger mixed with chilling fear. One man at the Immigration office with Hunt was a big man with a large black mustache. He looked like the same man who captured him in Guatemala. Could he be the same person who blew up Christie's plane? Of course . . . why hadn't he understood that earlier? What did Israel's secret intelligence service have to do with Hunt's explanation at the airport? He had done their work for them, once again. Now he was really in danger. The police, or possibly an international terrorist would label him mentally unstable. A manhunt would surely find him no matter where he went. No place on earth would be safe. He had come full circle. He had his memory back, but now he was the hunted again. He needed help, but who would help him now? He was a criminal, and alone. He had to get out of the country—fast.

FOURTEEN

Greg left the Hotel Casa del Balam in Mérida and drove all night. The flight from JFK on Aeroméxico couldn't have been easier. He began to think perhaps things were beginning to go right. He slept like a fugitive at the Temple of Frescoes at Tulum. A curious young pig looking for food woke him in the morning, snorting nostrils and wet nose in his face. He jumped up and chased the timid visitor out with a loud disparaging comment.

The events of the preceding twenty-four hours seemed surreal to Greg. There was symmetry here in the ruins of his life, among the ruins of a civilization. Now that he was here he didn't know what to do. The security of the jungle beckoned him. He had a hot need to retrace his nightmarish last voyage to Mexico and Guatemala. He needed to find out why he was somehow key to unlocking a powerful secret that ran through the dark heart of an international conspiracy. Only now awakening as if from a long sleep, did he begin to realize that he'd been a pawn from the very beginning; from the first time he stepped off the plane on his giddy first flight to Amsterdam.

In the radiance of the rising sun he understood the meaning of the myth of the Jaguar's heart. He saw himself in the jungle. He saw himself as the jaguar. It had become his symbol. This was what Dr. Rolf was trying to get him to understand. Instead he chose to be the jaguar. So to retrace his steps, he had to go back to the jungle, away from this illusion of the modern world. He knew he had to come back to the land of dreams and myth to understand the present mystery.

He slept all day in the shaded palms of the ruins. The blue sea crashed in his ears. The warm breeze filled him with energy. The peace of this place was overwhelming. Sleep came easily to Greg's troubled heart.

The successions of days that followed were eventful. Three days out of Palenque on foot and escorted by a native guide, Greg developed fever, chills and rigor. He knew the symptoms of malaria. He also knew he would be unable to travel. His guide, fearing he had a contagious disease, abandoned him to his fate in the jungle.

As Greg lay on his litter shivering in the sweltering humidity of the jungle, above him the light flashed an eerie message through the leaves of the trees. He had no fear. He was ready to die. In his pyretic dreams Christie appeared. She was dressed in native costume, as he remembered her. She was painted with bright colors. She took him to the village where they lived in splendid simplicity. These were the long languid days of their lives. The sweat, blood, toil and fear were gone. He was light, almost weightless, as she took his hand and followed her into the center of a circle of Maya.

From behind the green foliage he saw himself dance naked. The beating drums pound a rhythm of primal truth. His heart raced in fevered frenzy, like a drowning man who knew he was dying. Greg asked, what black purpose awaited him? What sealed destiny was hidden beyond the shimmering shadows of dreams? He wondered whether a Druid robed guide would take his hand and lead him through a bubble-like sphere; all sticky and wet into rushing colors; vibrating sperm, moving, cascading toward the calm clear light to God.

Greg opened his eyes. His fever had subsided. Around him these slight and strong people carried on their day-to-day tasks of living. They lived hidden from the world's probing eyes. Here, buried under roots, in subterranean homes, draped in animal skins, he was nursed to health by a shaman with round dark eyes and rough sandpaper hands. This doctor was schooled in the chthonic world cloistered from the trauma of passing time on the tiny surface of the planet. It was Greg's home. But it was also a lair, a den for lost and forgotten souls.

Around the world the earth's tension found release through faults or cracks in the fragile coating that floats on molten gases. Volcanoes erupted, buildings collapsed and in the civil unrest that followed, nations looked to the UN for help. And the UN is more than willing to intervene these days with food, money, advice, and politics.

Greg, safe in the jungle, recovered from malaria. He sought with renewed purpose and vigor to find out the meaning of the text at Igi-Balam. Day and night he poured over what he could remember of the codex. No longer depressed or obsessed with the past, he applied what he learned from his study of the mysterious medieval Knights Templar to the strange mathematical formulae in the codex.

There were too many unanswered questions. He had to return to Amsterdam. It wouldn't be easy now. He had to assume that he was being hunted. But if there was any place in the world where he could fade into the woodwork, it was Amsterdam.

FIFTEEN

If Greg, or for that matter, Inspector Kroode saw who was in the Great Hall of the Masonic Temple that night, they would not have believed their eyes. Just about every major business and government in the West, and some emerging Eastern European states were represented. From the general demeanor of those present, it was not hard to believe that this brotherhood (even the women were called brothers) was instrumental in contributing to nineteenth century revolutionary movements.

Secrecy cloaked the Knights Templar from their very foundation. They will remain a mystery because too many important people want it kept that way. This mystery and the perpetuation of the secret society have enabled them to protect some very dark secrets from the past. Books have been written and lives lost in the quest for the truth about the mysterious treasure of the Knights Templar.

According to legend, their treasure was lost when the King of France—some say at the request of the pope—began persecuting the warrior-monks. It all began at dawn, Friday, October 13, 1307 when Philippe IV ordered the arrest of all Templars within his territory. The next seven years saw the Inquisition extract confessions from Templars who under torture admitted to the vilest of acts: the sacrilege of spitting on the crucifix, and engaging in homosexual acts (including the kiss of recognition of another Templar; a kiss on the ass—the Mason's kiss). But that's the past.

The Temple at 39-41 Vondelstraat Oud comprised two large four story stone buildings situated on the southwest corner of Vondelpark.

High above Vondelstraat was a beautiful stained glass window overlooking a rear garden. In the center of the window was a massive bright yellow Star of David surrounded by an oyster blue stained glass background. Several of the other windows on the Vondelstraat side of the building held representations of a red rose surrounded by thorns.

The meeting of the governing Council of 33 was a special event. The Council of Elders, thirty-three in all, was summoned to Amsterdam to discuss the serious events unfolding. No one spoke at dinner. Candles on four sides lighted the large room; banks of sixty large candles gave a surprising amount of light. The moon outside highlighted the yellow in the Star of David enough to cast a golden glow over the entire assembly.

This was a special meeting; the 13th Grand Master of the Order of the Temple presided over the meeting, a lineage that traced itself back to the Crusades. In 1113 Godfroi of Bullion was the first Grand Master of the Poor Knights of the Temple of Solomon, or Knights Templar. Tonight his heir prepares to break bread in the name of the Prince of Darkness.

Since the time of their disbandment in 1308 (their leader Jacques De Molnay was burned at the stake in March 1314) the Poor Knights of the Temple of Solomon have been in hiding. They became a secret society with elaborate ceremonies and quasi-religious rituals. Over time, some were absorbed into other less militant monastic orders. Greg's discoveries at Igi-Balam indicated some escaped with a treasure and the entire Templar fleet to the New World long before Christopher Columbus bore the Templar flag westward.

Others gravitated to the secret society of Freemasons where they brought money, influence and power. But they also carried with them plans to vindicate their unholy order, and at the same time to secure their proper place in the history of the world.

It was here in the inner sanctum of the Mason's that rumor of a mystical skull—possibly the preserved skull of Dagobert II the last Merovingian king—was a matter of intense debate.

On the plane Greg had images of naked fatherly figures wearing nothing but leather aprons, set squares, interlocking diviners, and black rings. He couldn't shake the comical idea that portly potbellied men who collected money for charity, and had parades with funny shoes, and miniature cars could be involved in an international conspiracy. As he knew only too well, while this side existed, it was not the heart of the matter. Like an artichoke it was merely the outer surface. He chuckled. The lady seated next to him on the plane looked at him as if he were mad. Maybe he was mad. Maybe it was his destiny to peel back the artichoke to expose the rotting heart.

Greg's return flight to Toronto was uneventful. He arrived just after midnight. On the long flight his sleep was interrupted. He dreamed an inordinate amount lately. In one dream he was lost in a deep forest; Christie was calling out to him, but he couldn't find his way. An old man appeared and took his hand, and led him silently out of the forest.

He knew he couldn't just walk in to his apartment. He called his old friend Robin Fisher from a pay phone at Terminal 3.

"Hello."

"Robin?"

"Greg? Where the fuck are you?"

"I need a favor."

"Do you know what time it is? Where the hell have you been? The police have been looking all over for you."

"I need to talk to you."

"And a lot of people want to talk to you too. What's going on anyway? You wouldn't believe what I've been going through; the university, the police, and even a break-in at my house . . ."

"Look, can we meet somewhere? How about the Howard Johnson's near the airport. I don't have much time. I think I'm being followed, and our phone calls may be intercepted, so we don't have much time."

The sound of Greg's voice became urgent and impatient.

"Yeah, sure, okay. I'll be there as soon as I can."

After he hung up, Greg walked out the front door of the immense and empty terminal. He caught a cab to the Howard Johnson's. At the hotel he picked up the local paper and settled into a corner of the almost empty bar. In his head he went over the events of his life over the past two years. So much had changed. Could this be the real world, or was it a virtual world, a long and protracted dream?

Greg ordered a beer and returned to his paper. When the bartender came back with his drink, there was an envelope under the glass. Greg opened the note. It read: "Instruments that do harm may also heal; the final result depends on the proficiency of the user, and not just the instruments." It was signed, "Et Arcadia Ego." Greg puzzled the cryptic message. He knew it had to be from Hunt.

Just as Greg put the note down, Robin Fisher flopped down beside him at the bar. He was a middle aged academic of no special ability. He landed a job in the same department where he did his PhD shortly after he finished his thesis. He was a mediocre teacher at best, and the climate of political correctness on campus had tempered his appreciation of the opposite sex. He recently had separated from his wife of 17 years, and had gone through painfully embarrassing allegations of sexual harassment. Robin Fisher was a man who was past his prime. In Greg's eyes he was a charlatan and a sophist. But he was the only one Greg knew he could turn to for help.

"Do you know what time it is? I have a class in the morning." Robin was annoyed.

Greg took a sip of beer.

"Canadian beer all tastes the same to me."

"Is that what you wanted to tell me? You call me up as if the CIA is after you to tell me that Canadian beer all tastes the same?"

"Were you followed?"

"Are you crazy? I mean, I heard you were in some psych ward, but I . . ." He caught himself and colored with shame. "I'm sorry Greg. Sorry about Christie I mean."

"It's okay. I'm not crazy. Look, I don't have time to discuss the details of my situation now. But please try to understand, the less you know the better. I need you to do me a favor. I need you to call someone for me in Amsterdam."

"I think I need a drink," hailing the bartender with his thick muscular arm. "Get me a Manhattan . . . Oh, and make that double cherries."

"All I can tell you is that I've stumbled across something big, something to do with a group that plans to take over the United Nations and form a world government. It may already be too late."

"Are you on drugs or something?"

"Look, I can't go into it right now. I found several bodies, mummified bodies on my trip to Guatemala some time ago. Among the bodies was a skull. It seemed preserved or crystallized. That doesn't matter now, what matters is that among the papers in the tomb, there was a mysterious codex that didn't look Mayan. I only recently was able to make any sense of it."

Robin's drink arrived. There was a long silence. Greg took a sip of his beer.

"Go on," Robin encouraged, fascinated.

"Well in the codex contains interlocking pieces of a puzzle. A sort of master plan or schema that outlines events that will lead to the resurrection of the body."

"Christ?"

"No, I think the body is symbolic for the order of Knights Templar."

"And you think this means somebody is trying to take over the UN?"

"It was written in the 14th Century."

"But I thought you said it wasn't Maya."

"That's right. No, it wasn't Maya. It was European. In fact it was a medieval French attempt to disguise the codex to look Maya. Don't you see? It was made to try and convince anyone who found it that it was an insignificant fake."

"So what does it have to do with the UN?"

"As best as I can figure it, it's a timetable. I think it's a kind of puzzle clock. When all the pieces fit together it triggers a cascade of events, and something happens."

"And you think it's a signal to somebody?"

"Exactly. I think there are pieces of the puzzle that have been handed down by the Mason's from generation to generation. At the right time and place as specified by the document in Guatemala, something is going to happen. I don't know what, but something is going to bring all of these pieces together. And when that happens . . ."

"The timetable for a political takeover of the UN is unleashed."

"Exactly. Like Judas betrayed Christ with a kiss . . . only now it's a Mason's kiss."

SIXTEEN

"Rape hounds," Dr. Teunon was disgusted, after a preliminary examination of the body at the scene. He knew a more detailed analysis would include what she last ate, and DNA analysis of the semen would virtually give them the answer they wanted, if they had a suspect; but that was Inspector Kroode's problem wasn't it?

"Damned grim," Kroode looked down at the body of the young female lying in the hallway.

If there was a witness, they would have seen Kate run to the top of the third floor of her apartment at 252 Voorburgwal after an uneventful night drinking and smoking at Rick's Cafe. About 3 A.M. two men dressed in black crept into her apartment by climbing over the roof of three other buildings, and entered through an open third-floor window.

They found Kate fast asleep in the dark. One of the masked men approached her bed with the stealth of a cat, and quickly covered Kate's mouth with his gloved hand. She instantly awoke. When she tried to sit up she was confronted with a large hunting knife at her throat. She said nothing. She was told to kiss the blade of the knife. She whimpered as they tore the covers away, exposing her naked body. The same intruder took her tattered bra and wrapped it carefully around her neck and twisted the bra straps together, crushing her trachea with slow methodical skill. She lost consciousness after a brief but futile struggle; there was a final reflexive twitch of her arms and legs, and then a sudden calm.

The second intruder took a small-capped syringe from his pocket where he had kept it warm. He gently spread her legs and inserted a fluid into her vagina with a 20 cc syringe. They carried her body to the door, bound her by the hands and feet and threw her body down the stairs. Their mission accomplished they would retire to a Coffeeshop for a smoke.

"We got the DNA match up on the semen analysis," Pieter Teunon said into the telephone receiver in the mortuary. Behind him lay the naked body of another canal floater. The body was dissected in the usual fashion using a standard "Y" cut from the neck to the groin. The smell of death permeated the air.

"Anything interesting?" Hans Kroode asked sitting feet up on his desk eating a ham and cheese broodje.

"Maybe," Pieter Teunon hesitated. "At least it's unusual."

"Okay, you got me. I'm curious. What's the mystery in the semen analysis; we haven't even got a suspect. And don't forget we still have the other canal murder?" Hans Kroode cradled the phone between his neck and shoulder as his assistant Helga handed him another missing person report.

"For starters, would you believe this rapist has been dead of two thousand years?"

"Fuck! Doctor T, I don't have time for that kind of nonsense," Hans Kroode sat bolt upright in his chair, almost choking on his sandwich. Helga stopped and turned around at the door. She smiled and left when she saw he was okay.

"Well I'm afraid you'd better make time; because what I'm telling you is the honest to God truth; I couldn't believe it myself when I first saw it. I had them run the tests again, and again. And you know what, the same answers, the same goddamned results . . ."

"Are you telling me she wasn't raped?"

"Not unless he died and come back to life; no pun intended," Dr. Pieter snickered.

"So how would someone get two thousand year old semen?" the Inspector asked incredulous.

"I'd say they froze it, or kept it on ice."

"No shit!"

"No shit," Pieter reiterated seriously.

"Somebody wants us to think she was raped," Hans Kroode let the possibilities sink in. "Any idea who the rapist might be?" he asked half joking.

"Well, now that you ask, the tech Merel offered, probably Jesus Christ himself . . . '"

If he'd been listening carefully he might have heard a soft click as his word raced along the phone line to the technician eavesdropping on their conversation thousands of miles away.

SEVENTEEN

"The Great Book teaches us a time will come to pass when our destiny will be fulfilled," Hunt looked out over the Council. He looked down and read from the Great Book:

"The great and wondrous lady Maria of Quéribus let the young Lord of Montségor, a Templar of some distinction, into her chamber. The warmth of her bed replaced the cold and dampness of the room.

"And so for a thousand million years love conceives to achieve its ends in deference to social norms, or the self-serving laws of men. But the body being mere mortal flesh does wither and die, and so it is with the beauty of youth that it must wither and die like the fruits not picked languishing on the vine.

"But in her youth she died, poor Maria, still beautiful as a corpse all dressed in white like a wedding rose. So heart broken was her lover the pitiful Templar in his white *cagoule with* its red cross emblazoned on his chest; on the night of her burial, this poor beast so garroted by grief, cunningly and deceitfully he crept to her grave, and did take a shovel he had brought in hand and dug up the grave of his lovely mistress, deflowering her in her grave. From beyond the stars and majesty of the universe came a voice that beckoned him to return to this same place in nine months.

"As good a Templar there ever was, he returned as instructed and found the grave open again, and to his surprise saw a glowing crystal skull and crossbones. The same voice spoke to him: 'Guard this gift with your immortal soul, for it is from the supreme mover of the eternal wheels of the universe, and from whom all good comes.'

125

"The good Templar did as he was instructed and bundled it up in some cloth and disappeared off into the night again with his booty.

"It is said that in time it became his protector, and he was able to defeat his enemies by displaying the magical head. In time all things come to pass, and so it was with the head that he upon his death bequeathed the thing to the Order of the Temple."

Hunt closed the book and bowed his head in reverence.

EIGHTEEN

Inspector Hans Kroode arrived at *D'Admiraal before* Dr. Pieter Teunon. The last remaining rays of a warm October day were settling over the umbrellas of the outdoor café. He sat outside, ordered a beer, and began to soak up the sun, just as the doctor arrived.

"They were called the shock troops of the Crusades," Pieter Teunon sipped his beer, wiping the froth from his mouth with the back of his hand. "But it's difficult to get a handle on who they really were. So much of what has been written about the Templars is either crap or pure fantasy; and so, there is little in the way of reliable sources available."

"How is this bullshit going to help us solve two murders?" Inspector Kroode interrupted.

"I've done a great deal of reading on this bizarre sect of monks over the last couple of days. On one level they were simply warrior-monks, some would say mystic-knights in their trademark white mantle with splayed red cross. You see the very same cross on the sails of Christopher Columbus's fleet in paintings at the Rijksmuseum. Yet there is evidence to suggest that they were a much more mysterious institution—a secret order with obscure goals. Their clandestine methods were a cover for covert action; a sort of medieval secret intelligence organization."

"You mean like the CIA or MI6?"

"Yes, that's what I'm getting at. By the end of the fourteenth century they were accused of heresy. I mean really unspeakable acts in those days, including necromancy, homosexuality and spitting on the cross."

Pieter Teunon stopped briefly to sip his beer. A silent Hans Kroode sat looking out over the canal, watching the boats navigate the waterway.

"You know, over the centuries they have been depicted as bullies and greedy tyrants who abused their power. They were accused of Satanism. Some of them admitted—under torture—of practicing obscene acts of desecration. Today, some historians see them as victims of a high intrigue between the Church and French national interests. Of course, that serves the interests of the sect too.

"In the Freemason tradition they are seen as custodians of an arcane Gnostic wisdom that dates back beyond the time of the Egyptian Pharaohs to the building of the tower of Babel. Imagine how that would go over in medieval Roman Catholic France."

"I still don't get it Pieter. Are you saying some modern business men are running around dressed up like medieval knights rogering each other?"

"Guillame de Tyre wrote between 1175 and 1185 that the Order of the Poor Knights of Christ and the Temple of Solomon was founded in 1118. One day a noble by the name of Hugues de Payan from Champagne presented himself to the palace of Baudouin I, the king of Jerusalem, whose elder brother Godfoi de Bouillon captured Jerusalem from the Saracens some nineteen years earlier. According to the earliest accounts their *raison d'etre* at that time was to protect pilgrims on their journey to the Holy Land."

"I just don't see how this history lesson has anything to do with a double murder."

"I'll come to that. Tradition has it that they built their quarters on the foundation of the ancient Temple of Solomon . . . hence their name. Rumors over the centuries indicate they found something of great significance to Christianity there, something that has the power to turn the Christian tradition upside down. Some scholars believe they possess a secret knowledge or facts about the death of Christ—they claimed they had proof he didn't die on the cross—that threatened to destroy the authority of the Church."

"So you're saying there was a massive cover up. Some secret about Christ that had been suppressed by the Church flourished into a secret society that buggers each other and kills people," Hans Kroode was overcome by a desire for another cigarette.

"Killing to prevent the revelation of a secret with explosive implications for governments and the Church; for our whole notion of history, as we know it, over the past two thousand years. Yes, that's a motive."

"Maybe. What happened to them?"

"This is what is known: On Friday October 13, 1307 Philippe the IV of France (in cahoots with Rome some say) ordered all Templars arrested in France. Many Templars were tortured, imprisoned and put to death. Four years later, in 1312 Pope Clement II officially dissolved the Order. In 1314 the last Grand Master of the Order, Jacques De Molnay, was burned at the stake. Officially at least, the Order ceased to exist. Unofficially, however, there are reports that key Templars escaped from France. As a secret intelligence organization they might have intercepted intelligence reports. There is historical evidence that some moved to England and Scotland where they were absorbed into the secret society of Freemasons. Other more radical scholars say they immigrated to the New World with their treasure. "Recently a Canadian scholar by the name of Greg Fallows has written about evidence he says he found that shows the Templars may have lived among the Maya of the Yucatan and Guatemala a hundred years before Columbus. The big mystery, however, is what happened to their treasure. Some sources believe it was their treasure that prompted the attack on the Templars in the first place."

Hans Kroode didn't say anything at first; he quietly sipped his beer watching the light dance on the surface of the water in the canal. "Where does G2 come into all this? It's a branch of the United Nations Information Office, right?"

"Ah, ha! You do see my point. All the ingredients are there: power, money and a cover-up. But I don't know how G2 fits with all this medieval history stuff though."

"We need to find out more about this UN G2 thing."

"We also need to get in touch with this Greg Fallows character; find out what he knows."

"I hope he's not a Shriner." Hans Kroode ordered another round.

NINETEEN

As soon as Inspector Kroode finished his beer and bid the doctor adieu, Pieter immediately placed a call to Professor Leo Pauli in London from the nearest pay phone. A woman answered the phone.

"Just one moment please," She put down the phone and walked the luxurious hallway of the century old Belgravia apartment to a private suite. She opened the huge wooden double doors.

"Professor Pauli. You have a call from Amsterdam . . . a Dr. Teunon, sir."

"Hello."

"Professor Pauli, you asked me to call when I had something for you."

"Yes. What is it?" He snapped, sipping a glass of tawny port in his arthritic hand.

"I see the stigmata, but they are not recognized by anyone else," Pieter Teunon hung up.

He walked briskly back to his apartment alongside the canal on Spui Straat. Winter was approaching. He unlocked the door to his apartment and relaxed once inside, out of the cold evening air.

Moments later a red Porsche Boxster sped away from an underground parking garage somewhere outside of Paris headed for Charles DeGaulle International airport at a 160 kilometers an hour. At the KLM counter the driver bought a business class ticket to Amsterdam.

Renata Benoit worked for Mossad, the Israeli intelligence service. She joined the IDF, the Israeli army, just prior to the Six Day War.

She was in her late fifties and fit. On this day she looked like a schoolteacher. She was working as a translator at the Embassy.

Born in Rochester, New York, Renata was the youngest daughter of Jewish immigrants. She studied French at McGill University in Montréal before joining the IDF six weeks before the Arab-Israeli war broke out in 1967. As the youngest girl in a family of 4 boys she had a need to prove herself. Her father was a brew master for a local beer company; she grew up a middle class American. Much to the chagrin of her parents who emigrated from France after the Second World War, she joined the IDF after her M.A. at McGill.

Her innate intelligence was quickly exploited by the spooks in Army intelligence, an oxymoron in the IDF, as in any military organization. But the Israeli were far better than either the Americans or the Russians at employing women both in combat and as operatives in human intelligence gathering.

In 1972 she was sent to Munich as a part of the effort to neutralize the terrorist forces behind the murder of the Israeli Olympic athletes. Needless to say her cover has never been blown, and she has never failed in a mission. She was a single-minded woman with the grace and charm of an educated lady. She was also as cunning as a badger, who was both physically fit and emotionally aloof.

She was average height; weighing one hundred and forty pounds with round wire-rim glasses. Her salt and pepper shoulder length hair was held back with a leather beret. She wore a navy blue Tilley jacket and skirt—her favorite clothes for travel because of the number of pockets and their durability—with a brightly colored floral patterned blouse designed by Lucio, which she bought on a visit to Chartres. On her feet she wore sensible shoes, a pair of black loafers, none of those crazy spikes for her. She went for comfort, not style. But she was also a master of disguise.

Her real forte, however, was marksmanship. She could knock a fly off a bicycle seat at 300 hundred yards. Her code-name was Chameleon. She picked it because it suited her ability to blend in with her environment. She didn't have the magazine beauty of a model, but for Renata this was an advantage. She relied on her ordinary looks and sharp intelligence. She was a professional, and one of the best of the best in the most effective intelligence organization in the world—UN's G2. It was Renata who the American government wanted when they needed accurate intelligence about Saddam Hussein. For the past 2 years she had been seconded to the UN Department of Information, Paris section known as G2.

What was unusual about this assignment, and what has always been troubling about secret societies, especially secret societies with massive resources and powerful members, was their ability to use official assets for unofficial purposes—the perfect example of plausible deniability. An official organization like the CIA, or Mossad, would find itself taking the heat, or the credit, for a covert operation, but could neither confirm nor deny any connection, as is usual in Black Operations. In fact, the media saw any denial as affirmation of involvement, so intelligence directorates routinely issue neither confirm, nor deny press releases as a matter of standard operating procedure.

Renata had found that working with G2 she no longer had to worry about press releases and the cumbersome details of oversight committees. At the UN there was no overseeing body for the Department of Information. The joke at the UN was, the "UN has no intelligence." The work of the secretive G2 was, therefore, above suspicion and beyond the eyes of the Senate Intelligence Committee.

It was routine for her not to know what her mission was until she reached her destination and checked in with her contact usually through an embassy or consulate. This time she was to pick up a copy of the *International Herald Tribune* and instructed to check the very limited "personals" section. It would read: "WHERE ARE YOU MY OLD FRIEND? Call Judy, 31.020.625.27.75."

While the advertisement would appear innocent enough to most of us, to Renata the information was complete. A simple call to the Amsterdam number and a recorded message gave her an encrypted code and location of her contact. Anyone else who accidentally phoned that number would hear just a series of meaningless numbers and letters. She immediately opened her laptop computer and double clicked the map of the world icon, which brought a picture of the world onto her screen. She entered the series of numbers from the message.

Hunt stood with his hands behind his back, staring out the window overlooking Vondel Park. The sparsely furnished room had high ceilings and large windows. Every sound echoed through the spacious room like footsteps on an abandoned street. The autumn sky was overcast, and a light rain fell over the six hundred year old city. He was troubled by the Council's decision. Several hundred years had passed since the brotherhood had lost its position in the world and was forced to seclude itself behind the shadow of the Masonic Lodge. He would be glad to be rid of this false association. He had no use for the Masons and their arcane rituals. They were a tiresome bunch. He looked forward to the fulfillment of Jacques De Molnay's prophetic curse. The Templars would arise again, a true phoenix from the grave. Soon they would meet and all the pieces of the time puzzle would fit together. A New World Order had begun. It would be his Order. But even Hunt disliked killing. It was so primitive. He would be glad when it was over.

Hunt was a man of integrity. As he stood overlooking the city he loved so much, the stench of self-disgust rolled over him in waves of nausea. He knew what had to be done, and he would do it; he must have victory, at any price. Hunt ran the Order's international network, but the one asset he lacked was the most important. Prior to the Templars' dissolution by Pope Clement II in 1314, and assassination of Jacques De Molnay, the Order removed its treasure to Amsterdam where it was transported by sea to the New World. A few of the leaders who escaped made their way to Scotland far from their enemy's reach.

The Templar secret was so closely guarded by the Order that they were willing to go as far as murder. The medieval policy of plausible deniability maintained that the Templars' "proof" that Jesus Christ did not die on the cross must be maintained at any cost. The heresy, now well known, claimed Jesus Christ lived for another thirty years after his supposed death and resurrection. The heresy alleged Jesus married Mary Magdalen, and their heirs became the

Merovingian Dynasty—the true Kings of France—with legendary magical powers. To Hunt and his Order, the crystal skull was the real Holy Grail.

Hunt was determined to have it. It was their rightful destiny to rule the new United Nations, to bring about the fulfillment of the Gospels, the kingdom of God on Earth, as he would interpret it. The relic was the jewel in that crown, without it, the Order would never rise again to its former glory; forever doomed to obscure meaningless rituals; secret handshakes without purpose. He knew what must be done, for the glory of God, the kiss must be delivered, and the skull must be returned to its rightful owners . . . the Poor Knights of the Temple of Solomon. He clenched his fist tightly, digging his fingernails into his palms.

He turned around to his empty oak desk and dialed a number on the secure line. The years of searching and planning would soon be over. He would soon truly be the heir to the Merovingian Dynasty, the real sons of Christ. The heirloom would be returned to the family to which it belonged and so would its power, and the proof, lost for so long in the jungle would be revealed. The real heretics would be exposed to all, in the public forum known as the media circus. Perhaps there really is natural justice. He walked across the hardwood floor. His footsteps echoed like sharp spikes driven into the merciless souls of all those who died during the terrible nightmare of the Inquisition. Soon the biggest lie in history . . . the crucifixion and resurrection . . . would be exposed.

TWENTY

Renata spoke with a soft voice, an angel of death on a mission from God. She closed the laptop computer and disconnected the secure line. She was growing weary of the travel, and her missions were becoming more obscure. She threw herself onto the hotel bed, and switched on the miracle of CNN in time to hear a story about an archeologist and her team that were killed by guerrillas in Central America. She turned off the light, and drifted into another world of dreams.

Something haunted her; the hunter's breath on the back of her neck like a warm sea breeze, the click of claws on pavement. She watched the clouds drift over the ocean with the rhythmic droning of bees changing to faces; unhappy faces, shadows of souls snatched from life before their time. She felt the heat of the blast from the shotgun as it blew the back off her head into the clouds.

She awoke. It was time she got up. She had one more job before she completed her assignment. She couldn't shake the feeling that something was going to happen, something . . . strange was really happening.

Dr. Pieter Teunon closed the door without turning the lights on. It was a habit he acquired in medical school, a bad one as it turned out. He might have seen the face of a woman, and this would have surprised him. In his chauvinistic misogynist's mind to be killed by a woman would be the final insult. But he wouldn't know, except for that brief flash of light, and searing heat as it pierced his right temple that he had served the Order well, but in so doing had become expendable.

135

She carefully removed the silencer on the Beretta 9000s sub-compact 9 mm pistol, and placed it in Pieter's right hand. She walked over to his Macintosh computer and started it up by touching the return key. With her gloved hands she typed a cryptic suicide note. His homosexual secrets, and frequent outings to Club Gaeity hadn't gone unnoticed at Police headquarters. His suicide would be interpreted as the final desperate act of a despondent man tired of leading a double life. There would be talk in the morgue about how awful it was; what a waste of talent; if only he had said something; how terrible secrets were; how they could eat a man's heart and soul from within. To be gay these days, especially in the liberal city of A'Dam was accepted. Why would he feel he had to hide his orientation? No one would ever understand.

As Pieter's body lay on the pathologist's table—his table—and the morgue technician closed the door on this chapter, nobody knew how many people had suffered and died for the same secret over the past thousand years. It's a shame a secret can never be shared.

Greg never really liked Mexico. He stopped the rental jeep on the road and walked to the beach. La Joya de Mismaloya was a horseshoe shaped bay with a beautiful beach and mountains rising up on either side. The heat of the afternoon sun burned through his shoes as he walked along the sand, past the throngs of tourists and Mexicans selling everything from hammocks to cheap gaudy T-shirts.

He stopped at a little outdoor cabana on the beach, and ordered an ice-cold *cerveça*. It was the kind of place where the locals hung out, not the expensive tourist traps near the hotel on the cliff. It was too hot for anything except a cool *cerveça* and lime. He watched the tourists play in the warm pacific waters, and get sunburnt laying on the beach.

He scanned the ruins of the old abandoned movie set of *Night of the Iguana* on the hillside to left of the bay. He would continue his journey as soon as he regained his strength. The heat made it difficult to do anything except sit under the shelter of the cool palm leaves of the palapa.

He tried to recall that movie. He remembered Richard Burton say that he was going to commit suicide by taking "the long swim to China" from here. *Not a bad idea*, he thought. *If only life was that simple.* He remembered it was Ava Gardner who saved Richard Burton. And he thought about Christie and Kate. No one could save him. He was wild and free . . . and guilty. But he had his prize and he would profit.

"Mind if I join you?"

"Ah . . . no, not at all," not bothering to get up. The sweltering heat had a way of abolishing whatever remnants of social graces were left in him.

"Would you like a beer?" he waved for the waiter to bring two more. He wasn't sure of her age. She could be thirty-five or forty-five. It's hard with some woman, especially this one with the salt and pepper hair blowing around in the wind. She had a rugged sort of beauty about her.

"Staying at the hotel?" Greg pointed to the Hotel Joya de Mismaloya on the cliff to his right, built into the steep cliffs rising from the beach on the Pacific.

"Yeah," she squeezed the lime into a long neck *Tecate*. She wore a loose cotton beach robe over her bathing suit. She reminded him of Ava Gardner. Her silence made her all that much more attractive to Greg. He had to pinch himself. He'd had enough trouble with woman. It was his weakness; well, one of them. The other was money, of course, or the endless desire for it.

"You look as if you were waiting for someone," she took a sip from her beer, not looking at him.

He wasn't sure if it was a question, or an observation. He took his sunglasses off.

"I'm a medical archeologist."

"A movie archeologist?" She asked, drolly referring to what the locals called *El Set*. The broken down set was once the scene for the initial passions of Burton and Gardner.

"In a way," he gave a crooked smile. His tan and those dark eyes and hair made him look a little bit Latin. "What's your name?" He finally asked.

"Catherine." She removed her sunglasses. The silence chilled the air for a moment as their eyes met for the first time.

"Greg," he extended his hand. "From the States?""

"Yeah. You?" she asked taking his hand, smiling. She could tell a lot from a person's handshake, the firmness, the character, the heat, and the sincerity.

"No, Canada, originally that is, until I moved here."

"It must be cold in Canada now," she wiped the sweat from her forehead.

"Canada's a big country you know. It depends on where you are this time of year." In fact it was getting very cold in most of Canada in November. Some places have snow that will last until the spring, meaning April; while other places like Vancouver Island put up with the rainy season that comes with the more temperate weather of the Pacific Northwest, a mere five hour flight from Mismaloya Bay.

"Look, I have to meet someone at the old movie set. Would you like to walk over with me?"

"Will I be safe with you?" she asked peering over her sunglasses.

"Sure, come on," he stood up in the heat of the Mexican mid-afternoon sun.

"I think I'm gonna melt."

"It gets hotter in the summer,"

They walked along the beach and dipped their feet into the refreshing blue waters along the way.

A young boy ran up to them with a large iguana, and offered to let them take his picture—in exchange for money, of course.

Catherine laughed. "It's an omen."

"Sure, afternoon of the iguana," Greg laughed, giving the kid a few pesos from his pocket. There was something peculiar about this woman; the way she carried herself, her self-confidence. He couldn't put his finger on it.

TWENTY-ONE

The walk became increasingly more difficult as they made their way along the rugged coast away from the beach to the abandoned movie set. Not since Christie's disappearance had he experienced such a sense of total freedom. There was something about Catherine; her smile, her laugh, her carefree ways that seemed to put him at ease. It was a feeling he longed for, but had forgotten about. Since Christie's second disappearance and the messy skull business, the psychotherapy and everything, so much had changed. He walked relaxed and calmly along the edge of the cliff overlooking Mismaloya Bay with this stranger. He'd forgotten just how misguided some feelings can be.

Renata walked behind him, watching, studying his every move. He was just an animal, a target. Pulling the trigger would be the easy part.

They walked up the path along where Richard Burton ran to jump into Mismaloya bay for his long swim. At the ruins of the set, they sat on the old red brick steps to catch their breath.

Greg was particularly giddy after their exhilarating climb to the ruins. The afternoon sun was beginning its descent to its Pacific resting place when he had the sudden urge to tell Catherine everything. It was like a torrent of emotion; like a hurricane or an earthquake; he wanted to tell her everything: Christie, the Maya, the Templars, everything. And he did.

"Something about this place provokes the truth." In this magical place, she was tired of the deception and dishonesty.

"My name isn't Catherine." She heard her own voice say the words, but she couldn't really understanding why she saying them.

"My real name is Renata Benoit. I worked for Mossad, Israeli intelligence, until I was transferred to the UN Information Department in Paris. My mission was to retrieve your relic or whatever it is.

"But there was something strange about the way I was activated this time, something that up until now I couldn't quite figure out; that is, until something you said just now."

"What do you mean?" Stunned by her blunt revelation, he leaned back and turned to face her.

"I'm a translator, but in the past, I've been employed to . . . clear up problems." The matter of fact way she spoke made it seem so straightforward, like saying she was a teacher because she liked kids.

"You're a professional killer because you're good at it. Is that what your saying?"

"Greg, I don't know how to say this, but for a long time now I sensed I was being used by someone or something because I was a woman; because men find it difficult to kill women, even trained male assassins hesitate before killing a woman; its instinctive; but that one second is enough time for a trained woman to kill a man."

"You make it sound so clinical, like pest control." He thought about what he had done at the dig. *Maybe they had a lot in common after all.*

"Look!" She took both of his hands into hers, and looked him straight in the eyes. "I was sent here to kill you."

"I gathered that much."

But how could he be so stupid, again? When it came to women, Greg was a complete and utter idiot. He consoled himself with the rationalization that women weren't supposed to be professional killers anyway. Self-pity swept over him.

"Don't you see my point? There's something bizarre going on at the UN."

"The US government is planning to take control?" he asked hungry for information.

"No, governments don't get this sophisticated."

"I don't understand," Greg stood up, continuing to face her.

"Where's the skull?"

"Why? Do you think I'm *that* stupid. Give the skull to a hired killer!"

"Greg, I said, I *was* an assassin. Don't you see? Somebody or something is using me too. I knew it from the moment I picked up my contact from the *International Herald-Tribune*. I mean, it's just not SOP."

"Wait a minute. You say you picked up your contact in the paper?"

"Yes, that's right."

"That's strange. That's how I was told how to meet with Kate."

"Who?"

"It's not important now. But don't you think it's odd to make important arrangements by placing ads in the personal section of an international paper?"

"That's my point."

"Somehow I get the feeling this thing comes together with you and I."

The sun slowly slipped over the edge of the Pacific. In a few minutes it would be dark.

"Tell me what you know about the skull," she rose beside him. Her salt and pepper hair blew around her head in the wind.

"Wait, I heard something over there," Renata tilted her head toward a patch of trees.

"What could it be? An iguana?" Greg asked quietly. "You're the expert."

"Yes, and they never send just one," In a lowered voice coldly scanning the darkening ruins of the old movie set, she announced "there's always a back up; a watcher."

"Shit! It's probably the guy I made the deal with . . . to sell the skull. You know, my payback for all the shit I've put up with. It was my retirement plan."

"Well, that wasn't very bright! I suppose he approached you?"

141

"No, not exactly. Through a friend, in Toronto, on faculty with me."

"But the buyer contacted you, right? Right? Greg!" She suddenly raised her voice.

Greg was perfectly visible between the cross hairs of the watcher's high power night scope.

She shoved him down with a swift single motion "Get down," Renata yelled as a shot rang out over the tiny peninsula.

"The skull is hidden in a cave, just beyond that ridge over there," he pointed to a summit about three hundred yards from their position.

"Stay here, I'll take care of the watcher," and she disappeared into the orange glow of twilight.

"Wait . . ." But it was too late. She was gone into the emerging darkness after her prey.

Moments later he heard two metallic cracks, not like rifle shots, more like snaps, the crackle of metal against metal, and then a hard thud.

Renata appeared again minutes later. "Now take me to the skull."

"This way," Greg knew that sound had to have been a 9 mm pistol with a silencer. He led her to the entrance of a cave.

"I don't suppose you have a flashlight in that bag?"

She pulled out a small Halogen penlight.

"They teach you that in spy school?"

"No, Girl Guides actually."

The cave itself was a very inhospitable place. It was dark and damp, and smelled of human excrement. It was a place where animals, and probably people, came to die.

Inside a small black medical bag wrapped in a soft chamois Greg carefully revealed the brilliant crystal skull. Could this be the Holy Grail of Templar mythology? Even in the extreme darkness of the cave, this extraordinary masterpiece had an eerie phosphorescent, almost alarming, radioactive glow.

"If you look hard enough—according to legend—you can see the face of Christ in it," Greg proudly displayed his booty.

"Where did you get this?" She was dumbfounded.

"I robbed an ancient Maya tomb," his voice bold with the pride of his accomplishment. "And killed three people. Four people in total, but one was in retribution."

"I see now why you're such a formidable problem."

"It proves beyond a shadow of a doubt that there was pre-Columbian contact in the New World. But more important, it also draws attention to the biggest cover-up in the history of mankind; one that is sure to shake-up our entire understanding of Christianity . . . and Western history too."

He looked at Renata mesmerized by the skull.

"Jesus the Nazarene did not in fact die on the cross. Rather he was taken down off the cross before he died in order to fulfill the Gospels. He initiated a revolution that never came; at least not the political one that was envisaged. Imagine, a sort of 33 A.D. staged media bite. In fact, according to legend I mean, Christ fled to the Languedoc region of France with Lazarus, and some others, where he raised a family and spawned a dynasty. When he died at age sixty-nine craftsmen preserved his skull according to the Gnostic traditions; but time, nature and a force as yet unknown, has crystallized the thing and given it the iridescent glow it has now."

"I initially I didn't understand what the implications were. I focused on the Codex. For me, in the beginning, I thought it established my theory of pre-Columbian communication with the Europeans, but I quickly found myself in the company of people who were interested in my discovery for other, shall we say, less academic reasons. They took my translation of the Codex literally. Suddenly my life changed. I had no choice but to negotiate with these people; these so-called 'Heirs of Christ' as they refer to themselves. I now fear the skull is not something wonderful and good, but an internecine tool of the competing forces of nature: good and evil, or what the ancient Maya called the enigma of the Jaguar's heart.

"I found my initial proof of this buried in the archives at the Allard Pierson Museum in Amsterdam. I found a letter written by Jacques De Molnay, the last Grand Master of the Knights Templar just before he died. It had been smuggled to a Templar refuge in Amsterdam toward the end of the Hapsburg Empire.

"I have to get back to Amsterdam."

TWENTY-TWO

After the past few days, Greg found himself walking and thinking a great deal. He had much to think about, especially how he was going to sell this skull thing without getting killed. At Rembrantplein, the sky was a brilliant pastel blue. Coming into the square he stopped at the Schiller Café for a quick beer. He'd already had too much coffee, and after the hours of aimless wandering he needed to clear his brain. He knew he was in an untenable position. But he hated indecision. In the past whenever he came upon difficulties, he took the path of least resistance; but things had changed. He had proven to himself that he could be decisive. He really needed an ally; someone he could trust. But who would do?

Dr. Strumpf arrived at precisely 8:15 A.M. *These people are a precise lot*, Greg thought as he watched Strumpf get out of his black series 7 BMW. Greg wondered whether it was Kevlar reinforced. A bulletproof car like that at least it could withstand standard NATO 7.62 mm or 9 mm rounds. Greg also new it probably couldn't withstand anything more potent. He'd learned quite a bit over the past year. *So much for a sentimental education*, he reflected.

Strumpf sat down and ordered a coffee. Greg ordered another. The sun was very bright as they watched the Saturday morning traffic begin to build along Rokin. This was Greg's second visit to Amsterdam in a year. He knew that sooner or later the authorities were going to overtake him. He had to work quickly before Interpol appeared. He planned to get to Belize as soon as possible where there were no extradition treaties with the US or Canada.

Strumpf's baldhead glistened in the morning light of the outdoor café. He had a very direct manner. He came to the point straight away.

"How much do you want for it?" he asked point blank as soon as the waiter was out of hearing range.

"That depends on what it's worth to you." Strumpf seemed insulted by Greg's response.

"I should tell you, the Order met last night. Certain, how shall I phrase it for you Americans, contingencies have been arranged," he stopped and took a sip of coffee. He looked at Greg with his weasel-like electric blue eyes and sharp anteater nose.

"We know you have it," he continued. "There is no place you can escape. The police are looking for you. You have lost everything: your career, your wife, everything. You want to be careful. You are playing with powerful people, and forces. Bad things can happen, if . . ."

"If I don't hand over what you want?" A rage grew inside Greg that terrified him. *What's happening to me?* "Well, I don't see things that way. To me, it's my life insurance policy. If I simply hand it over—assuming I have it—you will have me killed, like everybody else who's gotten in the way over the past 900 years. No, to me, the best insurance is to keep what I have. As long as I have it, I'll remain alive."

"Don't be so sure. We only want what's ours. You've become a bothersome little fly that has to be crushed. We will get our property, you can take that to the bank." He got up. He didn't bother to offer his hand. He turned his large back in Greg's direction and climbed into the BMW. Before he stepped into the car, he looked back. "Think about it Dr. Greg Fallows. You are playing with powerful forces beyond your control. Natural forces of . . . cosmic proportions." He stepped into the car and sped along Rokin to Muntplein before the car quickly disappeared behind a tram.

TWENTY-THREE

The hearings began at 9 A.M. sharp. Room 419 of the Dirksen Senate Office Building was familiar enough to anyone who watched Col. Oliver North testify before the Iran-Contra inquiry, or the Watergate inquiry, or the Judge Thomas nomination hearings, or maybe you'll remember the room as the backdrop for the Clinton pardon affair. Today, however, the doors were closed to the public. The Subcommittee on Terrorism, Narcotics and International Operations of the Senate Foreign Relations Committee met to discuss the relationship of the Central Intelligence Agency to a little known secret society called G2, a section of the United Nations Department of Information.

The room was a bustle as members slowly arrived. There was a cacophony of shuffling papers, moving chairs, amid the gossip of Washington insiders. The Sub-committee, comprised of men only, something nobody noticed except the recording secretary Ms. Elloise Harper, a young African American woman from South Carolina.

At the head table sat Senators Robert Henry (D., MA), Michael Mahoney (R., N.M.), James McCloskey (D., CA), Matt Coyle (R., WA), Paul Wilson (D., CO), and Sub-committee chair, Senator John Clattmore (R., N.D.). Clattmore was a ruddy-faced western Senator with a reputation for cutting through red tape. He took his place in front of the microphone at the center of the long oak table.

"Good morning everyone," he bellowed as the echo accompanied by piercing feedback reverberated around the empty room.

The only two witnesses called were Nathan Hastings, the unctuous former investigator for the Sub-committee; and Malcolm Featherstone, a mid-level career bureaucrat with the CIA.

Hastings had an oily, suave personality. His hair was greasy and slicked straight back over his head. He was usually warm and easy going. But at times he could be moralistic and self-righteous on the subject of religion.

Featherstone was an analyst of some repute during the cold war years. By comparison he was cold and aloof. He was credited with blowing the whistle on the Agency and its connection to the Bank of Credit and Commerce money-laundering scam back in the 1980's. Unlike many of the more highly placed spooks within the CIA, the sub-committee believed Featherstone retained a modicum of integrity. Things really got hot for him after he blew the whistle on the Agency's covert accounts used to fund black operations in several foreign countries—including a number of so-called friendly democracies. However, he became the media's darling for a couple of years.

The committee requested his return. Senator Clattmore wanted details regarding G2 and whose interests it served.

The rumor inside the Beltway was that several of the world's intelligence agencies, including those formerly thought of as enemies during the Cold War were taking directions, and initiating covert operations on their own; independent of their own governments' knowledge or sanction . . . through a little known section within the United Nations. Notwithstanding public explanations about how the US government was concerned about administration efficiencies; this was the reason the US was withholding funds to the UN.

G2's purpose according to reliable sources was to foster the development of a New World Order. And in some ways it fit with Administration aims. On the other hand, some sources, often journalists who are less reliable—possibly contaminated for other reasons—held that a New World government would be supported, in fact, run by a cartel of private international banks and multi-national corporations who proposed a single world currency—But which one? The President was interested, very interested.

These allegations, if made public, would further erode the public's mounting mistrust of the US government's ability to keep the wolves of corporate self-interest at bay. The media was just starting to notice the issue. Allegations had already surfaced when several unsolved murders in Europe had been linked to a Canadian terrorist by the name of Dr. Greg Fallows. A Central Park murder had led Nathan Hastings to Amsterdam and the office of Inspector Kroode. An article published in *The Cherwell Review* exposed the story for the first time. The Sub-committee had hastily been called to investigate the credibility of the allegations; something political pundits in the backrooms were saying was too little, to late.

During his investigation of the BCCI affair, Hastings heard mention of a top secret committee run out of the National Security Agency, known as "The Blue Team." This top-secret group, according to information obtained by Nathan Hastings, and communicated to Senator Clattmore, in Hastings words, was "riding bareback." That is, without Executive branch approval; and therefore out of control, or as the crusty, pragmatic Hastings put it, "the Old Boys were wilding again."

"Gentlemen, I'd like to dispense with the usual formalities here today," Senator Clattmore scratched his silver haired head. "I've talked to each of you committee members in private, and you know why we're here. We are the heart, the soul, and the conscience of America. We bear a burden of oversight. The Senate of the United States has asked us to find out the truth."

There was little doubt that the good Senator from Fargo would be seeking his party's nomination for the Presidency in the next election four years from now. The way he bellowed, his jowls flapped as his fingers shot imaginary arrows at his political foes. Friend and adversary alike respected his mastery of rhetoric, his sharp, cunning wit. The Washington Post has called him "America's Churchill." He liked that.

In his tan suit and red tie, he burst out of his clothes. A robust man of at least two hundred and fifty pounds, "Clay" as his friends back home called him, liked his Canadian whiskey. But when it came to politics he was as sober as a Baptist preacher on Sunday morning. And he had a keen nose for scandal. This early autumn morning in Washington DC, Clay smelled a rascal of a scandal in this "Blue Team" story. It could be bigger than Watergate, and Iran-Contra rolled into one, and could be the catalyst that could land him in the Oval office in four short years.

Nathan Hastings was the first to testify before the sub-committee. He was experienced in testimony of this sort. It was his life. He started out in the Justice Department as a junior lawyer during the late Sixties after graduating from law school at the University of Chicago. For a while he worked with the Federal Bureau of Investigation, were he developed the unhealthy skepticism, and sixth sense that gave him the reputation as the one you wanted on your side in this town. After a fifteen-year stint at Justice, he abruptly left. He had just begun to build a name for himself as a freelance journalist when he came across the story of Steven Knight's death in *The Times*. He'd known Steven. And when his name showed up in the "Blue Team" file, Nathan found a whole lot on Canadian Greg Fallows.

And like Greg he had a weakness for women. He'd been married three times, each one ended in divorce. He always blamed it on his work, his lifestyle, and the usual male cop-out. How he laughed at that line. But the wives believed it was his inability to develop close relationships that had finally gotten to each of them. They sometimes got together, a sort of Post-Hastings support group, to talk about it. Once they tried to confront him about his problems. He would reply: "What do you expect me to be like in this dirty world?"

Now in his mid-fifties, Hastings spent his spare time writing, drinking, and traveling. It was no surprise that he and Senator Clattmore got along so well. Alcohol helped kill the pain temporarily, but only until the next morning when it amplified his misery.

This morning was one of those mornings for Nathan. He had stayed out too late the night before, even though it was a Sunday. He cleared his voice, which was normally husky. This morning it was gravel on glass. Taking the stand, he adjusted his tie and tried to focus his eyes.

"First off," Senator Clattmore asked, "Mr. Hastings, we are all familiar with your past achievements. As far as this Sub-committee is concerned, if you don't mind, we'll skip the usual protocol of reading your litany of credentials, in favor of a direct and full account of the events as you know them."

"Yes, sir, that's fine with me."

The Chairman turned to Senator Michael Mahoney, to begin the questioning.

"Thank you Mr. Chairman, in the brief you prepared for the Sub-committee you referred to 'diversionary tactics' on the part of this so-called 'Blue Team.' Can you elaborate on what you mean?" the handsome Senator from Santa Fe requested. Around the Hill he was known to be overly ambitious, mainly because he lacked both the intellect and the connections to advance any further up the Washington ladder. Nonetheless, in the past year he had proved himself nobody's fool, and had developed a growing reputation for 'removing the form from the argument and revealing its substance,' as he too often liked to quote himself at cocktail parties. His weakness (or perhaps his strength) was that he was a homosexual, and around the Capital in those days it opened a lot of doors for the handsome young politician from the arid plain.

"Senator, I think of it as the doctrine of plausible deniability in action."

"Are you saying covert actions have been sanctioned in the name of the President, but in fact these operations had nothing whatsoever to do with government policy?"

"Yes sir. Officials within the bureaucracy, primarily within the intelligence communities, but not limited to them, acted alone—are acting—in an organized way. I can't answer your question about the President knowing because I have no evidence either way. There usually isn't. Paper trail, you know."

"Do I understand you correctly, this unit is acting outside the law? Like a government Mafia?" Senator McCloskey asked.

James McCloskey (D., CA) was the intellectual on the committee, a Masters in political science from Harvard and a DPhil in jurisprudence from Oxford, he railed against lawlessness. He made his political reputation crusading against runaway big government. He was a liberal in the classical sense. And he was quick to see the implications, and the danger for the committee members if the allegations proved true.

"It sort of depends on what you mean by the Mafia? If you associate the Mafia with a cultural mob; the answer is clearly no; but if you mean a well organized group, crossing religious, political and cultural backgrounds penetrating every aspect of high office; I should say the highest offices, then yes, I would agree."

"Mr. Chairman, I believe we should not proceed any further without inviting the public to attend these hearings," the Democratic Senator from California sat back in his chair, very satisfied with himself.

"The Chair rules against that suggestion of Senator McCloskey, but reserves the right to do so, if further evidence supports such a move. Senator Wilson do you have any questions for Mr. Hastings?"

"Thank you Mr. Chairman, I would like to know how Mr. Hastings obtained the information presented to us, and is he able to back up his allegations?"

"Senator, the information presented to you in your package was based on information supplied to the Justice Department from several usually reliable sources."

The committee members looked around at each other; the mounting paranoia was palpable.

"Are there any further questions for Mr. Hastings?" Senator Clattmore looked at his watch. "If not we'll ask Mr. Hastings to step down for now, and standby. Thank you Mr. Hastings.

"Mr. Featherstone would you be so kind as to take the witness stand." Malcolm Featherstone was a mid-level career CIA analyst, of the so-called new school. He was too young to remember the glory days of the OSS or the Cold War. A new breed CIA man, Malcolm was a scientist. He grouped facts and looked for statistical trends downloaded from satellite and other electronic sources. He was deeply suspicious of unreliable human sources like Hastings.

Featherstone's background was electrical engineering, and he came to the Agency by way of the Massachusetts Institute of Technology. He was thirty-eight years old, but looked much younger. His clean-shaven face radiated innocence; his thin lips and brown lazy eyes betrayed a sense of wonder. His short closely cropped hair resembled the brush cuts fashionable in the Fifties. And he dressed impeccably in tailored suits that both flattered and conveyed authority. He exuded the air of a rising star. He had already proven his reliability. He was independent and owed no one.

Taking his seat in front of the microphone he shuffled his papers as the Sub-committee members sized him up. Clay placed his reading glasses on his nose and began. "Senator Coyle, I believe you wished to ask a question of Mr. Featherstone,"

"Thank you Mr. Chairman. Mr. Featherstone, I hope you will not be offended by my question, but I think it cuts to the heart of the matter, and I am not one who is known for beating around the bush when issues so great as this are before us. My question to you, Mr. Featherstone is this: what does the Agency know of this 'Blue Team' and what is it going to do about it?"

"Mr. Chairman, the Sub-committee asked me to explore this issue for it, and I have done just that. As you know the intelligence community is engaged in monitoring the telecommunications of all kinds from various countries. Over the past several months a great deal of activity has been noted arising from the European sector. That's my area of expertise."

"Can you be more specific in what you mean by activity?"

The CIA man hesitated, choosing his words carefully. Even if he wasn't in the covert operations end of things it was evident that the spy craft was in his bones. Featherstone searched through some papers like an accountant looking for the bottom line. Finally, he looked up.

"Activity means telecommunications traffic. Specifically, our NSA wizards noted that intelligence community frequencies . . . including our own, and some from the White House; others from Mossad, British MI6, and other western European intelligence agencies have seen an unusual convergence on Amsterdam."

"Do you have any idea where in Amsterdam?" Senator McCloskey asked.

"Yes, sir. A Masonic temple on Vondelstraat."

"The Masons?" The Senator from Colorado, Paul Wilson laughed out loud in disbelief.

"Not your average Masons," Featherstone retorted, not pleased with the Senator ridiculing his comment. "There is a powerful and influential secret society within the Masons who trace their lineage back to the Knights Templar of the Crusades. They use several names including connections with a little known section of the UN Information Department called G2. Sometimes they refer to themselves as 'the second pentagram.' In fact, the notion of a 'Blue Team' may in fact be a mistranslation of deux or second team. We frequently see the symbol of a circle within a circle in their communications. It appears that for security reasons nobody knows whom the others are outside their own circle. This core, or cadre, has allowed them to keep their secret society together, and secret, over many years. It's classic terrorist modus operandi.

"We do know that a certain Canadian medical doctor with an interest in archeology allegedly found something the Order claims is theirs. According to sources it holds the key to some secret held for posterity; something that if revealed would destroy our understanding of Western history, deeply threatening the very fabric of society. The intercepted satellite traffic clearly says, Dr. Greg Fallows, the Canadian physician archeologist, is compared to the Antichrist, or he could just be crazy."

"The Antichrist? Surely we don't take these conspiracy theories seriously?" Senator Wilson asked looking at Clay for direction. Clay shrugged and said nothing, however, he seemed troubled by the direction the hearings were taking. If what Hastings and Featherstone believed was even remotely true, all of their lives could be in danger. And it meant the White House, or someone in the White House could be involved; someone close to the President. The President? No, it wasn't possible. But he also knew Washington thrived on paranoia and rumor. In politics perception is reality.

"Everything you've told us is incredible. But why now, and why should we take it seriously?"

"I don't know that sir. It remains a secret; only that archeologist fellow . . . Greg Fallows knows, and of course, G2. At any rate, the only hope we have of penetrating them is through their target, Fallows. You could ask him yourselves, sir. I mean, if he were subpoenaed to appear before this Sub-committee."

"What do we know about him?" asked Senator Coyle.

"Only that he's an ex-patriot Canadian. He's on the run. His wife is missing after she apparently tried to convince him to hand over the secret. He may in fact have killed her. What we do know is that something or someone has changed him from the mild insecure doctor to a man wanted for the death of at least four people including a former NSA operative. He is engaged in a most deadly game of hunting and baiting the wolves. He's a bit of a wild card right now; unstable I think is the clinical term. We know he conveniently spent some time in a rural psych hospital after his wife disappeared."

"Where is this Greg Fallows fellow now?" Clay pursed his lips the way he always did when he was nervous.

"Hastings could probably tell you, but I believe Greg Fallows is in Mexico. We traced him there. The satellite digital real-time video can reach to almost any place on the planet. However, this is one of the areas we can't get a good view because of the coastal mountains and the sun's reflection from the ocean.

"We do know that a specific UN G2 communications channel is being used to direct their 'assets' to an area south of the Mexican resort of Puerto Vallarta. We believe they will attempt to limit any collateral damage by taking 'extreme measures' in the wilds of Mexico."

"We have do get to him before someone else does," urged Senator Wilson.

"What can we do?" Senator Coyle asked alarmed.

"Call him in sir, before he blathers everything on CNN," Featherstone stated coolly.

"Do you really think he would do something like that?" Clay asked.

"Sir, this man is desperate. He doesn't know whom to trust. He could be emotionally unstable. He's a wild card. He could do anything. He's just plain unpredictable."

"Mr. Chairman, this committee has to do something," Wilson pleaded with Clay Clattmore.

"Must I remind you, this Sub-committee has no authority to take such action. We would be as lawless as those we are hearing about." Clay wondered what the White House would think about a proposal to bring a wanted terrorist like Fallows in to testify before a Sub-committee hearing.

"Yet, if we raise an alarm, this secret society will know we are investigating the matter . . ."

"And we may be targets of reprisal too," Senator McCloskey looked around the room.

"Yes. But we can't give in to terrorism, no matter what, or who they are," said Senator Robert Henry adding the Administration party line.

"Then we have no choice but to act according to the rule of law." Senator Michael Mahoney ceased wagging his index finger at the chairman.

"We must find this Fallows, and then you will have your public hearings Senator," Clay Clattmore announced in a loud decisive voice.

Conspiracies have a funny way of ruining your day. But, if Clattmore wanted to be President, here was his chance to grab the dragon by the tail and give it a shake.

Hastings was quickly summoned from the outer chamber where he had been slumbering on the wooden bench. His head still throbbed, the regretful guilt of excess alcohol, as Senator Clattmore quietly outlined his assignment.

Hastings had to remind himself to stay away from tequila. He wasn't listening to what the fat Senator was saying. Clay, who was not normally given to emotion, put his hand on Nathan's shoulder.

"Be careful, you've got some powerful and influential people tracking this guy, and you're on your own, solo, got it. Just bring him back, and for God's sake stay sober boy."

TWENTY-FOUR

Renata knew the most likely time for an all out assault on their position was just before dawn. She prepared her 9 mm standard NATO issue pistol by threading a silencer over the end. Greg was asleep beside her on the cold ground. She focused the sights on his right parietal bone where she pictured the middle meningeal artery as she was trained in 'Country One' as the G2 code-named Israel.

Greg opened his eyes to see her sitting with the pistol resting on her knee, aimed right at his head. For a moment he thought his bizarre life would end on that rocky promontory overlooking the Pacific Ocean. The moment seemed an eternity as the gentle waves crashed on the shore below. And with the smell of heliconia in the morning air, it made him completely relaxed and unafraid of dying. He was a bit surprised by his reaction. Fear could rake his bones, and make him tremble like a pitiful child; but it did not. For the first time since the nightmare began he felt an inner peace. He wondered if Christie experienced anything like it when she died.

Renata drew back her weapon and smiled. The sun was rising over the thick jungle. The birds were making an awful racket for some reason.

"Quick, Greg, the cave!"

The sound of a helicopter was heard from across the bay, above the green jungle foliage. It zoomed over the Hotel La Joya de Mismaloya heading straight for them and the abandoned movie set. With one eye peering out from the darkness of the cave, Renata could see the black Jet Ranger landing on the flat surface of the former floor where Richard Burton and Ava Gardner kissed. Greg stood behind her and gently touched her shoulder. Like a movie, she saw the helicopter landing in slow motion. A squad of four men, wearing black from head to toe, prepared to jump from the helicopter, its rotor blades whirling madly, ready for takeoff.

She watched them, weighing the situation carefully. Then she turned to see Greg seated beyond the light in the darkness of the cave. He had unwrapped the skull, and was sitting cross-legged on the floor of the cave with the skull on his lap. The crystal skull cast an eerie green phosphorescent glow in the cave. Greg seemed to glow as well, his eyes two crimson reflections of the skull. In her eyes he seemed to gather supernatural energy from it. The ground rippled under her feet.

"An earthquake!" she cried, turning just in time to see the helicopter and its cargo tumble into the waters of Mismaloya Bay. The wayward rotor blades on the helicopter's final descent into the bay decapitated the ejected men.

"Did you see that?" She turned to look at the Greg-Buddha on the floor of the cave. "Jesus Christ!" She shouted.

"Yes, it is the skull! There is a power, an energy or something it taps in to."

"No wonder their willing to kill for it."

"Wars have been started—and millions have died—for it. What is this? Miracle or curse; the start of a new age of knowledge, or the release of a supremely evil force of nature?"

"Come on Greg, we've got to get out of here." She threw the skull back into the bag, grabbed a dazed Greg by the arm and dragged him out of the cave into the light of day.

The Chief of Staff put the phone back on its cradle. He was tired of the bad press, and the jibes that go with the role of number two. In his heart he longed to be number one. Sitting back in his leather chair, he believed success was near. It wafted over him like the fine bouquet of the Willamette Valley Pinot Noir in his glass.

Samuel Charles Paterson was a failed car salesmen from Boise Idaho who found refuge in arms of the legal trade and the mid-western politics of rage. He discovered at an early age the importance of connections to get things done, and more important getting ahead in the world, which to S.C.P meant plenty of money. He was good at the backroom business. The backstabbing came easily to him. He enjoyed the cigars and brandy; the fine wine; the dinners; the ingratiating people; the business class travel everywhere; the blatant superficial and hypocritical relationships. All these things he loved. But he lacked the personal charisma to be number one; which made him try that much harder. This time, what the press thought wouldn't matter, a higher court would decide.

In many ways Paterson was (perhaps he still is) an American hero. He was the mid-western boy who made good. He was the underdog—America loves an underdog. He'd milked that all the way through his legal career, but it was losing its shine. He was already fifty-eight, overweight, and bored. His short, curly black and gray hair sat above small armadillo-like eyes that swam in a hypertensive sea of red.

He took three blood pressure pills a day, and had a strong family history of sudden death. He drank too much single-malt whiskey, any whiskey in a pinch. He saw his internist at Bethesda Naval Hospital every month for a check-up. He adhered religiously to a low cholesterol diet, none of which seemed to make any difference to his overall health. He had nothing to lose; he couldn't wait forever to be number one; it was now or never. In many ways his weaknesses were also his strengths. He was above suspicion.

The society known to him as the Order recruited him some years ago when he was a junior Congressman back in Boise. He'd joined the Lodge because it seemed the right career move at the time. Many of the community's best and brightest belonged to 'the Church' as they called it. The more he learned about 'the Church,' the more he became impressed with the number of extremely successful people who were members. Famous men like George Washington, and Benjamin Franklin, and Leonardo DaVinci and Victor Hugo in Europe to name only a few. While these great men were known for a number of significant contributions to society and science, few knew of their connection with the secret order dating back to the white robed knights of the blazing red cross.

He was among those descendants of the warrior knights of the Temple of Solomon who to this day served in every corner of the globe, in every government and every industry. Up to now their purpose has been covert. But with the discovery of the skull, their mission to form a corporate world government was in full swing. And Samuel Charles was the man who wanted to be King. Featherstone's NSA contact phoned him at home in Virginia. She apologized for phoning so early but it was urgent. She had to meet him right away at the Smithsonian Institute. His NSA contact was a demure twenty-nine year-old by the name of Celeste Swan, a rather unfortunate name. The kind of thing parents in the Sixties did to their kids. She had walnut brown hair that she kept tied in a short ponytail at the back. Her dark, tanned skin, and hazel eyes revealed a soul desperate to please. Her small, thin red lips and long nose gave her a quietly desperate look. In her dark green overcoat and black dress, she looked as if she should be going to a funeral instead of standing outside the museum on that frosty morning.

"Thanks for coming so quickly," she reached for his arm as he walked up to her on the sidewalk.

"Thanks for calling," he joked. She looked away to avoid his eyes.

"What is it?" He sensed her uneasiness.

"Why don't we just walk a bit?" She hugged his arm tightly. They headed toward the Concourse, the Vietnam memorial, and the Lincoln Memorial at the far end of the park. The morning traffic was filtering in from the relatively safe suburbs.

"Look, you can pull out of this at any time, okay?"

"I know the rules," she smiled, an obvious lie meant to ease his conscience. "I intercepted more traffic last night . . ."

"And?"

"It came from here . . . Washington this time."

"From within the Agency?"

"No," glancing over toward the White House as they walked along the park in the crisp fresh air.

"Potus?" he asked bluntly.

"No, no," she looked up at him with those lonely eyes. "The COS."

"What was the traffic?"

"Amsterdam intercept via STARSAT 5 downlink."

"Are you sure about this?"

She looked over at the majestic Lincoln memorial.

"Absolutely."

"The content?"

"Bizarre stuff . . . a kind of poetry I think."

"The Chief of Staff is sending poetry to Amsterdam on a secure modem satellite line? Do you have a copy of the transmission?"

"That's what I wanted to see you about. I know I'm breaking all the rules by giving you this. I think it's in the national interest; but I don't know anymore. It could mean my job you know."

"I understand," he took her by the arm again. "If the COS is involved in something then he's no different than anyone else."

"Look at this." She pulled a neatly folded white piece of paper from her purse and handed it over to the former CIA analyst.

"Read this."

Whatever is that Knight's worry
Let the sound of Holy words soothe his brow
And let us go down to the shallow grave
As if by some great power or gust of wind;
For there are times now, much like those gone before
When women wore battle-dress and carried the Rosy-Cross
Not for our leaders they went into battle,
Yet proud of us who call them again out of darkness
But because of that Rose upon the cross
She forbade the telling of the vers
We can still see the old Temple from Malta and Madrid
Remember visions of Osiris wrapped in devil's cloth;
And cats in the Temple of Solomon
Remember who it was who told you this
As the puppet was kicking the Knights around

Let me go down, go down
They cried as they wen
Down to their deaths at the Fiery stake
On Friday 13 October, thirteen hundred and seven
And again when Jacques DeMolna
Was burned at the stake in the year thirteen fourteen
While fellow knights were driven fro
Merovingian shore
The last Great ships took our crystal shrin
Safely to foreign shore
Across that sea of peerless Chaos
So begins the time of our brethren from the Graal
Where the sacred shrine of Tummez still stand
Passed from one knight to the other unspoiled.
While the virgin and Madonna were safe at home
While we, the Son's of all that is,
Await the blooming of the rose
As he burned at the stake DeMolnay cried
'we keep the secret of Jesus protected
So hear this Priory Knights
When a Templar meets another knight
He will know her by his kiss
To each the other's ass affixed
As a sign of mortal servitud
Stamped upon each soul,
A true medallion of Merlin's gif
Like the real . . . Mason's kiss.

"Then there's a hand written note: Let the power reveal itself to you and you will understand the skillful art of the mason's of the Temple of Sion."

"I don't understand."

"I do," as he folded the paper into his inside breast coat pocket. "Thanks for everything. Now just go back to your life, and forget all this, okay?"

"I don't know if I can."

"But you'll try, right?"

"Right," she smiled from behind sad eyes.

Malcolm Featherstone made sure Celeste was safe in her car before he phoned Senator Clattmore from his encrypted cell phone.

"Senator Clattmore."

"Clay here."

"Sir, it's Malcolm Featherstone. I need to speak with you . . . *soon.*"

"How's lunch? Say 12:15, the Capital Club?"

"Better not. How about I meet you at the Lincoln memorial, and we can walk?"

"Fine. See you there,"

The rest of the morning Featherstone spent going over his files labeled LEGACY. All the signals intelligence (SIGINT) compiled from the STARSAT links and the human intelligence (HUMINT) gathered by Hastings and presented at the closed hearings of the Sub-committee was pieced together. He now had clear evidence linking the Chief of Staff to co-conspirators in Amsterdam who in turn were connected with power people around the world planning a quiet revolution at the UN. Everything pointed to the Grand Lodge in Amsterdam as the main hub of activity.

TWENTY-FIVE

By the time Hastings got off the plane and rented a car two hours had passed. To the car rental attendant, the word *manana* not only meant tomorrow, but also implied you had to *wait* until tomorrow to get anything done today. He was tired after his flight from Washington. The noisy crowds of holidaying yahoos in business class kept him awake the entire flight.

He drove from the airport along the highway into Puerto Vallarta, taking the bypass around the city center for as long as he could. He took a sharp turn toward the ocean and he headed down a narrow brick street filled with pigs roaming freely in the middle of the road. He wasted no time when he reached the coastal highway heading south; he hugged the shoreline rising above the Pacific the whole way. He passed the Sea Hunt restaurant on his left, perched precariously on the edge of the cliff on the way out of town. He remembered the last time he ate there he had gotten terribly ill on the oyster's. The sky was clear, and the air was beginning to smell clean and fresh again beyond the stench of the city with its throngs of vehicles without pollution controls, open sewers, and animals in the streets.

As he rounded a corner high above the ocean he saw Los Archos directly ahead. He knew he wasn't far from Mismaloya bay. The hotel could be seen jutting out of the rock above the crashing waves. Its terraced nightclub, with open dance floor under the stars, must have been a haven for the hopelessly romantic. He skidded to a stop at the top of the hairpin turn leading to the Hotel La Joya de Mismaloya.

He had no trouble arranging for accommodation. Because of the recession, tourism was down, and autumn was the off-season anyway; besides a recent earthquake was all the locals talked about at the airport. There was apparently little damage, however, since the quake was so geographically concentrated. As soon as he checked in, he walked to the balcony overlooking Mismaloya bay. Across the little bay he saw where the earthquake knocked a small helicopter into the waters of the bay. He could see divers pulling wreckage from the turquoise waters. As he watched the salvage unfold, he felt uneasy. Slithering black stingrays hovered around the wreck. A sense of foreboding overcame him, and he turned away from the balcony walking over to the kitchen counter where he poured himself a generous rum and coke.

The tropical breeze drifted about the room. The damp and musty smell of the place needed the fresh air. He took a step back onto the balcony and surveyed the beach with his binoculars. The tourists were setting up little territories on the beach—towels, and sun block amid throngs of local children selling everything from hammocks to contraband copies of 'Hard Rock Café' t-shirts. He scanned to his right along the beach past where a stream met the sea.

It was here that a little shantytown of locals on vacation sat under banana leaf palapas eating shrimp and drinking *cerveça*. He saw two gringos, a man and a woman. The man had a small black bag he was carrying under his arm. The woman, in her forties looked familiar, he'd seen that face somewhere before. He recognized Greg Fallows from the file photographs of the now infamous expatriate Canadian physician turned archeologist turned terrorist. For starters he was wanted in connection with the murder of Dr. Jana deVries in a remote area of the Petén jungle of Guatemala and Steven Knight in New York.

They stopped at a *palapa* on the tourist end of the beach. They each ordered a beer and smiled at each other. They had that self-satisfied look from other criminals he'd worked with over the years.

He put down his binoculars and drink. He changed into more comfortable tourist garb, and made his way down to the beach. He knew he had to make contact now, before someone else got to them. And before it was too late.

The beach was extremely hot, even early in the morning. When a little Mexican girl approached him with two hands full of hats, as he stepped off the concrete sidewalk onto the sand. After a half-hearted attempt at haggling, he bought the silliest of sombreros, one with a bright red band and fluffy little red balls around the brim. He placed it on his head, fastened the drawstring under his chin and walked casually over to the two smiling in the shade of the banana leaves. In his black and red boxer swimsuit, and matching beach top, he looked quite the sight, even for Mismaloya bay on that hot morning.

He peered over his plastic rimmed sunglasses.

"Hot down here. Isn't it?"

The voice startled Greg. Renata had watched the tourist with genuine curiosity as he walked up to their *palapa*. She was more suspicious than surprised.

"Mind if I join you?" Hastings pulled up a wooden folding chair from the next table. He didn't wait to be invited to sit down. He turned the chair around and sat down, straddling it like a horse, leaning on the back of the rickety chair crossing both arms. He called to the waiter to bring "three more *cerveça por favor.*"

Greg looked at the strange hat the man was wearing. He looked like a clown and he knew it. Renata sensed he wasn't carrying a gun, and simply smiled, a curt, thin little smile of minor irritation.

"I hope I'm not interrupting anything." Hastings smiled, not really giving the duo time to answer the question. "I'm from State-side." He thanked the waiter, as the stocky Mexican placed the beer and plate of limes on the little wooden table.

"I gathered." Renata took Greg's hand in hers, as if they were honeymooners. The change in her attitude surprised Greg who was compelled to play along.

"You kids just get married?" asked Hastings as he took a sip of beer.

Greg began to shake his head vigorously to imply the negative.

"Yes. How could you tell?" Renata piped in.

Greg looked at her with a surprised look on his face.

"Yes . . . is it that obvious?"

"Well around here just about everybody's either a newly wed or nearly dead," Hastings laughed solo at his own cliché joke.

"And what about you? Which are you?" Renata asked sarcastically.

"Neither." His attitude quickly hardened to cement in the torrid Mexican sun.

The hair on the back of Renata's neck bristled, and her pupils dilated, an autonomic response preparing for flight or a fight.

"Are you with the Temple?" Renata asked taking a calculated risk. Greg tightened the grip around her hand. He surreptitiously kicked the black bag by his left foot. He breathed a sigh of relief knowing it was still there.

"No." Hastings removed his sunglasses. "I'm with the Senate Foreign Relations Sub-committee on Terrorism, Narcotics and International Operations. I've been sent to help you. And bring you back to Washington to testify. We know you are wanted in connection with the disappearance of Dr. deVries, Mr. Fallows. Sorry, I should say, 'Dr.' Fallows. It is *Doctor* isn't it?" Hastings pushed a piece of lime into the long neck of his *Tecate* beer.

Greg sat silent. He didn't know whether to be afraid or relieved.

"You mean you're with the Justice Department?" Renate asked.

"Not anymore. Not officially that is. But I've been asked by the Sub-committee chair to assist in your repatriation."

"That's an interesting way to put it," Greg looked down and dug his foot into the sand.

"Since when has the Justice Department been involved with foreign operations?" Renate interrupted looking him in the eye with the intensity of a heat-seeking missile homing in on its target.

"Ever since the intelligence communities have been compromised," believing honesty to be his most poignant weapon.

Renata needed no further reassurances. He was either telling the truth, or he was a crazy liar. He didn't seem crazy. If he was a liar it was too much of a coincidence.

"Why do you want to help us?"

"Because we need your help to snare a fox," Hastings gave a crooked smile.

"What fox?" Greg asked.

"That's not your concern, my boy, Hastings replied in a condescending tone. He removed his sombrero to reveal a receding hairline and very shiny white forehead. Greg thought it was more distracting than the hat.

"Is he SX?" she asked, meaning a senior government official.

Looking away toward the tourists floundering in the waves of the polluted bay, Hastings didn't answer. But he knew where he'd seen her face before, in his file named T/A (terrorists and assassins).

"Look," he got up, turned his chair around, and leaned toward them. "You don't have much choice. If G2 doesn't get you, Interpol will, and as far as I can tell they're all one and the same. Your only chance of survival is to come with me. You'll be safe with me, and later on testify before the Sub-committee. You'll eventually get your day in court, so to speak, and perhaps, just perhaps, you'll get to spill your guts in public; let the dirty secrets wrapped up for centuries out for everyone to know. It's the only way. For you to survive, I mean."

"How does that catch the man you want? Won't that drive them further underground?" Renata asked astutely.

Hastings lit a cigarette. "We set a trap, a sort of reverse arms for hostages scam. It means one final job before we go back to Washington."

Renata nodded to Greg. It made sense. For sure it wasn't without risk, but at least they might have a chance. If the truth were made public they would have no reason to hide. Greg would have to take his chances with the legal system, but that was better than the alternatives. The press just might be able to do something good for a change; save lives instead of ruining them.

"Where's the skull?" Hastings asked.

"I have it right here." Greg kicked the bag with this foot.

"Good," Hastings smiled as he stood up. "We've got no time to waste. They may have more resources than we think. We have to move . . . now."

Greg exhaled with a surge of relief. Now they were three. Renata was still uncertain what they were in for. But she also knew she couldn't just go home to Paris. If she was lucky she could convince her boss she suffered from Stockholm syndrome—when the captor becomes emotionally involved with the captured. But that would be a stretch. If Hastings turned out to be a double agent for the Order, he would have to die—or she would die trying. She took her hand off the 9 mm in her purse as she got up. She hadn't noticed until then that she'd had her finger on the trigger ever since she set eyes on the odd tourist with the sombrero. But then again, she wasn't supposed to think. Look at where it had gotten her.

TWENTY-SIX

Paterson stroked the long slope of his nose as he waited at a table in the bar of the Hotel de l'Europe. No one would recognize him outside of Washington. He could walk with virtual anonymity, except for the occasional television newsperson that might by chance spot him. In Paris maybe, but in Amsterdam he did not worry about it. While he waited for his car to arrive he quietly read under the light of the bar. He glanced out the window every once in a while down the canal that ran alongside Rokin. The weather was sunny and warm, even on the cold November morning.

He scanned the small bar. There were only a couple of people in the bar at this time of day; most like Paterson were waiting for someone or something to happen. A couple next to the piano was drinking champagne, and laughed like lovers attracted by the city's salacious reputation. It was a notoriety that acted as an excellent cover for the even more pornographic traffic in diplomacy.

Paterson drank the last of his thick dark Dutch coffee. He stood up, left a decent tip for the bartender who smiled as he strode out the door. His black Mercedes-Benz was waiting for him on the other side of the revolving doors. As he stepped out onto the street, the noise and bustle of the morning traffic jolted his quiet reflection on Newburg's book.

He headed south across Muntplein Square in the back seat of the Benz. They crossed a sea of pedestrians and bicycles driving down Vijzelstraat where they turned right on Marnixstraat, and then left at Leiderstraat, over the scenic Singelgracht canal, past Constantijn Huygensstraat to 39 Vondelstraat Oud.

When the door of the car opened his armadillo eyes scanned the area before he stepped onto the sidewalk underneath the stained glass pentagram of the Temple. Another inquisition was about to begin, but this time things would turn out differently. He withdrew back into the safety of his shell as he knocked on the large wooden doors. He was at home among the gargoyles smiling down from their stony perches above the door. History loves revenge, and Paterson loved history.

The door opened, and a mustached gentleman greeted him with a kiss on the cheek.

"It is good to see you again Most Sublime Prince of the Royal Mystery." The greeter ushered Paterson in. He closed the large door with a click of the lock. The peace and quiet of the Temple foyer was in sharp contrast to the bustle of the city outside.

An almost sickly sweet smell of sandalwood filled the hall.

"May I take your coat?" The greeter smiled. Paterson handed his coat to the servant without expression, the way a king might to a footman, without so much as a hint of familiarity.

"The Council of 33 is waiting for you my Prince." The footman motioned for Paterson to enter another doorway to the left of a wide circular staircase. Walking just ahead of Paterson, he opened twin oak doors to a room filled with brilliant sunlight.

It had been many years since Sam Paterson had walked across that threshold. The immense room had a high vaulted ceiling and massive stained glass windows. He paused to appreciate the rich hues of blue, green and gold; the cascade of color flooded the governing Board of 33 assembled as they sat talking among themselves and reading newspapers. Each wore the white mantel with emblazoned red cross lapel pin.

A hush descended over the Board as Paterson walked into the assembly hall. The Board rose one by one. They needed no prompting. Paterson walked over to a pulpit carved in the shape of a gigantic eagle where two assistants dressed him in a simple hooded white frock with a red cross over the heart. He walked over to the pulpit and climbed the stairs to the top. When he reached the top of the pulpit, he looked down over the Board. A sense of immortal power came over him. He reached into his pocket and took out a small black crucifix and raised it to his lips. But instead of kissing the image of Jesus, he spat on the cross and raised it high above his head to the cheers of the assembled men and women.

"Let the Grand Imperial Council begin!" he cried holding the cross high, waving it from side to side to the great delight of the Board members.

"The Sons of Jesus rejoice this day. We are about to inherit our earthly kingdom as foretold. We will soon have Baphomet's head again in our possession, and we will avenge the name of our fathers." More cheers swept over the assembly.

He stepped down from the platform and approached a small group of men near the front. One of them was dressed in the white Templar cajoule. As Paterson approached, the man stepped out of his cajoule revealing his nakedness.

"To be of the Order requires obedience. Nakedness reminds us of our natural state. As with the Knights of old, we who are their sons do swear by the sword." As Paterson said these words he took a sword handed to him by one of the men and held it across the neck of the naked man kneeling before him.

"To swear by the sword is the most compelling oath, so we ask you to kiss this sword as a symbol of your submission to the will of the Order. Breach of this most sacred oath degrades you before your brothers and sisters, and" Paterson glanced down to read from a large leather bound book, 'which every Mason ought to preserve more carefully than his Life.'

When the plane touched down at Schiphol airport, Greg didn't think he'd ever be back in Amsterdam again. He nudged Renata who was sleeping beside him. Nathan Hastings read Anthony Trollope's *Can You Forgive Her* without bothering to look up, as the huge 747-300 pulled into the KLM dock. The dull November sky cast a dismal hand over the city. It was appropriate for his re-entry into this Fellini movie called A'Dam. The script was set. Hastings arranged to meet with a local police inspector who had been briefed on recent G2 murder/suicides. He had agreed not to talk about his activity to anyone—especially not his superiors. Nat knew Inspector Hans Kroode from his BCCI investigations; one of the main conduits for illegal funds came through the Dutch office on Herengracht Straat. But that was in the past.

Hans Kroode was at Immigration to meet the Trinity, as Nat code-named them. He also code-named their mission: *Chasing the Dragon.* He named it after the Amsterdam junkie slang for the unholy grail of perfect heroin highs. In this case, however, the Dragon was the White House Chief of Staff

Hastings met Malcolm Featherstone at Dulles Airport between flights, where he received his orders directed from Committee chairman, Senator Clattmore via encrypted digital cell phone. The NSA located Paterson in Amsterdam. Paterson had arranged for a brief stopover in Amsterdam after a meeting in Den Haig. The "script" called for a confrontation with the Dragon. Hastings conspired to bait him with an offer he couldn't refuse. The sum would have to be in the millions, but that wouldn't be a problem. Then they would expose the whole scam under the bright lights of the international media. Hastings could arrange this through his media connections. The scandal would rocket straight back to the White House, which in turn would demand the Senate Foreign Relations Sub-committee on Terrorism, Narcotics and International Operations hold open, public hearings. The revelations would scandalize the White House and catapult Senator Clattmore into the White House in the next election. At least that was Clattmore's plan.

Ostensibly Hastings was in Amsterdam to discuss European intelligence gathering for the TNIO Sub-committee. He arranged to meet Inspector Hans Kroode at the gate

"Hans," Hastings shook the blond policeman's hand. "How long has it been?"

"Six or seven years, I'd say," the handsome police inspector smiled. He cast a wanton gaze over Renata, who in her true chameleon fashion had metamorphosed into a European beauty with the help of some make-up and a black Oscar de la Renta body suit.

"This is Renata. She's . . . Fallow's body guard," Hastings screwed his mouth up, as if looking for a better description of her role in all this.

"Bodyguard!" Hans cried, nodding approval.

"Freelance, or professional?" the Inspector asked with a sarcastic grin on his face.

"Professional." Ignoring his attitude, she walked past the policeman.

"Nice body . . . guard." Kroode followed her with his eyes.

"*My* bodyguard," Greg asserted to the policeman.

"He's the famous, or should I say, infamous terrorist?" asked the Inspector.

"Don't believe everything you read. He's a medical archeologist. He's working with us now. The courts will decide his guilt or innocence."

"She looks familiar." Inspector Kroode watched Greg and Renata stop at the exit to the long hallway near the main shopping concourse.

"Leave it alone. They're with me. Afterwards, we'll talk. Okay?"

"You need a Heineken, old boy." Inspector Kroode patted Hastings on the back.

Hastings grunted something inaudible.

"Shit, I need a bath in Heineken."

"You've come to the right town my scurrilous friend." Hans Kroode laughed and put his thick right arm around the former Justice Department investigator.

"In the end, when you know the why, the who will be self-evident."

"The why is almost always self-interest of some sort." Nat Hastings sipped his beer. The pedestrian traffic bustled across Spuistraat on that fall Friday evening. A gentle freezing mist made the night air very damp and unkind.

They exchanged information: Kroode about the murders, and Dr. Pieter's apparent suicide right after telling him about the Templars. The whole unfinished business bothered him, and he let it show after he'd had a couple of beer.

Hastings on the other hand told Kroode about the skull and the modern day Templar plan to form a world government, based on a secret held for centuries concerning Christ. He stopped short of telling him about the allegation that Christ didn't die on the cross, and the alleged cover-up by the papacy and the King of France. He did say that publication of this proof could destabilize the entire Western world by calling into question the authority of both the UN, elected governments, not to mention the Catholic Church, and the affect it might have on the millions of faithful around the world.

What he didn't tell Kroode was that Senator Clattmore intended to use the whole affair as a platform for his Presidential campaign. And what the Senator didn't tell Hastings, but Nat Hastings could figure out for himself, was that Clattmore had no intention of letting the public know the whole truth. A partial truth would do, a scapegoat had been found, the Chief of Staff would resign amid allegations of unethical behavior; party officials who insisted on anonymity would say over the Christmas holidays from Camp David, that the Chief of Staff resigned. Amsterdam was an easy place. Rumors of sex, sex with boys would be enough to ruin his reputation inside and outside the beltway. The sources would go on to say, a hand written note would be handed to the President in the Oval Office on Christmas Eve. The President, of course, would announce a successor in due course.

Inspector Kroode stared blankly into his drink. He now knew why; it was just a matter of time before he knew whom. He was a policeman. He could relate to murders and motives. He had no interest in politics.

Renata and Greg came into the café at that moment. Both looked fresh and rested. They each pulled up a chair. Renate ordered a red Dubonnet on the rocks, and Greg ordered a draft beer.

"I think it's time we went over the plan again." Hastings raised his empty glass to catch the attention of the waiter who was eyeing a young boy reading a book in the corner.

"It's simple. I call up this Dr. Strumpf character, or whoever he is, and tell him to meet me at his place behind the Museum of Torture on Leidestraat. I agree to bring the skull, and he agrees to bring $3 million in cash. Right?"

"So far so good."

"At the same time the Inspector here leaks to the Press that the Chief of Staff of the President of the United States is trying to purchase a rare object of archeological value. The cash he brings will be used against him.

"During the ensuing confusion, Renata will sweep me and the skull away while the local police nab the 'Fox.' His picture will appear over all the wire services, caught in the act of some unethical scam in Amsterdam. He will be recalled to Washington after much embarrassment to the President, and in an effort to vindicate himself, he will testify about all he knows to the Foreign Relations Subcommittee. And the whole story will be made public."

Greg seemed extremely satisfied with himself. It all seemed so perfect, too perfect. Her instincts were better than his; they always had been.

"And what happens to us?" she asked.

There was an awkward silence for several minutes.

"What do you mean?" asked Hasting."

You know what I mean. After you kill Paterson."

Hastings hadn't counted on her being so intuitive; it reminded him of his past marital failures. His left eye twitched the way it did the night he was confronted by all his ex-wives. Shit! She was going to blow the whole plan.

"Nobody said anything about killing anyone," Greg piped in.

"That's right," Hastings recovered from his fugue state.

Outside the sleazy Museum of Torture a bevy of reporters from all the major wire services and networks waited in the cold. It was a great backdrop for a story.

"This better be good Inspector," from a red-haired androgynous photographer on contract with Reuters.

"Don't worry," Kroode said. "This one's going to get you promoted out of here."

"But I don't wanna get promoted out of here." The boy-girl looked a little worried.

"Yeah, right!" Another reporter piped in.

Inside something was going wrong. Paterson wanted to "talk with the head alone" before he'd hand over the money.

"I need to know it's authentic," Paterson stated sternly, his eyes blinked nervously.

Greg was wearing a wire. This had been a last minute decision Hasting had insisted on. It was uncomfortable and he felt exposed. He and Renata along with the Chief of Staff and a big burly fellow, who did not speak, except for the occasional grunt, stared at the black bag. Meanwhile, Hastings and Kroode were listening from a police car around the corner on Kerkstraat.

The room was dark, the rear windows let very little light into the room, and the small courtyard off Leidestraat was full of junk with redeeming features.

Greg took the skull out of the black medical bag he'd been carrying it in, and placed in on a small table near the center of the room. It glowed a luminous glow in the dimly lit room. The organic green light emanating from the skull began to pulsate in the room. It cast an eerie shadow and reflected in the window.

The four stood in silence, mesmerized by the throbbing light. The thing seemed to suck everyone's attention into it—like one of those lava lamps at a Sixties LSD party. The stronger the glow grew, the harder it was to resist the maelstrom of green light emanating from it. Greg's heart raced, in all the time he'd had the thing he'd never really wanted to play around with it. Especially after the first time when Dr. deVries found the thing, and then again in Mismaloya bay; both times terrible things happened. His heart seemed to race faster and faster. He couldn't hear anything except the beating of his own heart.

Renata stood transfixed by the glowing glass. An inner calm descended over her too. Her heart slowed to an incredibly docile rate. In fact, it should have been barely able to maintain cardiac output.

The bodyguard stood frozen, unable to move a muscle, his eyes a glassy glaze of fear hardwired into his skull. At the same time his face revealed a juvenile excitement, a small drop of saliva ran from the corner of his mouth; he looked as if he might lose bowel and bladder control.

The eyes of the Chief of Staff reflected the typhoon of pent up gases swirling about the room. His face, contorted and red, looked hideous and demonic. It cast a satanic shadow on the wall behind him. Suddenly, and without warning, a vibrating and crashing sound shook the room. The heat from the skull in the center of the room made Greg nauseated and light-headed. Suddenly, the skull couldn't be seen any longer. It seemed to evaporate into the swirling lightning. From the source of the energy, a large forked serpent tongue rose up, violently whipping, snapping the air with its wet force. It turned and with a violent snap, touched Paterson's head, and for one terrifying moment he glowed, one with the thing. Then in a split second, there was silence, the crystal skull was as usual hauntingly beautiful in its symmetry, and design, and the Chief of Staff lay on the floor, motionless.

The hulk of a bodyguard grabbed Greg and wrestled him to a corner away from the door and the window. Renata bent over to touch Paterson's lifeless body. She searched feverishly for a carotid pulse.

"Christ, he's dead!"

In the patrol car Hastings and Kroode heard nothing. The entire event was clouded with white noise.

"I think we'd better take a look, I don't like it."

In the street a crowd mulled about with the reporters and TV cameras. Hastings' staged media bite had turned into a public relations nightmare. There was no way out now; the truth was going to come out.

As the police doctor escorted the body through the crowd on Leidestraat the crowd and media pushed to see the lifeless body of Samuel Charles Paterson, White House Chief of Staff, carried from the seedy Museum of Torture. The cameras flashed as Greg was brought through the door of the little shop on Leidestraat.

The headline in *The International Herald-Tribune* the next morning read: MYSTERY SURROUNDS DEATH OF WHITE HOUSE CHIEF.

Alone in his prison cell at police headquarters Greg had plenty of time to think. He knew it was likely that he would be extradited to the United States, held in connection with the mysterious death of the Chief of Staff, as well as in connection with the death of Dr. deVries, and a few others if pieces of the puzzle were put together as he believed they would.

When the reporter, a bright young woman came to interview him for a story in *Rolling Thunder* magazine he wanted to tell the whole story. He wanted to tell the truth about the conspiracy surrounding the secret society, the international conspiracy to cover up, and alter historical fact. But he couldn't do it. Not just yet anyway. He couldn't forget what happened to Christie and Kate. He couldn't let it happen again; he couldn't draw anyone else into this nightmare, not just yet anyway.

Renata took the skull from the black box, and placed it on the table of the briefing room of the United Nations Information Department in New York. The perfect hair and face of news anchor Tracy Selman filled the television screen live from Room 419 of the Dirkson Senate Office Building in Washington DC. Around the table, all sixteen men and women smiled anonymous smiles.

"No one will believe a word he says." Renata began. "His medical records will be subpoenaed by the Sub-committee." She held up a manila envelope stamped 'confidential' in large red block letters.

"In his medical file, a history of a long-standing psychiatric problem known as a Schizotypal Personality Disorder will be found. Experts will testify that Dr. Greg Fallows has characteristic features of this disorder including eccentric convictions. He has expressed recurrent illusion, magical thinking, social isolation, undue social anxiety, paranoid ideation, and fringe religious beliefs. Because of this incurable condition, the Sub-committee will find his testimony unbelievable. And he will be confined to a suitable Federal mental health facility for the rest of his life."

"You have done well again, Chameleon," a cherubic little man said from the far end of the long table. "You have done the world and history a great service. You have returned the relic to its proper owners, to its proper home. We shall use it as it was intended, to protect and serve the chosen people. You have secured our future against our enemies. Well done.

TWENTY-SEVEN

The warm north wind signaled a change in the weather. Christie looked up from her coffee on the deck of the Palm Bay Inn and closed the book she was reading: Peter Carey's *Oscar and Lucinda*. She hoped she and Stephen were not like Peter Carey's pathetic characters. Today was the day Stephen Parmata arrived. He'd be coming on the noon ferry from Shute Harbor. After all he had done for her, it would be good to see him again.

"Could be the beginning of the wet." Margie, the Inn manager, sounded a bit depressed, as she directed her crew to clean up the debris from the overnight storm. The wet, or rainy season is often heralded by a change in the direction of the wind that normally blows from the south. It can also mean her already slow business could get even slower.

Palm Bay Inn sits on the south end of Long Island, the closest of the Whitsunday Islands to Australia in the Coral Sea of the Great Barrier Reef. It was here that Parmata had arranged for Christie to chill out while he finished his business in the States. That business had everything to do with securing a relic of great value for a European client.

Time seemed to stop in the Whitsunday Islands. With all that in the past, it was easy for Christie to forget how close she had come to being kidnapped in the remote Guatemalan jungle. As it was if it hadn't been for the device Stephen had given her, the Russian rescue team who risked their lives to save hers would never had found her in time. That was all in the past now. She surveyed the damage from

181

the storm and remembered how she lay in the humid cabin at the end of the beach last night watching a record 2600 lightning strikes an hour for three endless hours in the middle of the night. She was tired but anxious to see Stephen and hear news about Greg.

She walked back to her cabin along the beach. Even at 9 a.m. the sun was already unbearably hot for a Canadian. She retreated to the Mérida hammock on her verandah where she listened to the tropical wild life around her scurry in the jungle undergrowth: Goannas and skinks and Common Death Adders. The sounds of the cicadas droned a tropical tinnitus at times as she drifted into a timeless sleep.

She was awakened by the chugging sounds of the Shute Harbor ferry as it tried to remain stationary in the 16 knot current to transfer Parmata and another couple from the larger boat to the smaller motor boat for the trip to Palm Bay. The remote Inn has no dock, so the only way in and out is by small boat to the larger ferry to the mainland.

Christie was on the beach when the shuttle boat landed at the Palm Bay lagoon. Parmata stepped off the boat and threw his arms around her. He just held her for several seconds before saying anything at all. Christie was starting to get embarrassed as the other couple struggled with their luggage to get around them.

"Thank God you're okay" He kissed her tanned forehead.

"Fair dinkum," she declared leading up the path to the deck.

He laughed. "You're picking up Aussie pretty good too I see. "He grabbed two cold beers and headed to the shade of the canopy over the table on the deck where he told her the news.

"It looks like Greg will be going away for a very long time, that is, if he doesn't get the death penalty for the murder of a federal agent in New York."

"Is there anything we can do?" She knew it was hopeless.

"The best thing we can do is stay away from it. The best thing we can do is stay in Oz."

"And do what?"

"They do have cellos here you know."

"And poisonous snakes and spiders. I killed a redback in my cabin the other night, you know."

"You'll get used to it," he smiled. *What he didn't tell her, she didn't need to know*, he thought looking into her eyes; they match the sky.

His part had been well played and he'd been well rewarded for his efforts. They could live here forever, or maybe head inland to Charters Towers for a while. The red earth of the outback had a soothing effect on the soul the Abos always said. Or, they could get a boat and just trip around the Whitsunday Islands. Either way he had enough money for a while. Besides, he knew it wouldn't be long before someone would be looking for his freelance services again. And that's fair dinkum.

We are the "eye" at the top of the pyramid. I knew we would win everything, and without lawyers! But I couldn't have done it without the help of those faithful souls. Those selfless souls ready to give their lives for the cause.

Death is a reluctant companion to Life, as Pancho was to Don Quixote. I wish it could be otherwise. But only a fool thinks he can change something he cannot. I wish we could have avoided certain extreme prejudices: Kate, Dr. Teunens, Carlos, and the others, some were faithful servants of the cause. I don't like this wet work, you see. It seems so archaic, but it was necessary to achieve our goal.

We were more successful using modern methods with Dr. Fallows. His personality was ideal for modern psychiatric manipulation. And we were able to exploit his natural weaknesses—for the common good. This may seem hard for some of you to understand, but these are the kind of executive decisions a CEO has to make every day. Well, perhaps not most CEOs, but certainly the President and CEO of Templars.Net. Now, with a single world currency burgeoning, we will once again become the bankers to the world. And the wealth of knowledge stored in the electromagnetic field is ours to harvest and reconstitute as we see fit. We will of course only use it for the benefit of the corporation, specifically, for the benefit of the shareholders—all of you gathered here today.

There are mysteries of nature that cannot be rationalized away in pseudo science. Rivers will not change directions because we will it. History is not a celluloid shadow; it lives within us. Our DNA is our physical connection to a coil stretching back in time to that point where we intersect in the roiling primordial waters. We are wet-wired, riveted to each other and something outside ourselves. Each is knighted with glorious free will.

Now when I look south from my Upper East Side offices I see the United Nations building and I know that we have succeeded in bringing about the grand plan of Jacques de Molnay. He would be pleased with Templars.Net. He would be pleased with all of you.

I am pleased today to tell you, via our live Internet report, that share values have gone up 35.5% on news of our stewardship of the new world currency program proposed today by Heinrich Von Hartmann, one of our brothers, and the newly appointed Secretary General of the United Nations.

Rest assured, those of you who are anxious, globalization has finally matured from its roots in tribalism and nationalism, the scourge of all humankind, and the undisputed cause of every war. We will eliminate the epidemic of nationalism. We enter a new era, a post-modern corporate era; an efficient meritocracy the likes of which have never been seen before, where the science of government and public policy converge, and rational thinking means value for money—in the pursuit of the common good. We must overcome 7th century notions of privacy and individual rights when they clash with the rights, no, needs of society. Government is the voice of the majority of shareholders. Let that voice be heard. We guarantee we will be judicious in the exercise of our mandate, because I am your fool, and serve solely at your pleasure.

Parmata stopped typing. He selected *send now*, waited for the acknowledgement, and closed the laptop.

BOOK TWO

Where no counsel is, the people fall, but in the multitude of counselors there is safety—Proverbs XI/14 cited Israeli Intelligence home page

ONE

There is a place I love. It is in Jerusalem, near the Church of the Holy Sepulcher. I find the fresh fruit of the *phoenix dactylifera* not far from the crowds the very best in the world. They are the juiciest of delicacies when they are fresh, the sweet aroma of the oasis buried in each and every one. Kissed by the dry desert winds, they transport me to a simpler aromatic rendezvous. But you are not interested in my sweet fruit, although you should be. We have come to arrange a meeting. Let us say a meeting of Worlds. For if we look toward the Temple Mount, or the Dome of the Rock, as it is sometimes called, we see a dusty whirlwind, and a woman in prayer. She is why you and I have traveled so far. She is the song generations will sing. But, my friend, you have come far and already know this.

You and I have disagreed before about our roles. Mine is the mission from above, yours from below. I know you take umbrage in that description, but let us agree at least to disagree and focus our sights on the woman in prayer, for she is the ablution of all we seek. Yours is an eschatological mystery. Mine is teleological. Yes, my friend, you have labored long in isolation in the region of the damned. But it was not I who put you there. It was your actions, and yours alone. I know, I know, much is contested in the court of public opinion. But let us agree at least to discuss the lady in prayer over there, or at least the vortex above her head that compels us to meet.

"You, the prince of adversaries, know me as Saraqael, the angel of death."

"Yes, yes, you and I have much in common, blah, blah, blah," the voice of perdition, groaned. He took another cigarette from his beautiful dark navy Armani suit and lit it with a gold lighter embossed with the Seal of the President of the United States.

"A gift from an admirer." There was that crooked smile.

"But not as much as you might want." Saraqael replied impatiently.

"Angels are such weary creatures, and a wanton lot too, I know," the tempter chuckled. "Why don't we just make it easy? Why not let the poor girl know we're here? Give her an assignment and we're off. A couple of drinks and we say we've done all we can. No one knows the better."

"Let's not forget, these creatures are unpredictable, and unreliable. Remember Jeremy Duncan, the Canadian Taliban. He got some crazy ideas into his head and made a mess for everyone," motioning with his left hand toward Jerusalem.

"You know, the problem with you my friend, is that you're too damned serious. You need to relax. Now let's just get on with it, and you'll soon be buying me a drink. That was our bet wasn't it?"

Cut to fecund deities dancing, vital forces beyond our ken, perchance to dream for us each night as our own lives arc their way through diamond radiant gullies, bursting over harsh cold rocks in every near and distant moment, a mere drop of blue water sticks like sperm to find nothing, to become nothing. What is transition, movement from one place to another, from one dimension of space and time to another? What is a dimension, a slice of bread in some string bound universe? Fleeting thoughts, falling snow on already overburdened cedars? Is it a poetic river or a mere slight of hand, an illusion of some Divine wet software? The mystic surging river knows only change. Wipe to the toga clad philosopher crying, "you can never step in the same place in the same river twice." There is nothing but transition all round as the wind blows him into a cloud of squawking crows in the blood soaked mountains of antiquity as a door opens to a dimly lit bedroom filled with sadness.

Some say that when a child is born it is the fulfillment of a cosmic mystery each and every time, or at very least a celebration when a healthy child is born in the remote Guatemalan highlands known as the Altiplano. Others might say it is a miracle, but it is a mixed emotion for sure when the child is born healthy and the mother dies, and doubly so when the baby is suckled successfully by the dead mother. Yes, it has happened. It is not fantasy. But let us continue.

Lay pastor Miguel Martinez awoke from a sleep filled with beautiful angels dressed in golden robes, dancing in lavender clouds. And later, as he traveled the rough track at night he heard the sounds of guerrillas moving like panthers in the dark forests of the Highlands. It was routine in these parts to hear strange men swearing in the dark. He did not stop to notice, or think twice of the danger beyond the footpath. He kept moving forward toward the cemetery and the newborn child beyond it. The night sky was overcast and cool, and the smell of cattle dung filled the damp air.

At the edge of the pasture he scaled a rickety fence and along with his escort Francesca, he made his way through the multicolored flag-draped cemetery to the small wood framed huts on the other side beyond the abandoned Catholic Church. At feasts such as All Souls Day the people gathered to party all night with the dead. The flags were the remnants of that revelry.

As Miguel and Francesca marched through the cemetery the sound of barking dogs ahead of them seem to draw them closer to their nocturnal rendezvous. From the black night a child and several scruffy dogs suddenly appeared as if from nowhere.

"Quick, come quick," the boy pleaded.

"What's the hurry?" Miguel asked, already moving as fast as he could.

"Is that you Diego?" he asked.

"Yes, it's me."

"Francesca said we're going to your house." There was no reply from the boy. He and the dogs had broken into a run ahead of them. They followed as fast as they could.

A few minutes later they arrived at the small wood framed home of Eduardo and Maria Gonzalez. The house was quiet except for the sound of moaning and someone reading from the Bible . . . Revelations. Miguel recognized the words. *"Yo soy el Alfa y la Omega, dice el Senor Dios, el que es, y que era y que ha de venir, el Todopoderoso . . ."*

Inside he found Eduardo sitting beside his dead wife, baby at her breast. A gaggle of women wept, and beyond the light of the candles held by Eduardo and the women, Eduardo's eight children sat in the dark corners of the room.

No one looked at the visitors. All eyes were fixed on the newborn baby suckling the dead mother's breast. It was bizarre, perhaps even a miracle.

Miguel walked over to the mother and child, as he bent over to look at the child, it turned its small head and looked at him with unusual gray eyes. He gently removed the child, a girl, from her mother's breast. She did not cry. She seemed to smile at him, and then her eyes, her eyes lit with a silvery gray light that seemed that pierced his soul. She moved her mouth. Perhaps it was a sucking reflex, but no, she was trying to form words, and from her little chest the air in her gathered currents until she quietly squeaked, "Fah tee maa."

"The child speaks her name!" he stepped back in shock, and one of the women took the girl from him and placed her back on her dead mother's breast. Miguel looked at Eduardo who sat dumbfounded beside his dead wife, stroking her long black hair.

Eduardo looked at Miguel, as if searching for an explanation. She says, "Fatima. The child says her name is Fatima. Is it a Spanish name Miguel? Is it a sign from God? It must be a sign from God, Miguel. You should know this. The women have never seen a mother suckle a child so well . . . and the mother is dead," he pointed to Fatima nursing.

"I will get the priest." Miguel did not know what else to say. "I will go now. I will find Hermano Morales and bring him, he will know what to do."

Hermano Alvaro Morales was working in his crazy weed-infested garden outside Chajul when Miguel came down the dirt road that led to his patch of good earth. As a priest he couldn't afford to buy the land himself, but one of the parishioners, a finca manager, donated a small parcel of land so Alvaro could grow some vegetables of his own. And this he did, with love and thanksgiving. Mostly he grew maize because it was the most useful. He was weeding the patch when Miguel came upon him.

"Miguel, it is good to see you." He stood to embrace him. "It has been a long time, amigo. You remind me I should come to La Bala soon. But times like these are not safe for a priest to travel in the countryside alone. You have walked a long way. You must be tired and hungry . . . or thirsty at least. Come let us sit over here under this bountiful peach tree. I have a small lunch, praise the Lord, and we shall eat it together. Miguel, I'm so happy to see you, but I do run on and you haven't said a word. What's wrong my friend? You must have come for a reason my friend. Miguel why do you look so somber? Speak to me Miguel? Why have you come?"

Tears filled Miguel's dark eyes and his large leathery hands trembled as he took a sip of tea from the cup Hermano Alvaro gave him.

"Hermano you have been to school, and you have read many books. Is it possible for a baby to know its own name? To speak at birth; to suckle from the breast of its dead mother?"

"Well, my friend, I have never heard of such a thing. That does not mean they cannot happen, but only to say, I've never read about them . . . But wait! I think I may have heard of one case. The dead mother suckled the child. But these things are very rare, Miguel. Some might even say, miraculous."

"Miraculous? Can you be sure?"

"Sure of what Miguel? I don't know what you're talking about."

"Can you be sure they're holy signs? Unnatural things, I mean."

"You are scaring me Miguel. You look like you've seen a ghost, and all this talk of strange children. Why have you come to me?

191

What trouble's your heart? I can see something is. Does it have something to do with a particular child? Come my friend, it cannot be as bad as that. Tell me what burdens you so."

And so Miguel told Hermano Alvaro Morales why he had come. He told him about the child, the suckling, her strange eyes, and her naming herself Fatima.

There was no question now of Morales going to La Bala. There was only the matter of how they would avoid suspicion and the constant surveillance of the army, which was more paranoid now than any time during the thirty-six year civil war.

As he traveled, Morales was struck with the remarkable beauty of this country called Guatemala, the imposing volcanoes rising above the clouds against the orange sunset.

They arrived at the village, and Hermano Morales took a moment to give thanks to God for a safe journey here. They had encountered no problem beyond the difficult terrain. They left his rusting Toyota pickup at the end of a dirt track beyond the flooded road at Sacapulas then backpacked across a fallen tree over a raging river and climbed over gravel for many miles to a donkey path where eventually they were met by villagers and mules for the final precarious journey along the edge of the mountain to the village of La Bala.

They were immediately taken to the home of Eduardo and Maria Gonzalez where Morales also witnessed the scene as described by Miguel Martinez. By now there were hundreds of people outside the house and twice as many scrawny barking dogs. There was even a marimba band playing traditional funeral music and several villagers had brought pictures of the Virgin Mary that they placed outside the door of the house. Inside, the dead woman Maria Gonzolez, now covered in flowers, still suckled the child at her breast. Hermano Morales' instinct was to take the child from the breast, as if the whole scene was unnatural, obscene. Instead, he could see there would be resistance from the multitude of women and elders now occupying the room.

"Let us say a prayer," He looked to Eduardo, the child's father, for help. Eduardo nodded and they began the Lord's Prayer. Half way through, Hermano Morales heard the strange sound of a cat. But no, it was the child who turned her small head and looked at him with her cold silver gray eyes. She moved her mouth and made a sound. And as the multitude continued the prayer, he went over to the child, and put his ear to her head.

A second later he pulled himself away from the body of Maria Gonzales and the child called Fatima. He was seized by fear.

"My friends," he shouted, "we have an evil force among us, an unnatural force that can only be called by its rightful name! Jesus battled it in the dessert for forty days and nights, and we . . . we have it here among us now!"

Eduardo stood up and just as he was about to protest Hermano Morales raised his hands above his head

"Stop! Let not the devil confuse our souls. I sense evil among us! I must take this child and do the work of the Lord! She must die as her mother has died. This is what is natural and right!"

Although he expressed this with strong conviction, Morales was conflicted.

Several of the villagers nodded in agreement. As Eduardo began to protest, two of the men standing near the door came forward to restrain him.

"It is the will of the Lord!" Hermano Morales raised his hands up to the heavens. But he wasn't exactly sure what to do next. He wasn't sure what his role called him to do. Eduardo was staring at him in shocked disbelief, but everyone else in the room seemed to be deep in silent prayer. Even Miguel did not question Alvaro Morales' decision. But it was the first time in Hermano Morales' forty-eight years that he not only questioned his own judgment, but also the authority by which he made his claim. And how was it that people could so readily accept the claim of evil as the cause of an unexplained event? Could it not be just as readily a sign from God? But wasn't Fatima a Muslim name after all? Could he kill a child who might be a messenger from God? Or was she from the Prince of Lies? How can anyone be sure?

And so, doubting the correctness of his actions Hermano Morales took the child away with only a feeble protest from Eduardo, on his mission to send her back to God. But *how* does one send a child back to God? God doesn't give instructions on how to send a baby back.

As he carried Fatima close to him, this lovely special child made tiny movements against his body.

As he stood alone on the bridge and looked down at the swollen river below he searched in vain for guidance, for inspiration, for anything but this.

"If I cast her off and she lives, she is God's child. If I cast her off and she dies, she must be of the devil," he whispered struggling. Just then, a breeze blew up the valley, and he instinctively drew Fatima closer to him. It was a sign.

TWO

"When I look at her kneeling beside the wall. I see something entirely different. I see perfect, unbridled fanaticism. And it brings such joy to my heart. It is my favorite drink because it so deliciously frightens the angels of reason back into the towering amygdalae of fear—root causes and all."

"I know . . . you call it faith. But what is faith? Is it not a poverty of intellect that has led so many to my side; and this is the best part Saraqael: to do my sharpest work. I need not lift a finger, and yet I win! But it is you Saraqael . . . you are the one, the one with the greatest challenge. I sit back and watch.

"Look over there; a child is picking up a stone to throw at the woman praying by the wall. Did I do that? Did I bring her to Jerusalem? Did I cause it to happen? No Saraqael, you know I did not. I merely have to exist. I am possibility. I am always an option. I am the force-not-reason pop philosophers covet.

"Reason is such a stiff shirt isn't she? Or is it he? Never mind . . . no matter, as that guru-millionaire said . . . have another drink. Why not drive stone drunk and kill a mother rushing home? Don't you see, Saraqael, it's Bloody Fucking Nature!"

He sipped his drink. "I know you Abaddon. I know you'll find a way to be charming and irresistible. You perfected the art of rhetoric. So what will it be this time? Hmm . . . A priest? A Mullah? Another politician? Why is it you get to play the hero?"

"Come, come Saraqael, my rant is not important. We are creatures of the *Noosphere*, that land of possibility, of evolving mindscape. You always get so damn depressed. Give us a fight! A spanking good fight, I promise you, by Jove we'll have a good tale to tell.

"So I am priest." Turning to Saraqael he fingered his long black beard like a prayer wheel.

"Have you ever heard of the Fatima Prophecies, Stephen?" Father Burkholtz asked, handing a red file folder to Parmata.

It had to be two inches thick at least. Parmata took the folder and sat down on the black leather couch in Father Burkholtz's book-lined office.

"Excuse me, I should ask you if you'd like some coffee, or a glass of water perhaps?"

"Water's fine, thanks."

Father Burkholtz opened a cabinet door, took out two small bottles of Evian and poured a glass as Parmata began to read the file. "Let me begin by saying thank you for coming. I know it's a long way from Australia, and New York is not your favorite destination, I mean, after the attacks and everything. I know you've been busy with other things since then. But at any rate, I'm glad you could spare me the time."

"Your email was cryptic to say the least, Father."

"Some have called the Fatima prophecies the most well-known apparitions of the Virgin Mary. As you may recall, in 1917 during the First World War three shepherd children in Portugal claimed to have seen an apparition of the Blessed Virgin, and also at that time certain—how shall I say—unexplained events took place, witnessed by a number of local people including a vision of the sun dancing and darting erratically about the sky. And, as is well known, during her many visits to the children, Mother Mary supposedly gave the children several prophecies. The last, or the so-called third prophecy, has recently been released and some say it contains damaging information about the inner politics of the Vatican and our Holy Mother Church. What most people don't know is that there was another prophecy . . . a fourth. *That* is what I wanted to talk to you about." Father Burkholtz took a long drink of water and wiped the dew from his moustache before he continued.

In the pause, Parmata read the first paragraph from the file. *A mysterious child will come and an ancient prophesy will be fulfilled . . . the coming of the second Paraclete, or advocate of the Holy Spirit . . .*

And quoting the eldest of the three children, Lucia dos Santos during one of the long periods of questioning, " . . . but I tell you the truth, don't you see, it is to your advantage . . . the Holy Mother said, that I must go away, for if I do not, the Paraclete will not come to you, but if I go, I will send her to you."

"And of course," Father Burkholtz studied Parmata with kind compassionate eyes, "it was nothing more than a re-hashing of John 16:7."

"And you put it down to some kind of psychological mimickery."

"Yes. Exactly."

"So, what's the big deal then?"

"She said, 'her', not him, which up until now didn't mean much."

"But something has changed. I mean . . . something has changed your mind."

"Let me put it this way. The Holy See Mission to the UN has received certain information concerning a child who could be considered by some to be a candidate for the role of—how shall I say it—that special child."

"And you want me to find the child?"

"There is more you need to know. The fourth prophecy revealed the Paraclete would be a unifying force between Muslims and Christians."

"And you fear her falling into the wrong hands?"

"There is a risk she could be used for fanatic political purposes. She needs to be protected, educated, allowed to grow up on her own terms, to experience her own life, and not one manipulated for political ends. She needs to have a family, and grow up away from all this." He dropped onto the leather couch beside Parmata. "You of all people know what I mean Stephen . . . you of all people."

Parmata knew what he was getting at.

"So, this child, this girl from Guatemala, what are the next steps?"

"Not so fast Stephen. I think you need to know a bit more about her. I mean what we know so far. You see, the information we have isn't clear, but we believe the outcome, that is, whether the Paraclete is a force of good or evil is determined by the sex of the child. We just don't know which way it goes."

"You don't expect me to buy that medieval, good or evil stuff do you? Won't that depend on how she's raised? Or are we heading for a debate on nature versus nurture here?"

"We'll have that debate another time, I'm sure, Stephen. But first we, I mean *you* if you are willing, must find the child."

"And the child, the girl, is exactly where?"

"She is, as far as we know, still in Guatemala. A local priest, called by the lay minister, thought the child was possessed at birth. The priest went to the village and when he saw the child, and found her mother was dead, he told them he would take the child away, and . . . well, kill her. He said it had to be done. I guess he probably said she was possessed, and it was what God commanded, or something like that. I don't know exactly."

"And they believed him?" Parmata took a small notepad from his breast coat pocket. He unconsciously doodled the words 'random error' before closing the book. *What does that mean?* He couldn't put his finger on it, but he had to look something up: it had something to do with chance—probability, but he couldn't remember.

"Well, they're not exactly a sophisticated bunch. Look, if the most educated guy around tells you that something bizarre and unusual is evil, you'd probably agree. No?"

"I'm not so sure, but I get your point. I mean, we're talking potential infanticide here remember, Father Burkholtz. So, why ask me to find this child. I don't normally go hunting for lost children, or abducted children for that matter. I'm officially retired. I'm supposed to be taking it easy tending the BBQ—that kind of thing."

"But you *are* interested aren't you. I can tell by your eyes, and I see you've made some kind of notation, which I assume means you're going back to look something up. Or am I wrong, Stephen?"

"No, you're right. It's just that, I don't understand . . . why me? Don't you have priests, bishops, or FBI guys affiliated with Opus Dei who could do this?"

"Yes, you're right. There are others, of course. But you, Stephen, aren't one of us, and that's exactly the reason. No one can trace you back to us.

"But we're wasting time. You see if he kills the girl, I mean, what chance do I have. Ergo, what chance do we have of having that debate?" Burkholtz smiled for the first time since Parmata arrived.

"I see; so it's kind of a game, is it then?"

"Not exactly a game Stephen. But like games there is a statistical question of probability and random error in these things, wouldn't you agree?"

"I'll have to discuss it with Christie of course."

"Yes, of course you will.

THREE

"If we did not exist we would have to be invented, the Sage once wrote. That sage could have been me." Abaddon spoke, without emotion from behind his sunglasses. He was growing impatient. He was also very thirsty.

The jewel called Jerusalem reflected in Abaddon's sunglasses. "Let us move forward say twenty years then. The child has grown into a beautiful woman, like the one over there. Although, I admit, it is hard to tell from where we stand." An Israeli Defense Force convoy sped past on its way to a twitching slugfest in Ramallah. Saraqael looked at the army vehicles as they left a trail of dust behind them. "You have done some nice work, my friend."

"I cannot take all the credit myself. But we, we two are a formidable force; don't you agree Saraqael?" Abaddon ground the cigarette butt with his shoe. "Surely, you the Angel of Death have earned your stripes too."

Saraqael said nothing. He too was growing thirsty.

When Asma stepped off the plane in Halifax, the cold damp air sent a shiver down her spine. She was tired and in a foul mood. How she hated the cold and damp, and that was Canada no matter where she stood. She was raised in Queensland, and now, her parents decided to move back to her mother's native Nova Scotia. It was incomprehensible to her how her mother could leave Australia for this gray sky and barren rocky landscape dotted with grubby-looking excuses for trees. She was also upset about a recent phone call. Her father called to ask her to come quickly to Nova Scotia to see her mother who was diagnosed with metastatic breast cancer. It had already spread to her lungs and brain. Asma was angry and fearful at the same time. She'd recently started college in New York where the weather was not much better than in Nova Scotia but at least there the electrified energy of the place made her skin tingle with excitement. She was growing to love New York's devil-may-care attitude and in contrast Nova Scotia carried an air of disappointment about it. But her mother was born here, and she had to ask her something so profoundly personal she couldn't yet articulate it in her own mind. She simply knew she had to be near her mother, her adopted mother, before she died.

Now in her 21st year Asma spoke five languages fluently: English, French, Spanish, Arabic, and Hebrew. She took to languages with uncanny aptitude. Even more unusual perhaps was her skill in mathematics. She achieved a perfect score in her math SATs. She was very confident; some might say she was arrogant because she did not tolerate fools or adolescent frivolity. She was a passionate learner, a serious student. But whatever her classmates at Columbia University thought of her, no one could deny, she was a tall, radiant black-haired beauty with the most exquisite olive colored skin.

But Asma could also be cruel and manipulative. And it was a dark mood as thick as the maritime fog that held her that afternoon as she turned her rented silver Chrysler Sebring Coupe into her parents' driveway. Their leased white saltbox house overlooked Chester Basin on the South Shore. The sound of the groaner's clanging bell rang out its lugubrious warning to boats in the basin as she stepped out of the car. The salty sea air stung her nostrils as she inhaled the pungent smell of the seaweed.

Parmata stood in the door as she stopped by the car inhaling the fresh ocean air.

"Can I give you a hand with your things?"

Asma didn't say a word; she kept staring out toward Tancook Island. The island made famous in Frank Parker Day's novel *Rockbound*. The fog was so thick she could barely make out the outline of the black sleeping giant.

Parmata walked over to her standing by the car. "Do you want a hand with your things?" he asked startling her.

"Oh, sorry, I didn't hear you," turning to look him in the eyes.

Her sliver gray-blue eyes smiled, but he could tell she was tired. "You must be weary from your journey. I'll help you get all this inside. We'll get you settled away and I can update you later." He evaluated her with almost military precision.

"I'll be fine," she snapped back. "I just need a cup of tea or something."

"Right. We'll get right on it as soon as we get you tucked away." But as he carried her things up the stairs to her room, the tension rose higher with every step. No matter how he tried, there had always been a tension between them. It would always be her and Christie. They always had a unique connection, a special way of seeing the world. He'd seen it from the very beginning. He told himself he wasn't jealous.

"I think you're getting old, Stephen." She always called him Stephen, never father, that's the way he had always wanted it. "Yes, I guess I am. It's just all this homecare—it's made an old lady of me."

"Now let's not go there." Placing a kiss on his cheek she gave him a quick forced smile as a sidecar to it. "Let me freshen up. I'll be down in a couple of minutes for that cup of tea. Is Christie awake? I can't wait to see her."

"Yes, she's been looking forward to seeing you too. She's having a nap, but she should be awake in a while."

"What about that tea then?"

"Yes, that'll be the ticket, I'll go fix us a pot." Outside the bedroom door, he stopped, and turned around. "Is there a boy in New York?"

"Stephen, I'll be right down." And she closed the door to her room.

She walked over to the window and looked outside. The fog was thick as Devon cream as she tried to make out the outline of Tancook Island. And there she saw it, a small boat barely visible through the fog. It looked like an old fishing dory with two men struggling to gather up a lobster pot. *Maybe poachers*, she thought as she undressed and took a quick shower.

When she stepped out of the shower she took the towel off the rack and walked over to the window. There was something about the fog over the ocean that attracted her. It was a wet mystery with the promise of intrigue.

Out on the mirror calm water a man looked up from the dory at the naked woman standing in the window. "She has a rare beauty, Abaddon."

"And that is to our advantage," Abaddon replied hauling an illicit lobster pot and contents into the boat.

"She is still young and has much to learn about the world and its ways. Her moody, inquisitive passion will serve her well."

"I sincerely believe, my friend, that you are becoming sentimental," Saraqael nodded, and they both laughed. "That's a good one . . . The Prince of Lies and the Angel of Death become maudlin. Ha, ha, ha."

Asma pulled on her blue jeans and grabbed a pullover as she made her way out the door, and slowly down the steep staircase to where Christie was sitting in the living room. It was getting dark outside and the fog merely added a grainy texture to the night air.

Christie looked pale and older sitting there in a wooden rocking chair wearing a blue terry cloth housecoat and red Acorn slippers. She was getting to the point where it was hard to tell if you were looking at Christie or the disease. Either way she looked like she was dying of cancer. Asma fought back tears as she reached out for her mother's thin, dry hands. But it was the hair that really shocked Asma. Christie's beautiful blonde hair was gone. She had avoided looking Christie in the eyes, but when she did the fine wisps of fluttering hair on her scalp caught her attention again. It was just too painful.

"Good to see you Asma." Christie finally broke the interminable silence. "How are things going at school?"

"Fine Christie. Things in New York are fine . . . I mean it's really good. I love the place and the people are just so international. I love that."

"Tell me about your friends. What are they like?"

"They're like people," Asma snapped reflexively. And instead of apologizing she became defensive. "I didn't come to talk about my friends in New York. I came to see you. How are things going? I mean the chemo must have been hell."

"Yes." Christie understood Asma valued her privacy above everything. "After Johns Hopkins we came here to recuperate. There wasn't anything more they could do. So, I wanted to come home, to where I was born . . . to die." Hearing those words, Asma let go of her hands and walked over to the window turning her back on Christie.

Home, home, it was this notion of home that dogged Asma. She knew she was adopted there was no hiding that. Her dark hair and olive skin were a story she herself didn't know. Some day she would find her real parents. Stephen and Christie had been special parents but there was no escaping the fact that they weren't her natural parents. A piece of her was missing. That hollow was growing every day like the cancer in Christie's body.

"I have met someone." Asma turned to look at Christie. "But it's not a romantic kind of thing, I mean. His name is Dhul Fiqar. He's got a doctorate in philosophy from Oxford University. He's been teaching me about some of the Christian Gnostics and he's introduced me to the Koran and Islamic religious ideas. Talking to him has been, well, like an awakening, as if a black hole had been filled with a clear blue light. I don't know how else to describe it. I guess I find him enlightening."

"Is this a course you're taking?" Christie suddenly grew tired.

"No, nothing like that Christie; he's just someone I know. You asked, but enough of him, you look very tired; perhaps you should rest again."

"Yes, you are right, I don't seem to have much stamina these days. It has been good to see you. I'm so glad you could come. I know it's not easy to travel now between Canada and the States, with the border, I mean. But I do hope we can spend some time together. It would be good. I love you Asma." And they hugged each other in silence.

"I thought you might want that tea," Parmata offered walking into the room in his usual determined fashion holding a tray of tea and cookies. "I hope I'm not interrupting." He abruptly halted when he saw them embracing.

"No, no, tea is good," Christie invited him forward, taking a hanky from her pocket, drying the tears from her eyes. "Perhaps you and Asma could have tea. I think it's time for bed, if you don't mind Stephen."

"No, why should I mind," he set the tray on a coffee table in the center of the room. "Here, I'll give you a hand." And they both helped Christie to her bedroom adjacent to the living room.

"Have a good rest, mother." Asma lightly brushed Christie's cheek with her hand.

"Thank you Asma, it's so good to hear you call me mother," and she closed her eyes.

Asma and Parmata quietly retreated to the living room and Asma poured them both a cup of tea before throwing herself down on the leather sofa beside him.

"She doesn't have long, does she Stephen?" Asma searched her reflection in the hot dark liquid in her hands for a reason to life and death. "Does she suffer much?" She asked looking at Parmata who seemed to have aged this past year caring for Christie. Deep lines around his eyes and mouth tightened as muscles held back tears. He reached out and touched Asma's hand in silence.

A loud knock on the door startled Asma spilling her tea on the floor. Parmata went to answer while she stood watching him open the front door.

"Good day to you sir. I was wondering if I might use your telephone? Our truck seems to have broken down," the man explained.

"Sure." The visitor entered. "The phone's over there," He gestured toward the black analog phone on the wall in the kitchen. It was then that Asma first saw the tallish man of Middle Eastern origin, about 35 years old with long black hair tied to hang down his back and a wispy black beard. He wore a black leather jacket, blue jeans, and black runners. As he reached for the phone their eyes met across the distance of the room. He had a prominent mole on his left cheek. Asma had never seen him before, but she sensed she had. It was curious, but he looked familiar; it was very odd, and it made her uncomfortable. For a long time she felt she was being watched, or watched over; a shiver ran up her spine like perhaps she'd seen a ghost.

The stranger hung up the phone, thanked Parmata and left without looking at Asma again. "What was that all about?" Asma asked as Parmata closed the door.

"Nothing, a local whose truck broke down on the road. He called a friend to come pick him up. Why? You look frightened. Too much time in New York?"

"Yes, perhaps." Asma recovered her composure. "He just seemed so familiar in a strange way that's all."

"There are lots of immigrants around these parts now, if that's what you mean."

"Perhaps that's it. I don't know, just a feeling. Maybe I am tired after the journey. I think I'll head upstairs to bed."

"Fine. We'll finish that chat in the morning. I'm really interested to hear about your studies and life in New York. But that can wait."

He kissed her on the forehead and she disappeared up the stairs to her room. Parmata went back to the kitchen and turned all the lights out. He looked out the window and saw two men in a Toyota pick-up truck head up the lane toward Bentley's Road. *Maybe it was beginning*, he thought. Father Burkholtz had advised there could be a 'twisting point' or *torsade de pointe* as he had called it. *Something could click, like a switch had been pulled that would take her life in another direction*, he heard Father Burkholtz say like a voice from the past. *Maybe it was time she knew the truth.*

FOUR

The next morning Asma got up early. She quickly got dressed and took a walk along the rocky shoreline. The fog had lifted overnight revealing the green cookie cutter fields of Tancook Island in the crisp clear morning light. Waves rolled rhythmically along the beach as she carefully stepped over broken seashells and other debris cast-up on the shore; bits of black tarry rope, a small red plastic bucket, a child's salty shoe, and old broken lobster traps bore silent witness as her footprints along the sand were erased by the rising tide. The pungent smell of seaweed and a gentle breeze were as cleansing as any aromatherapy as she stopped to watch the Seagulls overhead perform their ritual dance, flying patterns darting between the island and the mainland in search of food. She wondered what it would be like to live on an island, to take a ferry whenever you had to go: shopping or to visit someone. It would probably make you reluctant to leave the island and what would that be like with nothing but books and the weather for company. She tried to imagine the people who lived over there and what their daily routines might be like. In some ways it must be like another planet, very lonely. But they must like it; they must be passionate about their choice; it would have to be a choice, or perhaps a self-imposed exile to escape the world. Like that man she saw last night in Stephen's kitchen. Why did she feel like she'd seen him somewhere before?

"You'd like the island," a man's voice came from behind, startling her.

"Geez, you scared the hell out of me," she jumped and turned to see the same man with the wispy beard she'd just been thinking about.

"Where did you come from?" She demanded with a combination of anger and fear. They were alone on the beach.

"Sorry, miss, I didn't mean to startle you." The soft-spoken man searched his pockets as if he were looking for something to give her.

"What do you expect when you sneak up on people?" She retorted in a distinctly angry tone. "Who are you anyway, and what do you want?"

"I live on the island," he reported without emotion, taking a St. Christopher's medal about the size of a quarter from his pocket and holding it in the palm of his hand in front of Asma. "It's for you. It means good luck."

She didn't accept the gift. Instead, she asked, "Why are you here?"

Still holding the medal in his hand, "I just saw you looking at the island and most people never get a chance to go over. I mean I just thought you might want to take a look for yourself. And I thought the medal might show you I intended no harm."

"I see." She took the medal in her hand examining it closely. It was exquisite and appeared to be made of gold. "Is this worth a lot of money?" she asked looking the strange man in the eye. "It looks like it could be an antique."

"I don't know nothing about that, miss." He looked down and nervously shuffled his feet. "When I saw you at the house last night . . . well, and I saw you again this morning . . . well, I thought maybe you wanted to go over to the island sometime; to see it I mean. Lots of people want to."

"Well, that's an interesting offer, I suppose."

"My brother and I do some lobster fishin', if you know what I mean," he smiled for the first time revealing discolored, irregular teeth.

"I don't even know your name."

"Excuse me, miss." He held out his large leathery hand. "People here call me Robin."

"But you're not from around here are you Robin," Asma shook his hand.

"No, miss, you're right. I was born in Britain, but my parents were from Sri Lanka, or Ceylon, as it was once known. My brother and I came over here to get away from the madness."

"What madness?" Asma asked growing increasingly interested in this strange, mysterious but gentle man.

"I guess you could call it fanaticism. I mean there are so many religious nuts out there these days."

"And you don't agree with them," she added, unsure of where this was going.

"Well, it's not that we don't believe in anything, but we just didn't like the way some people were trying to impose things on us. Society, I mean. You see, me and my brother are very devout, but not so much in a traditional way; more I guess as agents of social change."

"So you're politics forced you to leave. Is that it?"

"You should come to the island, and see for yourself," he looked with those dark eyes toward Tancook Island.

"I'd love to, perhaps some other time. You see my mother is very ill; dying in fact and I've come to see her. But perhaps another time," she allowed a brief smile.

"Yes, I see. Your mother is it? Another time it is then." And she began to walk back along the beach toward the house. Suddenly she stopped and turned back to Robin still looking at her.

"People call you Robin, but what's your real name then?"

"Saraqael," he smiled, twisting the hairs on his wispy beard. She nodded and turned away starting to walk back toward the house, and then, she didn't know why but she had to look back at the strange scruffy man again, but he was gone; vanished without so much as a sound.

When Asma got back to the house Parmata was watching CNN. Another terrorist attack had just been reported. Reports were sketchy but according to early reports the water supply of London had been the target of a terrorist attack. A large amount of an unknown chemical agent had been released into the city's water supply. Thousands of people were flooding emergency rooms with symptoms ranging from flu to difficulty breathing, and cardiac arrest. It looked like just the beginning, and authorities were warning people not to drink the water or take a shower.

"Here we go again," Parmata announced as Asma walked into the room. "More fanatics in London."

"It's hard to know what to believe," Asma's teeth clenched as an intense anger welled inside her. "They'll probably blame Muslim extremists again, no doubt."

"Nobody has blamed anyone yet, and no one has taken credit for this either. But there's no justification for this kind of action no matter who did it."

"You're so ready to believe the anti-Muslim propaganda aren't you?"

Parmata was shocked. He'd never heard Asma voice a strong political opinion before. "Is this what they're teaching you at Columbia?" he asked provocatively. She just stared at him with a look of deep disgust. "You don't understand Asma. Everyone you meet out there isn't a good person ready to help make the world a better place. I know, I've lived in it longer than you and had to deal with some of them."

"And that makes you a better person!" Her voice rose. She didn't understand the passion rising like a tide within her. It was as exhilarating as riding a horse bareback.

"It's got nothing to do with me. It's about right and wrong, surely you can see that."

"And who defines right and wrong: the government, or God; or maybe just you and your buddies when it suits you. You always act so superior but I know what you did to that poor Greg Fallows. How you destroyed his life with lies, and for what? How you and your cronies fabricated Greg Fallows was a terrorist and used him for your own ends. What exactly is a terrorist anyway? I mean, how can you sit there and define some people as terrorists and others as freedom fighters?"

"You don't understand Asma. I didn't create Greg. He was his own worst enemy. He killed that Dutch archeologist in cold blood.

It was his ambition, his greed, and his perverse personality that drove him to be in the wrong place at the wrong time. The best I could do was to rescue your mother from the nightmare he created."

"My mother that's a fine one. That's a good one. You know damn well I was adopted. You know I'm different, but you won't tell me why. I've always been different. Look at me! Why won't you tell me the truth for once? Just this once!"

"I will Asma, I will. This is isn't the right time. Your mother isn't well; she's dying. You can see that. Please do her the courtesy of at least waiting," Parmata rose and placed his hand on her shoulder, which she abruptly removed as she stood up to face him. By now she was boiling with anger.

"Fuck you, Stephen. Fuck all of you racist bastards. Fuck this charade. Why can't you admit it? You adopted me out of some racist guilt complex. I'm out of here."

She never got to the *root cause* argument, but she would; Saraqael was sure of that. He and Abaddon had hoped she would but there was plenty of time. They loved sophistry and pop philosophy. It could be used to justify so many actions and reactions. It's a bit of blame the victim thinking that could find the roots of anti-Semitism in the actions of Jewish settlers, or imply a justification for terror attacks on innocent Americans in abstract foreign policy terms. "Ah, but what can you expect Saraqael from those who think reason is a bastard?" he stirred the coals in the fire. Their less than opulent surroundings were in sharp contrast to their lofty ideals. But they go wherever they must, such is the price of righteousness—even to this god-forsaken Azerbaijan.

"They play the lyre of hedonism and put arsenic in the mullah's lunch! Ha, ha, ha," Saraqael laughed, putting another fist full of rice unceremoniously in his mouth, pieces clinging to his beard.

"In times of war, I ask you, is it wrong to kill someone on sight for disobeying orders?" Abaddon asked facetiously as he reached for the naan bread.

"Of course not, revenge is the sweetest spice of all," Saraqael poured a cup of mint tea. The vapors rose in the cold and darkened ruins of the charred government building. "And your mother and sisters are whores! Ha, ha, ha."

"But let us finish our lunch and get back to work. It's always better to make war on a full belly!"

"You are right in this my friend, but first give us some more hashish, your farts are making me ill."

FIVE

Asma unlocked the door to her apartment and burst into the room like an Alberta clipper bearing down on a helpless Chicago in January. But it was only November. Her icy mood had not been improved by the journey back to New York. She stormed into the darkness and threw her pack on the floor in the corner with a thud, slamming the door behind her and collapsing on the sofa in front of the window on the verge of tears. Her mind was a cauldron of dark emotion, twisting her spirit into a tight relentless purple knot. She had grown angrier every passing mile. The flight had annoyed her, the customs agents had hassled her about her student visa, and even the smell of the leather sofa irritated her. Nauseous, she ran to the bathroom in time to relieve herself of that 'Reubin made by a Cuban' at Philadelphia airport. That was another thing that aggravated her, why did she have to fly to Philie to get here?

As she stumbled back to the living room and flicked on the light, the phone rang.

"Hello," she tried to ignore the acid taste in back of her throat.

"Asma, you're home." It was Dhul Fiqar the former Oxford Don. Dhul was now teaching an epidemiology course at Columbia. The study of disease was his thing, and more recently he'd become interested in the development of an international computer network to alert health and government agents of any rapidly spreading epidemic such as anthrax or pneumonic plague. Without a linked dataset a bioterrorist attack could go unnoticed until it was too late. That morning he had been offered a position at the Center for Civilian Biodefense Strategies at Johns Hopkins.

"Dhul, how are you? This isn't a really great time for me. I just got back from Nova Scotia, and well, I'm not feeling great just now." Although she said these words, she wanted to talk to someone, to try and understand this turmoil within. She liked Dhul's quiet almost continental charm, his suave yet mysterious Johnny Depp look, and his unthreatening demeanor. He'd never made a pass at her, and that made her both intrigued and comfortable around him. He wasn't much older than her, only in his late twenties, and he already had a doctorate from Oxford's Radcliffe College. "You see, it's my mother, she's dying, and it's been difficult these past few days."

Yes, I see. Well, I don't want to intrude, but if you'd like to talk?" He poured on the charm.

"You know, you're right," she interrupted. "It would be good to talk. Why don't you come over? I'll clean up. You know what? I think I'm feeling better already," she laughed; that was a good sign the storm was breaking. Or it could be that she was beginning to understand that only through action and taking control could she tame the beast?

"That's the spirit. I've got some ideas I wanted to pass by you. And I've been offered a position at Hopkins."

"Dhul, that's fantastic!"

"Yeah, but it's in Baltimore, if you know what I mean."

"Look, you get yourself over here and we'll decide what to do from there."

A confident Dhul Fiqar stepped out of the taxi at 161 West 95th Street. As a child growing up in the south London borough of Bromley, the only son of Sri Lankan immigrant parents he dreamed of escaping to New York. In his parents' home in Bromley a family photograph sitting on the coffee table taken when Dhul was six showed all three of them agonizingly looking into the camera as if waiting for the pain to go away. The boy, with his straight black hair, already down to his collar sat uncomfortably nestled in the crook of his father's arm.

He was a quiet introspective child who showed immense academic promise. He was sent to Thomas Tallis secondary school in Kidbrooke, southeast London where the other students saw him as a loner. "He was a bit queer; studying all the time," one former schoolmate observed. By age 16, however, Dhul Fiqar had a stellar academic record and won a scholarship for early entrance to Oxford University. His parents were extremely proud of him, and although he rarely saw them after he left for Oxford they always sent him something special for his birthday.

It was this something he held in his hand as he rang the bell to apartment 1B. A thing of great rarity, a leather and gold bound copy of the Koran in Arabic Kufic script from 11th century Morocco together with a copy of the first Bible printed in the Western Hemisphere, the "Eliot Indian Bible" translated into the Algonquin language by John Eliot, the Cambridge missionary. His parents must have found it in a flea market in London. It was an odd combination of texts put together in 1881 by a University of London professor by the name of John Allan Tyndall, author of the little known and even less often read "The Tyrant of Syracuse." In fact, the preface by Professor Tyndall called for the education of what has come to be known as the "philo-tyrannical" leader. In it he argues the history of the West has been to conquer and suppress the East, especially the wisdom of the East. "The leader who has moved beyond merely being 'sunburned' by ideas into the world of action, of politics, in order to change the world, is consistent with the old Gnostic idea that Evil is often good in the making." It was an energizing idea on this misty evening as the wheezing sulfurous traffic snaked its way around Central Park. Dhul didn't really want to talk about Baltimore. He wanted to talk about action.

Asma answered the door wearing blue jeans and a tan sweatshirt with the word "Roots" written in large black letters across the front. "Dhul, you're always so punctual. What's that?" She pointed to the book in his hand.

"Oh, it's a gift from my parents. I thought it might cheer you up a bit."

"Well, that's awfully nice," she motioned him to come in.

"Look, I know you're under a lot of stress with your mother dying and everything, but I had to see you."

"Sure . . . no, actually, I'm glad to see you. I've been in such a dark mood since Nova Scotia. And I want to talk to you about this fellow I ran into there. He seemed so alien or something. I mean he had the air of an outlaw or something about him."

"What are you talking about," Dhul handed her his black leather coat.

"I met this guy on the beach in Nova Scotia, at my 'parents.'" She used the two-fingered hand signal for quotation marks when she said parents. "Things have been hell. I mean, I'm so glad to be back here, away from that dreary place."

"Nova Scotia?" Dhul followed her into the living room not really listening.

"No, not Nova Scotia; it's beautiful. I mean my 'parent's' house." She used that sign language again.

"Sorry, I didn't understand the hand gesture that's all."

"Well, that's the whole thing isn't it? I mean that's the crux of it. They're not really my parents, are they? I told you I was adopted."

"Yes, you did, but I don't understand. I thought you got along with your parents?"

"But I do, that's just it; I do," she threw herself down on the sofa across from him.

"Well then, I don't get it," he placed the rare book on the coffee table between them. "I mean, if you love your parents, and they are good to you, what difference does it make that they're not your biological parents?"

"That's just it; intellectually, I know that, but emotionally there's something else happening. You know, it's like I know something is right but feel it's wrong."

"I see," stroking his goatee. "I guess I understand the sweat shirt now!"

She laughed. "Yeah, I guess that was subliminal."

"So what's with the book?" She moved closer to the book on the coffee table.

"That you wouldn't believe. It's a rare book my parents gave me for my birthday."

"When's your birthday?" she asked with a devilish grin.

"Relax, it was last month actually. But my parents sent me this gift they bought in a flea market in London. It's fantastic is what it is. I mean it got me thinking about life and why we're here. Do you ever think about that?"

"Yeah, sure do. That's what put me in such a foul mood on the way back. What's the book about?" She picked it up to admire the craftsmanship of the binding.

"Well, it's a very old copy of the Koran and the Bible. It's rare for a number of reasons: not the least being the holy texts being in the same publication which of itself is odd. But the commentary is really very modern. It uses the holy texts to justify the editor's radical views. It's a kind of Gnostic revelation of the Prophet, truly remarkable and unique. You must read it."

"Wow! It's so timely too. I mean with everything that's happened lately," tracing the leather cover with her finger. "Do you believe ideas can change the world?" She looked past Dhul to the New York skyline.

"I sure do. Especially after reading this book."

"Have you ever met anyone exceptional Dhul?"

"What do you mean?"

"Well, I met this fellow in Nova Scotia, on the beach. Like you he was from the UK. But there was something oddly compelling about him. He gave me this medallion." She took the thing from her jeans pocket and held it out in her hand.

"Let me see that." Dhul took the coin from her hand. "It's very odd, very odd indeed. I mean, look, I can scrape off this superficial gold finish and there is another image underneath."

"Really?" Astounded, she drew herself closer to Dhul and the coin. "What could it possibly mean?"

"I don't know? Do you have a small knife?" he asked holding the coin up in the air for a closer look.

"Sure," and she went to the kitchen.

He took the knife and began scraping the gold off the coin. Sure enough underneath there was a silver coin.

"What is it Dhul?" Asma asked, shocked.

"I'm no expert but I'd say it was perhaps a Roman or Greek coin. Look a this odd cluster of snakes and what looks like a monogram 'Pi epsilon rho'."

"What does it mean Dhul?" Asma stood in front of him.

"I don't know Asma. I don't know. We'll have to ask someone who does." And he flipped the coin in the air in a mock coin toss. "Heads or tails," he called watching the medallion spin on the floor. "I know this guy in Jersey. He might know."

"Call him," handing him the phone.

"Now?"

"Sure, why not, traffic should be dying down. I have a feeling about this."

"What kind of feeling?" He handed the coin back to her.

"I don't know, like it has something to do with me."

"Let's just go," he stood up. "He'll be at home. He's always there."

SIX

Saraqael and Abaddon may do as they please because I created them. They come and go. We recognize them by their attitude, not their outward appearances. They act as they please because I have created them as a means to objectify daily phenomena. In that sense, they are real like Asma's coin. And yet we fear them, we fear them because we do not know what lurks beyond the blackness of the present. The past is filled with regret, and the future is yet to be sullied. We invent the hobgoblins of ideas to embody all those things we do not understand like death and evil, and why some people make the choices they do; because in the end it all comes down to choices, forks in the road, action, in doing or choosing not to, or perhaps the horns of a different dilemma. We have never been able to de-construct actions without recourse to moral motivation. And so it goes, and so it goes.

Asma was again roiling in the quagmire of her unsettled emotion when the taxi pulled up to the curb at 334 Broadway Ave., Paterson, New Jersey. The dilapidated three story red brick apartment building had a corroding white fire escape hanging off the front. The whole place looked like it was past ready for the wrecker's ball. Old newspapers glided about in the night gusts of wind mixed with the smell of exhaust and ganja. Screaming teenagers, mostly black and refugees from Medicaid bumped intoxicatingly into the remains of a rusting blue Honda Civic on their way down the street in search of more anesthetic to numb their pain. Was it any wonder it was so easy to recruit the new foot soldiers in the war? And what war you ask? That eternal, never-ending war that was known as the human comedy.

As you have seen, Dhul is intelligent, engaging, and as you are about to learn, passionate about one thing—action, not words, or ideas, or even philosophy. Such is the commitment of the converted, fervent believer in anything. It's as if existence itself breeds flies.

Asma stood staring at poverty, experiencing a youthful revulsion for what she saw as the greedy classes that kept the poor uneducated, narcotized, and unemployed. She kicked a rusting piece of muffler hard against the curb in solemn solidarity with the downtrodden of this world. The clanging ricochet scared a black cat that scurried from under the fender of a red Dodge parked on the street behind the Honda. It ran up the fire escape to a second floor balcony where the creature settled down to watch Asma and Dhul. Asma was outgrowing her sentimental schooling. She was acquiring the self-righteous arrogance of the believer. This was an important part of commitment to Divinity: act as the force of your Divine nature urges you. Is this not the foundation of all religions, the spirit within etc.? But therein lay the difficulty: the contradictory night and day of it, the essential antipodes of this realm of Being. But we're getting ahead of ourselves aren't we?

The smell of urine and decay filled the air as Dhul and Asma stepped inside the foyer of 334 Broadway and another world. It was dark and Asma sensed from the rustling noise that there were people lying about on the floor under the stairs. Dhul whispered, "Follow me" in Asma's ear and they quickly climbed the stairs to the second floor. Seconds later Dhul knocked on the door of apartment 2D.

As they waited for what seemed to Asma like an eternity, Dhul said, in a quiet melodramatic tone, "I've met the Devil you know."

Asma, unsure if he was joking, whispered, "What was he like?"

"Charming" he replied putting his finger to his lips to indicate the need for silence and stealth.

"In that case, I'd like to meet him too." And the door swung open. A very large black cat sat in the cluttered narrow hall of the apartment as if on guard, like a feline Cerberus.

"Good evening Moth," Dhul walked past the sentry. Asma followed. The cat didn't move as they walked by into the dimly lit living room, if you could call it that. Asma had never seen anything quite like it before. It was as if every newspaper ever printed was pilled at least four feet high. There was a pathway wide enough for a thin person to make their way through the maze-like squalor to another room where a bald overweight middle-aged man sat in an old wing back chair watching one of the all news channels on television. The same black cat that had been at the door was now sitting on his lap watching the news.

"How'd the cat get in here so fast?" Although Asma was nervous, the putrid smell of decomposing food and cat urine forced her to concentrate on not throwing up again. She didn't want an encore.

"Ah, you mean Mr. Moth, a most remarkable fellow," the man stroked the black cat with his long puffy fingers. "He is an exceptional creature, of rare lineage and intelligence. But we'll talk more of Moth later—of this I am sure. You have come to talk. But please, I am a dullard, please sit down, and let me introduce myself Asma." He motioned for Asma and Dhul to sit on a stack of newspapers. It looked as if this room was following the living room's lead. Dhul found a stack of suitable height and sat down. Asma followed his lead.

"My name is Jahaan Haddad. People call me Johnny," and he extended his cool right hand to Asma. "It is an honor to meet you. I've heard so much about you. And certainly your beauty has not been exaggerated. You're giving me a hard on just sitting here," and he laughed. Asma winced. "Dhul why don't you get us some tea, you know where to find it. Lapsang Souchong would be nice." Dhul disappeared in the corridors of newspapers leaving Asma and Johnny Haddad alone. He stroked Moth delicately behind the ears. "Moth likes to watch the news. It relaxes him. And you Asma what interests you?" The room was dimly lit—only the flickering from the television cast a glow on the unpleasantness.

"Life, I mean, people interest me, I guess," Asma gathered a picture of Johnny Haddad in her eyes amid the strobe-like light of the small portable TV. He had a benignly elfish grin with large dark circles around indolent green eyes that gave him a lemur-like expression. A small marooned island of hair on the top of his head highlighted an ocean of bald. He wore a green terry cloth housecoat and blue sweat pants with holes in the knees and old brown leather slippers on his feet. In his left hand he held a foul smelling French cigarette of the Gauloise variety.

"And do I interest you?" Johnny Haddad reached into his housecoat pocket pulling out a coin and holding it out so she could see the inscription. It was the same type of double snake inscribed coin Asma had in her pocket, the same coin given to her by that strange man on the beach in Nova Scotia. The reason Dhul had brought her to Johnny Haddad's.

"Who are you?"

At that moment Dhul came into the room with a pot of tea and four cups.

"Asma was just asking who I was. But perhaps we should have our tea first and I should tell her a story."

Dhul nodded and poured four cups of tea. He gave one to each of them including Mr. Moth, the cat, who lapped up the hot smoky Chinese drink with unusual noisy gusto. As Asma drank her tea, the room became increasingly foggy, almost suffocating her as if the smoke from Haddad's cigarette was filling up the room at hyper-speed. She saw Moth stand up on his hind legs and dance a little jig while Johnny Haddad and Dhul laughed like drunken sailors and clapped along with some Arabesque music playing on the television. In a flash everything seemed to slow down to the speed of a dial-up Internet connection. Now Moth turned summer salts in mid air as he twisted and turned in the fading light of the television. She was reminded of a miniature feline Cirque de Soleil act. And then the room faded to black.

Slowly a holographic image filled the room, which seemed to grow as well. One by one the pixels joined together like pieces in a puzzle to reveal a scene, a painting by Glyn Philpot, depicting the 12th-century English King Richard the Lionheart surrounded by followers preparing to embark on a crusade. King Richard moved his right hand high into the air as the crowd chanted his name, louder and louder; he threw his half-fingered gauntlet on his right hand; flinging it down with a thud where it landed at Asma's feet. When she looked up the vision was gone and the room was returned to its previous arrangement. Moth sat in front of the television wide-eyed, while Dhul and Johnny Haddad quietly sipping their tea. Moth looked at Asma as if to say, yes, I saw it too.

"I think it's time we had something a little stronger, don't you?" Johnny Haddad asked Asma.

"Not for me thanks," Asma placed her hand to her brow. "I've had plenty. Whatever was in this tea? It really went to my head."

"And Dhul, I know you don't take strong drink yourself, but you don't mind if I have a glass or two." And he reached behind his chair and pulled out a glass and large bottle of Stolichnaya vodka. He poured himself a large glass of straight vodka, and drank it down quickly.

"Pick up the glove," he told Asma who couldn't take her eyes off it. "It's for you."

"First the medallion, now this . . . I don't understand," looking at Haddad and Dhul. "Who are you? And what do you want with me?"

"We only want to help you," Dhul pointed. "Pick up the glove." So Asma picked up the gauntlet and put it on her right hand. It still felt warm.

"What do you know about the Crusades?" Johnny Haddad sat petting the cat on his lap.

"Dhul has given me a few books, which I've read, and my mother had some books on the Knights Templar that I read when I was growing up." She swung her gloved hand in the air above her head with an audible swoosh. "What's all this about?"

"It's about you," Haddad lit another Gauloise and taking a big gulp of vodka, he told her about her birth in Guatemala, how her father was asked to raise her, and that her real name was Fatima. "Your parents have perpetuated a great lie all your life. They've kept this secret from you, haven't they?"

"How do I know you're telling me the truth?"

"You'll have to trust us," Dhul knelt in front of her.

223

"Why should I trust you? You think I'm impressed with a holograph? You think bells and whistles are going to get me to buy what you're telling me? Give me a break!" She banged her gauntlet-gloved hand on the table beside her. "I admit the gauntlet is a nice touch."

"So what if I'm adopted? I've known that it's no secret. My parents didn't lie to me!"

"Did they tell you your name was Fatima? Did they tell you they intended to manipulate your life?"

"What are you talking about?" She looked down at Dhul, still kneeling like a supplicant before her on the floor. "Why did you bring me here?" she asked him, growing angrier by the minute. "I think you brought me here so your kinky friend here could drug and rape me. This . . . stuff your going on about is just bullshit, isn't? I should have known."

She stood up, exuding athletic strength. "Keep this glove!" She flung it at the black cat and said: "Let's get out of here."

"Ah, don't go yet," Haddad laughed. "I haven't fucked Fatima, ha, ha, ha."

"Come on Dhul! Are you coming with me? Or are you going to stay here with this drunken pervert?"

Dhul whispered something in Johnny Haddad's ear and left with Asma. Behind them the sound of Haddad's cackling laughter reverberated like the sound of procreating cats in a Lower East Side alley.

"I'm sorry." Dhul looked at Asma while flagging down a taxi. "I thought you'd like him."

"He's charming!" Asma retorted sarcastically shivering in the cool night air.

"But he has much to teach us." Dhul grabbed her hand, as she was about to step into the cab. For a second their eyes met in a frozen moment, and then she climbed into the taxi without saying a word.

SEVEN

The moment Asma closed the door her head and shoulders dropped the tension. "Those bastards drugged me," she said banging her hand on the door. She just stood there, behind the closed door as if holding back a horde of invaders. She was angry with Dhul and couldn't say a word to him on the long cab ride back to the city. She still couldn't understand why he'd taken her to meet this Johnny Haddad or whoever he was. She wasn't impressed with his techno-wizardry. And his psychobabble made her skin crawl. She was exhausted. She just wanted to a rest.

Sleep came quickly and easily to Asma. In her dreams: great battles, ancient armies fought over a medallion carried by a black cat on its back, in a silk purse. In the smoke of the battle the figure of bald man arose like a vodka swilling jinn. A turban wearing Johnny Haddad swooped down like lightning carried aloft on a neon blue carpet smelling of mould and vodka.

"You are wasting your life," the vodka drinking Haddad stopped the Persian knotted woolen carpet in front of Asma, and motioned her to get on. "Come on, don't be afraid, it's perfectly safe. It's made in Detroit, ha, ha, ha. Care for a drink? Ha, ha, ha." She didn't move.

"Come with me my beautiful Fatima. Let me show you your destiny. It's only a dream after all. Don't be afraid. Have a drink!"

"I don't drink," Asma stepped onto the carpet. In a millisecond she was whisked away to garden surrounded by aromatic flowers and a central fountain spouting cool spring water from the mountains.

"Where am I?" Asma asked in amazement. "This is the ancient garden of Alhambra," Dhul appeared from the passageway leading to the Alcazaba, or military zone.

"Let us sit down, in the old way, and begin your lessons," Dhul led her to a bench near the central fountain. Asma sat down with Dhul while Johnny Haddad rolled up the carpet and placed it carefully in the corner out of the way. A black cat rubbed itself against her leg. It was wearing a silk purse on its back. She opened the purse and took out the ancient coin and held it in her hand.

"The snakes are certainly not appealing," Haddad referred to the image on the coin. "Ugly but interesting. Observe the 'cista mystica,' or sacred chest with a snake crawling out on the one side, and then turn it over in your hand. Feel its power, and notice the two snakes entwined around a bow case. Some numismatists have called this coin the ugliest Greek coin ever make, but I think it's beautiful, don't you agree?"

The coin in her hand seemed immensely heavy. "What does it mean?" she asked. "The truth is before you, the past is filled with lies," the turban wearing Haddad sat next to her. He put his arm around her shoulder and gently squeezed.

"Get away from me," the dream Asma got up to avoid his clammy touch. "You're wasting your life Fatima. You can have wealth, knowledge, and power. These things are yours, and ecstasy. I can bring you bliss my child. What do you really know of the world? I can teach you. What of the strife and poverty in the world? Do you feel no compulsion to right past wrongs, to help the downtrodden? I know you do. You have the power to unite the great religions of Christianity and Islam."

Instantly they are riding his blue carpet, sweeping over dark clouds to orange mountains of fire. The tiny figure of Dhul back on the ground grew smaller the higher, and faster they flew.

In a second they were standing in a crowded room in a small house. She could tell by the multicolored fabric it was a Guatemalan household. A screaming child was born. She suffered the horror when the child spoke its name: the faces, the terrified faces of the people, and she saw a confused and conflicted priest holding the child, standing at a bridge looking down at a raging mountain river. Her mother, holding the child in her arms, rocks her gently to sleep, while her father strokes the child's head with his warm reassuring hand. All around them was the nauseating smell of Gauloise cigarettes from the dream Haddad's compulsive smoking.

"Don't you see Fatima, you are the 'cista mystica,' the sacred chest. Feel its power in your hand. It is your destiny."

Long fumes of cigarette smoke poured from the nostrils of the bull-like dream Haddad as he leaned over to kiss Asma with his big bull lips. "Sleep with me sweet Fatima my darling, daughter of the Caliph"

"No!" she shouted so loud she sat up in bed in a cold sweat. The digital clock beside her bed flashed: 3:33 AM. She turned on the television remote control. The theme song for the "I Love Lucy" show filled the room. She lay there, her mind racing, thinking about things she'd never thought about before: destiny, her place in the world, life, and this bizarre thing about someone called Fatima; how absurd, uniting Christianity and Islam. United against whom? How?

Eventually she drifted off, back to sleep. The light from the television reruns lit the room darting about the dark corners like a scared cat.

EIGHT

Saraqael pulled a cell phone from his jacket pocket and dialed the assigned number. He scanned the horizon, the sidewalks, and the street as if looking for someone. Here was the brief window of opportunity they had been waiting for. Abaddon sat silently in the driver's seat of the stolen Subaru, eyes hidden by dark sunglasses. Seconds later a blue Ford Escort stopped in front of the neo Art Deco MI6 building—Britain's Secret Intelligence Service at Vauxhall Cross—were it exploded into large chunks of burning metal and flaming upholstery shattered the clear glass windows of the covered walkway overhead. There was little damage to the rest of the building but Saraqael and Abaddon didn't care about that. It was a message they were sending to Daryl f, former head of the Middle East section that they cared about. They had grown tired waiting for him to come around to their way of thinking. They wanted him to know they had him in their sights. They wanted him to know there was an organization behind them, even if there wasn't now; there would be.

Abaddon started the parked green Subaru Outback and coolly drove to their lodging at 91 Albert Street in Camden Town. Later they would walk down the street to an Internet café and email Johnny Haddad the outcome of the day's events. They switched on the television to watch the live coverage. Apparently only one person had been injured crossing the pedestrian walkway at the wrong time. His name was being withheld for the time being.

Perfect timing. Soon they would be ready. Next year in Jerusalem!

Asma woke up to the sound of sirens on the television news. The lead story was about a car bombing in London outside the British foreign intelligence agency building. Miraculously only one person was injured, Mr. Daryl Spaulding, soon to be retired head of the Middle East section of MI6. Officials were investigating reports of a link to the Haza Narr (This Fire) organization in Lebanon. The phone rang.

"Hello." Asma threw an oversized Wellesley t-shirt over her head.

"Asma, it's me Dhul, please don't hang up. I know you're really pissed with me, but I need to see you. I need to talk to you. I can explain everything."

"Okay, try explaining why you drugged me, for starters."

"For one thing, I think I'm in love with you."

"I don't think this is a good time. Really, not a good time! I'm thinking this is a bit weird, if you know what I mean."

"I know, I know, this must seem strange, but I realized something last night. Please. I have to see you. I HAVE to see you."

"Okay, Dhul, but no weird shit, and I mean it.

"Absolutely. You name the time and place.

"Meet me at the university bookstore, at six. I have to pick up some things."

"Okay, great. I'll see you there at six."

Asma showered and got dressed, knowing something in her had changed overnight. A switch had been turned on. Her insight seemed sharper; yes, that's the word. It was very odd but she needed to read more philosophy, and the Koran, and the Bible too. And this was why she wanted to go to the bookstore. She wanted to pick up some books on Islam and Christianity. She wanted to learn more about Fatima, the daughter of the Holy Prophet Muhammad Ibn e Abdulla, and those Portuguese children of the visions. In an odd sort of way she understood she might someday know her true destiny, as if her search had come to end, like some sort of vocational revelation had appeared in last night's dream. For the first time she knew her destiny was real. But was it possible to unite the two great religions? Was this utter madness? How? Was a war the only way? A war had to be against somebody or something? No, not the Jews, she couldn't buy that. There had to be another way. She would have to learn, and fast.

And then the phone rang again. It was Stephen Parmata. Her mother had died. "Oh, God, so sudden."

"Yes," Could she come back to Nova Scotia for the funeral? Of course, she'd take the first available flight to Halifax.

What about Dhul? She'd have to email him and hope he got the message before he left for school. *First things first*, she thought as she logged on to Expedia.com to arrange her travel plans.

Dhul waited outside the bookstore for forty-five minutes before he acknowledged she really wasn't going to show up. His cell phone rang. He excitedly answered it, "Asma?" No, it wasn't her; it was Abaddon. He wanted to know how things were going with Asma? Was she on side or not? Dhul reported they were making progress, but there had been a set back.

"We need to get moving on this,"

"Yes," Dhul retorted, "I know, I know."

"You'd better. It would be a shame if we had to find someone else for the job—if you know what I mean."

"I understand," Dhul paced on the steps outside the bookstore. "It doesn't pay to get too close to Fatima—remember that." Abaddon hung up.

Dhul, the tanned Oxford Don from Ceylon, was worried. His confusion swelled, a tide of uncertainty crashing against his once solidly immutable conviction that violence was the only way to real change in this world, to revolution, not incremental change but Hegelian cataclysmic change. Could he really be falling in love with Asma? And if he was, how could he lead her into this war? What if she didn't feel the same way about him? Especially after the other night at Haddad's, he should never have taken her there. He wasn't thinking independently, he told himself as he waited for the subway to take him back home to Queens. But what soldier can afford that luxury?

Duhl was being followed. Yes, definitely he'd seen the same man, a gray haired white guy, parked in a late model American car at West 115th Street at Broadway when he left the campus. He noticed him because their eyes met as he walked past the car. He had thought that odd, but racists were everywhere, and xenophobia was rampant. Now, the same gray haired white guy was a few feet away on the subway platform. Could be coincidence, but he couldn't assume that. Out of the corner of his eye, Dhul tried to size him up. He was a tallish six feet with very polished black shoes, black pants, and brown suede leather jacket. Could be a policeman. Dhul put his right hand in his overcoat pocket and gripped the cold handle of a Glock 19 pistol. It was warmer now, almost inspiring. He grasped it in his pocket the way a drowning man might reach out for a life preserver. The only time he had used it was when he was in Chechnya. That was many years ago, before Oxford. He never believed he'd be called to use it. He always assumed it was his brain they were interested in, his powers of persuasion.

The subway train came roaring into the station. Dhul decided he'd miss this train, and see if the man was really following him. A large crowd appeared from nowhere, and after several nerve-racking minutes the train left the station. The man was gone, washed away by the tide of people. He ran up the stairs, taking two at a time, arriving on the street exhausted. He hailed the first cab home.

Perhaps paranoid is a higher sense of awareness.

On the long ride home he held the Glock firmly in his pocket. What glory there would be in Jerusalem the day she freed it. The day they freed all the oppressed peoples of the world. She had to understand that. That was their mission

He opened the door to his apartment and flicked on the light. Sitting there in front of him was that same gray haired man he saw standing at the subway station.

"Don't put you hands in your pockets if you plan to see another sunrise," the intruder advised in a calmly determined voice with a Canadian accent. Dhul didn't know what to do, or who he was.

"Who are you?" Dhul asked nervously. "You realize you're breaking the law. "He wished he hadn't said that, it might aggravate

231

the man. "Look, I'd like to know what's going on. I mean, why are you in my house," Dhul asked in his best Oxford accent walking closer to the man.

"That's far enough. Stay right where you are," the gray haired man ordered, "Or I'll have to kill you."

"Okay. Can I take my coat off?"

"No. Stay right were you are and this won't take long."

"Okay, but at least tell me who you are?"

"You'll know who I am when I'm ready to tell you."

Dhul just stood there. He glanced out the window wondering what his next move should be. The man just sat there looking at him; never taking his eyes of him.

"Okay, so what is this some pervert kind of thing? Is that it?" Dhul tried to find a way gain an upper hand. "And, you're a Canadian."

"Whatever you say," the intruder was growing impatient.

"Just a guess, that's all. The way you said, 'your' I suppose," Dhul said fishing for something to say that wouldn't come out sounding offensive.

"Why don't you sit down, over there," the man pointed to the sofa with his gun. It was then that Dhul got a closer look at the weapon the man was holding—a very cute black Kel-Tec P32, half the weight of its closest rival, but prone to rim lock jams according to Dhul's weapons instructor back in Chechnya. It takes at least three hands to clear a jam from one of these little fellows he remembered the former Brit SAS officer saying. And it's not much larger than a dollar bill, but potent at close range just the same.

"If you're looking for money, I don't have any," Dhul threw himself down on the worn pullout sofa bed held up on one side by red bricks he found in a vacant lot down the street as if to emphasize his point.

"I don't want your money. I want your soul."

"Ah, I see, some new kind of evangelism, and at gun point. That's effective. I mean it's worked for years. But I haven't heard of it here, in the States, I mean, well not recently anyway. Perhaps some of the colonial settlers used their rifles to finesse their Catholic rivals and convert the natives."

"Thanks for the history lesson. The weapon is really just for my protection, knowing as I do that you have a weapon in your pocket. But I can use it, so don't try any 'funny stuff' as they say."

"Okay, now we've got the pleasantries aside, how do you plan to save my soul?"

"I didn't say I wanted to save your soul. I want it."

"I see, and how does one go about gathering up souls like so many stray cats?"

"Have you heard of P2?"

"Yes, of course, there was popular novel about them that depicted some high ranking Masonic plot to bring about a single world currency. They were depicted as a shadowy ultra-conservative, perhaps cult-like Christian group. Wasn't that FBI counterintelligence agent, what's his name, I can't remember? You know, the guy who traded secrets with the Russians for cash and put nude pictures of his exotic dancer girlfriend on the Internet?"

"There are sick people everywhere," the gray haired man betrayed no emotion.

"So why me? You must know I'm not Christian. I mean just look at me? Or maybe you haven't noticed that I'm darker than you are."

"I'm concerned about what you're trying to do with Fatima. And I don't want you messing things up. I can see what you people are trying to do, and I don't like it."

"What's with this 'you people'?"

"I'm not being racist. No, you could say I'm in the information business. I know for a fact that some of your friends are in touch with the neo-Nazi Durk Juger. His financial company in Zurich has been the conduit to off shore banks around the globe helping to finance terrorist operations. I've been to his home; I've seen the photos of Bin Laden and Adolf Hitler beside each other on the wall. I've heard him quote Hitler saying Mohammed was the only true prophet, and how Hitler was most impressed with Islam. I've also heard him denigrate the Jews. Your common enemy, I believe?"

"Don't bring them into it; after what they've done to the poor Muslims in Palestine with the help of these Jew loving Americans."

"You see; this is what I'm talking about. And you want to enlist Fatima in your fanatical cause."

"Who's calling whom fanatical? What was it Churchill said about fanatics, can't change their minds or the topic? A bit like the pot calling the kettle black; pun intended, old boy!"

"I was hoping we could work this out intelligently. I was hoping you'd be reasonable . . ."

"You were hoping a few well phrased arguments, a couple of grand syllogisms would get me to forget what I've seen in places like Afghanistan. You want me to change everything I believe in, to change color like some chameleon, to betray the poor exploited people of those bombed Lebanese villages, and tell the Emir and his soldiers that it would be a really good idea to give up our religion and our history in favor of some American version of Wal-Mart democracy? You walk in the villages of Palestine, Afghanistan, Yemen or Bosnia and sense the history of a culture that is drowning in a tsunami of American Sodom and Gomorrah. Walk in the bazaars and mosques, smell the camel markets as they have been for thousands of years, and talk with the educated Mullahs. And you want to tell us to give it all up? She is the hope of our world. She can unite us. Your arrogance is simply stunning," Dhul threw his hands up in exasperation.

"I can see there is no convincing you to leave her to find her own destiny."

"This is her destiny as it was meant to be."

"Then we shall not meet again." The gray haired man dressed in black stood up. "But I'll be watching." And he left.

Dhul sat alone on the sofa stunned, a little bit angry, and slightly scared, silently staring at the empty chair where the intruder once sat.

NINE

From childhood Asma sensed she was different. Her parents doted on her, and sent her to private schools, first in Australia and later in Canada. She remembered as a child standing on the edge of the dock on Hayman Island watching the sun go down over Australia and how the brilliant rays of light, giant red fingers crept up over the island continent as if reaching out to her, the warmth of her mother's leg beside her and the firm reassurance of her mother's hand on her shoulder as they stood on the dock together. This is what she longed to remember, not the bitter arguments and shouting battles that had become their relationship of late. She loved her mother but the distance between them had increased since Christine's illness. Asma's guilt intensified now as she tried to read the in-flight magazine. Asma discovered it was becoming increasingly difficult to get from New York to Halifax. Air Canada, the only carrier it seemed with frequent scheduled flights to Halifax, required making connections through its hub in Toronto. Asma had come to hate making connections in Toronto. Only Chicago's O'Hare Airport surpassed Pearson Airport's reputation for delays. It seemed absurd to her that she should have to fly northwest from New York to Toronto to get to Halifax in the northeast. As she munched on the bag of salted nuts that was lunch she looked up over the seat in front of her at the commotion a few seats in front of her. A heavy set middle-aged balding white man was demanding another drink from the attendant who was reluctant to give the man another drink when clearly he had had enough. It was then the nervous looking

African American woman seated beside her dropped something on the floor. Asma reached down to pick up a small red notebook and gave it to the woman who took it quickly tucking it into her handbag on her lap.

"Thank you," without looking Asma in the eye. Just as Asma returned to her in-flight magazine the woman blurted: "Our whole life is in that little book." And she began to cry quietly. Asma didn't know what to do. She reached into her knapsack tucked under the seat in front of her, pulled out a handkerchief, and gave it to the small black woman beside her.

At 23 Asma had lived a rather sheltered, protected life. The woman beside her, probably only in her mid fifties, but Asma could tell she'd lived and suffered more than most people do all their lives.

"I'm sorry," the woman wiped her tears, brushing her straight black hair from her eyes.

"You don't sound like you're from the States. You're French aren't you?"

"Well, sort of, I guess; French is my mother tongue; I'm from Ivory Coast in West Africa," smiling at Asma with dark wet eyes. "I'm going to Canada to see my son, Banabase, who is studying medicine at Laval in Quebec."

"A good school," Asma searched for the right words to comfort the woman.

"My son, he is about your age. Oh, excuse me, I should have introduced myself; my name is Brigitte. My husband is the leader of the Sierra Leon rebel group UFR. He was arrested for breaking the ceasefire last May in Freetown by the combined UN/ECOMOG peacekeeping forces."

"I see, that must be difficult, I mean, for you, without your husband."

"Yes, but he left me well looked after; financially, I mean."

"Well, that's something, I suppose."

"My problem now is finding a place to put the money. That's why I'm coming to Canada now. My son has found someone, we think, who will help us."

"Why do you need help?" Asma asked naively.

"It's not easy to take money out of my country these days. And get it into the United States. Well, that's another matter. Canada is a good place for us." She smiled. Asma smiled back nervously.

"You see," Brigitte leaned over, whispering in Asma's ear. "Last February when my husband was still Chief of Army Staff, he 'intercepted'"—She made little quotation marks with her fingers—"a sizable sum of money, lets just say in the 200 million dollar range." Asma just about choked on the salty nuts. "The money was payment for a secret arms deal between our president, T.J. Kabutu and a fertilizer company in Moscow. My husband used some of the money he intercepted to buy weapons to fight the Sierra Leone dictatorship, but he also made a deposit in my name of 40 million dollars. He also bought some high quality gold and diamonds now held by a security trust company in Abidjan. The thing is the trust company doesn't know the exact contents of the boxes because they were told they contained family heirlooms, that kind of thing." She paused, looked around as if to check for surreptitious listeners, took a breath and continued her story.

"After a period of intense fighting, my husband was captured, and with some of the money he managed to bribe his captors to arrange a jet to take me out of the country to Abidjan. Now this is where it gets tricky. He also gave me the deposit certificates and documents to be able to transfer the money and remove the boxes containing the gold and diamonds. The plan was to find a buyer for the gold and diamonds. I have the papers here with me now."

"How can you get the gold and diamonds out?" Asma asked growing increasingly skeptical.

"My son, in Quebec, has been able to trace the trust company and confirmed the existence of the money, and boxes. But in order to take possession of them we needed someone with a different name, in a western country, to accept the transfer of the money and boxes. My son in Quebec may have found a doctor who will give us an account number for us to transfer the funds over here. Now, I am coming to America to settle with my son, and we will transfer the money from Quebec to the United States easily."

"I see. And what's in it for this Quebec doctor? I mean, if he gets the money in his account or whatever, why would he give it back?"

"First, we agreed to give him 15%, and second, if there are any problems my husband has connections around the world, if you know what I mean?" Brigitte coolly stowed her things in preparation for landing.

"But you're unsure if this doctor will go through with it, is that it?"

"I'm not sure my son is the best judge of character, if you know what I mean. He's young and naïve. That's why . . . if you could help . . . you seem so nice . . ."

"I'm afraid that's not really possible for me right now, you see I'm heading to my mother's funeral in Nova Scotia."

"Oh I see. I'm so sorry. How careless of me. I shouldn't have imposed on your good nature."

"It's okay, really. I hope you find what you're looking for." And with that their plane landed smoothly in Toronto. Asma made her way over to her connecting flight and never saw which way the African woman went. But she couldn't get her out of her mind the entire flight to Halifax.

An exhausted Parmata was waiting for her at the baggage carousel in the Halifax airport terminal. He gave her a big smile and a hug but she seemed cool, distant, and didn't return his embrace, or look him in the eyes. "You must be tired," he sympathized as he lifted her luggage onto the cart. She gave no reply, and followed him out to his parked car.

Once on the highway the silence was unbearable for Parmata. "Your mother left some things for you. Some things she wanted you to have."

"Tell me about my mother," Asma demanded bitterly. "Tell me about my real mother."

Parmata glanced over to Asma who stared straight ahead. Rain began to fall as sheets of big gray globules lashed the windshield. "Looks like a storm is heading in," trying to fill the void. Nature abhors a vacuum, and both the French and the Aussies like to fill it.

"Your mother loved you very much Asma."

"My mother, my mother, my mother! Where is my real mother? What is my real life? Why have you kept the truth from me? When were you going to bother to fill me? Huh? I have to find out from some degenerate in Jersey."

"What? You found out from somebody in Jersey?"

"New Jersey to you."

"What did he tell you?"

"That's not the point. The point is that you lied to me; you never told me the truth! Why? I don't understand. Why?"

"It's a long story."

"Well, geez, spare me; it's my life isn't it? Don't I have a right to know?"

"I was going to tell you . . . at the right time. It's just never been the right time, that's all. I mean we were concerned that you get your education and a career . . ."

"A career? Is that what this is about?

"No, I didn't say that."

"Yes, you did!"

"Look, we're not getting anywhere with this. We'll talk about it later. Okay?"

"Fine, it's always later." And an icy silence descended over them for the rest of the trip from the airport. The pitch-blackness of a Raven perched on the bell tower caught Asma's eye as they drove past St. Augustine's Church cemetery in Chester. Ever since she was a child her mother, Christie, talked about birds as omens. It was part of her Irish Canadian upbringing. And one large black bird meant somebody was going to die, for sure. But someone already had died. Or perhaps it was a warning of things to come. That's the thing with bird omens, you never know for sure.

By the time they reached the funeral home in Chester they were both exhausted. The usual stream of visitors came by to pay their respects. At the end of the small room was a closed casket with photographs of a young Christie on top of the coffin surrounded by flowers and cards from all over the world.

The wind outside had whipped up quite a gale smashing shudders and felling trees with a sudden thunderous "crack". The rain was just beginning to lash the windows in waves when in walked two soaking wet fishermen wearing rain gear suitable for the weather. And yet, they were still very wet.

They walked up to Asma. Parmata looked on with trepidation; he didn't know what to do, or what might be coming next. When they removed their Sou'wester hats, Asma recognized one of them as Robin (Saraqael), the man on the beach with the mysterious Greek coin. The two men stood dripping wet.

"We just wanted to say we are sorry for your loss." And then he added, "Allah is Great, we do not know his ways." And he reached out to touch Asma on the shoulder, as Parmata stepped forward between them to prevent Saraqael from touching her.

"For Christ's sake, this isn't the time for your games!" he pleaded to Saraqael quietly. "Please leave us, can't you see we are suffering enough."

"We mean only to comfort Fatima." The two of them stood there in front of the coffin not knowing what to do next until Asma said "Let us leave my mother to her rest."

Saraqael and Abaddon nodded and bowed their heads as a sign of respect and backed away. They sat in a blue Volvo station wagon across from the funeral home. A short while later Asma came out of the funeral home and walked in the pouring rain over to the Volvo wagon. She opened the back door and climbed in the back seat and sat down.

"Look, I know you're with Dhul and Haddad, and I know you think I should come with you, but the truth is I'm not ready. I don't know what to think just now. I need more time. I don't know enough. I still have lots of questions."

Saraqael looked around at her from the front seat. "We're only here to protect you."

"From whom?"

"From your step-father and his kind. They want to mould you into some kind of a perfect doll. We only want to help you discover your true nature; your special gift."

"Let me decide; okay guys? Let me decide." And she stepped out of the car back into the rain.

After the funeral the small group of mourners made up of friends and neighbors went back to Parmata's house. A kind of damp sadness clung to everyone like the salty rain. Asma went up to her room to be alone. Parmata knocked on the door. "Come in."

"I don't mean to intrude."

"No, it's okay, I want to talk to you. Come in." So he sat down in a big floral patterned armchair across from her on the bed, a defeated soldier, weary and beaten down, ready to hand over everything.

"I know you've just been trying to protect me Stephen, but I think it's time I knew the truth about my childhood. I mean, I've got these strange men following me around saying they're here to protect me. Protect me from what? From whom?"

And so he told her the story of her strange birth in Guatemala.

"Is the priest still alive?" she asked. "The one who saved me?"

"Yes, I think so."

"I'd like to meet him."

"I don't know if that's such a good idea."

"Stephen, don't you see. If I don't get the other side, I could be swept up in something here, and it would be your fault. I mean who are you trying to protect, yourself or me?"

"Okay, I'll take you to meet Father Burkholtz. He's at the Holy See Mission to the United Nations. I'll come back with you to New York. I'll get the whole thing arranged tomorrow."

"Good, now that wasn't so hard was it," she knelt in front of him. "This is my life Stephen. I know what I must do. Besides, we'd better get back to the people downstairs, they'll be wondering what has happened to us."

Just as they were leaving the room, one of the neighbors, George Schmelling, brought a telegram. "This just came for Asma."

She opened the wet envelope and read the message: *To Asma, although you have never known me, I knew your mother well. She was the love of my life until I became obsessed with an idea, an idea that destroyed me, and our relationship. Be true to yourself Asma; listen to yourself; trust only in yourself.* It was signed Greg Fallows.

On the flight to New York Parmata told her about Christie's first husband Greg and how he became totally fixated with the idea of an international conspiracy. How his fears became reality and how he was arrested for murder and tried as a terrorist. He was now serving a life sentence in a special federal maximum-security prison for terrorists somewhere in rural Pennsylvania.

She put her head back and closed her eyes. Greg's words resonated in the long wet corridors of her brain: listen to yourself; trust only in yourself . . . Be true to yourself. What was he trying to say? Here was a man who took a risk, followed his passion, and look what happened to him; he became something hated, a terrorist for a cause no one believed in, no one could understand but himself. What was this tug of war between one's self and the rest of the world? The twinge of a twisting began in her gut, a mounting tension and dread. She saw a bear, a great black bear; it's rancid breath and yellowed teeth snarling at her as it clawed the frozen ground to cover the distance between them.

She was startled when the plane touched down at LaGuardia, jolting her from her disturbed semi-conscious state that passes for sleep on airplanes.

She will come round my friend have no fear. The seeds of her discontent are beginning to sprout roots. She will soon begin to believe the easy rhetoric of sophomoric malcontents and see in root causes the shoots of evil. Soon she will become one of the blissfully naïve who chant anti-west, anti-globalization, anti-development slogans waving placards, wearing designer jeans and Nike running shoes, drinking lattes made from Guatemalan coffee, and listening to angry mostly nouveau riche black men sing songs of revolution from basements in a newly gentrified Harlem where the latest distractions are imported from countries where wars rage in poppy fields, not Flanders but Afghanistan and Iran. The root of causes runs deep Abaddon and we are here to see them watered, to fertilize the post-modern simplistic, polarized and paranoid view of the world. Ah, but when worlds collide my friend, so many souls to harvest next year in Jerusalem, so many autumn leaves will fall.

The child, as Abaddon called her, had grown up unaware of the special light that had been shone upon her. She was a precocious child. She liked all things animal and had many pets: from the brown snake she found one day in her Brisbane backyard BBQ to the injured Cane Toad she rescued along the road and nurtured back to life on a summer vacation to Charters Towers with her parents. She was surprised when her parents let her keep them. Life for Asma was literally a beach. She was always in the water, except when the weather or the Box Jelly fish prohibited it. She loved the outdoors. Her young, taunt body absorbed the hot Australian sun like a magnet and she developed a radiant golden tan in her favorite yellow and white striped bikini, which she wore in the winter of her fifteenth birthday, revealing her curvaceous figure to the delight of the Sunshine Coast's teenage boys. She literally drove them crazy. Her pouting lower lip teased but never revealed even to her first boyfriend, surfer Jay Patterson. The most she gave up to him was a hand job in the back of his father's red Corolla. And it drove Jay mad, but he was grateful for the temporary release, her loving, gentle, rhythmic stroking was the best Jay ever had, and he'd had a few hand jobs in his surfer career; most were fast and furious, but Asma seemed to know the rules; she stroked him expertly every Friday like a purring cat. "Asma!" he would scream when he came in her hand, his face buried in her neck, his right hand on her incredibly perfect breast under that maddening bikini. His blond hair and blue eyes longed to hold her amazing hips and pump his life-giving jizz into her, but it was not to be the case. A shark ate Jay the very next week. Friday's were never the same. She didn't go to his funeral. Paul Sander was screaming "Asma" into her hand at the exact time they were lowering Jay into the ground. Jay screamed it better. And soon she lost the allure of teenage sex—she did all the work—and she began to focus her energy on calculus and physics with the same enthusiasm and energy she once devoted to Jay's now buried member. For sure there were other boys, but Jay would always be special, but now he was gone, and she had other things to do.

College was Toronto, her mother's influence to be sure, and Columbia was a fight; Asma wanted journalism. She never knew that her father stepped in and agreed with her that Columbia was the best school if she wanted journalism.

The fog was thick, a cold wet cloth across the face when they stepped out of the airport into the choking air that was New York. The offices of the Permanent Observer Mission of the Holy See are located on 25 East 39th Street. Rev. Msgr. Doug Burkholtz, Senior Attaché greeted Asma and her father.

Father Burkholtz looked younger and fitter than his years. He had a short gray haircut, Marine style and a moustache. The haircut and agile spring in his walk reminded Asma of a cat, lean, all muscle, and no fat. His eyes were large and dark brown, almost dog-like. She sat down on the very same leather sofa Parmata had so many years earlier.

"Stephen tells me you want to know about your birth mother . . . The circumstances of your birth." Father Burkholtz offered her a glass of water that she refused.

"Yes," she looked pointedly at Parmata taking a sip of water. "I now know my name is Fatima, after the daughter of the Holy Prophet Muhammad Ibn e Abdulla."

"I see. And why could it not be that you were named after the mystery of Our Lady's appearance before three shepherd girls in 1917 Portugal?"

She stared into her glass of water as if waiting for a vapor to rise out it. Perhaps Parmata was right. Maybe she was being used.

"So tell me Father. What is the truth surrounding my birth."

"Let us begin with the Prophecies for it is only by understanding them that we can know the Truth."

Asma rolled her eyes in Parmata's direction. He took a book from the bookcase and idly flipped through the pages as if he were looking for a special passage, seemingly unaware of the conversation in the background.

"You've heard the story of the shepherd girls who claim to have seen Our Blessed Mother, and who learned from Her several future events, to confirm the authenticity of the miracle. Do you also know that one of the girls was still alive until recently; very old it is true, but still alive? She spent her life devoted to Our Lord's mission on earth, and she confirmed that in fact there were four prophecies, not three as is commonly believed. The fourth prophecy Asma is about the coming of the second Paraclete. Do you know what that means?"

"Like the second coming . . . of Jesus Christ?"

"That's what many believe, or should I say, choose to believe. But nowhere does it say that Jesus himself is the second Paraclete, only, according to John 16:7, Jesus said, 'I will send him to you.' And of course, we had always assumed, until you were born that is, that it would be a 'him.'" He couldn't help cracking a smile delivering that news.

"And this fourth prophesy, what is it?"

"Well you see, like most prophecies it is cryptic, and therefore subject to many interpretations. Simply put, it says the second Paraclete will be born of poverty, speak his name at birth, and he will go on to unify Muslims and Christians."

"What about Jews, Buddhists, and Hindus?"

"That's an interesting point. Scholars of the prophecy have debated the issue for years without any clear consensus emerging."

"But how? Are we talking about another pogrom? How could anyone unify such diametrically opposed perspectives without a common enemy to unite them? I mean it seems so absurd. And why do you think I'm that person?"

"Obviously I'm not the only one. You've met Johnny Haddad, I understand." Her spine straightened reflexively.

"Yes, a very strange dude to be sure. He gave me the creeps, and he spiked my drink, you know, him and that freakin' cat of his."

"Yes, the cat, an interesting species. But believe me Haddad wouldn't be wasting his time socializing if he wasn't on a mission. I mean beyond the obvious desire to get into your pants, as they say in the parlance of our times."

"Tell me Asma, do you believe in good and evil?"

"As concepts or as living things?"

"Let's just say, now that you've met Mr. Haddad, what was your feeling when you met him?"

"He gave me the creeps! Serious creeps!"

"And what does that mean? You sensed something compelling about him? Something . . ."

"Powerful."

"Yes, yes indeed. It's a beginning," he turned to Parmata reading by the bookcase.

"I think it's time she met Father Morales."

Parmata stayed in the office, content to thumb through the collection of rare editions, while Asma and Father Burkholtz disappeared into the maze of corridors to find the aged priest.

The Senior Attaché opened a heavy wooden door to a final hallway lined with doors. Walking to the end, Father Burkholtz knocked next to a small bronze plaque with the name Alvaro Morales written on it.

"Come in," came the reply after a few moments of rustling papers. Asma didn't look at Father Burkholtz while they waited for Father Morales to open the door. Instead she couldn't take her eyes away from the haunting picture of a suffering Virgin Mary above the door.

"Father Morales, I am very sorry to disturb you, but a young lady wanted to speak with you."

As Alvaro Morales looked Asma/Fatima in the eyes he was transported in a vortex of energy back to the bridge in the Guatemalan Altiplano where he held the child in his arms, praying for guidance to take a life or to save one.

"Fatima! It is you. Thank God. And you are a beautiful woman." He reached out to take her hand.

"Yes, she has come to hear the truth about her birth, about her parents, and the coming of the second Paraclete."

"Ah, yes," Father Morales nodded pensively, turning to shuffle toward an arm chair, as the dim light cast a shadow across the deep recesses of his wrinkled face. "You see Fatima, may I call you that?"

She nodded but he didn't see her. All his energy seemed focused on reaching the chair.

The room smelled like a nursing home—a combination of stale air, urea, and musty old clothes, unfashionable priest garments that hadn't seen the light of day for many years. And it was here in this old man's room, amid the refuse of a simple life, a long forgotten memory awakened from a dark primeval sleep. A small hummingbird, no bigger than a butterfly, fluttered its wings, drinking deeply from the sugar well of memory that stirred in her Amygdale, that tiny part of the brain where Saraqael and Abaddon drank their sweet mint tea in the Garden of Gethsemane, somewhere between the Then That Was and the Future Now.

"Fatima?"

"Yes," she answered reflexively.

"Come closer." And she walked over kneeling before the priest. He reached out to touch her face as tears moistened his tired eyes. "How could I have almost killed you?"

"What did you say?" She instantly withdrew to where Father Burkholtz was standing by the door.

"At the bridge," he muttered. "I almost killed you at the bridge."

"But why? What are you talking about?"

He told her the story of how he was summoned to that tiny village in Guatemala. He told her who her parents were; how she had miraculously spoken her own name at birth, and how he was conflicted when he held her in his arms over the bridge. He had never been certain about what to do, except that she should be taken from her parents. He thought it was the Will of God that she die as a small child before she could be corrupted, or worse perhaps corrupt the world. But there was something that kept him from dropping her in that river. And now he knew what that was.

"And what kept you from killing me in the name of God?" Asma demanded, her body poised, motionless.

"The Holy Spirit . . . It is written: 'You will be out of oil when the Paraclete returns for His bride.' You must confront the god of this world, Satan. It is your destiny, child. The Holy Spirit is among us."

"And how am I supposed to do that?"

"That my child is between you and God." And he closed his eyes, exhausted from the brief conversation.

"Come. I think it's better that we leave him now."

"Is he ill?" Asma looked at Alvaro Morales asleep in the chair.

"Yes, he's dying . . . cancer, multiple myeloma. There is no cure."

"I see." She followed Father Burkholtz back to this office where Parmata sat quietly reading.

"I see you haven't lost your interest in the antiquities." Father Burkholtz wearing a satisfied smirk, returned to his desk.

"Interesting stuff . . . *Malleus malificarum* by Dominican Theologian and inquisitor Heinrich Kramer."

"Ah, yes, *The Hammer of Witches,* 1487, I believe."

"And you are right."

"And why would a diplomat have a book about witchcraft in his office?" Asma was more confused than when she first walked through the door.

"The world is a confusing place sometimes, as you well know. Our forefathers struggled with that as much as we do; maybe even more. Our worldview is much more rational, dare I say amoral. While theirs was rich with a belief in angels, spirits, and devils, engaged in a titanic battle of good versus evil."

"Are you saying there are angels, devils, and spirits walking around the Upper East Side?"

"We must all be careful how arrogant we become. Arrogance is the foundation of fanaticism, for they must first convince themselves. For me, this is the lesson of Kramer's book on the inquisition, and why I keep it around: to remind myself not to become a fanatic. Maybe after all we really do live in Plato's cave and not Aristotle's empiric world."

"Thank you for your time Father Burkholtz," Parmata stood and stretched. "I think it's time we got back."

"Of course, but you are always welcome, and you too Asma; call me any time."

In the taxi on the way back to her apartment the silence was a well-deserved respite for both of them. Parmata, in that haze of delayed mourning, reflected on what he would do next. The future, an endless highway across the arid outback of his life, seemed to go on forever, and Asma in her own purple funk tried to make sense of this chaotic world of conflict, suffering, and greed. Yes, greed. It was hard to miss it. The juxtaposition of rich and poor, everything that is America, and the Western World, sprawled out before her eyes. Conspicuous consumption peppered with the garbage of a lost generation. That beggar, the one at the last stop light. He looked so familiar, almost like that man who she met on the beach in Nova Scotia. The world was a very small place; unless you could get away, find some place of your own. Maybe that's why great gurus and wizards liked remote mountains. The sheer physical isolation was part of their power source. Could that be what Nova Scotia was for Stephen? And where was her personal power source? Was life a quest for this? In a sense this is what she believed. And she longed to find that place, perhaps next year in Jerusalem. She resolved then and there to make the journey to Jerusalem. Maybe in Jerusalem she could find that sense of calm she longed for, and escape what seemed a madness of extremes. Surely Jerusalem was the eye of the storm.

Parmata's life had been turned upside down as it always does in grief; a feeling of helplessness crowded in, an unwanted visitor in the familiar fog of the daily grind. He had grown old and comfortable with Christie on that tiny fringe of North America. He wanted to retreat, to hide away from the nattering clatter of the patrio-commercialism; escape to his refuge on the edge of the world, a piece of heaven called Nova Scotia.

TEN

Abaddon caught Asma's eye as the taxi sped by him on the desolate mid-town corner as he fumbled for a cigarette in the pocket of his army jacket. Lighting the cigarette, he looked up at the swirling dust of a blue-gray cloud above his head. The world is different for angels. Everything has meaning. Abaddon could read the signs. And he smiled. *God is Great. She will deliver us Jerusalem.*

A gust of wind danced around Abaddon. In the blink of an eye he was gone, if he was ever really there. His smoldering Gauloise remained behind as evidence. Only a drunk on the opposite corner might have he'd seen a man standing there a moment ago, but no, he might have hallucinated it.

Abaddon stood next to Saraqael atop the 800-year old minaret of Jam 200 feet above the ruins of the ancient Afghan city, a remote area accessible only on foot, a two-week hike from Herat. The Jam tower rose from the dusty canyons of the Turquoise Mountains, where once the mighty Genghis Khan and his thundering hordes descended through the ravines from the wilderness to destroy this oasis at the base of two muddy rivers; the tranquil creation of the once mighty Ghiyath al-Din Muhammad, his piece of heaven on earth.

Abaddon and Saraqael have seen much destruction but it does not bother them in a maudlin modern way. Saraqael for one believes in the cycles of death and rebirth, destruction yields to creation. He sees his role as the midwife of that destruction. And so, they look down over the ruins of the ancient city with pride, and revel in the vast efficiency of modern destructive technology.

"When will she be ready?" Saraqael looked at Abaddon and tugged his beard. His black eyes betrayed a wolf's searching hunger.

"She grows more disillusioned with things of the West everyday. She turns toward Jerusalem. She is still in her cocoon, but she will soon break free. Of this I am certain."

"You are a fool Abaddon. We cannot wait. Now is the time for action. Enough of this endless talking; when do we see action?"

"You must learn patience, my scurrilous friend. The life of these people is not like yours or mine. You and I shape history. Do you know what that means? We are not content to plod away like beasts of burden in meaningless government jobs, pushing endless files of paper, attending dull pointless meetings all day. The cosmos is expanding every day, and they do not see it. We are accelerating expansion into the future by action. To explain this phenomenon they call it dark energy because they cannot see it, but they can detect it's effects; they assumed gravity would slow the cosmic expansion and now they see it's running amok and marvel that two-thirds of all the energy in the universe is what they call dark. And some of them may actually begin to understand that the reality they see is but a mere shadow. Soon she will understand the meaning of her name, and her destiny will become clear, as clear as the full moon in the desert sky. And as fast as the quantum fizz morphed the universe to its present size in 10^{25}th of a second she will be gone."

ELEVEN

Between dreaming and awake, where the glass rods of crystal light cut jello water, moving forward without oxygen, thick giddy children hold hands, never stopping to question the logic of impossibility, at the same time never ceasing to move forward. There in the distant egg-like horizon the Gnome Savant stands wearing a long white robe holding Neptune's trident. The children are not afraid of him. He is their solace, their security, and their earthly paradise, escaping the sticky world behind them. The air is filled with the sound of bees, buzzing impediments to progress; all this was known to them between dreaming and awake.

Asma awoke in her bed. The traffic along 30th Street was taking its revenge. The sky was filled with marshmallow gray clouds. She turned toward the alarm clock that she had forgotten to set. The red digital numbers flashed 7:26 A.M. She jumped out of bed, put the coffee on and hopped into the shower. Washing her hair she pondered what the old priest Alvaro Morales revealed: her real name, that is, her name from birth was Fatima. Why would her parents, her adopted parents, change her name? She thought about what the dying priest told her: about the so-called Fourth Prophecy. She suddenly vigorously scrubbed her scalp as the shampoo burned her eyes. New York was no place for a prophet, not after 9/11. The ideas seem to come from behind her burning eyes.

"New York is no place for a prophet," she whispered as if someone might hear. She rinsed her hair. The smell of eucalyptus was a warm balm that embraced her senses—anything truly was possible. School

252

is a pointless waste of time. What can be learned in books when the world is all around you? Isn't that what Dhul Fiqar was saying all the time? This was no time to be passive. Action was needed. She had to see Dhul. She needed to understand something. She needed to understand what it meant to be a prophet. She needed to understand what it took to strap-on explosives and walk into a crowded mall. She wanted to dive into the emotional source of these feelings, this passion for something more, a higher purpose, call it destiny, that invisible creature behind every move we make, as if someone was standing there; all the time unseen. A cold shiver raced up her spine and she dropped her coffee. Her hands felt alien, as the pottery mug crashed to the floor in what seemed a slow motion spiral. She was standing in front of the window stark naked. Suddenly very cold, she ran into the bedroom to get dressed.

Saraqael turned to Abaddon who was trying to roast a chicken over a dying fire. Abaddon was evidently frustrated with the lack of wood to be found in the desert.

"Should we call her a prophetess?"

"What?" Abaddon looked at Saraqael with tired frustrated eyes.

"I mean, can a woman be a prophet, or is she a *prophetess*?" He put his pen down beside him on the carpet.

"What difference does it make?" Abaddon snarled as he hunted the oasis for something to burn; other travelers had long ago taken anything that could be remotely considered a source of fuel. "Of course a woman can be a prophet or a prophetess! It's a matter of vernacular!"

"You agree with me then that she will be a prophet."

"I agree to nothing except that I am hungry, and this oasis lacks even a modicum of fossil fuel with which to convert this sorry fowl's flesh into a scrumptious dish fit for Angels!"

"Angels!" The both laughed at that one.

"Dhul, its me. I want to learn more. I want to do it. I am tired of just talking about things. I want to do something with my life. I don't want to just survive and die like my mother."

"Uh, huh," she heard from the other end of the telephone line.

"I mean I want to understand the meaning of conversion or whatever.

"Uh, huh."

She stared out at the New York skyline. "I have to get out of here. I have to or I'll die here . . . Can we meet?"

"Okay, how about the MOMA?"

"Sure, okay. Give me about an hour?"

"Okay, see you in the lobby."

Asma took the N train to Manhattan. She couldn't shake the peculiar smell of the room of that dying priest. There was something oddly familiar, yet foreign about the odor, almost fruity like fresh pomegranates. A Latino kid about 12 years old stared at her from across the train. It was mid-morning so the passengers weren't in any particular hurry to get anywhere. She tried to ignore him but he kept staring. The harder she tried the more self-conscious she became. The noise of the clattering train echoed in her head. She felt trapped and claustrophobic. The kid was carrying a music box blasting Astreaux World to the rhythm of the train. The subway car screeched into the Lexington Avenue station jolting her out of her trance. When she looked up the Latino kid was gone, and so was that odor, burnt papaya, as the train pulled into Fifth Avenue station. She decided to walk the five blocks to the museum.

When she arrived at the Museum of Modern Art, Dhul was pacing nervously in the front foyer. He was wearing his favorite brown Oxford tweed jacket and brown corduroy pants. His navy turtleneck completed the academic image he consciously nurtured.

"Let's get out of here," he gave a broad smile. "This place makes me nervous." He grabbed her by the arm swinging her around back out the door. "Too much security around these days. It makes me nervous. Let's head up toward Central Park."

As they walked Asma began. "You know my real name is Fatima. That's the name my real parents gave when I was born. The parents who adopted me, Stephen and Christie changed it to Asma to hide something about my past, but recently I just found out something,

something that has made me question everything. My entire life has been a lie. I can't go on like this. I want to leave New York. I want to leave school. I want to leave America."

"Why don't you go to Europe then?"

"Europe is so . . . Euro Disney. I need to go somewhere I can wear the *hijab*, the veil. I think I would find it liberating. I don't know why but maybe I'll find out."

"Where do you want to go? Lots of Muslim women wear the hijab here, all over the world. You don't have to hide somewhere to be a Muslim, even if these are difficult times for Muslims in America. Believe me I know it. If you want to be a Muslim, well, you have to believe that the Quran is the revelation of Allah to Muhammad. This declaration of faith, we call it *shahada* that says, 'There is no god but God and Muhammad is his messenger.'"

"I need to know about Fatima. Why were they so afraid of me knowing who I really am?"

"You don't become a Muslim to piss your father off."

"That's not the point, Dhul."

"I think it is."

"Are you going to help me or not?"

"I still think you're running away from something."

"Well, maybe I am, but you can help me run to something else, and that's what I'm asking. Help me, find myself, Dhul, please."

"Okay, I'll ask Johnny Haddad."

"I don't want to end up in a harem or the white slave trade or something."

"No, no, of course not. But I want to tell you something about me; something personal; something very few people know because it relates to my personal quest. You see I'm a eunuch. I was castrated in New Mexico three years ago, to concentrate my spiritual and sexual energy—think of me as a kind of spiritual being. You too need to accept your destiny Fatima." The name sounded so strange to her. He became oddly close after that but she couldn't entirely trust him—too many secrets. As they walked he began her religious instruction starting with the Five Pillars of Islam.

TWELVE

By the time they arrived at Haddad's place Fatima was planning her pilgrimage or *hajj*, the journey devout Muslims are expected to make to Mecca at least once in their lives. Dhul's words cast a spell as he described the magic of Mecca and Saudi Arabia, a misunderstood country poorly portrayed by the Western media. He had made his *hajj* already.

"It is site of the Kaaba, the most amazing building you've ever seen. It was the first house of worship, dedicated by Abraham to the one God." In lavish detail he described several rituals that are performed during *hajj:* circling the Kaaba, running between the hills of Safa and Marwa (symbolizing Hagar's search for water for her son, Ishmael), traveling to the plain of Arafat, outside of Mecca, and throwing stones at pillars that symbolize the devil.

As he described each one of these Fatima's heart raced. She scarcely noticed that loathsome creature Johnny Haddad greeting them at the door of his apartment. And how, in his special creepy way, he let his hands slide closer to her buttocks, than might be acceptable as he embraced her.

"It is so good to see you again Fatima, child of wonder and beauty," He undressed her with his eyes. "Please come in. You are always welcome, and you too, Dhul."

"We've been talking about the Pillars of the Faith, and I was describing Mecca to her," Dhul raced for the sofa. "Can we get some takeout, I'm starving."

"Why not, my treat," Haddad took Fatima by the hand. "Does our lady like Chinese?"

"Sure, that's fine with me, I'm not that hungry, but whatever you guys are having is okay with me," escaping his grip.

"Why don't you tell her about Angels, while I make the call." Haddad disappeared into the kitchen.

"What's this about Angels?" Fatima took her seat across from Dhul in a very worn out armchair covered in cat hair. There was that cat again, eyeing her malevolently from across the room, the way all cats do when someone has the audacity to sit on their favorite piece of furniture.

"Angels, yes. Besides the prophets including Noah, Abraham, Moses, Elijah, and Jesus, common to Christianity and Judaism, I believe in Angels, that is, spiritual beings that do the will of God."

"These angels, what do they do?"

"Remember that Greek coin we brought to Haddad the first time I brought you here?"

"Yes, I remember it."

"Johnny says it came from an Angel."

"How can he know that?"

"I know it because I have seen them," Haddad reappeared in the doorway.

"And what about the coin?"

"Ah, the ugliest coin . . . it's a token, or maybe better described as a toll. You have to pay the ferryman, you know, to cross the river Styx, that poisonous river of the underworld; the Arcadians took oath by it. Only one of nine rivers of the underworld mind you, but the one made most famous by Homer." He pulled the Greek coin from his pocket and tossed it at Fatima who snatched the coin out of the air with impressive agility.

"I still think it's ugly." She stood to examine it closely by the lamp. "Those snakes crawling out of the box are creepy."

"Ah, the cista mystica, the sacred chest. To the Freudians it was a sexual metaphor," he smiled. "But Dhul wouldn't know about that, would you Dhul?"

"Let's just say, that's all in the past, Jahaan."

"But you don't think it's a sexual cult thing?" Fatima examined the other side with two snakes entwined around a bow case. "I just think it's ugly, that's all."

"And you are right. It is certainly poorly crafted. Many of them were minted in what is now Turkey in the first century B.C. But its value to you is as enigmatic as its inscription—Pi Epsilon Rho, three letters of the Greek alphabet whose meaning has been lost in the sands of time. No one really knows what it stands for, except maybe the ferryman."

"And an Angel," Dhul piped in as the doorbell rang.

"It's the Chinese food," Fatima smiled, putting the coin in her jeans pocket.

Haddad opened the door and two Mujahedeen walked in carrying two bags of take-out food. "Well, I think it's time your political education began." Johnny Haddad looked at Fatima.

The two giants handed the take-out to Haddad and moved toward Fatima with conviction.

"No!" she cried. "Dhul, you have to help me! Please!"

"It's necessary; part of your education. You must learn how the other half of the world lives. Become a Mujahedeen . . . Take her away!"

"No, no," she struggled against the giants until one of them sprayed something in her face, and she fell limp in their arms.

When she awoke an oily darkness surrounded her. The air was stale with the pungent odor of gasoline. Her head throbbed and her mouth was as dry as an Australian riverbed. She had no idea where she was, or how long she'd been out. Alone, no one new where she was, or where she was headed. She heard a banging sound and then a door opened streaming light into what appeared to be a shipping container. In walked Dhul Fiqar dressed in army fatigues. He flicked on a light switch. One of the giants closed the door behind him.

"Where the fuck am I?" she attacked him with all her might, hammering him in the head with both her hands. He grabbed her hands and held them tight until she submitted to his superior strength. "I want to know what's going on, right fucking now!"

"Fatima, you need to get a grip."

"Stop calling me that, my name is Asma."

"You have a special purpose and you know it," Dhul released her hands. "You have been chosen. Jahaan says this is for sure. He has seen Angels following you."

"Jesus Christ this is so fucking lame . . . You expect me to believe this shit?"

"Believe me, it's important, a part of your political indoctrination," he led her over to a beanbag sofa. "Very soon, you will understand the root cause of things."

"This war on terrorism is a front. It is a religious crusade—Christians and Jews against Islam."

"No, I don't believe this shit. I really don't buy this. I lived in New York remember? I was there after 9/11. I saw what happened."

"And you think you know the truth!"

"What is truth Dhul? Kidnapping, huh? Is that your idea of some revealed truth? She slapped him hard across the face. "You people just don't get it! It's not about religion! It's about being attacked!"

"Fatima, listen to me. It's about oil. About who controls the oil . . . follow the money, like the man said about Watergate . . . Deep Throat."

"I've heard all this before, but I don't see how my expressing an interest in some religious ideas lands me here? Oh, by the way, where am I? And what was that with those goons? Geez Dhul, what's going on?"

"You're on a ship, a container ship, headed for Casablanca. This is where you'll become what your parents and that priest tried to keep you from discovering . . . your true destiny." He got up and walked toward the door. "You've got everything you need here. We know what we're doing. You've chosen sides. There is no turning back now. In a few days you'll commit to the greater jihad, the ongoing struggle within your soul to be a better person: to ward off temptation to return, to do the right thing, to follow your conscience and God's commandments, and to develop a closer relationship with Allah. This is what you asked for Fatima. This is what Johnny has arranged. This is to protect you Fatima. Just like the angels have protected you from birth. This is your sacred destiny. Soon you will understand. The day of judgment is coming." And he closed the door.

She ran to the door. It was locked. She looked around. Now there was light she could see. The container was small but comfortably furnished—even a small chemical toilet in the corner. There was a bed on the floor. Beside the bed were several books. She walked over and lay down on the bed. She picked up one of the books. It was the Torah. Then she picked up the other three: the Psalms, the Gospels of Jesus, and the Quran and she began to read.

THIRTEEN

Eventually Fatima fell asleep. Whether animals have dreams or not, philosophers have long debated. Asma, now Fatima, did dream that long howling night on the roiling ocean. Outside loud, fantastic winds raged as the Liberian registered cargo ship *Tantallon Castle* made her way through the rough salty seas. For vessels like *Tantallon Castle* and her skeleton crew the Atlantic crossing was routine. There were video games and movies to ease the boredom while the autopilot kept the *Tantallon Castle* on course for Casablanca.

As Asma/Fatima slept, the self-described Archangel Saraqael came to her in a dream dressed as her phantom father. It is the advantage of angels and dreamers that we may take whatever form suits our gnarly purpose. And as is the habit of angels, Saraqael perceived, oddly enough it was her father she trusted most, and it was this form he took in her dreamscape.

"Stephen!" she cried, spotting her father's silhouette amid the plane's smoldering wreckage. She touched his sad dirty face with her cold wet hands.

"You've been gone so long," he sadly looked around at the disaster.

"No, no, I haven't" cupping his face in her hands. "I've been looking for you . . . everywhere."

"And what did you find?" his face contorted with sadness.

"What?" her heart pounding madly.

"There is no god but God and Muhammad is his messenger," his face melted into a thousand bees swirling in an arid desert.

"Father!" she shouted, sucked into the vortex of bees as waves crashed rhythmically on the beach, under a fantastic pink crescent moon.

She raced to catch up to him, perhaps only a few futile yards ahead of her on the beach—but to no avail.

"What do you want from me?" she screamed crying, falling through the sand, as if some ancient chronometer behind the veneer of her eyes was sucking her to a place of infinite calm where the bitch goddess of ambition brooks no contradiction, and no one, no one ever wants something or desires anything more.

This is the prayer of the universe at the center of it all. That perfect note attained not through toil or suffrage but calm inner reflection; the silence between the music, the dark chaotic forces beyond reason's monoptic stare. The expanding ripples of the universe, spreading faster, stretching the very fabric of what we call Space and Time, propelled by dark matter or consumed by it. It doesn't matter.

It was here that Saraqael took Asma/Fatima in her dream to the place of oneness with the universe where the blue planet as we know it is a random error in the cosmos and the so-called laws of nature tick away time. So too a stochastic child born to a dead mother, suckled by that dead mother's breast knows the special significance in random events that sparkle in the twilight between dreaming and awake. This was a safe place that made sense to her heart and mind like a Raelian fascination with alien encounters, miracles great and small, and those haunted by life's sorrows. To leave behind the anxiety of everyday life, the mystery and meaning of being in the sea of ever expanding stars until it contracts to nothing again, that state of stochastic beginnings and ends.

She awoke to the sounds of shifting cargo on the tossing seas. She looked around, at first confused, and realizing where she was, she settled in to read in the flickering light. She was not afraid, rather she was resigned to find her purpose and make good. *This is what angels do*, she reflected.

It took a week to arrive in Casablanca. In the meantime Parmata called her several times. When he didn't get an answer he began to worry. He called a friend in NYPD, Sgt. Tom Slaughter to check in on her. When Sgt. Slaughter reported back that Asma hadn't been to classes in a week and her apartment was empty, he really started to worry. And like all fathers he assumed the worst.

While Sgt. Slaughter worked the official channels, Parmata made some calls to old friends in intelligence circles. What he discovered he didn't particularly like. He especially didn't like the part about her being seen with a suspected terrorist "sleeper" at the Museum of Modern Art. Both had disappeared around the same time.

This time when he walked into Father Burkholtz's office he knew exactly why he was there. He needed to understand what this was all about, and why Asma was in the middle of it. He knew it had to have something to do with that discussion they had had many years ago. He didn't know why he knew. He just knew it in his gut.

"Stephen, good to see you again." Father Burkholtz closed the door behind him. "Have a seat. I think I know why you're here." He walked to the window and peaked through the Venetian blinds before closing them. "I read something in the paper about Asma's disappearance. I'm very sorry. You mustn't blame yourself. You did your best for so many years. She's an adult now. What can I say? It must be a worry."

"Yes, it is. I need to understand what this is all about."

"There are forces we can see, and things we can't understand. It's outside our comprehension, Stephen. That's the eternal battle. The reason for faith, for trust."

Parmata looked right through the priest. There was no point arguing with him. This was not the time for metaphysics. He had to find Asma, even if he had to do it himself. He owed it to Christie. If this priest could offer him help, he'd take it, but he wasn't going to listen to his sermons.

"Father, the Vatican has resources, assets in place just about everywhere. Right? You have a network."

"Yes, that is the Church."

Parmata got up and walked over to the priest and whispered in his ear. "I'm talking about the circle within the circle . . . P2."

Father Burkholtz eyed Parmata suspiciously. "You know what's happening here Father don't you. You're either with me or against me on this." Parmata tapped the priest on the shoulder as if he needed to emphasize his point.

"Let's not get ahead of ourselves Stephen. We're on the same side. We brought Asma to you remember."

"Who's 'we'?" Parmata asked, a hint of anger in his voice. "Why did you bring her to me?"

"You know very well. She needed a safe haven, a place to grow up away from all of this. This is what we were hoping to avoid. You have to believe me Stephen."

Just then there was a knock on the door. Father Burkholtz opened the door just enough for the messenger to hand him a note that he read and gave back to the messenger and closed the door. Stephen couldn't see the messenger's face. He could only make out the black outline of a cassock.

"Stephen. The United States has invaded Chechnya. It looks like we could be in for another Iraq. The Holy Father wishes me to be in touch with the State Department to convey his profound concern for the safety of the people of Chechnya."

"This means?"

"It means I'll have to give my full attention to the diplomatic effort."

"Which means that I'm on my own. Is that what you're saying Father?"

"I'll do what I can Stephen. But I can't promise miracles. If something comes up, I'll let you know."

"Yes, I guess, I understand." Parmata lurched toward the door. "World events take precedent over the troubles of one father."

Father Burkholtz looked down at the floor as if the right words would appear on the floor like a teleprompter. "I hope and pray that Asma is far from our current troubles."

"The world is a very crazy place. Full of zealots of every stripe, I thought I'd retired, left all this behind me. But somehow, and Father I can't figure out how, but I think you knew something like this was going to happen to Asma; that she would be caught up in something bigger than all of us. And I'm going to find out why. Mark my words." And he closed the door behind him.

In Parmata's mind there was a growing clarity of purpose, his years in the shadows of government, his contacts around the world, and his stubborn self-reliance born of the rugged Australian landscape gave him a keen focus and ability to read people and situations. If anything, age had given him what some might call wisdom. Not that he was old, for 58 he was in better shape than many 40 year olds. Back home in Nova Scotia, he rode his bike 15 miles a day. He was fit and primed for this mission. He told himself, if he could sail around the world, as he had done, he could find and rescue his daughter—for Christie's sake.

But where to begin? He'd been out of circulation for some time now. Since he met Christie and then Asma came along right after that. They'd built a life together. He'd discovered a talent for making boats. A talent he never knew he had. But he always liked challenges, and the sea. He loved the salt air and the wind. And so, an idea became a passion.

The priest wasn't much help. He seemed so obtuse to Parmata, as if he were hiding something. He couldn't put his finger on it. It was just a feeling that's all. He couldn't go to the police. They'd label Asma as crazy, or worse a terrorist, if they hadn't already. And he knew where that led. He'd been part of that process in the past.

Exhausted, Parmata left the Papal Nuncio's residence and hailed a taxi back to his hotel on the east side of Central Park. He'd been going full tilt since he heard about Asma's disappearance 36 hours ago. He needed a meal and some rest, and perhaps a jog in Central Park in the morning. As he walked through the lobby of *The Pierre* hotel he had a sudden urge to read the newspaper. He picked up the *Daily News* and headed for the bar. Not one to drink alone, he sat at the bar where he ordered a draft beer and munched on the bar nuts while he dug into the news about Chechnya. The Organization for Security and Cooperation in Europe's (OSCE) mission had left the country in the wake of a renewed wave of Islamist inspired violence.

As he was about to turn the page a man sat down next to him and ordered a scotch and soda.

"Do you believe in angels?" the academic looking man took a sip of his drink.

"Pardon me?" Parmata looked over his paper, only slightly perturbed by the intrusion.

"Angels. You know . . . cosmic beings."

"Well, I don't know. I haven't really thought about it, but I'd have to say, no, I've never met one."

"Muslims believe in angels. Spiritual beings that do the will of God."

"Interesting. So you're a Islamic scholar?"

"No, no, actually, I'm in the technology sector, but since 9/11 like a lot of people I've been trying to understand why so many people hate us—Muslims, I mean, why do they hate us? Is it our money? No, I think it's their religion. I really do. I think it's all about religion. That' s hard for us secularists to understand. I mean who goes to church anymore, let alone prays five times a day? No one wants to say that of course, the truth would be dangerous to speak. It always has been. It is so politically incorrect. But I mean when you look at it, they think they've got the perfect socio-political system. If theirs is perfect, well then, ours must be corrupt. Ergo, purge it with fire. And when you look around, I mean, the garbage and erotica. Can you blame them? It's what the Islamists call the Luciferian New World Order: the Dajjal."

"Yeah, but haven't we, I mean the West, exploited the Middle East's vast wealth? All this talk about ideology; isn't it really about oil, and money? Wasn't the Middle East as we know it today carved up like a slaughtered lamb, the spoils of the First World War?"

"A sacrificial lamb?" And he laughed, downing his drink. "You see, my friend," gesturing to the bartender, "everyone wants more; desire is the human condition. It's what separates us from animals. When an animal has enough they settle down; they rest. Us humans? Uh uh, we always want more. We're just never satisfied. And religions try to calm that beast in us, rope it in, coral it, civilize it. But sooner or later it gets out, breaks free. And to the Islamists, that freedom we cherish; it's the very work of the devil, the illusion of paradise, when it's really a cycle of never-ending desire."

"So, the Islamists' view of the state and religion as inseparable actually got it right?"

"Exactly."

"If you buy the assumption all of this is possible in the first place and not just another human thought experiment."

"And you had proof."

"What kind of proof would that be?"

"The existence of angels, spiritual beings."

Parmata looked at him. Perhaps he'd made a mistake coming here. He had too many other things to do right now. He needed a plan: to find Asma. This was a waste of time.

"You don't believe me do you? You think I'm a nut. But I know this guy over in Jersey. He can drink a liter of straight vodka and not slur a word. He knows a lot of people, if you get my drift. He wrote a book in the 1960s, called *In the Shadow of God* in which he relates his experiences with spiritual beings, Angels."

"Well, look, that's really interesting, but I've got to be going, I've got things to do, and I can't really afford to waste my time running around meeting some sixties nutbar." And Parmata stood up and taking his wallet from his jacket he put a $10 bill on the bar. As he placed the money on the bar, the man put his hand on Parmata's.

"His second book is called *Fatima: Return of the Paraclete.*"

Parmata froze. He stared this strange bar fly in the eyes, searching for what he might know. Who was he? Why had he just been sitting at the empty bar at *The Pierre* hotel?

"Okay, you've got my attention," he pulled his hand away. "What's this all about? And who are you . . . *really?*"

"My name is Frank Pendergast, I'm with the Canadian Security Intelligence Service, CSIS. We've been watching you for some time. Years in fact, ever since you came to Canada after that messy business with that terrorist Greg Fallows. You married his wife and adopted a girl from Guatemala. A lot of people have been interested in your adopted daughter. And some of them have connections, profound connections with radical Islam in fact."

"Why are you telling me this? I mean, why now?"

"Our sources tell us she is in Morocco at a Jihad training camp."

"And you expect me to believe you?"

"I'm just trying to warn you. Don't do anything stupid. Don't go after her yourself. Leave it to the professionals. Remember what happened to Fallows. He got in way over his head."

"I know all about Greg. I helped create him." Parmata stared out the window as if the clean light of day could wipe away a bitter memory. "I was a different person then. People change."

"Really?" Pendergast stated sardonically. "Not you Mr. Parmata. You'll always be a con man at heart."

"What do you mean?" Parmata grabbed the agent by the collar.

"Easy, easy does it, Stephen. You might not believe it, but I'm really just trying to help you get your daughter back."

Relaxing his grip, Parmata sat back in his chair. "Okay, but I'm not Greg Fallows, you know, I'm not some amateur you can hang out to dry."

"No. But you can't do it alone either," the agent smoothed his ruffled collar. "This is bigger than your daughter Mr. Parmata. This is a battle that has been coming for centuries, and these people believe your daughter will be the one to usher in a future utopia, the perfect natural order, pure divinity in a single system, freedom from the modernist schizophrenic separation of church and state. There are two sides in this battle, and you daughter is in the middle."

FOURTEEN

"So, if I'm not supposed to try and get my daughter back, who will?"

"The British have robust assets in these areas. But don't kid yourself Stephen, they've got their hands full. It's not like she's the only one."

"What do you mean?" Parmata challenged as the anxiety crept up his back.

"You know as well as I do that the next wave of suicide bombers will be American and Canadian kids. Profiling has paid big dividends, but the blowback has been the terrorists' ability to recruit disillusioned young people willing to strap Semtex explosives onto themselves and blow themselves to pieces."

Parmata's hands grew sweaty and his mouth became as dry as his father's Queensland well that summer of endless heat and draught when he was nine years old. Thirsty exhausted animals wandered relentlessly searching for water, only to die at the edge of the salty undrinkable Pacific Ocean. Like them, he was desperately seeking a way to save Asma. Echoes of Christie were raging inside him; kicking and screaming from behind the chaos that he reasoned must be death's dominion. "So you're telling me she's being trained as a suicide bomber? Is that it you heartless son of a bitch?" Anger swelled up in him, a confusing mélange of emotion sweeping over him in a fury. He wanted to hit something or someone. "And you don't go after her because you and your friends have got something cooked up; to use her. Am I right? Is that it?"

"Stephen, Stephen, Stephen, calm down. All I'm trying to do is frame the scenario for you. You need to know what you're up against. This isn't something for amateurs. These people are passionately committed to their vision and your daughter fits the bill at the moment. But let's be clear on this, nobody really knows what she's going to do. Only Asma or Fatima, or whoever she becomes will know that . . . can know that."

"So you've stopped by to give me a little friendly advice. So what am I supposed to do now? Go home and rent a video, build a boat and sail around the world? What would you do if you were in my place? And what I would really like to know is: are you going to help me or not for Christ's sake?"

"It's not up to me," the agent reached into his coat pocket retrieving a small navy address book. "I'll give you the name of someone who specializes in tricky situations like this. His name is Michel Pichon. He's an Islamic scholar at Merton College in Oxford. He's a good man Parmata, and I think you'll like him. I'll tell you right now he has a weakness for French Burgundy wine. Take a bottle or two of Volnay with you when you meet with him. Don't be put off by his arrogant academic airs. He's well connected."

"What's his academic interest in Islam?"

"Angels," Pendergast rose, preparing to leave. "Spiritual beings, manifestations of the Divine and their Demonic equivalents. But you'll find that out for yourself soon enough when you meet him. You'll like him." And he abruptly left the bar.

Parmata was in a state of shock. He wasn't sure what to do next. Should he hop on a plane back to Nova Scotia to regroup, or catch a flight to London? He sat there for a moment uncertain what to do and he thought of how Fallows must have felt when he launched himself into a maelstrom chasing smoke and mirrors. How in those days, he played a part to lure Fallows into a trap he couldn't shake free. The address and phone number sat there in his hand. If Greg hadn't gone to Amsterdam, if he'd only gone home, everything would have been different. He wouldn't have gotten in over his head. Was he getting in over his head too? He of all people should have known better. At the moment, as crazy as it was, London was winning. Maybe Pendergast was right. Maybe, just maybe, he needed to understand more about what attracted Asma to these people. In a way he was partly responsible. He'd always encouraged her natural inquisitiveness. And his liberal humanism believed it was a good thing to explore ideas and traditions of other cultures. But he was beginning to sense there was also a big risk acting on information from someone he'd just met in a bar claiming to be an intelligence agent. That could be it, or it could be he'd uncovered a tragic flaw in his liberal roots. Either way he didn't like his options. If he couldn't just sit back and wait for something to happen and he knew he couldn't, then he'd have to either do more research or fire a shot into the dark. And he didn't like firing at targets he couldn't see. It made no sense to Parmata. How had Pendergast found him? He said he'd been under surveillance for years. But was Pendergast an intelligence agent, a Vatican agent, or something else? Why did Pendergast want him to go to Oxford? Why was he feeling as if both he and Asma were part of a conspiracy? Too many questions, but maybe, just maybe it was a good thing he was asking them himself. He wasn't so sure Asma was asking questions, and that scared him because that's how Greg had gotten drawn into the criminal jet stream. At least he was asking questions and that's what researchers do. So maybe it was time he visited Oxford again.

Asma awoke to the clear blue light streaming in her window and the sounds of traffic outside her window. The narrow streets were crowded with people, animals, and vehicles spewing exhaust fumes and exotic spices mixed in the morning air. This is Marrakech, a fulsome place where cultures collide on the edge of the desert.

She donned her veil for the first time and felt sheltered and protected from the prying eyes of the world. A familiar comfort enveloped her as she stepped out into the light to experience a new respect instead of leering eyes. Men averted their gaze when she walked past them on the street.

Asma now moved quickly along Rue Riad Zitoun el Kedim toward Jemaa el Fna Square heading for Ben Youssef Medersa next to the Marrakesh Museum where she had arranged to meet Dhul.

The Medersa is an old Islamic school next to the old mosque of the same name founded by Sultan Moulay Abdullah el-Ghalib in 1565. In it's day it was the largest Koranic schools in Morocco. While it was closed in the 1960s, it has been remodeled and is now open to tourists. This was the place Dhul had suggested they meet once she had adjusted to her new surroundings.

The Merenids constructed the original building in the fourteenth century. It was Sultan el Ghalib who added the Andalusian stylistic details such as the carved cedar, stucco and mosaic. Asma appreciated the overwhelming power of history as she crossed the expansive main courtyard into the elaborate prayer hall. There admiring one of the stunningly beautiful carvings was Dhul Fiqar. He smiled when he saw Asma walk into the room dressed in a traditional Muslim *niqab.*

"Fatima has arrived!" he beamed. "It is good to see you here in this ancient place of learning."

"Yes, it is a truly magnificent place. But the school is no longer functioning, so where will my education begin?"

"You will soon meet the Ones who will instruct you on your true destiny."

"When Dhul? I don't want any more games."

"There are no games here in this place, only the path to enlightenment."

"Take me to the teachers."

"You are in such a hurry Fatima. Knowledge comes at its own time. But yes we will leave at once."

"Where we going?"

"The desert," he walked toward the imposing door.

Asma watched him leave and weighed her options. Should she stay or should she go? What was here real destiny?

Asma suddenly reacted and followed him quickly catching up with Dhul but following at a discreet distance.

FIFTEEN

Professor Pichon was tending to the rhododendrons in his garden when Parmata arrived by cab on his doorstep at 86 St. Thomas Mews. Professor Michel Pichon had retired from active academic pursuits almost 15 years before, but even while he pulled the weeds from his tiny plot of earth he went over the classifications and significance of various religious and philosophical constructs in his mind.

Dr. Pichon was well into his seventies. He was a short portly man with fat stubby fingers that seemed to repel the dirt from the soil by some as yet undisclosed alchemical process. He always wore a three-piece suit, even while gardening. It was a habit he'd acquired at Merton's College. His hair was completely white and he kept it very short. His large unruly white moustache defined his face and personality. While he looked neat and organized, the untrimmed moustache in the middle of his face read the opposite.

Michel was the eldest son of a French schoolteacher and Italian mother who claimed a connection to Royalty in some Duchy or other. He was born in suburban Turin where his father taught English. His parents valued education and sent him to a private school in England and Oxford and the academy became his life. He became one of the three Angel experts in the world. His study contained one of the best collections anywhere, and his six volumes of Angelology was the undisputed definitive resource on the subject.

In his personal life he was like his moustache, less well organized. He'd never married, and in that sense he was a disappointment to his mother. Now she was long dead he was free from her criticism, but he still brooded around the garden the way his mother did.

The doorbell rang and Michel looked up toward the front door through the garden and the French doors half expecting to see his mother answer the door. Even after five years, he still looked for her. Searching, the grief counselor had told him, was normal in the first year, but after five years, that can't be normal. The bell rang again. He gathered himself up and trundled into the house.

"Good afternoon sir. My name is Stephen Parmata. I emailed you."

"Yes, yes, of course, I'd forgotten all about it, but of course you did. You see that's what growing old does for you. It gives you an excuse for being an idiot. But please excuse me, won't you come in . . . Mister . . . Pam . . ."

"Parmata," Stephen, with a smile walked into the foyer. "It's sort of Italian . . . an Australian variation, I guess you could say."

"Yes, well I'm Italian myself you know, at least my mother was Italian and I grew up there, but that's a long time ago. Please, let me take your coat. I've been trying to get things arranged in the garden. It's been such a late spring, and wet."

"I've just come from Canada, so it seems reasonable to me."

"Make yourself comfortable. I'll dust the dirt off and be right with you. The bar is limited, but I've got some decent wine," and he disappeared down the hall.

Parmata surveyed the disaster that was the living room. Books and papers were scattered everywhere in piles, some four feet high with barely enough space to walk between them. He flipped through a stack of loose papers held together by an elastic band. He quickly lost himself in the words. Just words, wonderful words, poetic words of music streamed across his mind like a symphony.

"You like Thomas Mann?" Michel was standing in doorway holding a bottle of Kistler and two glasses.

"I didn't know I was reading Mann," Parmata dropped the pages back in the pile. "How did you get the manuscript? I mean this looks like an original manuscript."

"Well, it is actually. Would you like a glass of wine?"

"Ah, sure, please, that would be nice."

"How did you get the Mann manuscript? I mean, why would you just leave it sitting in a pile?"

"You like wine, Mr. Parm . . ."

"Parmata."

"Yes, Mr. Parmata, to me, books are like fine wine. If you can afford the best why not have it?"

"So you're a collector then."

"You could say that, but that's not why you came all this way isn't it?"

"I don't really know why, I came, except, I was told you were an expert on Angels"

"Have a glass of wine, and why don't we sit down. Do you believe in Angels?"

"Is it a matter of belief? Somehow I can't imagine a God whose army of messengers he sends down on missions in some cosmic secret service. It strikes me as juvenile wishful thinking."

"You have thought about it quite a bit then, I can see."

"Well, it's because of my daughter," he swallowed a lump the size of his fist. A chink in his armor had appeared. He was a man, a father, a widow. His heart burned a cauldron of rage and fear to think his adopted daughter, his only daughter, could be held against her will by some fanatics. And it gave him no solace to think she might want to join a group bent on waging war. It made no sense to him. "Asma has fallen under, how should I say, the influence of some radical Islamic fundamentalists. At least that's what I think. I think they may have sold her a bill of goods, as they say." Parmata took a long sip of wine and stared out into the English garden. "How is it Professor that well educated people can buy into something, that frankly is on the same footing as Santa Clause or the Easter Bunny . . . at least to me?"

"That's the interesting part. It's a phenomenon of experience." And he picked up a manuscript from one of the piles. "The World my friend is divided into believers and nonbelievers. The world of the fundamentalists, and everyone else." He handed Parmata a treatise written by an Egyptian Islamic scholar in the 1970s. It screamed polemics, a flaming diatribe about religion, the end of the world, and global politics.

"Are you saying that people who believe in angels are extremists?"

"No, I'm implying that some people believe in angels in the same way."

"So, angels don't really exist, because I have a really hard time with that notion."

"Angels are messengers. Do messengers exist?"

"Messengers from God? Doesn't that require belief in God? That's the part I find impossible to accept."

"So it's God you have a problem with not angels."

"I have a problem with suspending reason."

"Because you believe in reason as the way to truth."

"Based on experience."

"And that's exactly the same argument believers use. So it's like I said, the world is divided into believers and nonbelievers. And to believers, the non's represent everything that's in need of cleansing."

"So, you're saying there's no proof beyond how one interprets reality? Is that what you're saying?"

"I would say that beyond scriptures, both the New and the Old Testament, there is no scientific evidence that will convince you. But what I find interesting, and why I've spent my whole life studying the phenomenon is the recurrence of the *leitmotif* throughout history and in many different cultures. Are you familiar with the work of Carl Jung, the Swiss physician psychoanalyst?"

"Yes, I've heard of him, of course. At one point in my life I was an art dealer, so would often encounter clients with an interest in Art History, and Jung would come up in that context."

"Jung put forward the hypothesis that dreams are a normal brain phenomenon that send messages to the conscious mind. Angels, from the Greek for messengers, are mentioned in scriptures and they frequently appear in dreams. So for Jung the scientist, angels could be seen as symbols whose presence can't be explained by anything in one's personal experience but seem to be present throughout many cultures and across time. For the scientist, at least if you consider psychiatry a science and not a dismal science like economics, then dreams represent inherited patterns, akin to the Platonic notion of *ideas*.

"Let me put it another way, if you can accept that our DNA has a long evolutionary tail physically connecting us back in time to our ancestors, should we not expect the mind to be constructed in a similar fashion?"

Parmata pondered that idea. "So, if the mind was constructed in a similar way to our DNA, fundamental or basic human concepts such as good and evil could have recurring manifestations?"

"Exactly, this is what Freud called 'archaic remnants,' or what Jung called Archetypes."

Parmata nodded his head and took a sip of his Kistler. "That's interesting."

"You see all I've done is explain the phenomenon in a language you can understand: the language of science. The language of the physical world can be used to describe the spiritual or unseen world. Isn't this what physics does? Is that not why physics was considered natural philosophy by the ancients?"

"So physics uses the language of mathematics to describe the unseen world, and mathematics describes diverse phenomena including so-called random events."

"Yes, the word is stochastic, from the Greek *stokastes* meaning diviner, in the service of deity or having the nature of deity about them."

"That's interesting, especially if it's applied to genetics."

"I suppose you're right but I'm afraid that's a little outside my expertise," Michel looked at his watch.

"I've taken up enough of your time, Professor," Parmata rose to his feet. "I can't thank you enough. Really, you've been a tremendous help to me. I can't thank you enough."

"It's my pleasure really. I don't have many people knocking on my door these days asking me about angels."

"No, I'm sure you're right," Parmata headed for the door.

"In your email you mentioned something about your daughter. Good luck with that. I hope this helps.

"Thanks. I hope so too."

They shook hands and Parmata left. He now had a small piece of the puzzle. But he knew he had to get his hands dirty and climb down into the sewer system called security and intelligence. There he knew he would find another piece of the puzzle.

SIXTEEN

A full moon draped the whitewashed landscape of Casablanca in a golden shroud. The taxi pulled up in front of the *Desert Rose Bar and Grill* on the outskirts of the city. Dhul paid the driver and Asma stepped out of the car and saw a revolver sitting on the front seat next to the driver. It sent a chill up her spine.

"What's wrong?" Dhul asked as they watched the taxi slip away into the night.

"It's nothing, nothing, really, I guess I'm not used to seeing guns," she nodded in the direction of the fleeing taxi.

"Ah, it's a hard business to be in here."

"Like New York," she agreed, walking into the *Desert Rose*.

"Yes, like New York, only more dangerous. The man we are about to meet is going to take us to a camp outside of town . . . way outside of town, about 400 kilometers out into the desert.

You'll learn to love the desert. There are so many more brilliant colors to a desert sunrise than you've ever seen before. I guarantee it. And the silence, the silence is maddening and awesome at the same time."

"That must be in a different country."

"It is. It is the land of sacrifice, and God's holy warriors; where God's law is the only law."

Everyone in the room seemed to stop talking when Asma walked through the door. But Dhul paid no attention to the bristling hostility that seemed to fill the place.

"That's him over there," Dhul looked in the direction of the long dark polished wooden bar.

"You have made quite a fuss coming in here, my friend," the man glowered. Then without taking a breath, he looked Asma in the eye and added in a low monotone husky voice, "There is no need for you to know my name. It makes no difference in the end. We are all just passing through this dimension anyway. Death is the only certainty. How we die determines our destiny." He took a sip of sweet mint tea and a long drag on a *Gauloise* cigarette, exhaling slowly. "It's hard to find good cigarettes anymore, you know, after they shut down the factory in Lille. But I've got connections in France."

Asma didn't know what to say. She looked at Dhul who was reading the menu. He made no attempt to acknowledge her presence.

"So, how does this adventure begin?" She removed her headscarf revealing her ample dark hair.

"It's already begun," Dhul piped in suddenly showing interest in the conversation. "Our friend here will take us overland to our next destination where you will be introduced to the ways of your destiny."

As he spoke a fat Fez wearing bartender arrived exhaling garlic and seven spices. "Anybody want a drink?" Dhul stopped talking.

"I'll have a vodka tonic please. These gentlemen may prefer Scotch," Asma shocked both Dhul and the stranger.

And so this is how the journey to Camp SRT 19 began. After 3 vodka tonics Asma was beginning to get used to the idea of thinking about dying for a cause. Even if she didn't understand it all, she was prepared to follow it through to the end. At least she was ready to follow it this far and maybe a little further too.

They left the bar about midnight heading due east to the border in a beat up old tan colored Land Rover. Without hesitation they suddenly turned south right before the border checkpoint where they continued along a camel track into the mountains and the desert beyond. The driver seemed to know exactly where he was going. The night was clear and the full moon cast an ethereal light over the landscape. Asma dozed off in the back seat of the Rover. The vodka tonics were working. She woke up when they pulled into an oasis to fill up with gasoline from the canisters the driver retrieved from the roof of the vehicle.

The night air was extraordinarily still and a malodorous wave of gasoline fumes unexpectedly filled the vehicle. A few Bedouin, traditional desert-dwellers, appeared around the truck peering into the windows and expressing a natural curiosity born of a less complicated time. Asma hastened to cover her head with her scarf for fear they would take her for a prostitute and start making lewd gestures like she'd seen before in Casablanca.

From nowhere several military vehicles descended on the oasis circling their Rover.

"Everyone out of the truck," the leader shouted evidently meaning business. Guns appeared everywhere among the black faces and olive green uniforms. Clearly they weren't in Morocco.

The driver came around from behind the truck where he'd been refueling and spoke to the officer in a language Asma didn't understand. The officer nodded a couple of times, smiled and shook the driver's hand. No one asked for papers or anything, and in the blink of an eye the military convey disappeared into the desert night. Neither the driver nor Dhul spoke as they climbed back into the truck. Asma, silent, stared at the back of both Dhul and the driver's heads as the headlights cast a faint light into the darkness ahead.

After many hours of driving over rugged landscape the Rover stopped in the darkness. A flashlight appeared first in the driver's window and then searching the whole vehicle with its narrow beam of light.

They had arrived at the Camp simply described by Dhul as SRT 19. It implied there were at least 18 others, but who really knew. It could also stand for a specific date but it didn't really matter, all Asma knew was that she was in a very different place. The anticipation was both frightening and exhilarating.

Saraqael and Abaddon sat around a glowing fire watching the Rover as it passed through the cursory interrogation at the Camp's main gate.

"She is with us my friend," Abaddon nodded in the direction of the Rover.

"God is great," Saraqael replied. They both laughed.

The Rover drove to a collection of tents beyond the campfire where Saraqael and Abaddon sat among men, regaling with stories of the desert over the fire. For centuries before radio or satellites invaded human consciousness, myths, legends and sagas told around countless campfires were the main entertainment. On a night such as this Saraqael recalled how he and Abaddon had escaped a fierce inferno during the last siege of Bal. But you are not interested in the stories of old, although you should be, you and I are interested in the girl over there getting out of the Rover, preparing to enter her tent and a new life beyond.

"You can settle and I'll see you in the morning," Dhul indicated the nearest tent.

"Yes, thanks that would be great. I am very tired after the journey and I'd really like some time to myself."

As Dhul turned to walk away, he paused momentarily and turning back to Asma he said: "Oh, yeah, I wouldn't venture outside the Camp. I mean if you were thinking of trying to find a place to go to the bathroom. The desert has nocturnal predators: human and animal alike. There is a very active white slave trade in Africa, and we wouldn't want to get distracted from our mission, would we? Good night."

"No, we certainly wouldn't want that," she climbed into the tent, exhausted.

Inside Asma became transported to a timeless place of rare beauty. A small oil lamp flickered light and licked shadows in darkened corners. Her bedroll had been prepared with loving care and the warm sweet smell of incense filled the air. She suddenly did feel very tired. Sleep crept over her in a tidal bore of memories; dreams seemingly connected together like paintings in a gallery rushing into one another on a crowded subway line of sub consciousness.

Asma awoke to the sound of gunfire cracking the silence with its impatient reveille. Then there was silence again until a Mullah's mournful sound called the faithful to prayer. Conflicted, and not necessarily religious, Asma didn't know if she should follow the sound of the call to prayer or not. In the end she decided to rouse herself and follow the call. She was after all here to immerse herself in the culture.

She found few women at the Camp. In fact it appeared that the only women were wives of some of the men. They tended to meals and cleaning for their husbands and kept a discreet distance from Asma at all times. And of course they covered their entire bodies to reveal only dark eyes that met Asma's gaze with inquisitive stares.

"Good morning," Dhul greeted her. "Your instructions begin today. But first we must eat. The body is the temple of the soul and must be cared for."

And so, after the meal of mutton stew, Asma began her training in what was known in Western intelligence circles as the most notorious terrorist training camp outside of the Middle East. As might be expected, in the weeks that followed she excelled at weapons training and took to the political discussion with fervor reserved for only the most ardent supporters of the cause. Abaddon and Saraqael were pleased.

"Dhul," Abaddon spoke. "We have a mission for you."

"But my mission is with Asma."

"Not any longer."

Dhul sensed what that meant. That he'd outgrown his usefulness and he was now a security risk. He knew too much and that meant only one thing.

"Dhul, you have been called to greatness. Now you must walk that path to your own destiny."

With that Dhul knew he would soon be walking some street, any street, it didn't matter. He'd be packed with explosives and with the flash of electrons zinging along a 3-cent wire he'd be blasted off the face of God's good earth. No way around that, he knew too much.

As the weeks flowed into months, one morning Dhul didn't come to her tent, and when she asked where he had gone they'd told her he left on a flatbed truck the night before. When she asked where he'd gone there was no reply; only a faint smile of secret knowledge. As she glimpsed this, she asked if he would be coming back? When there was no reply, she knew he'd been called to action. And she was both happy and sad. Happy that his action would strike at the heart of the beast somewhere and sad for that dark skinned beautiful man that one day long ago in New York—almost another lifetime ago—the first day they met at Columbia, she thought she might fall in love with those dark mysterious eyes. But that was a different time when passion meant something personal, not something political. She knew if she was to complete her mission, she must remain focused on her real purpose in life. That purpose she had grown to embrace with pure dedication and clarity of mind like she'd never experienced before. She was growing tired of this endless training. She envied Dhul. At least he was called to action, somewhere out there beyond the desert's blue sky. She had become Fatima. Asma was gone.

SEVENTEEN

Parmata stepped out his front door to pick up his morning paper and into the cold dampness that passes for winter in Nova Scotia. The headline of *The Chronicle Herald* read: Suicide Bomber Kills 14 in Jerusalem. Disquieted, he looked around as if someone was watching. It had been two months now since Asma disappeared. Everyday the news brought anxiety and fear to his doorstep. He couldn't watch the television news anymore it was just too much to bear. Too many suicide bombers, it was a daily event now somewhere in this troubled world.

He'd tried without much success to use his intelligence contacts. While they were certainly sympathetic; there was just no denying it, the jihadists were getting good at not using technology and therefore it was becoming increasingly difficult to track key suspects once they fell into the silence that is much of the Third World. Agencies were forced to rely on human intelligence. But reliable human intelligence in many parts of the world was very hard to find, where showing up Anglo-Saxon and white was the quickest way to land in a shit load of trouble. And local contacts were unreliable at best and quite often illusionary.

As he read the lead story Parmata froze. He recognized the name: Dhul Fiqar. There was a small call out box with a college photo of the suicide bomber. The article went on to describe the unlikely profile of a highly educated British man of Sri Lankan origin who had recently been offered a job at Johns Hopkins. Just then the phone rang.

"Hello?"

"Stephen?"

"Yes."

"This is Daryl Spaulding. Did you see the papers?"

"Yes, I was just reading it now. It's damned upsetting."

"Well, it could be the lead we've been waiting for." Parmata's heart jumped. "We've traced his trail back to a camp in Western Africa. It's not much to go on, and maybe she's gone by now, but we think; there's a chance anyway that she's still there."

"Now what?"

"We get you over here and we look at a Spec Op. SAS are up for it. I've already spoken to them."

"I'll be there as quick as I can. Gee, Daryl I didn't even ask you how you were? I mean after they tried to kill you."

"I'm fine Stephen. Nothing really, old boy, just a scratch. They actually gave me a good cover. Now I can be out of the Section and no one knows the difference!"

Colonel Randolph "Jimmy" Atkins met Parmata and Spaulding at Credenhill, the former RAF base. In a nondescript office inside the base Colonel Atkins laid out what they knew about Camp SRT 19.

In civilian clothes, Col. Atkins was a very fit man in his early fifties. He sported a trimmed gray moustache and carried an air of easy confidence about him.

"Why is it called SRT 19?" Parmata asked.

"SRT stands for special religious training, and 19 is most likely a secret network code of some kind linking the leadership to the central command," Col. Atkins tapped a pencil on his desk. "In any event we have a pretty good idea where Dhul Fiqar or as the media have dubbed him 'the Don Bomb' was prior to his terminal rendezvous in Jerusalem.

"We've been wanting to take down one of these camps for some time, so this is an excellent opportunity for us."

"Do we know if Asma is in this camp?" Parmata asked with trepidation.

"We can't be sure, old boy," Spaulding piped in, "But given that she was associated with this Dhul Fiqar character, there is a strong probability at least that she was at the training camp with him. At least that's what the best Intel suggests. We now have satellite coverage of the camp and we believe there is a woman who could fit Asma's description training at the camp."

"Our tactical plan," Col. Atkins added," includes using 25 men from "the Increment", former Regulars in 22 SAS or the British Army who've volunteered and received extensive training to conduct covert ops such as this for M15 and MI6."

Looking at Spaulding Col. Atkins added: "We normally don't discuss details of our tactical ops but Mr. Spaulding has indicated that you've worked with Her Majesty's Services on other Ops and you're cleared for this Op."

"Yes, that's correct Colonel. Please carry on."

"For this Op we'll employ a HALO or high altitude, low opening parachute insertion at night. Second, helicopters will swoop in to bring the assault force and extract our troops, any intelligence we can obtain and, of course, the package—your daughter.

"I have to tell you Mr. Parmata, this isn't going to be a walk in the park by any measure. I mean we believe she's been in combat training and she could resist rescue. Anything could happen. You must be prepared for any eventuality. We'll do our best, I can assure you, but . . ."

"Yes, I understand Colonel." Parmata reluctantly absorbed the message, "there is no certainty in life but she is my daughter, so please take care. That's all I ask."

Jumping out of an airplane at 25,000 feet requires oxygen, a pilot-like helmet and protective clothing from the extreme cold. Add a M-16 under your arm and 100 pounds of explosives and other high-tech gadgets and you might begin to understand the challenges facing the 16 man specialist forward team of "the Increment" as they tumbled out of the MC-130P on a moonless night somewhere over the West African desert. Operation Cormorant had begun.

The SAS "Increment" included combat air traffic controllers and other specialist forces to secure the landing zone so that assault helicopters could land the main force.

A blinding flash of light signaled the takedown had begun. Gunfire erupted from everywhere simultaneously. Confusion reigned as the true shock of the overwhelming force quickly neutralized any resistance. The soldiers immediately began rounding up survivors for transportation to interrogation locations at a pre-arranged undisclosed African nation nearby.

Back in London Parmata and Spaulding huddled near the corner of the bar sipping real ale at the Antelope Pub on 22 Eaton Terrace, in Belgravia.

"Hard to believe this whole area was a swamp two hundred years ago," Daryl made polite conversation.

"Yeah," Parmata replied fecklessly.

"They should be well on their way by now Stephen," Daryl stared into his beer. "How long has it been since we worked together?"

"Probably 20 years, maybe 25."

"We did have some fun back then. All that business with Christie's illness must have been terrible for you. I'm sorry, frightfully sorry, old chap."

"Thanks. But frankly I've been so worried about Asma I haven't had much time to think about much else. Asma and I have grown even further apart after Christie died. I just don't know what to do. And now all this; it's a nightmare. Really."

"What are you going to do when they find her?"

"Father Burkholtz at the Vatican UN Mission has said he'd help. I think she may need to be isolated, almost quarantined for a while."

"De-programming: isn't that what we called it?"

"I guess it is a bit like a cult, but how do you know, I mean, how do you really tell the difference between genuine religious fervor and fanaticism?"

"Well, my friend, we'll find out soon enough." As Spaulding spoke his cell phone rang. "Yes, yes, I see. I see. Okay." And he hung up.

"Stephen. She wasn't there."

"What?"

"She wasn't there! The mission was a success but they didn't find Asma. She'd gone, according to preliminary interrogations, she had just left at most maybe a day or two ago. I'm sorry. There's nothing more I can do at this stage. But we'll continue to see what useful information we get from the interrogations and let you know if anything worthwhile turns up."

EIGHTEEN

Saraqael was pleased. Angels of his stature, especially dark angels, rarely experience profound emotion. It's not that they don't feel. It's just that their nature isn't to feel the extremes or depths of emotion. That's why it's so easy for them to watch and influence events without actually having to get involved, because if they really cared about people they would have to get involved, and that is against their nature, as much as breathing under water is against ours.

Saraqael was pleased because Fatima had completed her religious and combat training, at least the first part of it. And all the residual security risks had been cleanly severed, including SRT 19, thanks to a little help from the Brits.

He hovered in his mind, as one might in a helicopter but without the aid of a machine, over the place they call Montréal. As his focus became more refined, a blue fog lifted and he could see clearly a woman enter an apartment complex in east Montréal at 5802 Avenue Malicorne.

"You're watching her because you are pleased, but pleasure is forbidden us."

"Am I not supposed to appreciate the arts?" Saraqael regarded Abaddon's glowing face.

"I think you are growing emotions my hairy friend and that we cannot, you cannot afford."

"No one believes in us anymore. We have been relegated to the stuff of fairy tales, to mythology and medieval ignorance."

"Now let's not put down one of our finest eras, well perhaps not our most productive, as the so-called Twentieth Century but the Black Death was a nice piece of work all the same."

"Science will never see us, reason is but the blind cousin of nature's children. Why do you think they refer to *dark matter* as mysterious and look for theories of strings to explain their ideas of nature when their ideas of nature are devoid of emotion? Because it is emotion they fear the most. That is the elegant irony of these creatures: they long to be immortal and to give up their very nature means losing emotion, the one thing that makes them different from everything else, the capacity to love, yet they choose to be like us, to follow us, to destroy life. This is the beautiful irony of why they choose not to see us, or believe we could even exist, which is exactly why we've been so productive of late. You and I know our natures. They don't know their own and so nature abhors a vacuum, and we help fill the void, you and I, the angel of death, and the Prince of Darkness. We give their lives the meaning they refuse to create for themselves."

"Look Abaddon, she is preparing to pray."

"That is a beautiful irony."

Asma rolled the prayer mat and stored it under her bed. It had been a long journey from Morocco and she was tired. Her handler, Abdul Azeem had arranged for her to rent an apartment in a part of Montréal favored by the Algerian community where she would have the protection of sympathetic refugees. It was in this neighborhood that Ahmed Ressam lived as he plotted to blow up Los Angeles airport. His thwarted "Millennium Bomber" attempt helped to consolidate American suspicion that Canada was a haven for terrorists.

It was from Abdul that she had learned about Dhul and the raid on SRT 19.

"Allah favors you. He has something special in mind for you Fatima. This is for sure."

"And what might that be Abdul?"

"Only He knows and he will reveal it to the world only when He is ready."

Asma left the building alone for the first time since arriving back in Canada. Dressed in black from head to toe her natural beauty was hidden under the protective veil. She hoped she was invisible among the people going about their shopping and business. The CSIS surveillance team semi-permanently stationed in the apartment across the street duly noted her exit from the building. Their report was passed to the field agents parked at the corner in the navy blue Ford E-series van with the ExpressVu logo on the side. They switched on the digital video camera that connected with the satellite uplink. Moments later Asma appeared on the large HD TV screen in the factory-like building that is the Ottawa home to the Communications Security Establishment, Canada's national cryptologic agency. In seconds her presence in Canada was known to other western intelligence agencies linked in the digital war against terrorism. And within the hour Parmata got word that Asma was located in Montreal. His relief was only surpassed by his anxiety about what might happen next. Why was she here?

Parmata sipped his coffee as he wandered among the sheep grass that was his lawn. The cool spring breeze swept from the East, a gentle reminder that winter is a reluctant departing guest in these Northern regions. The Nova Scotia winter was mild compared to the last few Parmata endured but he thought of Christie; how she would be thinking about planting flowers in the garden by the house where they would be sheltered from the cool sea breezes, even in summer. As he watched the Canadian Geese wing their way across the blue gray sky the phone rang back in the house. He decided to let the voice mail take a message as he continued his walk toward the crashing waves on the rocky shore. He could see the sheep on Tancook Island as they slowly made their way up the hill. How nice it might be to have some sheep, or maybe a dog for a companion. Since Christie died and Asma's disappearance he had forgotten the simple pleasures of friendship, even friendship with an animal was better than the solipsistic world he inhabited of late. Christie always wanted a German shepherd. Yes, that would be a good idea. The phone rang again disrupting his daydream. *Damn, better go get that,* he cursed the intrusive technology.

Spaulding was in Ottawa when the call came. The question was: should they pick her up or let her mission unfold? To bring her in now would only compromise the intelligence capacity in the war on terror. "Keep her under surveillance. I don't want her to disappear again, understand?"

By the time Parmata got back to the house there were two messages waiting on his voice mail. One from Daryl Spaulding that simply said call, it was urgent. The second was from Asma. Not to worry. She was sorry she had to leave so quickly but that she was okay and safe. And they would talk soon. He played the last message over and over again just to hear her voice. Then he saved it in memory. Her voice sounded relaxed, yet confident.

The phone rang again. He picked it up on the first ring.
"Hello?"
"Parmata, it's Spaulding."
And so, Parmata was briefed about what MI6 knew, or at least what they were prepared to share: how Asma had been tracked to Montreal and how they had lost her in a convoluted cat and mouse game among the close-knit Algerian immigrant community. But Parmata didn't tell Spaulding that he'd had a call from Asma (although Spaulding already knew that too). And so it continues, knowing very well that if she was under close surveillance as she probably was that they could have brought her in; instead they were tracking her in the hope that she would prove to be key in leading deeper into the network.

NINETEEN

Saraqael stood in the garden near the statue of the Goddess of Perpetual Love. He admired her slender figure and confident airs. She was, after all, only an ideal. In life love seems always to be at odds with the notion of perpetuity. He checked his watch. Abaddon was late again. How could an angel be late for anything? There was no traffic or other excuses. It could only be meant as an insult, to show who was the more influential.

Abaddon appeared on as if on cue wearing a navy blue suit cut from the finest Persian cloth. "How do you like it?" He spun around in front of Saraqael then stopping in mid turn to admire the Goddess. "Yes, I see you've been occupying yourself well!"

"We must proceed," Saraqael said growing angry. "We must get on with it. The girl is ready for her destiny."

"And we are ready for ours!"

"Never before has the World seen such a destructive force unleashed upon it."

"The uniting of Christians and Muslims against the Hebrew hordes. Who would have thought it possible? Only you and I Saraqael could conjure such a feat as this. And we have done it through force of Will and Power.

"May I remind you Brother of Darkness that we have no reason to celebrate yet?"

"You are right sweet Prince. We shall celebrate and celebrate we will . . . Next year in Jerusalem!! Ha, ha, ha, ha!"

And in an instant they were gone. Gone as if they'd never been there, never existed or invented in the minds of men. The subtle creaking of the ship of fools trusting in blind faith, failing to notice the rats eating away at the moral fiber stored in the dark underbelly of the aging ship of state. Ill prepared are we today for moral turpitude, content to sing hymns and think nice thoughts while the world groans under the aching strain.

Asma walked into the washroom of one of the many hundreds of Tim Horton's coffee shops in Montreal and removed her *niqab*, tucking it in a nylon satchel she had been carrying underneath her *abaya*. She wore jeans and a gray sweatshirt and tucked her long black hair through the Red Sox baseball cap. She stopped briefly at a mirror to look at herself as if to admire the artful transformation.

Abruptly she was out the door and down the nearest Metro station. *They'll have a hard time tracking me* she thought as she took the stairs two at a time. She caught the westbound train and got off at the second station where she caught a cab to the train station. At the train station she bought a ticket for the next train to Toronto.

On the train to Toronto she slept, her head propped up against the satchel and her dreams swirled in a desert thousands of miles away. Angels in suits and big dirty boots danced in a hurricane of sound. Their tarnished wings falling like rain absorbed by the thirsty sands, vanishing with the wind, leaving only silent twinkling stars as witnesses in the black moonless night.

At Union Station she took a taxi to Yorkville where she walked to a basement hair salon on Cumberland. Two very gay proprietors greeted her.

"Darling, where has the ugliest woman in the world been lately? How can we possibly to anything with this?" Mitch rushed to greet her at the door with a big kiss and embrace. David the other stylist looked over and smiled while continuing to blow-dry his redheaded patron's hair.

"Don't listen to him sweetheart, you look gorgeous as always!"

"Hey, guys, talk about gorgeous. You too are the most gorgeous pair I've seen in a long time; too bad for me you're both gay! No chance you could be bi?" They all broke into gales of laughter leaving the half blow-dried redhead rather flummoxed.

"Seriously, Mitch, I want to dye my hair."

"You want to change your hair from that radiant black?" Mitch drew expansive circles with his arms for dramatic effect.

"Yes, I've decided blondes have more fun, and I need more fun."

"Well, I'm going to give you the best color job ever! You just sit yourself down over here and we'll get started on this major makeover project. It ain't going to be easy but you've come to the right place kiddo. And where have you been girl? Your skin is mighty dry . . ."

The blonde Asma emerged from the hair salon with a dinner invitation and a place to stay overnight. She'd known Mitch for years through a mutual friend who was studying Theology at St. Michael's College. She would frequently have Mitch do her hair when she was in town and they became friends. She would sometimes stay at his place and they would talk long into the night. He was a kind person and a good friend. On this night she knew she it would be safe to stay at Mitch's and she could use a little distraction and a glass or two of red wine. She hadn't had a glass a wine in a very long time.

MI6 was unhappy with the Canadians taking the lead on this one. "They can't even follow this woman wearing a hijab in Montreal for Christ's sake! How bloody difficult can that be? Okay, okay, tell them that it's unfortunate and I'm sure they'll find her again. But wait, we do know that she made contact with her father. So we'll keep tabs on him. Right, tell the Canadians here's their chance to redeem themselves. And I want to speak to Frank Pendergast myself, right now," Spaulding hung up the phone.

At an Internet café on Bloor Street across from the Royal Ontario Museum Asma used an alias Yahoo Liberian account routed through a server in Europe. She knew the people following her would eventually track the message to the local ISP but by then she'd be out of Toronto.

The message to her father simply read she needed to meet Father Burkholtz. She had some questions that needed to be answered. She instructed him to reply to this email address and she would contact him again. She hit the send button and shut the system down.

"Excuse me lady, you're supposed to leave the computers on," the retro-looking punk with a nose ring rebuked, irritated by the thought of having to spend time away from his comic books.

"Sorry." She paid for her session. "Blondes you know. I guess I'm not used to using computers."

"Right, whatever," not bothering to look up.

She decided to do a little shopping. Her first stop was a used electronics store where she asked about the possibility of getting a refurbished cell phone. The way she said, "refurbished" raised the eyebrow of the salesman but he knew exactly what she was talking about. She was looking for a cell phone that couldn't be traced. "For privacy reasons, you know there's this one guy who won't stop calling me, and I was wondering if there was anything available using cell block technology. The creep is kind of a high tech geek and has all the gear to track me down using cell trace technology and GPS."

"Wow, sounds like a real creep alright," the clerk reached for a Motorola from a drawer under the counter. "I sort of re-jigged this one myself, so I kinda know it works," he smiled.

"That's great, I'll take two."

He looked at her, stunned.

"It's okay, I lose them a lot."

"Ah, okay." and he pulled another one from the same drawer.

Asma immediately couriered the second phone and prepaid phone card to Parmata.

By the time she connected with Parmata two days later she was on the Greyhound bus halfway to Guelph. Since her email Parmata had time to arrange for Father Burkholtz to meet her in Canada. It would also avoid Asma having to cross the U.S. border.

"The Jesuit Novitiate in Guelph. You can't miss it; it's on the old Highway 6 just past Woodlawn Road. Look for the Wal-Mart store. It's on the left. Can you be there tomorrow? 10PM?"

"Okay. Father Burkholtz is keen to help. He he'll do whatever he can to help you."

"Thanks Stephen. This really means a lot to me."

"To me too. I just need to know that you're okay."

"I'm okay, really I am."

"I love you, you know Asma. We did what we thought was best. Both of us, your mother and I."

"I know. See you tomorrow night. You've got some travel ahead of you, and by the way make sure you're not followed."

The encryption technology Asma had purchased was seriously out of date, at least as far as the Communications Security Establishment (CSE) was concerned. The wizards and their gizmos at CSE impressed Agent Frank Pendergast. Without these kids it would be a lot harder to reconstruct a destroyed hard drive, or burnt videotape. They mostly passed on information to the Brits or the Americans who did the real dirty work. But that was all about to change. Now Frank knew where they were meeting, he planned to be ready, and this time she wouldn't get away. And Frank would get all the credit himself; at least that was his plan.

Father Burkholtz met Parmata at Pearson International Airport in Toronto. He'd taken the Air Canada flight from LaGuardia. He met Parmata past the Customs and Immigration area.

"Thanks for coming Father, this means a lot to me."

"Yes, of course, I said I'd do anything to help, but I didn't think it would mean coming to Canada again. I haven't been here since I was in the Novitiate in Guelph as a young Jesuit."

"Well, Father that's where we're going;"

"You're kidding!" Father Burkholtz shrugged at the coincidence as they climbed into the rental car.

"No. That's where we're meeting Asma."

"Well, look if I call ahead I can probably arrange for us to meet in the Father Superior's private dining room."

"Excellent idea. We'll turn off at Campbellville Road and you can call from the payphone at the restaurant while we're waiting for lunch."

"You think of everything, Stephen. I should have known; some things never change."

298

The fragrance of apple blossoms from the old orchard trees greeted Father Burkholtz and Parmata as they drove in past the stone gates.

"Things have changed a lot since I was a young man first passing through these gates."

"I bet they have Father."

"I see the Chapel is gone," he pointed to the sign outside the former Chapel door that indicated it was now a computer facility for an insurance company.

"Yes, but there are a few aging Jesuits still here," Parmata waved toward the front entrance and the grey haired man waiting by the door.

"Well, I don't believe it," Father Burkholtz got out of the car. "If it's not Father Brian Murphy!"

"A little older James, but still the best hockey player outside the NHL!" The two priests laughed and hugged each other like lost brothers.

"You're still playing hockey Brian?"

"Yep, just turned 72 and I can give the young fellas a run for their money."

"By young he means the guys in their fifties,"

"Stephen Parmata, I'd like you to meet Father Brian Murphy, one of the least modest Jesuits around. Well, at least as far as hockey goes!"

"Nice to meet you Father. Thanks again for helping us out. I really appreciate it."

"Don't mention it. Any friend of the esteemed Father Burkholtz is a friend of mine. Enough of this—please come inside. I have someone I want you to meet."

A blonde haired woman wearing a dark green tracksuit stood looking out the bay window of the wood-paneled dining room.

"We have a lovely view of Wal-Mart now."

Asma turned and smiled. "Stephen, and Father Burkholtz, so good of you to come,' she walked over to shake Father Burkholtz's hand and kissed Parmata gently on the cheek.

Parmata couldn't get over the way she'd changed. It wasn't just the hair, but of course the blonde hair was in sharp contrast to her natural black. It was the way she carried herself, a sense of self-confidence she radiated. Perhaps it was just maturity but to Parmata it was something else, something powerful, like someone on a mission, a no nonsense attitude. That's it: she seemed to exude purpose.

"Asma, we . . . I've been so worried about you,' Parmata reached out to embrace her.

She pulled back. "Yes, it is good to see you too. There is so much to say, and there is so little time."

"What do you mean? We've got all the time in the world."

"I wish we did Stephen; I wish we did."

"Come my child," Father Murphy invited, "Let's sit over here where can be more comfortable. Would you like some tea or coffee perhaps?"

"Tea would be nice Father," she agreed sitting down on the sofa.

Outside Frank Pendergast and his team of five federal agents encircled the old Novitiate. Pendergast had been waiting for years to lead a team that apprehended a suspect. Standard operating procedure required that the Royal Canadian Mounted Police take the lead on any arrest or apprehension of suspects. But this time Frank intended to go it alone. He was going to do it his way; he wasn't going to let the police get the credit for his team's analytical work. Even those uppity Brits would thank him.

"Ready on all points," the radio crackled.

"Hold still," Pendergast barked back. "We move on my order and only my order. Confirm."

One by one the radios squawked affirmation.

"Mike, are you getting their conversation?"

"Affirmative," the radio snapped.

"Then we wait," Pendergast commanded into the car radio parked in the shadows at the end of the long tree-lined driveway leading up to the Novitiate.

TWENTY

Parmata stared at Asma in amazement. Who was this woman? Where did she get her energy, her power? *Christie would have been so impressed.* He took a seat in one of the large leather armchairs Father Murphy gathered around the small coffee table across from the sofa where she sat. She seemed to have really matured, and yet at the same time changed in some strangely quixotic way these past months.

"You look well Asma," as he accepted the coffee from a young novitiate. "I see you still have some recruits Father Burkholtz."

"Ah, but there aren't very many. Not like in our day." Father Murphy looked at Father Burkholtz with bright eyes.

"Alas, you are right my friend. The days we spent here were among the best in my life Brian."

"And mine too. Remember the size of the strawberries!"

"How could I forget, and young Father McDermott. He ate so many he broke out in a rash! We called him Father Strawberry!"

"Poor Jim. He died last year."

"I didn't know that. What happened?"

Father Murphy became silent and suddenly serious. "The Lord works in mysterious ways, wouldn't you agree Asma?"

"Yes, definitely." She had obviously not been listening to the conversation.

"He took his own life. God rest his soul," Father Murphy made the sign of the cross. Father Burkholtz nodded and blessed himself as well.

301

"Do we know why?" Father Burkholtz pressed.

"They say he suffered from mental illness. Manic depression, bi-polar disorder I think they call it now."

"I'm sorry to hear that. But Asma you have things you wanted to ask me?" Father Burkholtz turned to her, putting his coffee down on the table.

"Yes, you see, my instruction, my religious instruction that is, is only half complete. I need to understand the teachings of the prophet Jesus."

"Well, my child, we see Jesus as the son of God."

"Is the God of Jesus not the same Allah of Mohammed?"

"Why yes of course He is."

"Then you will teach me of the ways of Jesus?"

Father Burkholtz gave Father Murphy a puzzled, 'what should I say,' kind of look? "Why of course. This is what we do," he smiled at Asma.

"Good. We can begin right away."

"But Asma, aren't you going to tell us what happened to you? Where you've been? I mean, I've been worried sick." Parmata flinched, exasperated with the conversation so far.

"Stephen, I know you love me, and you have suffered a great deal in my absence. But I need you to accept it when I say I'm okay. All you need to know is that I'm back now. I did what I needed to do to learn more about a part of myself, and I needed to do that alone. This is all you have to know. Please Stephen, leave it at that.

"Now Father Burkholtz, you are a learned man. I believe you have a PhD in philosophy from the University of Pennsylvania?"

"Yes, that's true," the white haired priest wiped his black framed glasses with a handkerchief from his breast coat pocket.

"And your area of interest was epistemology, was it not?"

"Yes, but that was years ago. Today I spend my time in diplomatic activities for the Papal See."

"What's this all about Asma?" Parmata asked growing irritated. "I didn't come all this way to discuss philosophy."

"Well, I did!" She snapped back.

"I don't see how this has anything to do with where you've been and what you're up to."

"Up to! You think I'm up to something do you?"

"Come on Asma. Who do you think you're talking to? Your every move is being tracked."

"Tell me something I don't know Stephen. Now either sit down and shut up or leave. Your choice."

She'd never spoken to him like that before, with such verve and passion. He sat down fuming.

"Now look," she glanced sideways at Parmata. "The West, that is western thinking, western philosophy has been enthralled with reason as a means to explain reality; how things really work. Right?"

"Well, yes, I suppose some have argued over the years that is how we know truth."

"But surely religion and religious truth is not founded on that belief?"

"You imply the belief in reason is just as, shall we say vague an idea as faith itself?"

"I mean why does reason work? In science for example, we face the abyss do we not, when we refuse to see the bizarre spectacle of theory and practice at the very heart of the scientific method, or any logical construction of the universe for that matter."

"What have you been reading?" Parmata asked dumbfounded.

"I've been thinking a great deal. I've been thinking that at the very core of the Western quest for knowledge is a moral question: whether the work or activity is good or bad. Knowledge might be power, but the real issue is whether it is used wisely or foolishly, is it not Father?"

"I would have to agree."

"Then in real political terms, the conclusion is both strange and very depressing. Once confidence in reason is lost to the sham arts, the west can no longer be differentiated from those irrational cave dwellers glimpsing reflections on the wall. That is, those who believe what they see or experience are actually reality."

"We do have our faith in God. And a belief in good and evil"

"But if good and evil are equal and quaintly both unreasonable then it is impossible to differentiate among the senses in which reason has been said to be 'beyond good and evil' leading ultimately to nihilism—that is nothing. Is this not the moral reality of modern western society and culture?"

"You paint a harsh picture of the West."

"Is this what they've been teaching you?" Parmata interjected.

"I'm talking to the priest!"

"What are you trying to prove Asma?" Father Burkholtz asked calmly taking Asma's hand in his.

"I need to understand Father, why we are so far apart. I need to understand my place in all of this. I mean, if I am to fulfill the prophecy."

"Okay, let's move!" Pendergast shouted into the microphone attached to his earpiece.

In seconds the wooden door burst wide open as the plain clothed agents descended over them. Asma made a dash toward the large bay windows. It was obvious now that she has been checking her escape route when they came in the room.

"Stop or I'll fire!" Pendergast shouted aiming his pistol at the fleeing Asma.

"No, don't shoot, stop," Father Murphy sprang up in front of Asma as she went through the window tumbling to the lawn below.

Three shots rang out. Two of them lodged in Father Murphy's chest sending him crashing to the floor, while the third smashed a pane of glass widely missing its intended target.

"Are you nuts? Look what you've done now, you idiot!" Parmata shouted at Pendergast. He dashed to the window but couldn't see where Asma had gone. He was torn between following her and racing back to attend Father Murphy.

Dark red blood oozed from Father Murphy's chest soaking the red Persian rug on the floor. Father Burkholtz held Father Murphy's head whispering the prayers of Last Rites and motioning the sign of the cross with the crucifix from around Father Murphy's neck.

"He's dead," Father Burkholtz looked up at Parmata.

TWENTY-ONE

Asma cleared the brush behind the Novitiate in one sweeping leap. She dashed to her waiting rental behind the Wal-Mart. Pendergast's men had left their positions to rally to the aid of their leader when they heard the sound of shots fired. *Amateurs*, Asma thought as she climbed into her car and speed past the cemetery on Woodlawn Road.

Saraqael checked the position of the detonator in the Semtex explosive package while Abaddon silently strapped the belt around the young Palestinian girl. The child's hollow gaze betrayed no emotion. She pulled the brown leather coat over her head. She removed her hijab and let her long black hair flow around her shoulders and she walked out the door of the small bakery into a waiting car that would take her through the checkpoints along the road from Ramallah to Jerusalem where she would walk into another bookstore and buy a book. She would be disguised as an Israeli university student doing volunteer work. At the bookstore she would buy Karl Marx's *Das Capital* and walk over to the checkout counter where she would, in a brilliant flash of light, detonate the package around her waist and in one overwhelming moment she would join her brother in Heaven, killing herself and the non religious Jewish store clerk, a girl about her age by the name of Anna. She wouldn't know that it was Anna's first day on the job. Or how Anna had struggled to let her parents still in bed back in Idaho let her take a year off college to go to Israel. In that split second of explosive light their eyes would meet for a second before the curtain of darkness gave way again to the fractured light from the street, and another developing story on CNN.

The flashing red and blue lights outside the Novitiate converged on the front entrance where City police were having trouble understanding why the Security Intelligence Service had mounted an operation without their involvement. Let alone that someone had been killed, and that someone was no other than local hockey legend Father Brian Murphy. The media would have a field day with this. It was going to be impossible to keep the Operation under wraps. Pendergast was in serious trouble now.

Inside the Novitiate police questioned Father Burkholtz and Parmata. Pendergast kept yelling that this was a national security counter-terrorism issue that was outside their jurisdiction. The uniformed police officers nodded and took extensive notes. Father Burkholtz and Parmata sat quietly on the sofa as they watched the Coroner's staff remove Father Murphy's lifeless body from the room.

"Now what Stephen?" Father Burkholtz asked with tired bloodshot eyes.

"Dunno, Father. I just don't know."

"You did get to see her at least. You know it's times like these that I wish I still smoked," the priest sighed.

"I know what you mean Father, but I'm just not sure who she is anymore."

"She will always be a child in your heart. You're going to have to trust her Stephen. She's a woman now. She has to make her own choices. And I can tell from our brief conversation tonight that at least she's asking the right questions. She's nobody's fool Stephen. You've got to trust her, and to do that you've got to trust yourself first. Don't forget you and Christie raised her."

"Well, for me, it's back to New York. For one thing, I think we need to do a bit more work on the fourth prophecy I told you about years ago. I need to understand more about what it means and how much we really know about. It might be good if you came with me Stephen."

Parmata's eye's lit up, recharged with a sense of purpose. "Absolutely. Of course, you are right. I don't know why I didn't think of that earlier. It's an obvious place to start."

"Frank," Parmata signaled to Pendergast. "If you don't need us anymore tonight, I think we'll be heading out."

"Sure, sure. Look, I'm really sorry about all this, I mean, I didn't intend for this to go sideways like this."

"I know, I know. But you tried to kill Asma. What's with that? You've got to understand I'm just looking out for my daughter here Frank. But if you ever try that again, I'll kill you myself. Understand?"

Frank Pendergast stared at Parmata. He nodded and told the City police he could vouch for the priest and Parmata.

As Parmata and Father Burkholtz headed toward the door, Pendergast offered, "Oh, Stephen, don't worry, we'll keep looking."

"That's exactly what does worry me, old boy," Parmata countered as he headed out the door.

Asma reached into her bag and opened the make-up case applying the red lipstick with relative ease. *It's been a long time* she thought as she readied herself for the meeting. She dropped the keys for the car at the rental counter at the Hyatt hotel then headed out on foot. At Bistro 990 she greeted the *maître d'* with a big smile.

"Table for one?" with a faint southern Italian accent.

"No, actually, I'm meeting someone here?"

"What's his name?"

"Rupert. John Rupert."

"Ah yes, Mr. Rupert is already here. Come with me." He led Asma to a table behind a planter in the back of the very crowded restaurant.

"Asma," Rupert stood offering his hand.

"Mr. Rupert, nice to meet you finally," she took a seat across from him. "Thank you for agreeing to meet with me on such sudden notice."

"The pleasure is entirely mine."

Asma was good at sizing up people quickly. She'd always had an uncanny knack for reading people. She seemed to sense people the way an animal could sense fear. Maybe it was the same instinct after all. In Rupert's case she sensed what might be called a tendency toward sexual perversion such as ephebophila, a desire to have sex with teenagers. She didn't know it, but she was right. For in this case, Rupert was a middle-aged man who liked to dress up in woman's underwear. He's chosen perversion was paraphilia. In fact he was wearing a pair of his favorite Victoria's Secret red panties. He sometimes followed women around, or called them up to make obscene phone calls. Generally, he's what might be called a creep par excellence. Maybe it was those cold steel gray eyes that betrayed his obsessions.

"So, you defended Greg Fallows at his trial?"

"Yes, not one of my most successful cases, but then again, he wasn't as good looking as you are. You are gorgeous you know."

Asma smirked. *Nailed it*, she thought to herself. *Creep-o-supreme-o.*

"Do you stay in touch with him? I mean have you been in touch with him in prison?"

"Dr. Fallows' case was extremely complex. He was his own worst enemy you know."

"You weren't his only lawyer then?"

"Shit no. He had three of us. Two Americans and myself to cover off the Canadian angle."

"But you didn't answer my question."

"What was that again?" looking around for the waiter. "I could use a drink. What about you?"

"Tea's fine with me. Thanks."

The waiter brought a pot of tea for Asma and a double Scotch on the rocks for John Rupert.

"Well? Are you going to tell me or not?"

"Yeah, he emails me from time to time," he sipped his Scotch with obvious relish.

"Did he ever mention to you why he did what the did. I mean kill that lady archeologist?"

"Look Asma, I guess I know you're sort of related to him, right?"

"Actually he was my mother's, my adopted mother's first husband. She divorced him. So he's not related to me at all."

"And you're not some journalist or writer looking for a story?"

"No way, I'm a religious studies student" she lied.

"And your interest in Fallows is what exactly?"

"My interest Mr. Rupert is purely personal and doesn't concern you."

"Of course, yes, I can appreciate discretion." He waved his drink in the air at the waiter.

"Look, if you help me with this, there might be something in it for you." This got Rupert's attention as he raised an eyebrow and sipped his second Scotch on the rocks.

"Like what, exactly," he probed smiling.

"I know some people who might be able to supplement your income," she lied for the second time.

"That's interesting."

"Can you connect me to Fallows? I mean a personal conversation?"

"How much are we talking about, exactly?"

"How much do you need? Why don't we just say that the people I know can make your life much more relaxed," she smiled recalling the extreme hardship of the SRT 19 camp.

"Well, in that case I guess we have a deal," Rupert raised a finger for a third tumbler of Scotch, his eyes starting to glaze over the way alcoholics do when they get a snoot full. "Okay, this is what I'll do. I'll talk to Greg. If he agrees to talk with you I'll arrange a time for a prison visit,"

Asma knew it would be taking a huge risk to venture into the belly of the beast that is to walk into a prison when she herself was being pursued by intelligence agencies on at least two continents. But on the other hand what could be safer. It would be the last place they would look. And as far as Rupert's reward was concerned

Saraqael and Abaddon would make sure he got the reward he deserved.

"It's a deal. My friends will make sure you get exactly what you deserve."

"Well, in that case, I think another drink is definitely in order, don't you agree. Did anyone ever tell you how beautiful you are?" He reached over to kiss her hand.

Asma quickly rose from the table. "Great. I'll call you tomorrow afternoon." She knew better than to expect anything from him in the morning, It was obvious he was just getting started.

Pendergast rubbed his aching head. It would be very difficult to explain the dead priest; meanwhile his superiors would be busy trying to explain to the Brits how they had let Asma slip through their fingers twice in one week. The media would be all over this story, and the local cops weren't about to back up an Operation when they hadn't been briefed about it in the first place.

He sat in the Tim Horton's donut shop staring into his black coffee when his cell phone rang.

"Frank?" the Oxbridge accent asked.

"Yeah, Pendergast here. Who's this?"

"Spaulding. Daryl Spaulding, old boy."

Frank swallowed a gulp of black coffee prepared for the worst.

"Look, I know this hasn't been a good day for you Frank, but you boys need to know that we've picked up some fresh Intel that might be of interest. I mean, some of our people have picked up a few bits of information from some sources close to the group Asma aka Fatima was training with in the desert."

"Uh, huh," Pendergast looked at his watch.

"And it looks like they have plans for something big in Jerusalem, and if it's true what they're talking could put Asma/Fatima at center stage."

"That's very interesting," Frank yawned. He was pretty sure that by 0800h he'd be at his desk back in Ottawa waiting for his pension or that ever prosaic pink slip.

"Frank, old boy, are you still there?"

"Yeah, sure. Yeah, I'm here."

"There's more. A guy by the name of Michel Pichon, a retired professor of Islamic Studies in Oxford contacted us. He said Parmata had been to see him asking questions about the Fatima Prophecy and angels."

"That's interesting." Pendergast eyed two teenager girls pushing each other around by the door of the donut shop. "What's this angel angle?" Frank quipped pleased with himself.

"Not sure, old boy, but we think there just might be a connection with her trek back to Canada. I mean it's possible, conceivable at least that she's on some kind of quest. And Parmata is there too, right?"

That could explain a great deal, Pendergast thought. It would certainly explain why Asma, Father Burkholtz and Parmata were meeting with Father Murphy tonight. This was not good. He'd let Burkholtz and Parmata simply walk away. His headache just got a whole lot worse.

TWENTY-TWO

By the time Father Burkholtz and Parmata arrived at Burkholtz's apartment at Fifth and 71st Saraqael and Abaddon were on a plane headed for Toronto. It was important for them to cover Fatima's trail. The grand scheme was unfolding according to their plans for what they hoped would be the performance of the century. As the plane's thin vapor trail etched its way across the horizon Parmata tucked his suitcase under the pullout sofa in Father Burkholtz's guest room. He couldn't help but think about the events of the night, how good it was to see Asma, but how strange it was at the same time. She seemed to have matured so much over the past few weeks. It was both exhilarating and frightening. How shocked he had been to see Pendergast take aim and fire at her. And that poor Father Murphy, he hadn't done anything wrong. Somehow the world just kept getting stranger and stranger. A knock on the door brought him back to reality.

"Sorry to bother you Stephen. I've just poured myself a Glen Livet if you're interested?"

"Sure, be right there," Parmata called from behind the closed door.

In the spacious living room Parmata found Father Burkholtz searching online Vatican archives accessible only to those with special permission. As the Papal representative to the United Nations, he certainly warranted access to the most amazing volume of historical records ever digitized.

"Really nice place you have here." Parmata admired the view of Fifth Avenue from the large pre-War windows.

"One of the perks that come with the job." Father Burkholtz fixated on the laptop screen.

"It has occurred to me Father that I don't know your first name."

"Forgive me. How inconsiderate of me. Really. Douglas, Doug for short. Please call me Doug."

"Okay Doug, what do you think about this prophecy business. I must say I've been skeptical from the start."

"I knew you were, but sometimes we have to accept things on faith."

"Yeah, that's the part I have trouble with Father, I mean Doug."

"Well, what I've been able to glean from my brief review of the original testimony of the Fatima girls, it would appear that the so-called Fourth Prophecy has always been viewed with suspicion. It appears there was some disagreement among the girls. Not all of them agreed that the Virgin Mary communicated a Fourth Prophecy at all. But as with many issues concerning faith it was better to document it and worry about the veracity later. After all, none of the Prophecies can be subjected to the bright light of reason, can they?"

"I'll get my research assistant Simon Rochefort to dig deeper in the morning. For now, let's have that drink. You must be exhausted. It's been a terrible night."

"Especially for Father Murphy."

"May he rest in peace." They raised their glasses in unison.

Asma sat in the visitors' room of Millhaven maximum-security prison outside Kingston, a three-hour drive east of Toronto. John Rupert had arranged for her to meet with Greg in private for thirty minutes. It was the best he could do. Prison rules were prison rules.

A door opened in the far corner of the sterile off-white room. A middle aged graying and slightly balding man walked through the door before it closed behind him.

Asma stood reflexively as he entered the room. He looked tired and defeated, and hunched over, as if he'd lost the last of many battles. And maybe he had. He extended his hand and smiled looking up at the security camera in the corner.

"You can never get away from those things in here," he gestured to the camera with a glance.

"My name is Asma. Nice to finally meet you," shaking his hand. A great deal can be learned from a handshake, Asma had learned. *This certainly wasn't a typical American crushing handshake. No, far from it, it was weak and uncertain.*

"Likewise," Greg took a seat on one of the orange plastic chairs scattered around the room. "Christie was everything to me, you know."

"Yes," she nodded, her eyes instantly flooded with a salty emotion. "Where does one begin?" she said aloud not really expecting an answer.

"I suppose you're here to ask me what happened?"

"I need to understand some things. For some reason, I don't know why, our lives are interconnected like we are standing at the same crossroads at different places in time. I know that must sound weird but I have these insights or intuitions where I sense with amazing clarity a kind of deeper meaning."

"Greed. That's all it was." It was just a statement of fact, neither more nor less. "I discovered a place where dreams and reality converged, and in the end it was a nightmare. A dangerous place, a place you don't want to experience," he glanced at the clock on the wall.

"But that Dutch archeologist, Dr. De Vries, wasn't she a friend of yours? How could you just up and kill her? It doesn't make sense."

Greg stared at her, took a deep breath and succinctly recounted the story of his murderous madness.

"So I packed my bags and headed for the seclusion of the west coast of Mexico."

"Does killing someone ever make sense?" he asked staring at Asma.

"Well, I suppose there are circumstances when it's justifiable, if not necessary. World War Two for example, or perhaps a Holy War."

Greg raised an eyebrow. His face was older but still had the handsome features of his youth. "So, as long as the cause is just? And who and what determines a just cause?"

"You've turned the tables on me now, and you're interviewing me," she frowned.

"I suppose that's because I never really understood myself what happened that day in the Guatemalan jungle; that day we discovered the most amazing thing I've ever seen. I've gone over it again and again in my head a million times. What motivated me to commit murder? I can't really answer that, except an overwhelming sense of power, call it ego, call it greed; I had to have it. I knew she would take it and place it in some museum in Holland. That would be the end of it. I wanted to use it. I had a special purpose in life—a mission—and this strange crystal skull seemed to be the fork in the road. And it was. But not the fork in the road I thought it was, or was hoping for."

"So you're telling me you were deluded? Temporary insanity?"

"No Asma. I've come to understand that actions and even nature as we know it doesn't follow a linear path. And reason is subject to the same stochastic or random error. It might even be a law of nature. Look around; see the clichés living on the edge of arguments, seek exceptions to finely tuned rhetoric, and the seductive words that flame our emotions into causes. Search the dark recesses of history's blurred panorama. See the blood stains behind the reasons why killing is justified."

"Your time is up," the obese corrections officer appeared beside Greg.

"Good luck," Greg stood up and shuffled toward the door as if venturing for the last time toward a time portal from which he knew he would never return.

"You too." Overwhelmed and confused she whispered "you too."

Rupert swaggered into the Faculty Club at the University of Toronto. As adjunct professor of criminal law he was entitled to the crumbs the academy offered to lesser beings outside tenure track positions. While he resented the snobbery of the academy he secretly longed to be accepted by them. Therefore, he made a point of dining at the Faculty Club every Friday. On this particular Friday he had arranged to meet a female colleague he'd been harassing by phone for years. He was obsessed with her even though she was happily married with five children and told him so ever time he called her cell phone to express his fondness for various parts of her anatomy.

Dr. Glenda Rasmussen was a full professor of philology and had had enough of Rupert. A tall, slim brunette who was strikingly beautiful in her mid forties, she'd discussed the situation with her husband who worked for the city police. He spoke to a friend who knew someone in the organized crime branch who spoke to an ex-con who needed a break. The ex-con spoke to a former colleague in the extortion business now in the car theft business that knew a couple of Nigerians in the export business.

Glenda intended to give Rupert one last chance. He'd already been called before the Dean of the Law School for sexual harassment. One of his students had filed a complained but he'd managed to convince the Dean it would be better for everyone if the matter were dealt with quietly. The university didn't need a sex scandal on the front page of *The Toronto Star*. Glenda's husband convinced her that it would be better for her academic career, and the family if she kept things out of the spotlight. And so, after six years of harassment, she was giving Rupert his final chance to cease and desist.

Glenda had had enough. And when she left the Faculty Club that warm Spring Friday afternoon she knew she had to do something. What she didn't know was that Asma had already made arrangements to cover her own tracks. And that meant a convergence of misfortunate events awaited Mr. John Rupert.

When Rupert walked home that evening he was surprised to see the garbage collectors working so late. As he walked past the truck one of the men bumped into him.

"Sorry man," the handsome dark skinned man leered at Rupert as the other man came behind Rupert lifting him in a swooping arch, tossing him into the open trash truck as the other man pushed the red button that churned the garbage that was John Rupert into the mix, soon to be on its way to a distant landfill somewhere in Michigan.

The two overly tattooed Hell's Angels waiting outside Rupert's house on Pears Avenue were disappointed when he didn't come home that night. It meant they still owed a favor and they'd been hoping to make a deposit in the favor bank that night. But as luck would have it John Rupert would never be seen again. And who said there weren't Guardian angels? Saraqael chuckled before he disappeared into the subway station.

Parmata walked into the kitchen and poured himself a steaming cup of coffee.

"Good morning Stephen," Father Burkholtz hailed as he entered the spacious kitchen. "You slept well, I trust."

"As well as can be expected I guess. I just don't understand why Asma is doing this."

"Her quest you mean?"

"Yeah, if you want to call it that. To me it's juvenile, like she's off trying to find herself."

"And that strikes you as a waste of time does it?"

"I guess when I was her age I was interested in other things . . . making money."

"And so for you, a personal search for meaning in life; one's place in life is trivial?"

"Yes, I guess you'd say that. After all, does anyone ever find anything? I mean, don't we create our own meaning?"

"I take it then you're not a philosopher. The unexamined life is not worth living and all that . . . Socrates?" Father Burkholtz heard his Blackberry ring and quickly read the email missive, saying to Parmata: "Excuse me. I'm going to need to make a phone call. Please, make yourself at home. I'll be back as soon as I can." Then he disappeared into his study.

Parmata sat at the kitchen table and picked up the *New York Times* as he sipped his coffee. Instinctively he always scanned the paper for any sign of news about Asma before he settled on an Op-Ed page piece about alleged rampant healthcare fraud in a leading HMO. Just then Father Burkholtz burst in.

"Stephen . . . we have to talk," he gasped, clearly out of breath.

Parmata looked up and saw the wild look in the priest's eyes. "What is it Father, I mean Doug? Has something happened?"

"I texted my assistant Simon Rochfort last night before I went to sleep. He's a very dedicated fellow and he did some checking."

"That was fast," Parmata eagerly attentive, obviously impressed.

"Again, he's very dedicated and this is exactly the kind of challenge he relishes. Anyway, he came across some original documents in the archives. In one of the testimonials, one of the very first debriefings, one of the girls, her name is not important, said something very strange. The second Paraclete would be a woman and she would unite the great religions of East and West. So of course everyone took it to mean she was talking about the Roman and the Eastern Orthodox Churches. Until that is, she revealed the Paraclete would be called Fatima. Now, you must remember it was bad enough that the second Paraclete was going to be a woman let alone that she would be called Fatima. So, one of the interviewers, they were called interrogators at the time, interviewed the girl privately on her own on several occasions, On one of these occasions in her parent's home he saw a copy of the Holy Koran. He asked about this oddity and was told that her father had studied in Cairo as a young student. Moreover, it turns out for a brief period of time he flirted with Islam, attracted by the mystical teachings of Sufism. In his report the interviewer determined the Fourth Prophecy was a hoax or a corruption influenced by the girl's father."

"And that has to do with Asma exactly how?"

"It's highly likely Simon thinks that others have picked up this corruption and are using it to further their political ambitions."

"And how would they do that?" Parmata speculated, perplexed."

"By convincing certain elements that there was a Christian element to takeover Islam."

"You've got to be smoking something illegal Doug. That's the craziest thing I've ever heard."

"Is it? Crazier than Asma is the second Paraclete sent to unite Islam and Christianity?"

"Well, now that you put it that way . . ."

"So it's likely that whoever is behind this is also connected to Asma's mission, quest or whatever it is."

TWENTY-THREE

Asma sat on the patio of *Le Select Bistro* on Wellington Street West in Toronto. She sat enjoying the remains of the day as she sipped a glass of red. It has been a long time since she took the time to soak in the ambiance without thinking, just feeling the warmth of the late sun on her face and the bustling conversation around her. Her mind drifted as Saraqael sat down next to her wearing his trademark sunglasses and dark navy suit.

"I see you're enjoying the decadence," Saraqael said gesturing to the wine as the waiter appeared.

"I'll have the same," he said smiling.

He is a handsome and somewhat charming egomaniac, Asma thought. She searched her bag for a note pad and pen. *Even if he is the devil personified.* "Look, I think I deserve an explanation. I mean the killing of the priest and everything."

"Nothing to do with us."

"I see. Then when do we get it started?"

"Oh, it's started. You are ready for your defining moment."

"And what might that be? I'm tired of the secrecy and the running. I've been doing some thinking and I need to have some questions answered."

Saraqael raised his considerable eyebrows behind the Ray-Ban Aviators. "There is no more time for study. You've taken the courses. You understand the mission. You have been sent to disturb the order of things, and that's all you need to know. That is your job," Saraqael asserted hotly.

"I've been doing some thinking."

"Thinking is not your job!" Saraqael no longer smiled.

"Well, you can't stop me from thinking. Not even you can do that, and believe me I know who and what you are."

"Then you can appreciate the consequences of diverging from the path that has been chosen for you."

"I've come to understand the risks on both sides of the equation," she made a note on the writing pad.

"What are you doing with that pad of paper anyway? You're starting to piss me off."

"I'm making careful notes, in case something happens to me. I mean I want to make sure my side of the story is told."

"Why would something happen to you?"

She looked at him incredulously. *He is a good liar,* she thought.

In the moments that followed, screeching tires and black cars descended on the patio like a dark bird of prey. In the first milliseconds Asma reacted like a cat running in one rapid athletic movement down the narrow alley between the buildings as the police and security forces surrounded Saraqael in a textbook takedown.

Parmata and Father Burkholtz sipped wine on Fifth Avenue as the traffic raced by in a river of fumes. "So do you think whoever is behind the mythology of the Fourth Prophesy is connected with one of those international terrorist organizations?" Parmata asked puzzled looking at a map of New York City.

"I don't know Stephen. I think we know very little about what the intentions of these folks are. I mean, what the media know is very limited isn't it? The terrorists seem to appear and disappear like characters in *War and Peace.* One day Saddam is a friend and the next he is the face of evil. I can see why people are confused; especially young people."

"You sound almost sympathetic," Parmata took a sip of Kim Crawford Marlborough Pinot Noir.

"No so much sympathetic but understanding. I mean, when you look at the poverty and conditions on the West Bank, Gaza,

Iraq and Afghanistan. It's no wonder there are so many kids willing to blow themselves up."

"Interesting. I mean doesn't the Bible say 'the poor we will always have with us?'"

"Ah, but you forget Liberation Theology inspired us to seek Heaven on Earth."

"Really. I would have thought you would be more inclined to traditional theological perspectives." Parmata glanced up at the sun compressed between the buildings.

"Stephen. Who was it that brought her to you?"

Yes, it's true, Parmata thought. *It was Father Burkholtz who arranged for the baby girl Asma to be adopted by he and Christie. It was Father Burkholtz who told him the story of the girl who spoke her name at birth.*

The sun disappeared behind a cloud. "It's starting to look like rain. Maybe we should head over to my office and check in. See if anything has come up."

"Sure," Parmata downed the rest of his wine.

When they got to Father Burkholtz's office there was indeed a message waiting from Daryl Spaulding. In brief, Frank Pendergast had lost Asma again but Toronto police had nabbed a known terrorist going by the name of Saraqael D'Aqiz who was with her at the time. Spaulding said Pendergast was anxious to make up for recent blunderings and so had called him with the quasi-good news. Spaulding was of course only too happy to point out that Asma had indeed gotten away . . . again.

"Who is this Saraqael character who was with Asma?"

Father Burkholtz stood carefully studying the message, as if there was another meaning or a hidden message that he'd missed.

"Are you okay Doug?"

"Yes, I'm fine. I guess all the events of the past few days are getting to me. All the travel and trauma, I mean."

"Maybe you should lie down."

"That might be a good idea. I'll just be in my study. You don't mind do you? Really?"

"Absolutely not."

Father Burkholtz disappeared into his study and closed the door behind him. Parmata pulled up a chair in front of the flat screen computer monitor and began a Google search: Saraqael + D'Aqiz. What he found shocked him—thousands of references. Saraqael is the name of an Archangel, he read. Some say it is a female angel. Although Parmata wasn't sure how that worked with angels anyway. According to Angelology Saraqael was one of the good or holy angels who presided over humans who had committed serious so-called "spiritual" sins. And in Arabic Angelology she was the one who assisted with exorcisms. But this Saraqael was a man. Then Parmata recalled his conversation with Michel Pichon in Oxford. "The World my friend is divided into believers and nonbelievers. The world of the fundamentalists, and everyone else," Professor Pichon had taught. If a person wanted to take on a persona of someone with *cosmic influence* the sex of that persona would be of little concern; especially today and especially if the world is divided into believers and nonbelievers. But what does that have to do with Asma?

Asma couldn't get her conversation with Greg Fallows out of her head. He was pretty direct about his own mistakes and the dangers of not being critical: of people, their motives, ideas and beliefs. Wasn't that the legacy of Spinoza and the beginning of modernity? Was the post-modern world spiraling inevitably into Jane Jacob's new *Dark Ages Ahead*? What was she looking for anyway? She was waking up from a dream, or was it a nightmare? But how could she get out now? She sat staring at the computer screen on the second floor of the Internet café on Bloor Street West across from the Royal Ontario Museum. She opened her web browser connecting to the Yahoo site to access her alias email account. Once the spam and other junk mail downloaded, an email from Dhul Fiqar appeared. She hadn't heard from Dhul since her training in West Africa. She wondered where he had gone when he left the camp. She heard that his mission was terminal, and she had her suspicions but the

323

email confirmed her worst fears. Dhul's message had obviously been written some time ago and it confirmed his commitment to the cause of the Palestinian people and the willingness to give up his life for that cause. It was that expression that hung in the air for her. What good could that do? He was convinced he had gone so far down the road it wasn't possible to back down now. In that instant she knew she was different from him. Was this what they had in mind for her too? She ached to be home. Home, yes, home in Nova Scotia. She longed for the dreamy days of laughter and warm breezes, and nights of pounding rain and maddening winds. She knew Parmata was trying to find her. She knew she had been cruel to him. She was confused and getting more so. She needed his help to step out of this quagmire, but how? Suddenly she felt very cold and alone . . . and scared. She wasn't a terrorist. She hadn't done anything . . . yet. She knew that Saraqael, Abaddon and company wouldn't let her go simply because she'd decided she didn't want to play with them any more. But she couldn't deny it; she had awakened; her passion for their root causes argument didn't ring true anymore, if it ever truly had. She needed to connect with Parmata. Thank you Greg, thank you.

Saraqael sat in the interrogation room in the basement of the Metro Toronto Police 13 Division on Dundas Street West. Pendergast and Staff Sergeant Etienne Allard from the RCMP counter terrorism special task force stared at the captive, waiting for him to say something, anything. Instead Saraqael sat with his eyes closed ignoring the security and intelligence officers. This was really starting to annoy Pendergast who had been through a great deal of embarrassment the past few days. He was in need of serious redemption. Saraqael was a big fish on the international most wanted list. He had the Toronto Police to thank for that but if he could find and contain Asma/Fatima before she was going to do whatever was her mission, what Spaulding had alluded to, he would not only be redeemed but also possibly promoted.

"C'mon, we know you are here for something. You might as well give us the goods," Allard coaxed in his French Canadian accent.

In his mind Saraqael was miles away flying on a magic red carpet eating dates, watching the tuna fleets somewhere haul in their catch.

Pendergast knew he had to shock this monkey into coughing up something useful, but how? He seemed incredibly resistant to standard interrogation techniques. For instance, sleep depravation didn't seem to bother him, and second he seemed to be able to tune out things around him with extraordinary skill. There had to be something that would crack this guy's façade. Then he thought of something.

"We have Fatima you know and we know what you're planning in Jerusalem." Saraqael opened his cold brown eyes and stared Pendergast to the core as if trying to determine the veracity of the statement.

"Bullocks."

"No, it's true. We know you are planning to blow up the Temple Mount. You intend to blame it on the Israelis," he was creating it as he went along.

Saraqael had to think about this for a minute. How could they possibly know that, he had to be guessing! Was it possible they had been compromised? No, there were very few who knew the plan. It wasn't possible, or was it?

"If you know so much, tell me who is the Primate?"

Pendergast looked at Allard who was puzzled by the whole conversation.

"Primate, yes, primate, that is a good question. I should think the Primate is a man,"

Frank smiled, pleased with himself.

Saraqael smirked and closed his eyes again, heaving a huge sigh of relief. Pendergast looked at Etienne Allard in disgust.

TWENTY-FOUR

The cause of righteousness is a tortuous path. The first casualty is always the plan. True leaders know this and adjust tactics to circumstances. Jerusalem is our destiny. After more than a thousand years, the great religions of Christianity and Islam have come face to face in that great political game of chicken. Since the Crusades had left matters unresolved, East and West have grudgingly co-existed. But events of late have exacerbated the need to take action, decisive action. One angel down, while important, isn't enough to alter the plan. Abaddon is my angel of detail and direct action, and he will ensure the completion of the mission.

Parmata shut down the computer as Father Burkholtz walked through the door.

"Feeling better?" Parmata stood and walked to the large bay window overlooking the FDR Expressway.

"Yes, thanks, much better. Recent events must have caught up with me. It's not every day you see an old friend gunned down."

"I suppose that's true," Parmata considered the options. "Look Doug, I know you want to help but I'm thinking the best thing that I can do now is to head back home and wait."

"Really? Don't you think you'd be better off here? I mean you're company and with my connections we'll find out what she's up to before anyone else."

"I'm sure you are right, but I just think I need to get back home."

"Are you giving up Stephen?"

"No, no, I think I need some time to think about everything. You understand."

"Yes, of course, but it seems we've made so much progress together . . . I mean, what will you do?"

"Not sure Father, I mean, Doug."

"I think you're making a mistake Stephen. We'll have a better chance of locating her from here with my resources and connections. You can't do this alone Stephen. How long have you known me? A long time for sure. I brought her to you. I want her to succeed too."

That's an interesting word, Parmata thought. "Succeed?"

"Succeed in life, as a person, as a woman."

"I see. Okay, I'll think about it. But if we don't make any progress by Friday, I'm heading back to Nova Scotia."

"Sounds reasonable. That gives us a couple of days to sort this out; make some real progress, I mean."

Asma opened her pack searching for a tissue when the coin Saraqael had given her, the one Dhul had scraped off the gold paint to find an ancient coin underneath tumbled onto the concrete floor with a loud clanging sound. It must have been in her pack since that horrible night they drove to Patterson. Asma quickly scooped it up, admiring it. Her thoughts drifted to Dhul, how handsome he was. His lonely eyes that first attracted her seemed now somehow lost and desperate. Holding the coin tight in her hand she need to see Stephen more than ever. On impulse she opened her web browser and connected to her webmail and fired off a missive to Stephen: meet me. It's urgent. You know how I cried when the blackbird screamed. Meet me Friday at noon where the blackbird screamed. Then she shut down and fled.

Father Burkholtz seemed distracted all evening. He drank only one glass of Port after dinner and went to bed early. They had eaten quietly without saying more than a few words. Parmata was beginning to wonder if Doug was more depressed by his friend's death than he had appreciated. After Doug excused himself and retreated to his room, Parmata re-entered the priest's study to check his email again before bed.

And there to his surprise was an email from Asma. It was exactly the missive he was looking for; she needed him and he needed her. He would leave the next day for Toronto. He didn't need Doug Burkholtz right now, he needed Asma, and perhaps more important, for the first time since she was a child, she needed him. *Meet me Friday at noon where the blackbird screamed.* But where had the blackbird screamed? Then suddenly he remembered: the SR-71 Blackbird. Of course! They watched the Labor Day air show on Toronto Island and the supersonic reconnaissance plan flew low over the island screeching over their heads startling everyone, and Asma had cried with fright. She couldn't have been more than 10 years old. It was startling and unforgettable even to this day. They had been in the field behind the Yacht club. Yes, he knew her message, and only he would know it.

In the morning over coffee and pan chocolate Parmata told Father Burkholtz of his plan to leave that day. He'd already booked a flight online and he'd be home by late that evening.

"Well, I guess I haven't been a very good host." Father Burkholtz refilled Parmata's cup.

"No, it's not that Doug. I think I just need to get home for a while. I think it's catching up with me too. We'll stay in touch. I promise," he lied, as he downed his coffee, grabbing his bag.

"Thanks for everything Doug. I mean it." They shook hands and he left. Moments later he was flagging down a taxi and on his way to LaGuardia, feeling that he had escaped just in time.

TWENTY-FIVE

The air was humid and thick with the acrid smoke of stop and go traffic from the Gardner Expressway as Parmata took a seat on the Toronto Island ferry. He looked around half expecting to see Asma but there were only couples with children and dogs on leashes and picnic baskets overflowing with food, and an excited gay couple with matching red bicycles and yellow and red riding gear. It was a beautiful day for a rendezvous. But Parmata also knew he could be followed. He walked the upper and lower decks of the ferry and honestly couldn't detect anyone who might fit the image of an uncover cop. *Then again,* he thought, *what better cover than a happy gay couple or a family on a picnic?* Without an obvious tail, he decided to simply be another tourist and enjoy the rest of the short trip to the islands. Since he'd gotten on the wrong ferry—he'd taken the Ward Island ferry—he had quite a walk ahead of him but at least he'd given himself plenty of time.

When he walked behind the Yacht Club he saw someone sitting at a picnic table underneath the large Oak trees about fifty meters across the lawn behind the Club. He knew it was Asma and his heart raced. But instead of walking straight for her he walked over to the waterfront and doubled back making sure he wasn't followed. Once he was sure everything was okay, he casually walked up and sat down at the picnic table.

"I remember that day like it was yesterday." Asma looked up through the trees to the sky. "I remember my blue flowered dress, the hundreds of butterflies and the smell of charcoal and barbequed ribs burning on the grill.

"Okay, so I wasn't a great cook," Parmata smiled as their eyes met.

"But they tasted the best," she laughed. "There is so much to say, Stephen. I don't know where to begin."

"It's okay. It's just so good to hear you laugh again. I was afraid I'd never see you again; never hear your voice, or hear your laughter again."

"I've been caught up in something . . ."

"I know, I know, there's plenty of time for that. Right now we have to get you out of this. And we will."

"I have to show you something." She took the coin from her pocket. "It was given to me a long time ago. At least it feels like a long time ago now. I showed it to Dhul, you remember Dhul, and he scraped off the gold paint. Underneath is a silver coin of maybe Roman or Greek antiquity."

Parmata took the coin in both hand and like any kid from the street tried to verify its worth by trying to break it in two. And sure enough it cracked like a cheap imitation. He looked at Asma startled.

"What's this?"

"What?"

"I think it's a chip or something," he broke the coin completely in half and removed a wafer-thin filament. "Asma, I'm no expert, but I think this could be a GPS tracking device of some kind. We need to get out of here now!"

On the patio of the crowded Hemingway's pub in the trendy Yorkville area Parmata ordered a Foster's. "Old habits die hard," he said while Asma ordered a club soda and lime.

"I think we should go to the police, seek some kind of immunity, States evidence or whatever it's called here."

"I don't disagree, Stephen," Asma stirred the lemon around in her glass. "I just don't want to go to jail Stephen. I don't want to end up like Greg Fallows."

"No worries on that front my girl. I've got it covered. We'll seek immunity from prosecution in exchange for information that will put the real culprits behind bars."

"But if those people were . . . . I mean are tracking me, they won't be pleased with the turn of events."

"No, which is why we need to get official help as soon as possible. Don't worry, I know some people who I think we can trust."

"Trust, that seems like a luxury to me," Asma scanned the room.

"Don't worry sweet pea, it will come."

"You haven't called me that since I was a kid."

"I guess I was afraid you'd bristle with any term of endearment."

"Was I really that bad?" she clutched Parmata's hand. He didn't say anything. He just held her hand in his and thought of Christie. *She would be so happy.* A breeze blew the napkins off the table.

Frank Pendergast and Etienne Allard were now virtually joined at the hip. There was practically nowhere Frank went that Etienne didn't follow. Frank's superiors in Ottawa had decided it was best for everyone, especially Frank if the RCMP officer accompanied him from now on. Frank tried to not see it as a slight. He rationalized it as a temporary necessity like a cast or a colonoscopy. In either case it had to be endured.

Hot off their less than spectacular success interrogating Saraqael they were eager to respond to Parmata's call for help. Etienne was also pleased that they were leaving the very boring police station to meet Parmata and the object of their search at a local watering hole. It was likely he'd be able to have a smoke too; something that even other cops frowned upon these days.

They looked like cops when they walked onto the upstairs patio off Cumberland Street. "You guys look like you could use a drink," Parmata gave an Aussie wave to the waitress on semi-permanent sabbatical at the bar. "It's hard to get a drink here," he was clearly frustrated. "Especially when the World Cup is on."

"This is Allard. He's with the Special Task Force, RCMP." Frank took a seat beside Asma. "And this is the famous Fatima."

"Asma," Parmata corrected.

"Right you are. So what is the proposal? On the phone you said you wanted to crack a deal." And so Parmata outlined his proposal for immunity in exchange for information and a place in the Witness Protection Program.

"That all sounds fine Frank," Allard piped up for the first time. "But I think we're going to need her help to snag the big fellas. Especially since we're not getting anywhere with the guy we've got in custody." Frank nodded in agreement.

"Do we have a choice?" Parmata asked facetiously. The cops looked at each other in that way cops do when they know they hold all the cards.

TWENTY-SIX

These are difficult times for sure. The best laid plans thrown into disarray by chance. We have labored long to bring events to this point, years in fact. You do not see the careful selection, down to every detail and then, suddenly as if propelled by an unseen wind, events outside of our control conspire against us, against me, but we will not be deterred. Saraqael is out of commission for now. He will reveal nothing. He is my committed angel. Abaddon is still in place. Together we can make the long journey to Jerusalem where the child will fulfill the mission I have given her.

Abaddon's call did not bring welcome news. Somehow we have lost her.

"Find her. She is critical to the mission."

"I don't know what could have happened to the chip. She may have lost it'

"Or found it," The anxiety was palpable and I wanted to throw up.

"That's impossible," Abaddon declared. "It was well crafted by the best in the business."

"I know, I paid for it, I paid for everything, and used my extensive network of connections to see she received the best training."

"We'll find her. I know she was in Toronto. She has to still be there. If everything is okay, she will contact us at the prearranged time."

"And if she doesn't?"

"Well then, we'll know we're dealing with a rogue element."

That's an interesting way to put it. I might have said a stochastic element, or a stochastic child to be more precise. Either way we will have our answer.

"She is scheduled to contact me at 1900 today."

"Good. In a little over 5 hours we will know. And I pray to God that we haven't lost her."

"I'll let you know immediately when she calls."

"Tell her Zacharias is waiting."

"So it begins."

"Yes, she will know she is to meet you in Jerusalem on Friday."

"So it begins."

"You and I will talk again once you have made contact."

"It is the beginning of the end."

"No, it is merely the beginning of the beginning. The cobra strikes back."

Asma quickly hung her clothes in the hotel closet. She didn't have much time. Pendergast and Allard had arranged for separate rooms for Parmata and Asma at the Sutton Place Grand Suites on Bay Street in Toronto. This time it was the police that placed the surveillance chip in her watch. But this time she knew and this time she would be using her training to prevent something from happening. *Time to stop playing games*, she thought. *Time to take control, to do the right thing.*

Allard made it clear she wouldn't be allowed to see Parmata or anyone on this side of the veil as he put it, until things were concluded. He seemed to be in charge, which made her much happier. Pendergast couldn't seem to plan his way out of a port-a-potty. In any case, she had to make contact by phone in under an hour. She would use one of the pay phones off the lobby.

At precisely 5 o'clock she made the call to Abaddon. He gave no indication of any problem. He told her that Saraqael was out of commission for the time being. It would just be the two of them from here on in. He gave her the code word for the commencement of her mission. In a sense she was relieved it would soon be over, one way or another. She also knew the real danger was just beginning but there was no turning back now. Abaddon gave her a series of numbers she knew were GPS coordinates confirming the location and time of their meeting in Jerusalem. Things were happening quickly now. She wondered if the police would be able to act as fast. She looked around the empty corridor and abruptly confronted her own terror. What if no one was there to help her? The brief conversation was over. Asma stood there still holding the receiver to her ear as if waiting for an answer where none would be found. She began to quietly cry.

"It's okay we'll be with you every step of the way." Asma looked up. It was Allard. "We do this occasionally," he smiled. "You need to get some rest. We need to go over a lot of things tomorrow morning. I'd suggest a quiet evening to decompress. We'll see that you and Parmata have dinner in your suite. It will be the last time you two see each other until this is all over."

"Will you be there?"

"We'll talk about that in the morning. Now it's time you got back to your suite."

The next morning the sullen sky and blinding rain epitomized Asma's mood as she opened the curtains gazing out over the lead colored city. A city she knew and yet she didn't really know. A knock on her door jarred her back to reality.

Pendergast, Allard and Parmata walked in and sat down at the dining room table without saying a word. Allard threw a stack of paper on the table and immediately began handing out sheets to everyone. Asma quietly sat down too. It was if as if everyone had absorbed the mood of the gray city outside.

"We need to go over a bunch of things: logistics that kind of thing," Allard clearly now taking the lead. "Asma we'll need to know what your instructions are. It's critical from here on in that we stick to the plan as much as possible."

As much as possible, Asma thought. *That doesn't sound entirely reassuring.*

"But we will keep her in sight at all times, right?" Parmata piped in.

"Yes, of course, but we're going to have to get clearances with the Israeli security forces because it's going to be their lead."

"It *is* on their turf after all," Pendergast added.

"What does that mean?" Parmata asked with growing anxiety.

"Officially, it means we'll be assisting the Israelis."

"Which means?"

"It's on their turf. It's their show. We've been trying to coordinate things with them, but you know how things are in Israel."

"No, I'm afraid I don't," Parmata retorted.

"Relax, Stephen, everything will be okay. Won't it?" Asma gazed at the two policemen smiling an obvious attempt to break the tension in the air.

"There's nothing we can do," Pendergast replied. "It's Israel. They do these things all the time. It's a matter of sovereignty."

Parmata nodded his reluctant concurrence looking out the window. He didn't like it but he had no choice. He wondered what else would go wrong.

Asma took a direct flight to Tel Aviv from Toronto where she met an Israeli woman by the name of Jackie who drove her to a nondescript apartment near the Hilton. She didn't say a word to Asma the entire time from the airport to the apartment. When she pulled the car up in front of the gleaming white building she parked.

"Its number 10. There's food in the fridge. Stay indoors. Someone will contact you." She threw Asma's luggage on the ground beside the car and sped away in a cloud of dust. *That's nice*, Asma thought, as she covered her head with a red bandana and picked up her bags. At the apartment she threw her bags in the tiny bedroom and switched on the small television while she looked in the fridge for something to eat. All she found was a package of chicken salad and several cans of Coke.

"Beggars can't be choosers," she said loudly as she took the booty back to eat in front of the Israeli television news predicting the start of the "100 year war of survival" as one commentator put it.

Parmata and the two policemen followed a few hours later on a flight that connected through New York. Arrangements had been made for someone from Israeli's secret intelligence agency (Mossad) to meet them at Ben Gurion Airport. As they made their way through the city the tension in the air was palpable. It had been years since he'd been in a war zone, but he was here now, in another kind of war zone. Military convoys were everywhere heading north to the border with Lebanon. Intense fighting had erupted again and militants had streamed across the Israeli border for the first time killing hundreds of Israelis near Haifa. *It was certainly a very tense time to be here*, Parmata thought as they pulled into the Hilton hotel parking lot.

As soon as they got settled they met in the spacious lobby bar and headed down to a permanent safe room Mossad kept in the basement of the building. Once in the room with the door secured, the burly Mossad agent Isser Weisbart threw himself down on the sofa.

"Okay, what's all this shit about? We've got a fuckin' war goin' on here, and I don't need to be babysitting some friggin' Canadian bitch."

Allard stepped up to the plate without missing a beat. "Look, we're here to prevent a major terrorist attack against Israel. We're here to assist you. As I indicated in the Intel prelim report, we believe we have access to a major source, aka Canadian bitch to you, who could avert an attack. We don't have details at this stage but the MO calls for her to travel to your country. We know this has been developing for several months; the Brits have been working on this thread for years. It seems to be coming down here now; we'll know more soon. In fact we should contact our double soon. She probably needs sustenance; that's reassurance, Stephen. And it's probably no coincidence it's happening when you're heading into the biggest military mission in years." He paused looking the Mossad agent in the eyes before continuing. "Yes, we've got limited resources but that's to our advantage. We don't want to attract attention and we'd like to stay as close as possible to the girl. Several people have already died. It seems things are heating up fast. We need to know we can count on you." Parmata nodded. He couldn't have said it better himself.

"Who the fuck is he?" Weisbart glared at Parmata.

"He's the father . . ."

"Well that's fuckin' great! We got the family here! Let's break out the Bargee rolls."

"It's okay Weisbart, he's a former operative. He's cool and most importantly, she trusts him. Without him the double could get scared and run again."

Allard summarized the Intel report just in case Weisbart hadn't read it; which was quite likely given his overall attitude. Weisbart seemed be listening, waiting for something to criticize. When Allard finished he looked to Pendergast to add anything he might have left out.

"Okay," Weisbart said. "So we have a sitting duck and no target. Is that the general run down?"

"Basically, that's the situation. Yes," Allard sheepishly realized how well the agent actually grasped the situation.

"How is she?" Weisbart asked.

"Well right now she's probably scared as shit," Pendergast glanced sympathetically at Parmata pacing by the small basement window.

"I'd stay away from the window if I was you," Weisbart advised.

"Right," Parmata walked into the kitchen for a drink of water.

"I should call her, but we should decide on what we're going to tell her. I mean it's really your call Weisbart."

"I'll be right back," Weisbart left the room. When he returned a few minutes later he seemed to have had an attitude adjustment. His demeanor was relaxed and friendly. Not at all the tough disinterested veneer he wore on their initial encounter.

"Look," Weisberg walked over to Parmata. "I understand this is going to be difficult for you. But you should know we are extremely grateful for your cooperation, and your daughter's cooperation as well."

"Thanks. I appreciate that."

"Okay we've got lots to do. It appears their target is the Temple Mount."

"What?" Allard shouted.

"We've been tracking some chatter that has been indicating a major attack on the Temple Mount. We haven't been able to triangulate all the coordinates but it would appear your Asma is the 'Fatima' referred to in their oblique references to religious texts."

"I see, well that would be a major attack on their own site wouldn't it?" Parmata asked in disbelief.

"Exactly. That would draw the maximum heat and inflame the situation further. The devout would interpret it as an attack from our side, and the violence would undoubtedly escalate in the entire region, and perhaps world wide."

"Absolutely," Pendergast agreed. "And our response would be to clamp down on the Islamists further which would only serve to fame the flames."

"Where does that put Asma?" Parmata asked knowing the answer to the question wouldn't be good.

"In the thick of it for sure." Isser looked at Pendergast who was studying the wood grain of the oak coffee table.

"But you've got a plan? Right?"

Silence. Parmata glanced up at the window as 4 Apache attack helicopters headed north along the Tel Aviv beach. The weight of an idea, a random decision taken hours ago in Toronto that seemed so right, so possible now seemed so wrong and so potentially misguided.

"Stephen, as you know, the first thing that goes out the window in combat is the plan. We will be relying on Asma's wit and reflexes. This is combat. I know you know this."

Hope is a fickle lover. It soars in romance then hovers over the desert of the doldrums of ennui until it finally vanishes, a star in the distant nebula of a cold dark eternity. Parmata's hands grew damp, the autonomic response to anxiety. He thought of the first time he and Christie held Asma. The child's sweet, radiant face, even the cold autumn breeze that presaged winter couldn't dampen their excitement as they bundled her into the car for the long drive home. Mostly it was seeing Christie's eyes radiate love. Her eyes . . . he would never forget her eyes. How he longed for her now, her steady as it goes way. He missed her more than he had in a long time. She was gone and he'd have to get Asma back or die trying.

"Then I need a role in this," Parmata walk up to Isser.

"No way. This is going to be risky enough for professionals. We can't have family running around."

"Wait a minute. It might not be such a bad idea," Allard suddenly engaged again. "He would be unknown. I mean he would look like a tourist. He could blend in with the crowd."

"And he has past experience," Pendergast added obviously pleased with himself.

Weisbart screwed up his mouth.

"We've done it before. But you'd have to be on a short leash. Understand?"

"Yes, I understand," Parmata let the implications slowly permeate his entire being from the tips of his fingernails to the top of his thinning grey hair. *I walk alone.*

"Okay. Get some sleep. Allard, come with me. We need to reel in Asma. She doesn't know me, but she knows you."

Parmata looked as if he were going to follow the Mossad agent and the RCMP Officer out the door. "No. You are staying here. You can't be seen anywhere near her at this stage. Understand?"

"Yes," Parmata took a seat on the sofa. He knew it was useless to push it; at least he was in the game. The door closed behind Weisbart and Allard leaving Pendergast and Parmata to the deafening silence.

"I'm going to hit the sack," and Parmata headed off down the hall to one of the bedrooms. "You can have the sofa."

TWENTY-SEVEN

Asma put the cell phone on the table. Allard had given it to her before they left Toronto. She stared at it the way a child might try to bend a spoon with mental telepathy after hearing about such phenomena on television. Then suddenly it rang as if on command.

"Yes?" The rendezvous was set. She hung up the phone and dashed out the door into the darkness.

Abaddon gingerly packed the explosives and detonator into the vest. He had carefully replaced the Down feather lining with enough explosives to blow a truck size hole through the side of a building. Admiring his handiwork he carefully inserted a medallion similar to the one Asma showed Parmata. Then he placed the vest in a padded steel lined suitcase. As he shoved the case under the bed, over his shoulder he saw a shadow in the doorway.

"Is the package ready?"

"Yes," he smiled. "Is Fatima ready?"

"Tomorrow will be especially bright over Jerusalem."

Abaddon was pleased. "This angel's work is almost completed."

"And after so many years, the angels will soon be revealed."

"Where the fuck is she?" Isser said spitting in the shadow of the café as sirens wailed past them on the boulevard across from the dark green sea. "She was supposed to be here by now." Allard looked at the flashing lights announcing the Dolphinarium music club across the street. It was 2 AM and Asma was over an hour late. He was nervous. A cop learns from experience to trust intuition and this wasn't good. Things had gone wrong from the get go.

"What now?" he asked in a low languid tone half looking at Isser and half watching the kids pouring out of the music club into the warm Tel Aviv night.

Isser threw his cigarette to the ground in disgust. "I'll have to talk to the Colonel. I'll meet you back at the hotel. Man, this is seriously fucked up and it's only begun," he shook his head as he disappeared down the alley toward the market.

Isser burst in the door of the hotel room just before dawn. Allard was sleeping on the sofa and Pendergast was standing at the sink drinking a glass of water. "We have to get moving! Now!" Isser shouted as Parmata appeared in the hallway rubbing sleep from his eyes.

"What's happening?" Parmata asked sizing up the situation.

"No time to explain. I'll brief you in the car," Isser, tense, lit a cigarette.

"Lets go!" the three Canadians cried in unison as they dashed after the Mossad agent out the door.

Asma recoiled at the sight of the explosive package. As soon as she'd stepped outside Abaddon had been waiting. She sat in the small kitchen staring at the vest. Abaddon smiled as he held it in front of her like a victory trophy. It wouldn't be long now she knew. The pieces were clicking in place like a fine old Swiss watch counting down the end of history, or the beginning of the next hundred years war. This she knew was the real purpose behind the fiction about to unfold. Abaddon knew she was scared. He saw it as a sign of weakness, a failure to grasp the greater cause. Angels should have no fear of death. And she truly was to become a messenger of the highest order. The clock on the wall crept past 5 AM. Asma knew dawn was less than an hour away. She told herself she had to remain calm. She needed to think. Everything was possible.

When I conceived this journey so many years ago it was only an idea. The child from the Altiplano, the myth of her naming herself, it was all so well crafted. The selection of Christie and Parmata as parents to raise the child, it was all so perfect. It was an idea that we kept to ourselves at first, then we brought "the angels" in: Abaddon and Saraqael. This small, close-knit cadre allowed me to reduce the risk of contamination and because I was patient, content to plan the seed and wait for it to grow; satisfaction would soon be mine.

I came to Jerusalem myself to see the end of the beginning of the great awakening of fire, the start of the final battle between the Truth and the Lie, a battle that has been raging for 3,000 years. The wick of the candle is Fatima: that name that sparks such fervor on all sides. I can see you cringing. How will a great battle reveal the Truth? Only in the purge of fire will iron be forged and the dawn of a new age be revealed. This is the cleansing effect of fire and the birth of a new, old religion in the clash of three great religions in the post-modern epoch.

Enough. How did I conceive of this? That is a good question. It was in the old way, in a dream. One night many years ago, during a night of high wind, thunder and lightning, sleep sent an angel sailing down a wine green river in a mystic fog. Fear sweated from my pores like tears as the eerie red night sky on the horizon cast its glow across my face. I am alone, strapped to the mast of an ancient vessel like some dream Odysseus. I don't know how this occurred, I might have been there all along, anyway the fog seemed to clear, I can remember it as if it was yesterday, revealing a light on the water, a street light, very odd I remember thinking as the vessel headed toward the light, revealing an opening in the water below the light. Down, down I slipped into a fire beneath the sea. Surrounded by the fire, I was comforted by the clean heat, the enormous heat that consumed everything. It was then I saw the Temple Mount, the ruins of the Temple of Solomon, the spiritual home to the great religions of modern times. And in the conflagration of the Temple I saw the rebirth of another great religion, the first new religion to do battle with the Lie in eons. From the ashes a figure like Aphrodite was assembled from the rising smoke and she spoke the words, "Fatima" to me. And I remembered the Fatima Prophesies. My mind was suddenly clear and I knew exactly what I had to do. I woke up. And the rest is, as they say, history.

In the Jeep Isser said Intel was pretty sure something was set to go down near the Temple Mount.

"How do you know that?" Parmata asked, bracing himself in the back seat. Isser didn't answer but scowled in the rear-view mirror at him. Parmata wanted to ask Pendergast and Allard how they could think Asma would be at this location? Even if there was an attack on the Temple Mount, how could they know Asma would be there? *So much for plans*, he thought.

As they made their way to the Old City in the predawn darkness, the streets were already crowded with military convoys without headlights bearing north and east.

"Hang on, I know this city like the back of my hand. We'll have to take a detour." And with that Isser made a sudden turn to the right down a narrow alley filled with pushcarts and people, honking his horn as he sped along.

Isser parked in front of the Intercontinental Hotel across from the entrance to the Western wall, or Wailing Wall as it is variously called. He didn't like what he saw. There were no police or military vehicles to seal off the area.

"What now?" yelled Parmata from the back of the Jeep. Pendergast sitting beside him looked at Allard in the front. He seemed to be wondering the same thing. Their silence frightened Parmata more than the fact there was no plan, or whatever plan there was had long gone out the window.

"Give me a walkie-talkie," Parmata ordered getting out of the Jeep. "I'll walk around to the front of the building. I can scope things out."

"Wait!"

"Give me a fucking walkie-talkie or I'm going without one! Your choice . . ."

Isser tossed him a small cell phone size walkie-talkie.

"Always channel 9. Got it? And leave the heroics to somebody else. Just walk down the street and find a secluded spot and call me. Okay?" Parmata took the walkie-talkie and shoved it in his pocket.

"Absolutely, mate," Parmata smiled, donning his Australian accent.

"Walk with purpose. Just do this one thing and we'll take over."

"Right," nodded Parmata quickly moving away from the Jeep.

They watched from the darkness of the Jeep as Parmata disappeared down the street and around the corner.

Asma sucked in her chest as Abaddon snapped the last button of the explosives vest around her looking her in the eyes. She looked away. He then handed her a plain leather jacket that would complete her disguise.

"You look like an academic. Once you are at the front door, you will complete your destiny Fatima. The vest will be detonated remotely by this cell phone," he said showing her the razor thin phone. "Nothing can stop us now." As Abaddon said this Father Burkholtz stepped into the room.

"This is truly a great moment my child." He walked up to her, kissing her on the forehead. "You will be remembered throughout history as the flame that lit the fire of the great awakening. This great fire is necessary to forge a new religion from the remnants of the old three. In a way it is the die that will cast a new Trinity, for out of this maelstrom something magnificent will arise. And she will be your church Fatima, for you are both the catalyst and the glue of the new covenant: out of the three shall be one, and the mother church shall be Fatima's, the return of the feminine principle as the leitmotif of Gaia's great Earth shall once again proclaim the Truth and stamp out the Lie."

Asma was shocked. "Father Burkholtz," she stammered. "What are you doing here?"

"Fatima, my child, your whole life has been my creation. Together we are fulfilling a prophecy revealed to me in a dream. It has been the purpose of my life, and the purpose of yours."

345

"Are you crazy?" she pulled away from him in horror. "Everything I've been told is a lie! You've manipulated my entire life! Everything!"

"Fatima there are greater things at work here than you and I can possibly understand. We are the servants of a greater power. We are mere instruments. Our lives mean nothing," he gestured to Abaddon and himself and softened his voice. "But your life will be for a higher purpose. This is your destiny, what we have trained and disciplined you for all your life. Your life will have great meaning."

"I don't believe this!" she screamed reeling backwards. "This is insane!"

"And what did you think this was all about? The politics of root cause alienation? Anti-globalism, or other such tired rhetoric of the Left?"

She reached inside her jacket to disconnect the vest.

"I wouldn't do that if I was you," Burkholtz warned as Abaddon grabbed her arms from behind. "Remember I control the detonator. Besides you can't take the vest off or it will set off the backup."

"You mean booby trap!"

"I like to think of it as contingency planning. But enough talk. It's time for action. Enough talk Abaddon, get her in the car."

Parmata ambled down the street to a dark archway in a wall across from the Temple. The smell of urine and feces reminded him that he should be careful not to sit down anywhere. He took the walkie-talkie from his jacket pocket.

"In position across from target. Nothing happening . . ." Just then, a car pulled up in front of the Temple. "Wait, it's her! I don't believe it!"

"What? Can you see her? Say again."

"Yes, I see her. She's getting out of the car. She's with Father Burkholtz for Christ's sake!"

"What?" Allard's eyes threw a sharp query at Pendergast.

"Who's that?" Isser asked nervously fidgeting in his seat.

"Never mind. We don't have time. It's going down . . . *Now!* Get on this *now*!" Allard screamed at the Mossad agent who called in the tactical team that as it turned out had been on standby off the main thoroughfare all along.

Suddenly the streets were a wash with blue and white flashing lights as tactical vehicles raced to the target. Meanwhile Parmata, not content to watch Asma explode in front of him dashed across the street as dawn was breaking in the eastern sky. He knew the security forces would be prepared to kill Asma rather than let her complete her mission. Meanwhile Parmata headed for Father Burkholtz standing in front of the black Mercedes. From inside the car Abaddon saw Parmata running toward him. He stepped on the gas leaving Asma and Father Burkholtz standing alone while he headed for Parmata just as security forces crashed into the Mercedes and grabbed Parmata sweeping him into a security vehicle.

"No, I'm one of you!" Parmata hollered as they threw him in the back seat of the minivan. "I'm with you!" he yelled, grabbing his walkie-talkie. He called Isser complaining bitterly. In the ensuing melee Burkholtz leaped across the police barrier and headed for the same hole in the wall Parmata had been waiting in earlier.

Security forces surrounded Asma with pointed weapons and instructed her to lie down on the ground.

From the minivan Parmata saw Burkholtz run into the hole in the wall that had he had mistaken for an archway. He bolted from the van before the agents could stop him. Bullets zipped around him but he was too focused on Burkholtz's shadow disappearing into the shadows to worry about anything. As he reached the hole in the wall a bullet ricocheted off the stone beside his head just missing him. Unfazed he disappeared into a walled olive grove, transported back in time.

Allard ran to Asma but was stopped by security forces. "It's okay. It's okay! She's with us!" But the security forces didn't move. They stood a safe and measured distance from Asma who was lying face down on the concrete.

"Are you okay Asma?" he yelled.

"Yes, I'm fine, but Father Burkholtz has the detonator code. It's controlled by a cell phone number," she yelled.

"Shit!" Allard cursed looking at Isser and Pendergast.

"And I'm booby trapped!" she added with a sense of humor in her voice.

"Fuck!" the two Canadians and the Israeli cursed in unison.

Parmata didn't know if the fugitive had a gun but he stayed away from the wall knowing that bullets tend to ricochet along walls. Crouching by an old olive tree he spotted a figure about 50 meters ahead making for a road beyond the top of the grove. He scrambled to his feet and dashed along the footpath beside the olive trees triangulating a straight line to where a gate at the top of the field led to the road. As he reached the top of the hill he had a clear view of the fleeing Burkholtz in the early morning light. Just as Burkholtz made a dash for the gate and the open road behind it Parmata pounced on the priest with impressive force knocking them both to the ground. Parmata, arms around Burkholtz, tumbled with the priest to the ground.

"Give it up!" Parmata yelled breathless.

"Never," Burkholtz gasped, fumbling for something in his pants pocket under Parmata's determined grip. Finding his cell phone he managed to flip it open with the flick of his wrist. In an instant he pressed the red send button and a brilliant red yellow flash lit up the morning sky. Almost immediately a dozen police and security personnel surrounded Parmata and Burkholtz.

Parmata sat stunned as the police took Burkholtz into custody. Tears filled his tired eyes as he sat cradling his head in his hands. "No, no, no," he muttered under his breath. "It can't be true."

He gradually became aware of someone standing next to him. "Good work," Allard gently acknowledged.

"But Asma, poor Asma."

"What do you mean?"

It couldn't be, he thought opening his eyes. "Asma!" he exclaimed.

The Israelis, experts in explosives, had quickly disassembled the detonator and reassembled it in a couple of minutes without setting it off in order to track the location of the detonator when the signal was sent from the cell phone. "That's how they made it to us so fast," Parmata said sipping a coffee watching the clear morning light kiss the gentle Mediterranean surf. It was good to have her here, and he reached out to hold his only daughter's hand.

"Thank you for everything you've done for me Dad. All my life I mean."

"Just hearing you say 'Dad' is enough thanks for me."

"What do you say about getting some lobster?"

"Sounds great. I'm starving. But I want real lobster," Asma said laughing.

"There's only one place for *real* lobster."

"I know," she said. "Nova Scotia."

"Are you ready to go home?" he said.

"Ready if you are."

"Let's go get some lobster kiddo."

"Let's go home."

—The End—